'Cauvery Madhavan's evocative narrative spins together the intriguing lives of her charact...  ... makes *The Tainted* a riveting ... conversations among the p... tale of the Anglo-Indian con... uncertain future. The intricate details of every experience are captured in simple language and with great precision. A moving story, compellingly told'
Shashi Tharoor

'A compelling and assured novel of conflicting loyalties and conjoined pasts that resurrects forgotten histories of the Irish in India, exhuming tragic loves and foiled mutinies, and examining them in the clear light of the present'
Namita Gokhale, Director,
Jaipur Literature Festival

'Loved it, an incredible book! This hugely accomplished novel shows all the shades of Indian society. Combining history with humanity, it wears its research lightly. I loved its intricacies, and the characters have lingered in my mind'
Sue Leonard

'Beautifully written . . . gripping and moving. A natural talent!'
Mary Stanley

'A beautifully crafted Indo-Irish novel which is both compassionate and heart-wrenching in equal measure. The pages of this rich novel transports the reader to India under the British Raj: the author weaves a seamless thread to India in the

21st century. Want a "diverse book" to read in 2020? This fits the bill. It is a must-read'
Leela Soma

'Cauvery Madhavan juxtaposes the colonised, the colonisers and something in between, amidst two cultures, to capture the complex hierarchies, social taboos and uncertain loyalties of a century ago, and then, astonishingly, somehow manages to weave a skilfully crafted love story into the mosaic'
Eoghan Corry

'Beautifully written. Not just a powerful story with an unexpected dénouement but a nuanced portrait of the post-colonial condition both in India and Ireland, and of the systematic silencing of female outcasts everywhere'
Felicity Hayes-McCoy

'An absolute triumph, which uses a little-known episode in Irish history – the mutiny of the Connaught Rangers in 1920 – to bring a fictional recreation of colonial and modern India to life. It is another important piece in a century-long legacy that continues to shape both Indian and Irish identity'
Dr Mario Draper, lecturer in military history

'*The Tainted* pivots around this staggering notion: generations must grapple with the consequences of a single night of forbidden love. Written with an affectionate familiarity for the Anglo-Indians, the "tainted" by-product of British colonial

rule, Cauvery's brilliant saga treads lightly with engaging conversations . . . all the while stealthily moving towards a punch-in-the-gut ending'
Indu Balachandran

'As an Indian-born but Irish-based novelist, Cauvery Madhavan is uniquely positioned to understand two countries that could hardly be more disparate but are united by the legacy of British colonialism. The love affair between Private Michael Flaherty of the Kildare Rangers and Rose Twomey plays out against a fictional retelling of the Connaught Rangers Mutiny of 1920, in which Irishmen garrisoning the British Empire turned against their masters because of events during the War of Independence in Ireland. This beautifully written novel tells the tragic story of two people caught in a no man's land of identity and how trauma can transmit itself from one generation to the next often in ways that we never fully understand'
Ronan McGreevy, *Irish Times*

By the same author

Paddy Indian
The Uncoupling

The Tainted

Cauvery Madhavan

HopeRoad

HopeRoad Publishing
PO Box 55544
Exhibition Road
London SW7 2DB

www.hoperoadpublishing.com
First published in Great Britain by HopeRoad 2020
Copyright © 2020 Cauvery Madhavan

A CIP catalogue record for this book is available from the British Library

Supported using public funding by
ARTS COUNCIL
ENGLAND

ISBN: 978-1-9164671-8-7
eISBN: 978-1-913109-06-6

Typeset in Perpetua
Printed and bound by Clays Ltd, Bungay, Suffolk, UK

10 9 8 7 6 5 4 3 2 1

For
Sagari, Rohan and Maya

'Language, identity, place, home:
these are of a piece – just different elements of belonging
and not-belonging.'

Jhumpa Lahiri

PART ONE

1920-45

Mutiny

CHAPTER ONE

Nandagiri, January 1920

'I know you're anxious to meet the fine Eastern beauties of Raja Bazaar, Flaherty, but the first thing we've to do is pay our respects to the dead. I tell you, lad, this is where your lessons about life in India should begin – right here.' Sergeant Tom Nolan of the Kildare Rangers crossed himself before lifting the latch at the entrance to the military cemetery.

Private Michael Flaherty crunched down the broad gravel path, thankful for the shade provided by the majestic tamarind trees that dotted the acre and a half of the graveyard. He was startled when two natives rose suddenly from behind a large marble headstone – short, curved scythes in one hand, salaaming obsequiously with the other.

'Don't you go encouraging them, Flaherty. They're waiting for baksheesh, that's what they're always after.' Tom led him across to the left-hand side of the graveyard. 'Look: "Here lies Pat Walsh". Young Pat came out to India in 1913 with the Kildare Rangers, before the war. You knew him, didn't you? His ma worked for the Aylmers up at the Big House in Straffan. In fact, Colonel Aylmer paid for this headstone and us lads in C Company, we had this angel especially ordered all the way from the monument-wallahs in Madras. Fine-looking thing, isn't it?' The big man sighed. 'Three weeks was all that lad knew of India,' he said sombrely.

'It was the dysentery that took him, wasn't it?'

'Aye. Shat himself to death, he did.'

Sergeant Nolan was running his fingers along the inscription on an elaborate stone cross. 'Did you know we lost twenty-seven men to cholera when the Regiment was first posted here back in 1913? Good men all and lucky, too, I'd say.'

'Lucky?' Michael followed the Sergeant along a row of older tombs, watching him flicking out fallen leaves from the crevices in the sculpted headstones with the tip of his cane.

'Jaysus, lad, I'll tell you why they were lucky – because they died in hospital, dosed with opium and Father Jerome by their bedside. Think about it – a year or two later and they could have been rotting in the sludge of some rat-infested trench in France, gassed and dead with no absolution. Which would you prefer, eh?'

'I don't plan to die anywhere but at home, Tom.'

'Ah, cocky as always! Look around, Flaherty – there are many ways to die in India. If the heat doesn't kill you, it could be cholera or consumption, and if you keep those at bay you could go to your Maker from the bite of a mosquito, a dog or, quicker still, a snake. And then there's the worst of all – the venereal. Jaysus, I wouldn't wish it on my worst enemy.'

When Tom began to go into details of soldiers slowly going mad in the sanatorium in Deolally, the younger man wished they could just leave and head for the bazaar, as promised. The orderly rows of headstones and the Sergeant's commentary had brought back the misery of the three-week voyage from Plymouth in England to Bombay when, in the few respites from severe

4

seasickness, Michael had had to endure stories of death and dying from seasoned India hands with a relish for morbid details.

'All right, Flaherty, stop your moping.' Sergeant Nolan slapped him on the shoulder. 'The bazaar it is. We'll head on to Mumtaz Bibi's in Black Town. Her girls are clean and I swear none of them smell of Condy's fluid like the girls from the Rag.' He lowered his voice. 'Truth be told, lad, I can never bloody get it up in the Rag. Jaysus, could anyone blame me? There are thirty whores working there and six hundred of us, including the Fusiliers and the two companies of the Welsh lads up from the plains. The girls do a brisk trade, so you can't take your time when there are others outside getting impatient.'

Michael wondered what his mother would have thought, should she have overheard this conversation.

But the Sergeant was continuing: 'God-awful place it is, for sure. I've seen the Welsh and the Fusiliers get into fights while waiting their turn. The Military Police don't like to see any trouble in the Rag. They'd double march you to the Guard Room in no time at all – no ifs and buts. There are plenty of do-gooders that want the place closed, but where the hell would that leave the likes of us poor soldiers? Sure, it's a well-known fact that abstinence in the tropics can do you terrible harm.'

By now Michael was thoroughly put off. 'I haven't too much money, Tom,' he tried.

'Go on with you, you miser! You've a week's pay in your pocket – sure that's enough to keep you shagged up till Kingdom Come.'

Half an hour later they were in Black Town, Nandagiri's native quarter, making their way through the filthy laneways. In Raja

5

Bazaar, the main market, Michael lingered in front of a stall selling birds of all kinds and was captivated by a large green parrot. Within minutes he had parted with one rupee, having been repeatedly assured by the fast-talking proprietor of the stall, a giant of a Pathan, that he had secured a bargain.

For a while after, Michael had been followed by a ragged crowd of children, who shrieked with laughter as the bird squawked abuse from its cage. They grew bolder by the minute, taunting the parrot with whistles and loud screeches until Tom Nolan turned on them suddenly and let out an almighty roar, clipping a few ears into the bargain.

'Flaherty, you've bought yourself trouble,' he said sternly. 'Dogs and monkeys are a nuisance but at least they can't speak.'

'I'll put manners on him, Tom. You can see he's intelligent.'

The older man responded with a loud snort just as they halted in front of a two-storey house.

Through a tiny iron grille set high in the wall, a child's eyes regarded them for a moment and then they could hear her call out, her voice shrill and excited. Seconds later, a heavy latch was pulled back and the child, no more than six or seven, opened the door, her mouth agape. Behind her, an elderly woman bustled down the corridor towards them and the little girl, still open-mouthed, clambered back onto her place on the small ledge beside the door.

As she came closer, the old woman threw her hands up in delight.

'Eye-rish sahibs! Tom sahib! Oh, so happy Regiment is come back! I having plenty new girls, clean girls. Doctor sahib give clean chit. Always, my girls very clean.'

Michael flinched as she stepped closer, leering at him, her teeth stained an alarming red and her spicy breath overwhelming.

She clutched him by the forearm, saying, 'Come, come, sahib, very good time here.'

'Jaysus, Tom, would you tell her to stay away from me?'

Tom laughed. 'Lighten up there, lad. Wait till the Colonel gets wind of this: Nandagiri's finest ladies are happy to have the Regiment back!'

They followed the woman down the cool dark corridor, and as they emerged into the inner courtyard, Tom turned to him and winked. 'Mumtaz Bibi will sort you out with whatever you fancy. Mind yourself now – make sure you see the girl washes herself before, and you've heard the good Surgeon-Major say it often enough – wash yourself after.'

Michael nodded wordlessly. This was nothing like the exotic experience he had been anticipating: rose petals and peacock feathers, fragrant dusky skin and bejewelled fingers that could work all sorts of magic . . .

Mumtaz Bibi made Michael sit on one of the dilapidated chairs in the shade of the narrow verandah while she fussed over Tom Nolan, pulling aside one of the grubby curtains and ushering him dramatically into the last of the dozen or so rooms that flanked the courtyard. Michael placed the parrot's cage on the floor beside him and looked around.

A low brick wall surrounded a well that dominated the centre of the courtyard; beside it, a brass bucket caught the late-afternoon sun and shone blindingly, its handle tied to a very long coir rope. A young woman stepped out from the room that Tom Nolan had been taken into, a large earthen pot held casually to her hip, and headed for the well where she threw the brass bucket in. Michael heard a dull splash and the woman shook the rope vigorously from side to side, her big breasts swaying with the motion until, satisfied that the bucket was full, she steadied the rope and began to pull it up. She filled the earthen pot then set off back to the room.

The parrot must have spotted the woman for he stopped his preening and, cocking his head this way and that, he began to rock gently on his perch, chanting, 'Nice girlies! Girlies! Girlies! Plenty good jig-jig!' Every minute or so, as if clearing his throat, he paused before giving an ear-splitting squawk. Michael could hear muffled giggles and plenty of cursing from the occupants of the hidden rooms.

The young punkah-wallahs who sat beside each of the doors with their backs to the rooms, stopped their work and grinned at each other, glad for the break from the monotony of their work. Their sole function was to keep a steady rhythm as they pulled the ropes that were attached to enormous cloth fans which hung from the ceilings inside the rooms. Nodding off to sleep was a hazard of the job, one they paid for with a kick in their shins and the loss of the tip that might have been thrown to them by departing customers.

Michael had already tried in vain to distract the bird, but the parrot carried on undeterred: 'Quickie jig-jig! Good jig-jig!'

There was a growl of frustration from one of the rooms across the courtyard. 'Abdul, you *sowar ka baccha! Punkah chalao*, you bloody fool!' The punkah-wallahs immediately stopped smiling and set upon the ropes vigorously as if possessed. The boy Abdul pulled as hard as he could, but he had begun crying in anticipation of the hiding that he might get, and with every sob his rhythm got more and more erratic.

In his cage, the parrot heard the abuse hurled at Abdul and within a few seconds he countered enthusiastically, his raucous voice ringing loud and clear all around the courtyard: *'Sowar ka baccha!* Son of a pig! Your sister is a whore! She do plenty good jig-jig!'

'Flaherty! Would you keep that bleedin' bird quiet?' bawled the Sergeant. 'You're never coming anywhere with me again.'

There was a quick flurry of movement in the dark corridor and Mumtaz Bibi hurried into the courtyard carrying a large black shawl which she flung over the cage with an apologetic smile at Michael. The parrot went quiet immediately.

'Sahib, come,' she said, and led Michael to another enclosed courtyard, much smaller than the first, with just two rooms at one end. A huge peepal tree grew in the middle, but there was no shade, for the sun streamed in regardless, finding its way through the canopy of leaves. In a natural hollow, low down in the trunk of the tree, sat a roughly-hewn stone idol, its menacing black eyes rimmed heavily with grey ash and its body smeared all over with a thick yellow paste.

'Sahib picking girl?' Mumtaz Bibi gestured towards the door of the first room. Inside, four young women sat together on a low sagging charpoy bed in a companionable tangle of arms and legs, combing and plaiting each other's hair. They looked up at him unhesitatingly and waited. Michael was taken aback by their bold demeanour and the frank curiosity on their faces. Mumtaz Bibi gave Michael a quick glance and snapped her fingers at one of the girls, who got up immediately and jumped off the bed.

Once in the adjoining room, the girl unhooked a rag that hung from a nail and dusted the thin mattress on the charpoy. The punkah on the ceiling slowly came to life, pulled by a wretched little creature with a cleft lip who had been asleep on his haunches outside the room. Mumtaz Bibi had given his ear a sharp twist and the boy had sprung up, gathering the ropes that lay limp beside him. Michael sat down on the charpoy, the coir ropes squeaking with his weight. The girl headed to the corner of the room where the floor dipped towards a rudimentary drain; a cockroach that had been lurking under a large earthenware water-pot scurried away through it, heading outside.

Lifting her skirt up around her hips without any ceremony, the girl picked up a bar of Lifebuoy soap from its place on a wooden ledge, squatted in front of the drain and began washing herself.

She was very dark but not a smooth inky black like the Negro lascars on the troopship that had brought the Regiment out to India from Plymouth. Instead, her skin was coarse and she was heavily built; her feet were badly cracked at the heels, he noticed. Her eyes were lined with kohl, and her palms and the tips of her fingers were decorated with a red stain. Her hair, very long and loosely plaited, glistened with coconut oil, the rank smell of which Michael found most disagreeable. Sitting uncomfortably on the charpoy, he wondered how he had let Tom Nolan convince him that this was the best way to spend his first weekend furlough in India.

When she was finished, the girl loosened her skirt, wiping the inside of her thighs dry with the garment as it slipped off her hips. Michael stood up and fished in his pocket for a few pice and held them out to her. With one eye on the doorway, she slipped the coins into the water pot and then salaamed gratefully before continuing to undress. She had lifted her cotton shift over her head, exposing her large breasts, when she realised that Michael was leaving. She gave a small cry of dismay, and as he strode across the courtyard, nearly tripping on a knot of the peepal tree roots, he heard her call out for Mumtaz Bibi. The wide-eyed stone idol glared at him from its nook in the tree and he shuddered.

Mumtaz Bibi followed him quietly to the bigger courtyard. The parrot was silent in his hooded cage and Michael, a little unsure of what he should do next, looked towards the room that Tom had gone into.

'Tom Sahib having two girls.' Mumtaz Bibi came closer, smiling at him. 'Girl not good? Sahib better liking white girl?'

Michael picked the shawl off the cage, handed it to her and headed for the front door. 'Tell Tom Sahib I go. To barracks.' He spoke slowly, wondering how much English the woman really understood.

Mumtaz Bibi accompanied him all the way to the front door, where the little child had nodded off to sleep, her cheek pressed against the grille. The old woman drew the latch open and Michael stepped past her out on to the narrow street. As he walked back towards the bazaar, he heard the parrot squawk softly in his cage, dipping his head from left to right, and Michael walked briskly, hoping the beggar children wouldn't latch on to him once again. The bazaar meandered in haphazard fashion. Shopkeepers called out to him as he walked by, some sending their lackeys to follow him, which they did for a distance, the more persistent ones running alongside, imploring him to stop. They only gave up and slunk away when he turned around with a raised fist and let out a roar as he had seen Tom do.

He was sweating profusely by the time he reached the dusty road beyond which lay a large reservoir, the rather grandly named Lake Victoria, which separated the native Black Town from the rest of Nandagiri. On the far side of the water, to the north, was the lower end of Kildare Avenue with its fine hotels, elegant tearooms, tailoring establishments, bookshops, taxidermists and hardware emporiums.

Michael walked up and onto the bund – an earthen dam that enclosed the lake from east to west. The bund, which was about twenty feet high, had been built eighty years earlier to blot out any views of Black Town from Kildare Avenue and its pretty lakeside bandstand. The bund was out of bounds to all natives and animals from Black Town; their only access to Nandagiri was a circuitous route around the western shore that brought them into the town via the civil lines. The semicircular bund came to an abrupt end on either side of the gardens that surrounded the bandstand, with steep steps leading down to the large expanse of manicured lawns and flower beds.

Michael jogged down the steps, hoping that he hadn't been spotted coming from Black Town, since soldiers were not permitted to go there. Tom Nolan had a well-founded theory that neither the Military Police nor the officers would be out and about on Kildare Avenue much before four-thirty in the afternoon: 'No better time to head to Mumtaz Bibi's so we can get shagged and be back in time for tea.'

Michael followed a gravel footpath through pergolas weighed down with rambling roses and jasmine, and past neat borders of dahlias, cannas and carnations. He couldn't take a shortcut over the grass, for the lawns themselves were out of bounds to soldiers in the ranks. Passing through the ornate gates of the park, he stood for a moment in the shadow of a bronze enthroned Queen Victoria and, resting the parrot's cage on the stone plinth at the base of the statue, he surveyed the length of Kildare Avenue before him.

The wide cobbled street ran in a straight line all the way up to St Andrew's Church, where it branched out in three directions, one of which he knew led to the military cantonment a mile away. It was only three weeks ago, on their arrival via train from Madras, that the Regiment had paraded smartly up Kildare Avenue to cheers and cries of welcome from British civilians, who had paused along both sides of the street, ordering their tongas to stop, coming out of shops, clapping as the soldiers had marched past, heading towards the regimental barracks.

Now, as Michael set off up the street, he could see the bhistis, weighed down with their goat's bladder water-carriers slung on their backs, watering the cobbles around the church before working their way down to the gardens at Lake Victoria. The sweet scent of fresh wet earth filled the air, and Michael breathed it in deeply, knowing that it would last but a minute or two. Coolies and jampan-bearers called out to him as he walked by, offering to carry the parrot or take him back to the barracks in the comfort of a jampan – a type of sedan chair.

Michael lingered at the elaborate window display of the Empire Medical Hall. He knew that Tom had intended to stop by at this well-known establishment to stock up on remedies, which he claimed were far superior to those supplied by the regimental doctor. Bottles of pink calamine lotion and Milk of Magnesia were arranged in precarious pyramids, ringed by a fine selection of eau de colognes and talcum powders. Rows of tinctures, syrups and balms occupied the remaining space. As he marvelled at the variety, Michael spotted the stylish façade of the Emerald Tearoom across the street and crossed over, confident that if he entered and sat at a table overlooking Kildare Avenue, he could wait in cool comfort for Tom to show up.

A haughty head waiter walked up to Michael just as he put the parrot down by the windowsill, under the fronds of a giant potted palm.

'These tables are reserved, sir – for officers and their wives,' he said stiffly. 'Please follow me: we've another section.'

'It's fine, Victor. This gentleman is with me and there's no one else here yet. Michael, come along here, lad.'

'Father Jerome! I never saw you when I walked in – fancy meeting you here.'

'This is one temptation I can't resist,' the priest informed him. 'They've the best fruit cake in India, I reckon, and their jam sponge is as good as you'd get in Dublin. Sit down, sit down.'

Michael ordered tea, and the waiter, his lips compressed in defeat, agreed to return with the cake trolley.

Father Jerome leant over the table and lowered his voice. 'Pay no attention to his manner, Michael. These Anglo-Indians all have a chip on their shoulder. They've mixed blood, you see, and are highly complexed as a result. Ah, I see you've bought yourself a parrot. Native birds are fierce rude, don't you know? Here, take a napkin and throw it over the cage. It won't look good if the regimental chaplain is caught fraternizing with a foul-mouthed creature, will it? Now tell me, lad, how are you settling in?'

'I've my name down for the Signallers course, Father, but it'll be many weeks before we know who's been selected to go to Madras. As for everything else – the rations aren't too bad and a man can afford to buy a roast chicken if he wants to, and bread and butter are cheap. I thought the bacon was grand till that route march to Ooty. Did you hear about it, Father? Young Captain Milne turned green. Lord, he was sick as a dog! We were crossing the river at the ford at Pykara and saw a herd of filthy pigs on the bank, their snouts buried in whatever they were eating. It was only when we got closer that we realised it was a body, a human one! Sergeant Nolan said the natives let their dead off in rivers.

Apparently, river waters are considered holy or something. I tell you, Father, I haven't touched bacon since.'

'Indeed, it's a strange religion, Michael. It has the natives in a vice-like grip that even dying cannot release, for they believe in reincarnation.' Father Jerome slurped his tea before adding casually, 'I could do with a little help on Sundays – you know, in the half-hour before I serve Mass. It would get you off duty for an hour or so if you volunteered. You'd do a fine job, Michael, and your mother, God bless her, would be proud of you.'

Michael was grateful that the waiter timed his return at that precise moment, followed by a flamboyantly turbaned Indian bearer pushing the three-tiered cake trolley. Although he liked the regimental chaplain, he was a bit taken aback by the suggestion and wasn't quite sure how to respond. There were many others in the Regiment who could be described as God-fearing Catholics, far more committed than him. And the slagging he would get – it would be painful. Why, he would be crucified in the barracks every Sunday.

Then he had a desperate thought. *I could get out of it by telling Father Jerome where I was barely an hour ago. Let's see if he still wants a sinner like me ironing the vestments and polishing the silver for Mass.*

Father Jerome was looking at him genially. 'Try the sponge or even one of those cream buns. The jam in them is particularly delicious.'

'I'll have that slice of custard pie.' Michael pointed out the confection to the waiter.

No sooner had he ignored Father Jerome's recommendation and declared his choice than Michael felt churlish. Cream buns were actually his favourite, and the last time he had eaten one was when the troopship had docked in Aden on the voyage out to India. But he felt a sudden resentment at having been put under unfair pressure, for he couldn't possibly refuse the priest's request to volunteer, could he? And anyway, why did Father Jerome have to mention his mother?

'Good choice, Michael lad. The pie is in fact excellent.'

Michael cut into the edge of the pie and it crumbled softly. Perhaps it was a good thing, he thought, as he savoured the taste of the smooth vanilla custard, that he had shown a degree of contrariness. Maybe it would dissuade Father Jerome from pursuing the matter of Sunday Mass.

'So, what did you think of Black Town then?' the priest asked unexpectedly. 'Did you buy the parrot there? Raja Bazaar holds enticements of all sorts, eh, Michael?'

The young man wiped his mouth with the back of his hand. So, this was what the more experienced soldiers had implied when they said that this priest always managed to wheedle things out of people. Father Jerome was going to get him to admit to being at the brothel, in the bazaar and out of bounds all in the one go, without so much as making an accusation.

'Yes, I bought the parrot for one rupee, Father. Sergeant Nolan thinks I bought myself trouble.'

'Ah . . . so Tom gave you the tour, did he? I should have known. You both go back a long way, I believe. Your fathers were both ghillies up at the Aylmer house in Straffan.'

'Yes, and my sister – my eldest sister, Bridget – was to marry Tom, but she drowned the year I turned ten. It was a dreadful thing altogether. My Da reckoned it was one of the biggest funerals Ardclough had ever seen. The Aylmers even came down from the Big House – although not into the church, of course. You see, Father, she was the nursery maid and a big favourite with the children.'

Michael stirred his tea and tried hard to picture his sister's face, but all he could really remember was her cheery disposition. Her scapular lay rough against his chest, causing him a good deal of discomfort in the heat but he bore it stoically because, though he had hesitated at first when his mother had asked him to wear it, in the few short months since he had left home become convinced of its efficacy in keeping him safe from harm's way. Often he had wondered how the very same scapular that had left Bridget to struggle in vain to disentangle herself from the reeds at the bottom of the canal, had somehow managed to save him – the first time at Plymouth from being kicked in the head by Colonel Aylmer's charger when it broke loose below decks on the troopship – and the second time, barely a few days ago, when a sudden sharp sag in the mosquito net above his bed had alerted him to the fact that a snake had fallen from the rafters in the high ceiling and lay hissing barely a few feet away, directly above his face. The punkah-wallahs had managed to kill the young cobra, having cornered it in the latrines after a quarter of an hour of high drama, but Michael had no doubt that Bridget's scapular had saved him.

Michael sighed and looked out at Kildare Avenue. Surely Tom Nolan would have finished at Mumtaz Bibi's by now. If he turned up at the pharmacy across the road at this very moment, Michael could make his excuses and leave before Father Jerome steered the conversation back to helping at Mass.

The priest dabbed his lips and then brow with his napkin. 'A heavy cross to bear, it is – the death of a child. How difficult to believe that such a thing could be the will of God – and yet such a cross couldn't be borne without His help.'

Michael looked away quickly. Any talk of heavy crosses brought back the wretched sight of his mother, crippled by the weight of her grief as it had slowly and surely crushed her spirit. He knew what Father Jerome was going to do next. It was what most people did when they were powerless – they prayed. For weeks after Bridget drowned, the whole family had prayed constantly for her, and through it all and ever since, Michael had often wondered why they had bothered petitioning for her soul when she was so obviously in heaven – for where else could his sweet and beautiful sister have gone?

To Michael's surprise, Father Jerome said nothing but scraped back his rattan chair and stood up instead. He smoothed down his hair, which sprang up as coarse and unruly as before.

'I must head into that fine establishment across the street, the Empire,' he said. 'They've something for everything, and as you can see, my hair needs subduing.' He turned towards the head waiter who was striding across the room, solar topee and cane in hand. 'Ah, Victor, you've everything ready. Now be sure you put Private Flaherty's tea on my chit, good man.'

Michael stood up. 'That's decent of you, Father Jerome, but I have money. We were paid yesterday.'

'No need for any of that, Michael. I'll be seeing you before Mass tomorrow; an hour ahead should do.'

The priest jammed the solar topee on his head and marched off briskly without waiting for a reply. Michael flopped back into his chair and groaned in disbelief. He had just sold himself for a custard pie! No jig-jig but plenty of pie – was this what the Mysterious East had in store for him? The turbaned bearer began to clear the table while the head waiter hovered impatiently.

I bet that bloody Anglo-Indian would like to clear me out of this room as well, thought Michael as he got up and headed for the palm by the window. The parrot squawked as the napkin was lifted off and when Michael turned, cage in hand, the man was waiting, solar topee at the ready.

Out on Kildare Avenue, Michael scanned the now crowded street, wondering if he would be better off forgetting about Tom and making his way back to the barracks on his own. They would anyhow have had to present separately at the Guard Room, in the same fashion as they had left, for strictly speaking Tom Nolan, as a Non-Commissioned Officer, was forbidden from fraternising with a Private.

As he tried to make a decision, a tonga-wallah pulled up just outside the Emerald, where Michael was standing. The vehicle heaved as the passengers alighted and Michael found himself face to face with his Commanding Officer, Colonel Aylmer. Instinctively standing to attention, he saluted smartly.

'At ease, Private Flaherty.' The Colonel returned the salute and turned to help his wife down, his two children and their ayah following with small nervous squeals as the tonga rocked from back to front.

The children stared at the parrot and Michael froze, fearing what was to come.

'Mother, look – a parrot! You did promise we'd have one as soon as we got to India.' Colonel Aylmer's son was a delicate-looking boy and his eyes were wide with excitement.

'I'd prefer a monkey.' The little girl made a face at Michael.

The parrot shifted on his perch and squawked loudly, and the children were delighted.

'Oh, look! Does he talk? Oh, do make him talk!'

'Now in you go with Ayah and make sure Victor has the table under the punkah for us.' Colonel Aylmer waved the ayah on.

Mrs Aylmer, who was adjusting her hat, which had got dislodged as she stepped out of the tonga, smiled and shooed the children ahead of her into the Emerald Tearoom.

Colonel Aylmer watched them disappear into the building. 'I see you've applied for the Signallers course, Flaherty. Good, very good, but it could be a while before we know how many from the Regiment will go to Madras. I've been thinking – you might take on duties as my batman in the meanwhile.'

'Sir! Yes, sir!'

'Have you heard from the family? Your father, old Donnie – he's well, I hope? I believe it's been a bitterly cold spring at home. The lower lake in the East Woods was frozen over for days.'

'Sir! They're well, sir! I had a letter waiting when we docked in Madras, sir.'

'That's good. I'll speak to Captain Milne. You can start with me straight away.'

'Sir! Yes, sir!' Michael came to attention and saluted, and as if on cue the parrot fluttered around in the cage and squawked, *'Sowar ka baccha!'*

'Native birds have no manners, Flaherty. Mrs Aylmer will have none of that in our house.' With that, Colonel Aylmer strode into the Emerald Tearoom to join his family.

CHAPTER TWO

Nandagiri, March 1920
I swear I'll never touch another bottle of Lion Beer — and Jaysus, I won't ever sing myself hoarse again. Please God, I will remember these good intentions the next payday.

Michael fingered the scapular around his neck as he made these resolutions, his head throbbing like one of those small native drums beaten by the crazy old Pathan who came around the barracks with his troupe of dancing monkeys. The chai-wallahs claimed they had a cure for a hangover, but it was common knowledge that all they did was lace their syrupy-sweet tea with flecks of opium.

Wincing, Michael put the heavy iron, hot with glowing coals inside it, down on its brick stand and lifted the old cotton sheet off the priest's satin stole. He checked the stole for creases and any tiny burn-holes from the embers that sometimes spat unexpectedly out of the iron. Father Jerome had shown him the near-invisible darning in several places on the alb and stole that he had had to get repaired at his own expense, sending the garments all the way to Ooty to the French nuns who were the acknowledged experts at mending delicate fabrics.

Satisfied that there was no damage, he hung the garment carefully on the wooden clothes horse. Michael had fashioned the stand for Father Jerome just a few days earlier, using rough lengths of teak salvaged from the woodshed at one end of Colonel Aylmer's house. He had finished it off neatly, using brass thumbtacks to cover the wood with strips of green baize that he had managed to coax out of Captain Milne, who had ordered several yards of the fabric for repairs to the billiard tables in the Officer's Mess. Father Jerome had been delighted with Michael's handiwork.

'You're a good lad, so you are. I knew it straight away.'

Michael had taken more than two months to fall into a routine at Sunday Mass, for Father Jerome was far more particular than he could ever have imagined. The priest refused to accommodate any shortcuts or alterations when it came to the serving of Mass just because they were, as he put it 'in this heathen, idol-worshipping land'.

The Regimental Chapel stood at one corner of the north end of the parade grounds and was partially shaded by the overhanging branches of three large Flame of the Forest trees. Originally a barrack room, the Chapel's distinguishing feature was a slim wooden cross, painted white, that was fixed to one gable end. Screwed on the door was a smaller but heavier brass cross, and on either side of the steps leading up to the door were regulation whitewashed terracotta flowerpots, each overflowing with masses of marigolds and tumbling nasturtiums.

Michael's first job when he arrived at seven o'clock on a Sunday morning was to unlock the small anteroom that served as a vestry, and to open the wooden shutters that were meant to keep out the dust. The parched red earth yielded copious quantities of fine dust that swept across the vast parade grounds, penetrating even the tiniest of cracks in windows and doors.

This morning, as always, the two sweepers squatting by the steps of the Chapel had jumped up to salaam Michael as he approached. He let them in to sweep and mop the Chapel while he began the task of preparing the anteroom for Father Jerome. A large wooden ammunition box, on which the faded remains of a stencilled cross were still visible, contained two brass candle-stands, several large candles, a pair of small silver dishes, an ornate chalice and an assortment of embroidered altar cloths, loosely wrapped in an envelope of soft muslin.

Michael dabbed polish sparingly on the silver and brass items and lined them up on the small desk by the window to dry before buffing them to a high shine. *If only my Ma could see me now,* he thought. He had brushed the maroon velvet altar cloths and was ironing out the kinks in the fraying silken tassels when the priest walked in, dabbing the beads of sweat off his forehead.

'Ah, Michael lad, good – good, you've made a start. This heat, it'll be the death of me and it's only March as yet. What will we do when it turns hot? We'll have to shift Mass times to earlier in the morning.' The priest examined the polished chalice as he spoke, holding it at arm's length, up towards the light streaming in from the open window. 'Are we down on the polish?'

'There's enough for another few weeks, Father. That bottle from Madras is much better than the foul stuff issued by the Quarter Master. The brass shines up as good as new.'

'You go easy with it now, lad. There's no more where that came from.'

'I'm watching every drop, Father.' Michael grinned secretly as he looped the altar cloths lightly over his arm and headed into the Chapel. Everyone knew the priest had a knack for procuring things that even the Quarter Master could never lay his hands on. The list included a Dundee cake sitting snug in its shiny tin, untouched since it had left the famous London store that produced it, a dozen tins of condensed milk, two brand-new football bladders and a tropical field-set of first-class emollients for all manner of bites, stings, blisters, corns and calluses. 'The kindness of others knows no bounds,' he would say, but they all knew that it was never that simple.

Michael draped the three altar cloths one next to the other over the long wooden trestle table and then stepped back, to make sure that the three silken tassels were level with each other. Father Jerome was particular about the appearance of things.

'The tassels are level but the space between the altar cloths isn't equal.'

Michael swung around. A young woman was standing in the aisle about halfway up the Chapel. She caught his eye for a moment, before looking up at the ceiling, checking exactly where the punkahs were before picking the pew she wanted to sit on.

'The best spot is not necessarily directly under the punkah, but you must know that by now,' she said, glancing at him again as she smoothed down her pale-yellow voile dress and then placed her wide straw hat on her lap.

Michael nodded, not knowing what to say, convinced that he had seen the young woman before and yet not quite able to place her. She was slight, very pretty, and her light-brown hair, fashionably crimped, framed her face closely. It was the colour of her eyes that held his attention. From where he stood at the altar, they looked green but now, as she sat in the second pew looking directly back at him, so confident and unhesitant, he could see they were flecked brown and amber.

'I'm Sean Twomey's daughter. I look like my father, so people always think they know me from somewhere. You see, I have his colouring and eyes, all Irish.' She patted down her hair with deft little motions of her wrist. 'In fact, I had red hair when I was born.'

Just then, Father Jerome walked in from the anteroom bearing the silver chalice. 'We've an unexpected helper today,' he announced. 'You know Mr Twomey, I'm sure.'

A tall man with receding hair and a sheepish smile shuffled in behind the priest, carrying the cruet set and candlesticks.

'The Bacon-wallah?' Michael knew instantly it was the wrong thing to have blurted out.

'My father does have a name, you know!' the girl said, bridling.

'Now, Rosie pet, don't get in a huff. The lad meant no harm – sure, that's how they all know me, for don't I produce the best bacon and sausages east of the Suez. Aren't I right, Father Jerome?'

'Too right, Sean, too right you are. It can keep me going all day, the thought of two thick bacon chops on a plate, surrounded by a mound of buttered potatoes and some peas from the Convent of Mercy. Rose, hold your head high, child, for your father is a mighty fine Bacon-wallah.'

The priest signalled for Michael to ready his vestments, and as Michael made to leave, he glanced back at Rose Twomey, who looked far from mollified.

Father Jerome returned to the anteroom followed by the Bacon-wallah, who waited silently as the priest put on his alb and stole and finally the chasuble, saying the prayer for each as he did so. The heat in the room was stifling and as Michael fanned the priest with a hand-held punkah, he wondered why the Bacon-wallah was here in the Regimental Chapel when it was the custom for most civilians to attend Sunday Mass at the larger and more comfortable St Andrew's Church on Kildare Avenue.

The priest adjusted the chasuble and then crossed himself before addressing Sean Twomey. 'I'll speak to the Colonel myself, Sean, but I wouldn't like to promise anything. Rose is only eighteen, and you know as well as I do that Mrs Aylmer's a very particular memsahib. Still, as I said, I'll do my best. And now I'll advise you to take your place in the pews; there's little enough sitting room once the lads file in.'

When the Bacon-wallah left, Father Jerome sat down on the only chair in the room and closed his eyes. Michael knew he had to keep quiet and continue with the punkah, for this was the five minutes before Mass that Father Jerome spent praying and thinking, his fingers drumming the arms of the old chair as he mentally ran through his sermon.

But today the priest was in a talkative mood. 'What do you make of it, eh, Michael? He wants me to put in a word with the Colonel. The Bacon-wallah has a notion that Mrs Aylmer might be persuaded to take on his Rose as a lady's maid or even a nanny for the two little ones. But the girl is Anglo-Indian. I know her mother was from a military orphanage so there is plenty of Indian blood running in her veins. No, I don't think Mrs Aylmer will care for an Anglo-Indian in her household. Like every self-respecting Mem in India, she would rather have a native ayah than take on a chee-chee girl, though I must admit young Rose doesn't look like one. Takes after her father, don't you think, and speaks like him as well.'

The priest dabbed his forehead with a large white handkerchief. 'Sean Twomey's a good man, but he should have gone home to Ireland when he finished up here. But so many of these time-expired soldiers tend to stay on and end up making

26

disadvantageous marriages with half-caste girls. What's the draw, eh Michael? What would make anyone want to stay on in India?'

Father Jerome still had his eyes closed and Michael wasn't sure if he was really expected to reply. He couldn't imagine what would make anyone want to linger on in India. Now if it was Canada or Australia, he might jump at the chance himself, and to America he'd go in a flash – but India, hell, you'd be lucky to leave with your life and limbs intact.

The priest sighed and stood up. 'The Missal please, Michael.'

The Mass book in his hand, Father Jerome moved to the door and waited for Michael to open it, stepping out after a considered pause and walking in a slow, ceremonious fashion to the altar. Michael had found it amusing at first: the priest's solemnity seemed out of place in this dilapidated old barrack with its terracotta roof and dusty punkahs that didn't so much stir the air as occasionally dislodge all manner of creatures from their dark sanctuaries in the tiled roof above. No falling scorpion or disorientated bat or even the odd snake was allowed to disrupt the Mass for any more time than it would take to have it caught and killed. Two Indian coolies sat waiting on their haunches right outside the Chapel door, their pronged sticks, nets and lathis at hand in case any such occasion should arise. It was Father Jerome's demeanour that lent gravity to the occasion. His unhurried preparations for each stage of the Mass, combined with his sonorous voice, transported the congregation to a place far removed from the modest building.

When he first started his Sunday Mass duty with Father Jerome, Michael had been taken aback at what he saw from his vantage point a few steps behind the altar. The sincerity of the devotion had really surprised him. These men who swore, drank, gambled and visited the Rag as often as they could afford and with no compunction, sat Sunday after Sunday, making their weekly peace with their Maker and queueing patiently to receive Communion.

Michael wondered if Bridget ever featured in the prayers that Tom Nolan recited with his eyes closed and head bowed. Or was the man, like so many of the other soldiers in the Chapel, just praying for himself? Michael often watched Tadhgh Foley, who always sat up in the first pew, his hands clasped together so tightly that his knuckles turned white even before Mass began. The whole Regiment knew he had lost three of his children in quick succession – and as if that had not been cruel enough, the three separate letters from home telling him about their deaths from scarlet fever had arrived at the very same time. Father Jerome, who helped the men to read and write their letters, had had the dreadful task of relating the tragic news to Tadhgh. The man had borne his grief wordlessly, which the others had put down to shock, and even now, he spent most of his time in silence, obsessively carving a set of wooden animals for his remaining child, a baby boy not yet a year old.

As casually as he could, Michael glanced over to where Rose Twomey sat. She was looking directly at him and her frank gaze didn't waver a bit. He had seen that kind of look before and it had always led him into trouble. Mary Cullen had given him that look and so had her sister. And there was Nuala. Everyone in Ardclough had thought her a bit slow – except they hadn't seen the speed with which she could undo her buttons.

Michael looked away, staring instead at the embroidered cross on Father Jerome's stole, trying hard to pick up the thread of his sermon . . . but memories of those dangerous afternoons back home in the ruined keep of Reeves Castle interrupted his thoughts. Nuala had shown him a huge breast that had left him so speechless that she stuffed it back tearfully, rebuffing all his subsequent overtures with vicious name-calling. Mary Cullen had pulled her drawers down for him but would only let him look, and her sister, who had asked him to go first, had at the sight of him, fallen to her knees sobbing that she had gone too far. Weeks later, he had been waylaid near the stone bridge at the canal and given a good thrashing by the girls' brothers. 'That'll teach ye!' they shouted as they flung him into a bank of nettles.

Rose was still looking at him. This time he didn't look away but held her gaze, even as Father Jerome asked the congregation to stand for the Creed. She closed her eyes and began to recite, her lips barely moving, her hands smoothing down the white satin sash on her dress. The Chapel filled with that strange hissing that always came when the Mass-goers collectively chanted the Lord's Prayer.

After the Mass, when the soldiers had regrouped and marched smartly away back to their barracks, Father Jerome walked down to the door of the Chapel, where he stood majestically beside the pots of marigold, like a king outside his castle, acknowledging individually the few officers and civilians as they slowly made their way out. Michael began clearing the altar, carefully putting things away in the anteroom. He could see Surgeon-Major McArdle and his wife in animated conversation with Father Jerome before they finally said their goodbyes. Sean Twomey and his daughter were next, and Michael lingered at the altar to see if Rose might turn around to look at him again, but she stood dutifully by her father till the Bacon-wallah shook hands with Father Jerome and then, unfurling her umbrella, she stepped out of the shade and walked away without turning back.

Michael waited in the anteroom for the priest in order to help him disrobe and lock up. Often Father Jerome would just sit back for a few minutes and ramble on about the sermon, usually being very self-critical about the content of his homily. He would then repeat some of the conversations he had had after Mass. Today, as usual, he was dabbing beads of sweat from his forehead when he walked in and sat down heavily.

'Lord help us, Michael, the letters from home in the next dak will bring nothing but the worst news. I've been hearing about it from Surgeon-Major McArdle, and I tell you he was very good to have given me notice of what's to come.'

'What is it, Father? Will there be another war?' Michael was putting the silver candlesticks away as he turned to look at the priest.

'No, Michael, the trouble's at home. Killings, beatings – all indiscriminate and cruel. There's bound to be repercussions. Have any of the men said anything? Have you heard any talk? Come, lad, you must know what I'm talking about. Weren't you home on furlough before Christmas when those devils tried to shoot the station-master and his son in Sallins? They burnt the cottage down as well. There was no compensation and never will be.'

'Aye. My Ma was so afraid – she put her foot down and wouldn't let me out of her sight, but there was no stopping my Da and some of the neighbours. That whole week they kept vigil at the station in Ardclough where my cousin is the linesman. So, the news is about the Black and Tans?'

'Yes, although I'm not sure what to make of it, lad, as it seems our own newspapers have been censored. The good doctor was quoting the American papers, which he laid hands

30

on yesterday. Apparently, the violence has spread the length and breadth of the country. People are fearful.'

The priest disrobed in silence, passing the vestments to Michael, who shook them out, folded and hung them on the wooden stand, before draping a sheet of muslin over the whole arrangement to keep it dust-free till the following Sunday.

'But right now, I must put aside Surgeon-Major McArdle's news, for duty calls – the men will be waiting,' said Father Jerome, looking at his watch. 'You be a good fellow, lock up and drop by my office with the keys. I've a nice little packet of coffee to give you. Did I ever tell you that my brother's a shipping agent in Singapore? He knows all about the small comforts in life, and this coffee from Java is one of them.'

Michael thanked him. He often wondered if the generous 'shipping-agent brother' in Singapore was just a good cover for Father Jerome's natural penchant for those 'small comforts in life'. However, the priest was just as generous as the brother he claimed to have and Michael was grateful for whatever came his way, whether it was coffee or shaving balm or even the occasional book.

Father Jerome headed off briskly to his small office on the far side of the parade grounds, next to the NCOs' Mess; it was here, every Sunday after Mass, that he spent two hours or so reading out letters and writing replies for the soldiers in the Regiment. A good many were illiterate, barely able to sign their own names. Michael felt desperately sorry for the men who were dependent on the priest to relay news from home. Reports of births and deaths, intimate declarations of love and longing, litanies of complaint, requests for more money, news of illnesses and tragedy filled the letters that arrived from Ireland, and the priest was privy to them all. The men had no choice but to share their most personal details with Father Jerome as he read letters from their wives and sweethearts, their parents and children, and then patiently wrote out the replies back.

There had been chatter all right, about the Black and Tans, but much of it was futile 'wet canteen' talk, fuelled by the beer sold there, only to be put aside the next morning, when all that mattered was surviving another viciously hot day. The bugles sounded at five o'clock in the morning, an hour before dawn, but most mornings Michael found the heat had roused him earlier, and if it wasn't the heat it was the foul breath of the wizened old native barber as he leant over Michael's sleeping body to shave his face. The Regiment paraded while it was still cool, just as dawn broke, the early-morning marches taking the same old routes with hardly a variation, in order to avoid the local sholahs – the patches of mountainous forest surrounded by grassland. These areas were considered a malaria risk; also, they were frequented by wild boar that invariably caused the officers' horses to bolt.

The hill stations in the Nilgiri Range could not compare in altitude with North Indian Himalayan towns like Darjeeling or Simla, which Michael had heard were very cool even in the summer. With spring at its end in South India, the temperature in Nandagiri had been rising steadily, along with everyone's irritability. Morning parade was the only major exertion of the day and it was followed by breakfast at nine o'clock, after which the men headed back to their barracks with nothing to do except lie on their beds and threaten the punkah-wallahs with fates worse than death if they should dare slacken their efforts.

Camp followers arrived in a steady stream all through the morning until lunch, squatting outside the barrack verandahs and setting up impromptu stalls on the bare ground. They cried their wares unceasingly: tea, tailoring services, mynah birds and tame mongooses, coffee, postcards of naked women, cigarettes, fruit, buns and cakes, nasty-looking herbs and potions to keep your dick from shrivelling up while you queued impatiently at the Rag, and medicines to cure you if you got anything more from the native whores than you paid for. If you were awake, too hot to read, and if you hadn't the money for a game of cards or the energy to listen to another man's woes, you could spend your time in a hammock under the punkahs on the verandah, watching the whole *tamasha* – the great Indian circus of chancers, swindlers and crooks – unfold before your very eyes. And even if the scene was no longer as novel a spectacle as when the Regiment had first arrived in Nandagiri a few months ago, without this daily performance, life in the barracks would be unbearably dull.

In the afternoon everything came to a standstill. The fragrant khus-khus tatties were lowered over every window and door, and the bhistis drenched them with water. The barracks became cool, dark havens as the punkah-wallahs got a steady rhythm going on the ropes. As the water evaporated from the sweet-smelling grass blinds and the punkahs circulated the cool air around the darkened rooms, it was possible in those couple of hours to drift off into a hypnotic sleep of the sort that only a tropical afternoon could induce. The only soldiers not supine were the ones on Guard-Room duty.

Not too far from the barracks – for Nandagiri was but a small cantonment – in the officers' bungalows, a siege mentality struck entire households every afternoon, and memsahibs and their male housekeepers, the khitmatgars, prided themselves on the degree with which they could seal the whole house from the debilitating heat. Nothing stirred but the fine red dust that swirled across the parched parade grounds as if possessed.

Evening did not always bring relief. If the air was still, the insects would be out in greater force, and sweat seemed to attract them in droves. But at least there was more to do than during the day. Colonel Aylmer was keen on the Regiment playing sport, and there was always a game of football or hockey to be had. The swimming pool was only two years old and had been constructed by the Madras Sapper Regiment, who were based in Wellington thirty miles away. B Company took their turn in the pool on Tuesday, Thursday and Saturday evenings, and Michael, along with some of the other younger lads, always went to the wet canteen afterwards.

The wet canteen was the highlight of most days in the barracks. There was drink to be had and it was served cold. Here a man could buy a beer, on credit if needed, play cards, take a gamble on a game of dice or place a bet on a boxing match. If you hadn't any money and had accumulated too many unpaid chits, the talk, some of it loose and careless, was always free. And talk there was, of the trouble in Ireland. A couple of the Fusiliers – Shinners no doubt – had started the rumours going while queueing up at the Rag, but Tom Nolan, who had overheard Captain Milne discuss it with Major Symes, was able to tell everyone at the wet canteen on Thursday that the rumours were, in fact, true because the dispatches from Army Headquarters had expressed concern about the possible effect on morale amongst Irish regiments.

The men had listened quietly but some muttered that they wished they were back home to be able to give the Tans a swift kick in the bollocks and a slow bullet to their heads. The canteen had drunk a round to that idea. Fighting talk always got their blood up, and many a fist was slammed into a palm as one by one the men raised their bottles and vowed to string up the Tans and bugger them with rifle butts. 'Tie them down to railway tracks at night,' suggested the lad whose father was a linesman. 'Weigh them with stones and drown them alive in sacks,' said the lad who had worked in the flour mill at Naas. By closing time, they found it hard to decide between nailing the fuckers to a cross, leaving them swinging by their scalps at the crossroads or setting them alight, crotches first.

But the next morning was just another day in India, where the only constant was the company of other men suffering equally from sunburn and featureless routine. It was little wonder, thought Michael, that all mention of the Tans was left for the wet canteen.

Though Father Jerome had, after Mass today and in a deliberately casual fashion, slipped in his questions about how much the men in the barracks knew about the events in Ireland, Michael had held his tongue as he always did. Much as he liked Father Jerome, he had decided that he wasn't going to be the priest's inside source on the thoughts and activities of the men in the Regiment.

As he locked up the anteroom of the Chapel, it struck Michael that if Surgeon-Major McArdle was right and the newspapers at home were indeed being censored, things must really be as bad as the priest feared. Tom Nolan would want to know about that, he thought. Much like Father Jerome himself, the Sergeant wished to be in the picture about everything and anything – but he garnered his information very overtly. It was hard not to be truthful, when Tom looked you in the eye and asked what he wanted to know directly to your face.

The keys to the Chapel in his hand, Michael headed to Father Jerome's office. To the east of the parade grounds he could see the weekend bazaar in full swing beneath the intertwined canopy of three majestic peepul trees. All manner of things could be purchased, all sorts of services were available, but it was the Bacon-wallah who was the king of this Sunday market. Seated on a folding canvas chair, set on a high wooden platform, between puffs on his pipe, he barked commands to his three Indian servants, who scurried around, weighing and packing as per his orders. Two urchins kept the dogs and monkeys away with sling shots, which they used with great precision, and painful yelps punctuated the air now and again, but the smell of the dried and cured sausages, the smoked bacon and the aroma of chickens being grilled over red-hot coals kept the creatures coming back.

Michael had seen the Bacon-wallah at the Colonel's bungalow a couple of times while there himself on his daily orderly duties. Sean Twomey home-delivered the Aylmers' requirements four times a week, like he did to the rest of the officers' bungalows. Mrs Aylmer normally left such routine kitchen matters to her very able khitmatgar, but when the old soldier called once a month to settle the chit, she received him on the verandah, paying him quickly and with the minimum of small talk.

Regimental memsahibs were notorious for not paying their chits on time. The proper stabling of polo ponies and the upkeep of children in boarding school back home was a drain on a military salary, and Indian tradesmen were always the last to have their chits settled. Perhaps that was why the Bacon-wallah transformed himself into Sergeant Sean Twomey for his chit-collecting trips. Bathed and shaved for the occasion and wearing his old Rangers uniform, all his service ribbons displayed proudly and a shamrock on his cap badge, he did his monthly collection in the cantonment on a smart bay Arab that he had got from a retiring cavalry officer in exchange for settling his very large unpaid chit; he even employed a syce to accompany him for the occasion.

Two weeks ago, Michael had been polishing the brass on the Colonel's dress uniform when the Bacon-wallah arrived at the Aylmers' bungalow. Peering through the dressing-room window that overlooked the verandah, he watched the old man stand up, nearly to attention, as the Colonel's wife swept out of the house, her purse and her leather-bound account book in hand and the khitmatgar in attendance.

Mrs Aylmer believed that India was to be survived, not loved, and in order to do that she ran her household with clockwork precision; as for her chits, they were always paid on time. Her native servants respected and feared her both in good measure, for she expected them to take their duties just as seriously as she took hers. She spoke passable Tamil, first learnt nearly twelve years ago in Nandagiri when her husband, then a young Major, had insisted that his bride take lessons in conversation from the Regiment's own Brahmin tutor. She had quickly realised the wisdom of this; speaking Tamil allowed her the freedom to go riding out in the country every day as she had done all her life in Ireland, and, equally importantly, it meant she didn't have to rely on her khitmatgar to translate between her and the rest of the servants.

The Kildare Rangers had been posted to India, to the regimental centre in Nandagiri, twice in the last ten years, and though she did not much care for coming back to India, this time Mrs Aylmer was top of the pecking order in the cantonment. She came only after her husband in the moral and social authority she commanded amongst soldiers of every rank, their wives and absolutely any civilian whom she came across. This time around she was the Burra Memsahib, with nearly the same set of household servants as during her previous tenure in Nandagiri. They had turned up, all unsummoned, at the Colonel's bungalow the night the Regiment arrived, the khitmatgar heading the line-up, greeting the family with folded palms and tears in his eyes.

The same khitmatgar, Gajjapati, stood right behind her chair this evening, looking at the Bacon-wallah with ill-concealed envy. Michael knew what was running through the khitmatgar's head. Here was a tradesman – a bazaar tradesman, even if it was the Gorah Bazaar – who was able to sit in the presence of the Memsahib.

Michael picked up the scabbard of the Colonel's ceremonial sword and as he dabbed on the polish, he listened to Mrs Aylmer questioning the items listed on the chit that Sean Twomey had just presented to her.

'The smoked bacon has become far too dear, Mr Twomey. Why, it's eight annas more than it was in January when we arrived, and there's another matter – it's far too salty. Cook has to soak it for a whole night and the next day as well, and that'll not be possible once the hot weather comes. Surgeon-Major McArdle has been talking to the Colonel about the dangers of eating too much salt.'

'Ah, the Surgeon. He's newly arrived in India, Mrs Aylmer. The body needs plenty of salt in the tropics, sure, we lets out more salt than we could ever eat. With sweating and such, you know.'

Leaning against the window with the polish-soaked rag in his hand, Michael had laughed quietly at the expression on Mrs Aylmer's face. She, like her husband, placed great store by loyalty. To gossip about the Regiment's new Surgeon would

38

be unthinkable, as would discussions of any bodily fluid. So, ignoring the Bacon-wallah's remarks, she ran her finger through the bill, comparing it now and again with her own account book, checking details with Gajjapati. When she was satisfied that the account was correct, she paid the chit in full and placed the order for the following week.

'I won't be ordering any more of the smoked bacon, Mr Twomey, unless you're willing to use less salt. I'll be forced to order it from the Jesuit Fathers in Ooty. The rest of the weekly order will be as usual, with a leg of lamb for this Sunday, plus an extra seer of lamb bones every second day from now on. The children are to have good bone soup daily.'

The old soldier stood up and bowed slightly. The Jesuits were the bane of his life. How could his pigs ever compete with those who were fed on the leftovers from the tables at an Irish seminary? 'Less salt if that's the way you want it, Mrs Aylmer. And you can be sure there'll be no charge for the bones if it's for the young ones.' He twirled his greying moustache and smiled. 'They're neat little riders, the pair of them. They looked very smart trotting down Kildare Avenue on their ponies.'

Michael had nearly finished, with just the puttees left to whiten up with Blanco, when he heard the children shout out to their mother that Father was home. The family gathered on the verandah and fell happily into their evening routine. The bearer kneeling at the Colonel's feet eased off the master's riding boots and proceeded to sponge his feet with icy cold towels. The small ivory-inlaid teapoys that the Memsahib had recently bought from the Kashmiri dealer in town were brought out from the drawing room and on to them the khitmatgar placed crocheted doilies before bringing out two tall glasses of very cold homemade barley water and little rounds of puff pastry filled with minced chicken and peas. He waited quietly, smiling indulgently at the children, while the Colonel and the Memsahib decided what they would like to drink. Mrs Aylmer handed him the key to the drinks cupboard in the dining room and he duly returned with two glasses of gin, a bottle of cold tonic water, and slices of lime.

'Dinner will be a bit early, Gajjapati,' Michael heard Mrs Aylmer say. 'We'll be going to the Club immediately after. Ask Ayah to get ready. She'll come with the children and they can stay at the Club for an hour or so. Tell the syce to bring the carriage around in half an hour.'

Colonel Aylmer, an accomplished artist himself, was admiring his children's artwork. 'James, son, this is wonderful – our gulmohur tree with Tippu Sultan sleeping under it! How did you get that silly dog to keep still? I think you'll be coming with me next weekend, to Lansdowne Ridge. Would you like that?'

'I should like to paint the mountain, too, Father. Don't you like my drawing just as much?' Alice Aylmer had climbed onto the Colonel's lap. She was eight years old, with far more artistic ability than her older brother. Michael had seen her deft little water colours and well-proportioned sketches pinned on the cork board in her parents' bedroom and he waited to hear what the Colonel would say.

'Alice is too young, isn't she, Mother?' James objected before the Colonel could speak. 'She's too young to ride with Father and me all the way to the Ridge. Anyway, her pony has lost a shoe, and the farrier can't come for another few days because his baby turned blue and died.'

'Oh James! Wherever did you hear that?'

'But it's true, Mother. Ask Ayah or even Gajjapati. The baby died in the most horrible way – it was a cobra bite. I heard the syce tell Ayah this morning.'

'You mustn't listen to the servants' talk, James. I've told you that before.'

'I wasn't listening, Mother, I promise. I just heard them.'

Colonel Aylmer ran his fingers through his son's hair. 'The poor man must be in a bad way,' he said. 'That's not the first child they've lost, if I remember right.'

'I suppose I'd better make inquiries, though you know yourself, Charles, that these Eurasians can get too familiar, given half a chance. Do you think you might send him something towards the child's funeral? That should be enough, don't you think?'

'I'll send on an envelope to Father Jerome, or better still, I'll suggest a collection at the Club this evening. That'll help the poor chap.'

James put down his lemonade. 'Ayah said the farrier should be happy he has one less mouth to feed.'

'Like we'll be when you go home to Ireland.' Alice had her hands on her hips.

'Alice!' snapped her mother. 'You're being very unkind. And James, that's quite enough.'

Colonel Aylmer pulled his daughter close. 'Now, let's see your sketch, Alice. I see you've used your new pastels and very well too. It's a fine drawing, wouldn't you agree, James?'

'Oh, I know she's a better artist than me, Father, and she's made Ayah's face look just as ugly as it does in real life. But you've another two years in India before you're sent back, Alice, so I should like to have Father to myself at Lansdowne Ridge.'

'Really, Charles, do put them out of their misery,' his wife frowned. 'We can't have the children fighting over you like this.'

41

The Colonel laughed. 'Beatrice, my dear, they know I'll have a fair resolution. Now, let me see . . . how about if Alice gets a new paint box maybe?'

Alice cried, 'Oh, thank you, Father! That is very fair, perfectly fair!'

Michael watched the child skip around the verandah in excitement. The Aylmers were well off, unlike most of the Irish officers of the Kildare Rangers. Colonel Aylmer's father had commanded the Rangers in 1895 and had been decorated twice for his bravery during campaigns in the North-West Frontier. However, the family fortune had been made by Aylmer men a few generations earlier in the sugar plantations in the West Indies. Charles Aylmer was the eldest of three sons and his marriage to Beatrice had been considered very advantageous, for she was the only daughter of one of County Kildare's largest landowners, bringing with her an independent income of four thousand pounds a year.

As a child who had grown up in Ardclough, barely a mile away from the Aylmer estate, Michael was much more familiar with the family's personal life than most men in the Regiment. Other soldiers' families had traditionally found work on the estate, but none had the access to the daily goings-on that Michael and his family had had, for when his sister Bridget started at the Aylmers' as a nursery nurse, she regaled them at home every night with stories of the life at the Big House.

The two years between 1916 and 1918 had been a difficult time for all in Ardclough, and on the Aylmer estate it was no different. Charles was a career soldier and his two younger brothers, who had volunteered in the first few months of the war, had been sent into the thick of the action as soon as they were commissioned.

The Kildare Rangers were away fighting in France, and every week brought telegrams: casualties, deaths and men missing in action. In the autumn of 1917, when she was just thirty years old, Beatrice Aylmer took over the running of the estate completely when her frail in-laws died in quick succession, barely a week apart, unable to bear the news of the deaths of their two younger sons at Gallipoli. Colonel Aylmer came home on leave twice during the four years of the war and both times left secure in the knowledge that his wife, with the help of the Estate Manager and numerous staff, would not let the Aylmer estate fall apart.

Bridget had been very fond of little James, who was just two years old when she started work at the Big House in 1913. But it was Baby Alice who was her favourite. Bridget was there the morning the child was born, had cradled her nervously for a few minutes while the doctor and the nurse had attended to Mrs Aylmer, and had fallen in love with the sweet-natured infant, a love that was reciprocated by the little girl. The children's nanny was in her sixties and having looked after Beatrice Aylmer and her four brothers themselves when they were small, she was not jealous of the children's fondness for Bridget but encouraged it instead. The girl took them to the lake to feed the ducks, she walked and ran and played ball with them, read to them, made dresses for the dolls and costumes for all the pretend play that kept them busy for hours.

By the time Colonel Aylmer returned home from the war Bridget was indispensable.

Looking at the family gathered on the verandah in the fading light of an Indian dusk, Michael remembered how his sister used to pray for Colonel Aylmer's safe return from the war. 'My poor little mites must have their father back,' she would say as she knelt, the rosary beads moving swiftly through her fingers. *If only Bridget could see the children now, together with both their parents,* he thought, then cleared his throat softly before stepping out on to the verandah. He came to attention and saluted smartly.

'Sir! Good evening, sir.'

'At ease, Flaherty. I take it you have me sorted for tomorrow morning?'

'Sir! Yes, sir. It's all cleaned and polished, done and ready, sir.'

'Good, good. How are they getting on in the Mess with the regimental silver?'

'Sir! Captain Milne stopped by at the Mess at four o'clock. The lads must be done by now, sir.'

'We must show the Fusiliers how we do things here in Nandagiri. It'll be a splendid St Patrick's Day dinner. The Band Master's assured me the music will be fit enough for a Coronation Ball.'

'Sir! The Band have been practising all month, sir.'

There was a small tug on his tunic, and a boy's eager voice. 'Will you bring me a bird's nest tomorrow, Michael? With eggs in it?'

'I'll do my best, Master James,' Michael promised. 'I've spotted one in the eaves of the Chapel roof. I'll see if I can tease it out.'

Mrs Aylmer was quick to intervene. 'James, you mustn't trouble Michael. He has a lot of duties and his own things to do in the barracks.'

'It's no trouble at all, Mrs Aylmer. I'd be happy to do it for the young lad.' If only she knew, thought Michael, that it was probably going to be the most interesting thing he'd do all week.

'Well, you'd better get going, Flaherty,' the Colonel put in. 'Take the khitmatgar's cycle if you wish. It is rather dark and we do have a big day tomorrow.'

Michael came to attention and saluted. 'As you say, sir. Good night, sir, Mrs Aylmer.'

'Will you wear the shamrock in your cap badge tomorrow, Michael?' asked Alice.

'Sure, Miss Alice. I'm an Irishman, aren't I?' said Michael, bending down and giving her a little salute.

CHAPTER THREE

20 March 1920

Dear Diary,

Aunty Mags says that's how real English and Irish girls keep diaries and this is how they start – 'Dear Diary' – and then they pour their hearts out, writing down everything that happens to them, good and bad, sad and happy.

Dear Diary, you were my eighteenth-birthday present from Aunty Mags, so here I am, and this is what happened to me today.

Mrs Aylmer said no followers, but Private Flaherty is *not* a follower. He is the Colonel's batman and works in the same house as I do: how could that be *my* fault? I think he's taken a fancy to me, but I can't help that.

I shall now confess what happened today. The family had gone to the Polo Grounds, to watch the Colonel and the Chokra Sahibs practise for their return match against the Fusiliers next week in Ooty. I was on the verandah sewing buttons on Mrs Aylmer's blue riding jacket, when out he walked with his mug of tea and a mouth full of Gajjapati's coconut macaroons. The cook has been told to give the Private tea and something to eat before he goes back to the barracks. I know that because I heard the Colonel ask Mrs Aylmer whether the servants had remembered to feed his batman.

'Old Donnie's son', the Colonel called him. 'Did Gajjapati give Old Donnie's son his tea?' Mrs Aylmer said, 'Yes, of course, Charles, they do as they are told. Do you see how like Bridget he is? It unnerves me sometimes.'

So, there I was on the verandah and he sits down beside me without so much as a by-your-leave and begins to talk, mostly questions about me. Aunty Mags said that's what men do when they're really interested in you. Anyway, I said it was my turn and I asked him about Bridget. It was a sad story, and when he had finished, I asked him about the Aylmer estate. And wait till I tell you this, Dear Diary – the estate's nearly as big as the entire cantonment in Nandagiri! No wonder the family can afford the fancy new motor car that is being driven up from Madras. The Colonel bought it off a retiring Brigadier who's heading back home to England, the lucky man.

The motor car arrives next month, just in time for when Mrs Aylmer plans to stop going out on her horse. She's expecting, you know, and how lucky that turned out for me because the Colonel felt Mrs Aylmer would need some proper help for herself and someone far more superior to the native ayah for the children. So, Mrs Aylmer agreed and took me on, though Michael said that back home in Ireland, in the Big House, the Aylmers had no less than forty servants!

But when I asked him about my father's hometown, Michael wasn't very helpful. 'I've never heard of a Crossterra near Glengarriff,' he said, 'nor, in fact, of any Glengarriff.' Maybe he hasn't travelled like I have. I've been to Madras and Bangalore, and me only eighteen. Aunty Mags said we'll be going to Calcutta next year. Uncle Dennis will be eligible for passes for us on the train. Imagine – Calcutta, the heart of the Empire! We might even see the Viceroy as he drives by in his carriage.

I told Michael this, but he laughed. 'I've crossed the Suez Canal and I'm only twenty-three,' he said, 'and I've seen the King and Queen at a hundred paces while parading at Windsor Castle.'

It made me a bit cross to think he was making himself out to be a man of the world so I told him that I'd probably be crossing the Suez myself before I was twenty. 'I'll be going home, you see, back to Ireland.'

'Back home? To Ireland?' he repeated and didn't even try to hide his surprise.

I told him what Father has promised me – that we'll be going home to Glengarriff soon, leaving this horrid hot country of dirty natives behind to be with our own people.

This put Michael in his place. He went quiet for a while and then he told me, 'I bet you'll get to see them too – Their Majesties,' he explained. 'If anyone does, Miss Rose Twomey, it will be you.'

I stood up then, to show him how I would curtsey, just for fun, and that's how it all happened. The button box on my lap fell to the floor, and we were both on our knees picking up the little brass ones and the big camel-bone ones and the special ones made from mother-of-pearl, when he leant forward and kissed me on my cheek.

I stood up, Dear Diary, I stood up straight away and I told him Mrs Aylmer had said no followers. But he squeezed my hand, gave me a wicked big wink and walked away, down the verandah steps and towards the gate, whistling loudly with his hands in his pockets. I shouted out to him that Mrs Aylmer didn't allow whistling either, but he never looked back. I'll have something to say to him tomorrow. What do you think I should say, my Dearest Diary?

CHAPTER FOUR

29 March 1920

Dear Diary,

How difficult this week has been, so very difficult. The poor Colonel . . . winning the polo match against the visiting Fusiliers and holding the huge silver trophy aloft was no prize at all, after he'd had to put down three of his best polo ponies.

It was a horrible affair. I tried to pull Alice and James close in towards me so they wouldn't be able to see what was happening, but both times they managed to push me away and stand up on the rungs of the fence, looking across the polo-field to where the poor creatures lay writhing in agony. The Colonel shot them himself, taking the gun from the vet, the first two between chukkas, as soon as they fell and right where they lay, one with a snapped ankle and the other a broken knee, and the third – the bay mare, his favourite – at the end of the match when the vet gave his verdict with a gloomy shake of his head.

It put a real damper on the win and Major Gordon, the captain of the Fusiliers team, stood talking very solemnly to the Colonel for a long time after. Everybody could see the Colonel was heartbroken and Mrs Aylmer was white as a sheet when she, being the Burra Mem, had to hand him the trophy.

When we got home, Mrs Aylmer asked Uttam Singh, our new Sikh chauffeur, to take the children and me for a little drive up to Lake Victoria and the bandstand and back. I didn't mind at all, for when I'm in the motor car I feel like Lady Rose, especially when we drive down Kildare Avenue, there being only six motor cars in the whole of Nandagiri. All the natives stop whatever they are doing and salaam us many times over, and everyone else stares so enviously.

But that day wasn't quite the same, even for me, and when we returned to the house an hour later the Colonel and Mrs Aylmer were still in the bedroom, with Gajjapati standing guard outside like he does when he knows his Sahib and Memsahib don't want to be disturbed. It irritates me when he takes it upon himself to do that, but these native servants get too possessive of their masters sometimes and forget their place.

Anyway, I know that if it wasn't for the visiting team being there, the Aylmers wouldn't have gone to the Club for the dinner dance later that evening. Michael, who was on point duty at the portico of the Club for the night, told me the next day that the Mess Steward had said that the officers were so subdued, the only talk, even before the cigars were brought out, was of horses, terrible accidents at polo, shikar mishaps, the best guns for putting down animals and the serious expense of replacing three polo ponies all at the same time.

'The Aylmers wouldn't be thinking about the money,' I said to Michael. 'They would be thinking about the ponies.'

'You're right. We thought it odd in Ardclough, the way the animals got priority on the Aylmer estate. My father always said if he were reborn, he'd want to come back as one of the

Colonel's gun dogs.' Michael was joking, but I told him that love of animals was one of the things that set us apart from the natives.

Alice and James were miserable and insisted on hanging around their ponies in the stables at all times of the morning and evening, causing the lazy syces – the grooms – to work harder than usual. Thankfully, two days later, the children brightened up at the prospect of heading off with their father, who was motoring down to Coimbatore in the plains to strike a deal with the Raja of Pudunagari who had sent word that he had some fine young polo ponies for sale.

Mrs Aylmer was rather irritable that morning after the Colonel and the children left. She has been sick these last few mornings and I think it tires her out. Gajjapati watches her like a hawk, keeps trying to coax her to eat some food and I think she tires of his fussing, too. She wasn't happy with the kedgeree he had made; she felt the chopped boiled egg that was sprinkled over had gone off and she asked me to smell it and see what I thought. It smelled fine to me and I told her so. She pushed the plate away and closed her eyes, saying, 'You people can't tell when things are spoiled.' I don't see how she could possibly class me as 'you people' along with the khitmatgar. Really, I should have said something, but I made excuses for her; she did look so pale and drawn.

That evening, she apologised to Gajjapati for being so tetchy and he fell at her feet so dramatically that I longed to give him a smart little kick, the way Father does when he wants the natives to stop their grovelling. Mrs Aylmer asked him to get up, which he did after another dramatic interval. I was tidying away the books that the children had been reading aloud to her earlier and I wondered if she would turn to me next and apologise.

I would have smiled and said she was not to worry, but no apology ever came.

You know, Dear Diary, I met Father Jerome the other evening on my way home and he asked how I was getting on at the Aylmers'. I told him all the good things – that I was happy and was kept busy between my duties with the children and Mrs Aylmer. I help her with her toilette, brush her hair, look after her clothes and help her to dress and do her hair for her if they are going out in the evenings. She was so surprised when she saw my beautiful handwriting. I had to remind her that I'd been educated by nuns! So, she has asked me to make a list of all the books in the small library and I am to do this on little cards and arrange the cards and books alphabetically. Father Jerome was very impressed, I think. I didn't tell him that I am not allowed to read to the children, as Mrs Aylmer said they will become good readers only if they read for themselves. I believed her until that awful Dolores Cooper told me it was because they didn't want the children to start talking like me! I asked what she meant and she told me not to get so high and mighty and to just scratch my skin to see what showed beneath. I tell you, I won't be talking to that darkie ever again.

Nor did I tell Father Jerome that Mrs Aylmer isn't very friendly. I mean, she hardly ever talks to me except the bare essentials – orders, requests to do this or that. The other day as I was doing her hair, I asked her if she knew of a place called Glengarriff and she smiled and said she had honeymooned there after her wedding. I told her that it was my hometown and she lifted one eyebrow but did not respond. Soon afterwards, she told me she'd manage the rest of her toilette on her own and could I go and make sure the children were being good for the ayah.

No, I didn't tell Father Jerome those things, nor that when the children go to the Club, they always take the ayah but never me. Michael says it's because they wouldn't know what to do with me once we get there. 'Well, you can't wait around under the neem tree, next to the playground, along with all the children's ayahs and grooms, can you? Where would they put you?' I was annoyed when he said that.

As a matter of fact, staying behind when the Aylmers go to the Club every evening suits me fine – it's the only time I get to talk to Michael. I wouldn't dare do that when any of them are around. When they're gone, I sit on the verandah and sometimes, if I haven't any chores I might leaf through the fancy catalogues that arrive from Madras and Calcutta, or even read the ladies' journals that come from London. Michael has usually finished his duties by then: it's mainly uniforms, boots, belts and buckles that he has to clean and polish, and he is quick to join me with his mug of tea. Dear Diary, it's the best part of the day. The servants are busy on the back verandah with the preparations for dinner, the beds are being made, mosquito nets hung, animals being stabled and we, Michael and I, are left alone to talk.

I've seen the mali look at us curiously a few times, but Michael threw his boot at him once and he's never dared lift his eyes away from the flower beds again. Michael has learnt quickly – the natives must always be kept in their place if they are to know their place.

Of course, I never told Father Jerome about me and Michael either. I know exactly what he would do, the same as he did when that flirt Dolores Cooper was seen talking and laughing with that boxer fellow Gerald O'Gorman in the Emerald Tearoom. She hasn't seen him since that day, but I'm not surprised; she hasn't a hope even though she's been trying to catch a soldier for herself for the last four years. Lord forgive me, but I'd rather die than have her colouring. Dear Diary, I remember how Mother made me promise again and again that I'd always stay out of the sun. Michael laughs at me, at my hats, long gloves and my aversion to the sun, but I don't care. I'm Irish and I intend to stay that way.

As I said at the start, it was a difficult week. Yesterday morning, Mrs Aylmer was unwell and she stayed in bed. The Colonel came back to the house at eleven o'clock and I was at her side, just applying a cold compress to her head, when he and Surgeon-Major McArdle came into the darkened room. The Colonel told the Surgeon-Major: 'The real reason for my wife's misery is that she hasn't been out on her horse, and the Planters' Hunt have been out twice this week. I'm only teasing, Beatrice my dear; another week or two and you'll be back in the saddle.'

The Surgeon-Major was shocked. 'Surely, Colonel, Mrs Aylmer will not go out with the Hunt. I must insist that she refrains from doing that. It would be most unsafe, for her and the baby.'

Mrs Aylmer sat up at this point. 'Not hunting, Surgeon-Major, but up in the saddle I will get,' she said. 'Just with the children, and with Charles – there is plenty of safe hacking around these hills. The syces will accompany me on foot at all times.'

'Very well, but my professional advice is that you *not* ride after August. We don't want any problems in the last three months, do we?'

When the men had left the room, Mrs Aylmer asked me to prop up her pillows. 'Rose, ask Gajjapati to fetch the syce. I'd like to hear directly from him what he's been up to these past few days. Have you seen him riding the mare out?'

'Michael told me he saw the syce riding the mare by the parade grounds.' It just slipped out, I should have called him Private Flaherty, but it was too late.

'Michael? You mean Private Flaherty?'

'Yes, Mrs Aylmer. I was talking to him yesterday, when the family was at the Club.' I quietly excused myself and left the room.

I remained with the children for the rest of the morning, in the schoolroom where they were finishing the work set by their mother. The Colonel had decided to stay on at home till lunch, and while waiting, he read the papers to his wife. It wasn't till the entire household had roused after their afternoon nap that she sent for me.

'Rose,' she said, 'I don't want you getting mixed up with Private Flaherty or any other soldiers, for that matter. They've nothing to offer a girl like you except trouble. Your father won't be pleased and neither will I.'

What was I to do, Dear Diary? I was fit to cry but I wasn't going to let her see that. Only Indians indulged in that sort of pathetic behaviour.

'You needn't worry, Mrs Aylmer,' I said to her. 'I'm not looking for any trouble.'

Why would I, I thought to myself, *when I've found an Irishman to love?* I was as shocked with that unexpected realisation as Mrs Aylmer would have been, had I blurted it out aloud. While I trembled at my thoughts, Mrs Aylmer seemed happy enough with what I had said, and by the time Captain Milne's wife called to the house at four o'clock, she was quite herself again.

That was yesterday and today she was even better still, managing to eat a light breakfast and riding out with the children for the first time in two weeks. I spent all of this morning thinking about what I hadn't said to her – that I had found an Irishman to love. Oh Diary, could it be possible that he would love me, too? To think that, soon, when Father takes me back to Ireland, I may have someone there of my very own waiting for me!

CHAPTER FIVE

Madras, July 1920

Michael had a big tin of caramels in his hands as he walked into Madras Central Station. All of Madras city seemed to be there – natives with their dirty bundles and battered tin boxes, soldiers in transit asleep against their canvas holdalls as they waited for the troop trains, well-to-do Brahmins with their retinue of servants carrying food and water for their journey, Europeans milling around the first-class waiting rooms and red-shirted coolies squatting in small groups smoking beedis but alert for the arrival of the next train.

Michael dabbed his neck and face with a large handkerchief and looked up at the huge clock above the station-master's office. It was barely eight in the morning and already the July sun had turned the cavernous space into a heaving oven. The air stank of soot and sweat, and he decided to walk to the far end of platform 2, where the roofless stretch made waiting a bit cooler.

He hadn't seen Rose for a month, one month in which he had missed her pretty face, her happy chatter and the kisses stolen whenever they had the chance. So, when her telegram arrived stating very simply that she was reaching Madras the next day, arriving by the Nandagiri Mail and that she was staying at 32, Railway Lines at Egmore, he was grateful that he had the next two days completely to himself. He was on leave from the Signallers course he was attending at the Battalion Headquarters at Fort St George in Madras, where he and fifteen other soldiers on the course had sat their examinations last week. They now all had a few days off while they waited to see if they had passed, before heading back to their own regiments.

Having spent the first six months in the relatively mild and pleasant climes of Nandagiri, nothing could have prepared Michael for the heat in Madras. The mosquitoes tormented him at night, and during the day the extreme humidity kept the course instructors on a short fuse, tempers flaring at the mildest of irritations. The Signallers course was intense, with much to learn, and he had worked hard for the whole month, hoping he had managed to pass; the extra pay he would be entitled to would come in handy.

Rose had written to him nearly every day, but he had only managed five replies in return. He had asked to be excused, because doing anything in the oppressive heat of the evening was an ordeal: he couldn't even bear the touch of paper under his palm.

Dozens of coolies suddenly began racing across the station, swarming like an army of red ants towards platform 2 – a sure indication that the Nandagiri Mail was on its way. Michael was certain there would be someone else as well to meet Rose off the train, most likely the aunt and uncle she had mentioned who lived in Madras. He knew Rose wouldn't be expecting him at the station and the thought of surprising her amused him.

The Nandagiri Mail was a sight to behold as it pulled into the station with slow majesty; great puffs of steam billowed out of the jet-black monster as it ground to a juddering halt. Long before the train came to a final stop, all hell broke loose as coolies jumped into the still-moving carriages and passengers tried to ready themselves at the doors to alight, all at the same time. As Michael walked briskly along the now stationary train, ignoring the third- and second-class compartments, he observed with mild irritation the manner in which Indians of every rank travelled.

It seemed they took along with them every single thing they possessed, tied in bundles of various shapes and sizes: charcoal stoves and utensils to cook and carry food so they didn't have to break their unfathomable caste rules, rolls of bedding, brass pots filled with water – and to top it all they were accompanied by their faceless women, in purdah. So overloaded were they, that their disembarkation from the train was a long-drawn-out affair, creating total impasses within the compartments and on steps of the carriages, and causing mayhem on the platform itself. It was a good thing Indians were confined to the second and third class, he thought, or train travel would become completely intolerable.

He spotted Rose as she stood at the door of her first-class carriage, looking up and down the platform briefly, then smiling and waving to someone before picking up her small valise and stepping down. She was greeted affectionately by an older man who kissed her on both cheeks, took her case from her and gave her his arm. Michael took a couple of long strides and caught up with them.

'Hello, Rose. Fancy a caramel?'

She turned around and uttered a small scream of delight. 'Michael!'

He handed her the tin of caramels and kissed her on the cheek then stepped back, waiting to be introduced.

'Uncle Dennis, this is Michael Flaherty.'

Michael's hand was shaken firmly. 'Ah, you're Rose's Kildare Ranger. I'm Dennis Roberts – good to finally make your acquaintance, young man. Rose has written to us about you. Well, shall we talk as we walk, for I've a gharry hired and waiting.'

Rose squeezed Michael's hand lightly. 'Will you come with us to Egmore, Michael? Do say yes. Aunty Mags would love to meet you. Will that be all right, Uncle Dennis?'

'I'll never stand in the way of anything that your Aunty Mags might love to do, Rose. It's never worth the trouble, I learnt that long ago.' The man turned to Michael. 'My wife will be pleased to meet you and there's room enough in the gharry. Now, what about you, Rose? Are you to stay with us a while? Give me some news of your father. I haven't seen Sean for eight months now. Are we to expect him in Madras soon?'

Michael insisted on taking the valise from Dennis and they headed down the platform towards the waiting gharry outside the station.

'I can stay for a week, Uncle Dennis, and as for Father – the piggery comes first, especially since the two new sheds were built. He doesn't trust his labourers fully and he's right because they'd cheat him at the first opportunity if he went away. You know how adept Indians are with petty theft – a few handfuls of feed here, a couple of coins there, a day-old chick or two from the henhouses. He's looking for an overseer – not Indian, of course – and when he gets one, he might relax a bit, but then again, knowing Father, he might not.'

She unfurled her cream lace parasol as they walked out from under the porch of the station and stepped into the morning sun. Michael knew it was one of her prize possessions, obsessed as she was about keeping the sun away from her face. The Bacon-wallah had ordered it for her birthday from the Army and Navy catalogue and it had arrived a week after her birthday, a large package with impressive London postmarks.

Dennis Roberts took the valise from Michael and handed it to the gharry driver. As he helped her climb in, Michael caught the faint smell of Rose's cologne, with its hints of lavender and camomile. The gharry-wallah picked up the reins, clicked his tongue and they joined the other lines of carriages, carts and rickshaws in order to reach the gates from where they could make the right turn on to the Egmore Road.

Rose heaved a sigh of relief when they were finally able to pick up a bit of pace. 'People in Nandagiri think Kildare Avenue is bad,' she said, dabbing at her forehead with an embroidered handkerchief. 'They should see this!'

Her Uncle Dennis laughed loudly. 'And my dear, if you think *this* is bad you should see it in the evenings, when the trains arrive continuously from four o'clock all the way up to ten at night. Even the presence of the Railway Police doesn't stop the chaos.'

'In that case, I'll remember never to arrive on an evening train, Uncle,' she replied, before turning to Michael to say, 'I wasn't expecting to see you at the station and I even feared you wouldn't have a day off at all. But to think you've two whole days! I couldn't have come at a better time. Do you return to Nandagiri immediately, if you pass the course?'

Michael told her about his month at Fort St George in Madras and how hard he had had to study for the examinations. He confessed his anxiety about the results. 'The Sergeant-Major takes pride in the number of hopefuls that he can fail each month. He told us he'd a reputation to live up to.'

Dennis Roberts patted Michael on his knee. 'Don't fret, my boy. You've done your best, it's obvious.'

Rose gave her uncle all the news from Nandagiri and asked for news in return. 'How's Cousin Ronnie? He promised to write to me as soon as he got to Australia, and he hasn't done so as yet.'

'Rose, you can discuss that with his mother because your Aunty Mags has the same complaint. Ronnie seldom writes. I keep telling her it's because he's hard at work, making his mark in a new country, but she still worries constantly.'

As they talked, the gharry made its way to the Railways Lines and wound through a series of leafy lanes before coming to a halt in front of number 32. Michael followed Rose and her uncle through the small wooden gate and down a short path to a large verandah that overlooked an enclosed garden to one side. Rose flew into her Aunty Mags's arms and explained who Michael was.

'You'll stay for breakfast, of course,' the kindly woman said immediately. 'I'll get the cook to start on it right away. Dennis, you must stay too. It's a special occasion, after all. We didn't expect to meet Rose's young man today.'

'I can't, Mags dear. I've an inspection coming up in a week's time and more work to be done than there's time. You'll excuse me, Michael, my boy. I've told the gharry-wallah to stay on, Mags. No doubt you ladies will want to head to Spencer's Emporium or perhaps even the beach this evening.'

Mags allowed her husband to kiss her on each cheek, and as she watched him walk down the path she grumbled good-naturedly, 'I've told you, Rose, many times over, never marry a railway man and this is why. There's always an inspection in the depot, especially when you need them. Well, come in all and make yourselves comfortable. Rose, you are in Ronnie's room as usual and everything's ready for you. You'd better freshen up, my dear, after that train journey; you can unpack later. I myself won't be too long with the cook, and then, Michael,' she said, ushering him into the sitting room, 'we can sit and talk.'

Michael sat down on the large overstuffed sofa and looked around the modest sitting room, which was dominated by an upright piano piled high with music-sheets and songbooks. Two armchairs and another smaller sofa took up the rest of the space. Hanging on the wall in pride of place behind the sofa was a sepia print of a scene from the Coronation Durbar of King George V and Queen Mary. The framed print had two small Union Jacks flying each side of the picture, and in the china cabinet was a display of more royal memorabilia than he had ever seen.

This was the first time since he had left Ireland that Michael had been in a real home, a welcome visitor in a household run by a woman – a far cry from being one of forty soldiers in a soulless barrack room.

He closed his eyes for a moment and tried to remember the details of domestic life at home, how his mother moved so gracefully from one side of the kitchen to the other, constantly wiping her hands on her apron, her look of utter satisfaction if she had got a good day's drying, the way she would talk to the cat when she thought no one was listening. As he settled back into the comfort of the sofa, he realised just how much he missed home.

When Rose came back into the room and sat down beside him, they moved closer, holding hands and kissing each other hungrily, and then he stopped, buried his face in her neck and murmured, 'I missed you, Rose.'

She pushed him away lightly. 'You're a tease, Michael Flaherty. Is that why I've had barely five letters but dozens of excuses from you?'

'Come now, Rose, I thought I'd be forgiven by now. I brought you the caramels specially to make up for not writing, but better still, I'm going to take you out today, just you and me. Will your Aunty Mags let you come out for the day? I thought we might go for a stroll to the Marina in the evening and then to a dance maybe?'

'Kiss me again, Michael, before Aunty Mags comes in.' Rose pressed herself against him and he kissed her, his heart bursting with tenderness. As he brushed his lips against her forehead, his overwhelming emotion was one of helplessness. His initial infatuation had grown into something more serious – and the more involved he had become, the greater his despair. Her obvious love for him was flattering and he found himself going along with her girlish notions of life in Ireland and ready to tell her all that she wanted to know about home if it made her happy.

It was the tender moments like this that triggered his despair, that reminded him of the reality of their situation. Michael knew he would never be given permission to marry her. The military rules were strict and clear – marriage for young soldiers was forbidden. It was difficult enough for senior NCOs, who were considered very fortunate if they had managed to put their wives and children on the regimental books. There was always a scramble for that privilege, despite the fact that married soldiers led a hard life, with very cramped quarters and little or no social facilities.

What's more, Michael had signed on for seven years with the Colours, with a regiment that could be sent to any part of the Empire at any time. Seven years before he could ask permission to marry. No wonder the lads in B Company thought him a bloody fool to have got tangled up with the Bacon-wallah's daughter.

He could think of no one to turn to for advice now except Father Jerome, for Tom Nolan had been totally dismissive about Rose, warning Michael that Eurasian girls were always on the lookout for a quick and legitimate passage out of India.

'You'll be making a right idiot of yourself!' he'd scoffed. 'Nobody waits seven years in India. Jaysus, lad, that's time enough for an entire family to be dead and buried in these climes, and anyway, what's to stop her from latching on to some other gullible sod the minute the Rangers get posted out of Nandagiri?'

Tom had then dug him in the ribs. 'Haven't you heard the cavalry regiments cut a dashing figure in their uniforms? She won't wait seven days for you, my lad, when one of those young stallions comes riding by, but I tell you, even the Cavalry fellows won't be fool enough to take the likes of *her* home.'

When he had protested that the Bacon-wallah would take his daughter back to Ireland himself, Tom had told him straight: 'You asked me what I thought and I'll tell it to you as I see it. Assuming she'll wait for you – seven years, Jaysus, she'll be an old maid! Haven't you seen what the weather does to women out here in the East? And think of it, man – your children could turn out to be darkies. When blood's diluted, the colour will always come through. It wouldn't be fair on the poor things – what would they do back in Ardclough? You'll have to pick the ones to take and the ones to leave behind. Ask Rose why her mother was in an orphanage: I'll bet you she wasn't white enough to take back home, that's why. And why did Sean Twomey, the Bacon-wallah, marry her? It was because no white woman worth her salt would've wanted to marry an old Irishman gone native. So, the Bacon-wallah goes to the orphanage and picks a girl, as light a one as possible, and does her the big favour of marrying her. Colour can skip a generation, you know, Michael, so you might get a few nasty surprises along the way.'

Tom had stopped to take a long drink from his bottle of beer before putting his elbows on the table and confiding, 'And you can be sure the Bacon-wallah *won't* be going home. He's been saying that for twenty years or more, since the day his time was up with the Rangers. Why would he want to go back to a hovel of a cottage in West Cork when he can live here with a bungalow to call his own, a business that more than pays the bills and native servants salaaming him night and day? The daughter may have notions of all kinds, but the Bacon-wallah's no fool. He's a tradesman now, with a good name and reputation. Sure, there's no living to be made down the sodden boreen that he was born in.' He finished sternly: 'You don't be a damn fool yourself, Michael, and don't let her make one of you.'

Michael had sprung up from the table where he had been sitting with Tom and had walked out of the wet canteen in anger. He knew that the only useful advice he would get would be from Father Jerome, and he had been planning to speak to the priest as soon as he got back to Nandagiri, after the Signallers course.

Michael looked at Rose on the sofa and felt sorry for her, as he had many times before. He would never dare say it to her, for she had made her feelings very clear on that subject. 'It's respect that I want, Michael,' she had told him, 'not sympathy. Sympathy only ever makes me feel small.'

Aunty Mags walked into the room to announce, 'Breakfast will be ready in a short while. We've a new cook, a bit of a duffer, and Lord knows it's taken a while to get rid of his dirty Indian habits. Rose, do you remember how your own dear mother struggled during the war years with untrained natives who used to turn up at the kitchen door looking for work?'

Aunty Mags launched into an explanation for Michael. 'During the Great War, the best cooks and khitmatgars joined the Army and we poor housewives were left to manage with the dregs. Rose's mother Evie, may she rest in peace, used to say she wished she could roar like Sean: just one holler was all it took. She, poor thing, was so soft-spoken, they all just took advantage of her.'

Rose was looking at a collection of framed pictures arranged on the teapoy beside her armchair. She picked up one in a pearly frame and handed it to Michael. 'That's her, that's my mother Evie. She died from malaria when I was six.'

Michael looked down at the photograph in his hand and Tom Nolan's words came back to him in a rush: Rose's mother was undoubtedly several shades darker than Rose whose pale complexion belied her mixed blood.

'Evie and I, we grew up in the same military orphanage. We became close, closer than most sisters. No one would have ever guessed that we weren't related.' Aunty Mags was wiping a tear from her eye before suddenly becoming all business-like. 'Rose, put that picture away, dear child, and let's talk about what we can do today. Your Uncle Dennis has kept the gharry-wallah for the whole day, so we mustn't let that go to waste.'

Over breakfast, Aunty Mags was full of ideas for different excursions and entertainments. Deciding it was now or never, Michael put his cutlery down on his plate and said: 'I was wondering, Mrs Roberts – that is, if it was acceptable with you, and Mr Roberts as well, of course – if I could take Rose out today.'

Aunty Mags looked surprised. 'Mrs Roberts? No, no, dear boy, it is Aunty Mags to you as well.' She thought for a moment. 'There's music and dancing at the Connemara, and I'm sure Rose would like that, wouldn't you, my dear?'

Rose nodded her head enthusiastically and Aunty Mags smiled. 'There you are, Michael, it's settled then.'

'Where's the punkah-wallah, Aunty Mags? This heat's making me quite silly.'

'He'll be here soon, my dear. I've sent him round to the bazaar for a few things. I thought I'd make a lemon cake for teatime. It's your favourite, Rose, I know. I haven't forgotten.'

Michael stood up and walked to the window. 'Shall we take the gharry to Spencer's before it gets too hot? We can have lunch there and ice cream, as well. How about that, Rose? Their ice cream is even better than the Emerald's up in Nandagiri.'

'Only if you'll bring her back before the afternoon heat. Rose, remember you aren't used to our Madras afternoons. I'll have the khus-khus tatties lowered and ready immediately after lunch. Your Uncle Dennis comes home for a rest then and Michael can lie down here on the sofa. It's good to rest. We old India hands know that only too well.'

Rose had stood up as soon as Michael had spoken, saying excitedly, 'I'd love that, and then in the evening the beach and some dancing at the Connemara. Oh yes, let's make the best of your days off, Michael. Will you come with us, Aunty Mags?'

'Oh no, my dear, I couldn't leave right now. I've the sewing machine out and my darzee is supposed to call by today. If I'm not here he'll head off straight next door to Mrs McKay's and I won't see him for another three weeks. Her son, you must remember him, Rose, the boy with the squint, he's heading off to Sydney in a month's time. We thought we had Ronnie kitted out fit for a king when he went away, but this McKay boy is getting no less than a Raja's trousseau – six trousers, six shirts and would you believe it, two suits – one black and one navy blue. All that fuss and he doesn't even have a job lined up for when he arrives! Our Ronnie, God bless him, had barely a day to get used to Sydney before he started work there, all organised by your Uncle Dennis, of course.'

She turned around to Rose. 'But talking of his evening, you must come back home for dinner before going dancing at the Connemara. It'll work out frightfully expensive to do both there. Rose, you don't want this young man to be throwing his money away, and anyway, your Uncle Dennis will want some time to talk to Michael.' She explained, 'Dennis's grandfather on the maternal side was Irish, you know, from Connemara, but lived out his life in India. He was a railway man and survived the Mutiny only to die a terrible death later. Rabies – he was bitten by a bat of all things.'

A shadow appeared at the doorway and Aunty Mags summoned the khitmatgar into the room. She fired off orders for the day's meals, discussing in detail every dish that was to be prepared, writing down all that was required and calculating the amount of money needed to the very last pice. She finally handed the man some money and dismissed him with several warnings about being prudent with the shopping.

Aunty Mags shook her head as the man left, salaaming. 'That fellow's a crook by trade and a khitmatgar by chance,' she sighed. 'Ready to cheat me at the slightest opportunity.'

She suddenly got up and exclaimed: 'But up! Up! Just look at the time! You really must leave before it gets too hot. Your uncle will be annoyed with me, and with you both, too, if he knew you were gallivanting outdoors in the heat. Leave now and you'll be back in time for lunch and then you can rest awhile before your evening at the beach.'

In the gharry, Michael put his arm around Rose's narrow waist and pulled her close. To think he had a whole day in Madras with her, away from the prying, censorious eyes of a small-town cantonment, away from the ribald sniggering in the Nandagiri barracks and the certain annoyance of Colonel Aylmer who, shortly after Rose had taken up employment in the Aylmer household, had passed on his wife's displeasure at his batman's obvious infatuation with the new lady's maid in no uncertain terms.

CHAPTER SIX

20 July 1920

Dear Diary,

I didn't take you with me to Madras and you know why. Aunty Mags can be so nosy; she wouldn't have hesitated to ask me to read it out loud to her and I couldn't have said no – she just won't take no for an answer. I love her very much, and she says I'm as good as her daughter, but I don't think Mother would ever have asked to read my diary: in fact, I'm sure she wouldn't have.

I had such an adventure in Madras, because of the native uprising. Michael was so brave, the hero of the hour. I know he loves me truly, but I can't say more than that. There are some things a girl cannot tell anyone, not even you, Dear Diary. However, you must believe me when I say he's the gentlest, kindest, most handsome young man a girl could ever want.

I've been kept so very busy since I got back, which is why I haven't written in a while. Mrs Aylmer and the children returned to Madras from their few weeks in Ceylon and I travelled back to Nandagiri with them. It's so good to be here in the hills again; anything's better than that wretched heat of Madras. Uttam Singh had met us at Mettupalayam with the motor car but to my disappointment he was there only to take the luggage up to Nandagiri.

Mrs Aylmer had arranged for us to take the Toy Train up the mountain despite the fact it would take twice as long, all because she had always wanted to see the Kurinji flower in bloom. On the night train back from Madras, Mrs Aylmer talked to Alice and James about the rare blossom that flowers just once in twelve years. The children were excited, as excited as the many hundreds of people who will be travelling to see the blooms over the next few months, sometimes travelling long distances to do so. The last time the Kurinji flowered, the Viceroy himself, with the Vicerine and their entire staff of four hundred, journeyed all the way from Delhi just to see the Kurinji cloaking the hills. I remember the occasion well because, along with four other six-year-olds, I'd been picked to stand in line and hand the Vicerine a posy of Kurinji when she visited the regimental school. Unfortunately, my mother, who'd been so very ill for three months, died the night before my big day. To my shame, I think I cried as much for the missed chance of curtseying to the Vicerine and having her smile back at me as I did for my poor dead mother.

The station-master at Mettupalayam was waiting for us when the Madras Mail pulled in and we were immediately escorted to the first-class carriage at the front of the Toy Train. He informed Mrs Aylmer that the Colonel had telegraphed that he would join the family on the train at Conoor station, at which news Alice and James whooped with delight. The station-master had placed two railway attendants at Mrs Aylmer's disposal for the whole journey, and no sooner had they stepped forward and salaamed than James begged to be allowed to go with one of them to see the locomotive being stoked up. Alice pleaded, too, and Mrs Aylmer sent me with her, with instructions that she was not to get her clothes dirty.

This was difficult, for even though we stood a good bit away, great black clouds puffed and billowed from the engine as it was loaded up with huge shovelfuls of coal. When James returned, his face looked like Alice's favourite golliwog, and I had to take him to the first-class restrooms to get washed and cleaned. His mother said he would need a soak in one of Gajjapati's extra-hot baths.

The rare flower lived up to everyone's expectations, and once we had left the water stop at Kallar and began to climb in earnest, every now and then there was a collective intake of breath as the train rounded a bend or emerged from a tunnel to reveal the glorious sight of Kurinji blooms stretching as far as the eye could see.

The children had a happy reunion with their father when he boarded the train at Conoor, and it was only a matter of a few days before I'd settled back into the routine of the Aylmer household. Mrs Aylmer's pregnancy is beginning to show now but she seems to have more energy than before.

Michael came back from Madras a week ago, straight into the thick of it. The Regiment went on route march to Ooty, where they were to have a joint exercise with the Fusiliers. Father left a day ahead to set up and be ready for the Regiment when they arrived at the halfway camp at ten in the morning. Having left Nandagiri at four o'clock, when dawn was still two hours away, and having marched uphill for six hours straight, he knew the men wouldn't be satisfied with just what the regimental cooks were going to provide. Father's clever that way – he took three of his men, two chokra boys and two bullock-carts laden down with fifty pounds of bacon, bread, sugar, tea and coffee and eighty chickens who must have woken up the whole cantonment with their squawking.

Dear Diary, Michael burst out laughing when I told him that every night Father says a prayer for hungry soldiers all over India. 'God bless the ravenous Regiment,' he says, crossing himself solemnly. 'They're my bread and butter, Rose. Where would we be without them?' I know he's right, but I'd much prefer it if Father would buy up one of the tearooms on Kildare Avenue instead of setting up his stall under the gulmohur trees, having to cope with dogs and monkeys, in the middle of all the noise and terrible smells in the Gorah Bazaar. He could call himself the proprietor of a real 'establishment' and all the officers and their families would come, too. Father could even hire Dolores Cooper's cousin, Lionel, play on a piano just like they do in the Emerald Tearoom. He'd do fine – at least he hasn't her unfortunate colouring – and I could write out all the menus beautifully in my best handwriting. But Father won't even consider it. I think he just loves being right next to the parade grounds and amongst soldiers. Mother used to say it kept him alive, the feeling that he was still part of his Regiment and the great Army that kept the Empire in order.

Dear Diary, how I've rambled! I really wanted to tell you about all the things that happened today at Theppakadu. For the last few months, Colonel Aylmer and some of the other officers have been planning a tiger hunt in the Masinagudi Forest: they're eager to have it before the rains come. The forest cover is sparse at the moment and that means animals are easier to spot, but just one heavy rain can change everything, turning the forest lush and green and impenetrable.

All of last week, the Colonel waited on news from the headman at Masinagudi about the arrangements for elephants and beaters. When the message came through that everything had been organised, Mrs Aylmer told me that she and the children would be driving down to the elephant camp at Theppakadu which is just a few miles from Masinagudi village, and that I was to go with them. Michael and three other soldiers, who were orderlies to Major Deacon, Captain Milne and Surgeon-Major McArdle, and who were raring to experience a tiger hunt, volunteered to accompany their officers. I wondered if Father would be anxious about me going but his eyes lit up when I told him that Mrs Aylmer wanted me to help her with the children and I knew immediately he was thinking of the good old days, when tigers were plentiful. 'Just think of it,' he reminisced. 'It wasn't that long ago, between 1896 and 1905, that more than nine hundred tigers were shot in the Nilgiris and would you believe it, child, the government was happy to pay a bounty then for every single beast that was shot.'

Poor Father, he's never shot a tiger, it's such an expensive business, but we've a few black buck heads mounted on the dining-room wall and a bearskin, too. How Mother used to hate those heads. She always said the eyes followed her around accusingly. Mother – she was so gentle.

This morning Mrs Aylmer, the children and I made an early start just after dawn. Ayah, Gajjapati and three other servants had been sent ahead yesterday. Uttam Singh had polished the car till the brass shone like gold and he was ready and waiting to leave, the dog boy sitting in front beside him, gingerly holding Uttam Singh's loaded rifle. Colonel Aylmer never lets Uttam Singh drive anywhere without a loaded rifle on the seat beside him because elephants are not uncommon on the forest roads around Nandagiri and lone tuskers especially can be dangerously unpredictable.

When we arrived at the halfway point at Pykara, the Forestry Ranger was waiting for us. Mrs Aylmer and the children strolled along the grassy slopes, admiring the views of Mukurti Peak and other landmarks pointed out to them by the Ranger.

Meanwhile, I got Uttam Singh to lay out the rugs and fetch the large wicker basket, and very soon we were having our picnic breakfast overlooking the vast valley, to way down below where the Pykara River flowed, though it had been reduced to a mere stream at this dry time of the year.

We stayed on for a while in Pykara, because Uttam Singh wanted the car's brakes to cool off completely before the final run down to Theppakadu. The Ranger got the villagers to bring up two bear cubs that had recently been captured when their mother had been killed by local shepherds and, with that little encouragement, we were soon surrounded on one side by a semicircle of natives all eager to show off some pathetic creature or other – porcupines, a mongoose or two, a tiny spotted fawn – all in exchange for a few coins and if not that, for just a glimpse of Alice and James with their white skin, blue eyes and golden hair. I was glad we had Uttam Singh who stood between us and the natives, keeping the more curious ones well at bay.

The rest of the journey to Theppakadu didn't take as long as expected, maybe because we all slept most of the way. The children were the first and not long after Mrs Aylmer nodded off. Dear Diary, I was a bit rude, but Mrs Aylmer will never know. I stared at her from head to toe. I've never been able to have such a good look at her before, not from such close quarters. She's so very fair, her skin quite flawless with not a freckle to mark her. I've a sprinkling of freckles on my shoulders but though Mother always consoled me, saying that they were a sure sign of Irish blood, still I'm glad they can't be seen.

I gazed at her as she slept, her hands crossed over her swollen stomach. Her gloves are exquisite, fine silk satin. Mother used to have a pair like them – but not as nice, I admit. Father bought them in Madras for her as a wedding present. When she died, she was laid out wearing her gloves, and sometimes I think it was a pity they weren't kept for me. But I suppose it's like me and my umbrella; if I were to die, I'd want to be buried with it! I know you are laughing, Dear Diary, but I wouldn't go anywhere, not even to heaven, without my face kept out of the sun.

Ever since I started working for Mrs Aylmer, I've tried hard to keep note of the things she places great store by. You know, how she likes her tea tray arranged, her particular liking for flowers like lupins and sweet peas; she thinks the native flowers are so vulgar, and I agree. I mean, what's there to admire in a marigold? Mrs Aylmer always has a soak in the big copper bath that was ordered and brought up from Madras, and how I'd love that instead of a tin bucket and a mug. If Mother was alive, I might have many more ladylike things. Father is generous, but if he can't see the need for something, then he won't buy it. A man simply cannot understand that you can want something even if you don't really have a need for it.

I must have fallen asleep in the car myself soon after, because the next thing I knew, we'd arrived at the riverside camp at the Ranger headquarters in Theppakadu. Even though I don't care too much for Gajjapati, he's faultless when it comes to housekeeping and he had everything ready for our arrival. The tents were pitched fifty yards from each other in a wide semicircle facing the river, with rugs and chairs laid out under the shade of their awnings.

We were barely twenty miles from Nandagiri, but having descended two thousand feet the heat was nearly as bad as Madras! The saving grace was that our camp lay in the shade of a dozen huge teak and rosewood trees. I just love the sound of water, and the Moyar River separated our camp from the elephant kraals in the distance. But how deceptive some things can be! The peaceful Moyar is notorious for its crocodiles, and the horrid creatures are known to attack men sometimes. I remember Father telling Mother and me about seeing crocodiles at this very site when the elephant camp was just being set up ten years ago.

On the other side of the river, over a wooden bridge, were the Forest Rangers' offices, the coolie lines, the elephant kraals and the tribal huts. Most of the elephant trackers and trainers are tribals, and no sooner had we arrived than their women and children gathered in a noisy group on the bank opposite us to stare and point. Alice and James stared and pointed back, for they were close enough to see that the women were bare-breasted.

'Mother, look! Savages! Do you think they are cannibals?'

'You're never to point at others, James, for that makes you a savage, as well,' said Mrs Aylmer, sitting down on the chair that Gajjapati was holding out for her.

I totally agree with her. It's our good manners that separate us from the natives – that and cleanliness and honesty, of course. I've had to deal with Indians much longer than Mrs Aylmer, and sometimes I think she doesn't realise exactly how careful you've to be. Aunty Mags says it's not enough that they have to be afraid of you, you've to be afraid of them, too, or you could get careless, and they love it when you're careless. A little here and little there, and before you know it you've been cheated.

It was late afternoon when we arrived and so Gajjapati didn't waste any time before serving lunch. We had mince cutlets with kedgeree, and Gajjapati was about to serve the rice pudding with spoonfuls of marmalade stirred into it, when I spotted a familiar figure cycling towards us across the bridge from the elephant camp on the other side.

Dear Diary, I dislike Lionel so. He's Dolores Cooper's first cousin, though I wouldn't hold that against him. (I mean, you can't help who your cousins are, can you?) Lionel has recently managed to get into the Imperial Forest Service and is one of the new Foresters. It's the lowest grade but that's all he'd get anyway since he is too much of a duffer to sit any exam for the upper cadres. Well, you should have seen him – all cock of the walk he was as he dismounted and came up to greet Mrs Aylmer. Kept looking at me, but I ignored him. He told Mrs Aylmer that he had everything ready for when the Colonel and the other officers arrived later in the evening. The way Lionel went on, you'd think he'd organised it all himself, when it was actually the Colonel who had made all the advance arrangements. I wouldn't believe a word that Lionel said. He was supposed to go off to Australia but never made it – drank and gambled away his passage money within two days when he was sent to Madras to board the *Spirit of Australia*.

That was two years ago, and last year he had the nerve to corner me at the Christmas Dance at the Railway Club, pin me against the wall and say he'd marry me if I gave him a kiss! I told him Father could spot a gold-digger a mile away, and that truth must have hit home because he left me alone that night and hasn't dared speak to me since.

The Colonel arrived at five o'clock in grand fashion, driving a Rolls-Royce on loan for the occasion from the Raja of Pudunagari. They've become friends ever since the Colonel bought those three polo ponies from the Raja, after that dreadful day in March. The Colonel is arranging for the Raja's son, the Prince, to go to school in Ireland, the same school that James will go to next year, and the two boys are to travel to Ireland together. The Prince has come to the Colonel's house a few times now, to get to know James and to learn some of our ways, such as how to use a knife and fork, proper manners and etiquette and things like that, just so that he isn't an embarrassment to himself when he arrives in the school. Mrs Aylmer thinks he will make a proper Gorah Sahib by the time he finishes his education and, the last time he came, she made him pour out tea and pass the sandwiches around and then praised him no end for doing everything correctly.

The Prince is a plump little fellow and he looked so funny the first time he came, with his kohl-rimmed eyes, all dressed up in a long gold brocade tunic with a double row of pearls around his neck and shimmering pearl studs to match in his ears. I think Alice's comments made him very self-conscious, and the next time he visited, he was wearing a linen suit, and though he wasn't wearing the earrings, the string of pearls remained around his neck.

In the Rolls-Royce with the Colonel were the Collector Mr Myers and his wife, Mr Smythe the Superintendent of Police and Major Deacon. The vehicle swept up into the camp so majestically I nearly expected the Viceroy to step out! A few minutes later, the second car also arrived, bringing Captain Milne and his wife, accompanied by Surgeon-Major and Mrs McArdle.

Just as the sun was setting, hot water was carried into the tents, canvas baths were filled and the ladies got themselves ready for dinner. I don't know whether I should have been pleased or put out that Mrs Milne and Mrs McArdle asked Mrs Aylmer if they could possibly 'borrow' me in turns to do their hair for dinner. But they were both so happy with what I was able to accomplish with so little of the usual toilette at hand, that they pressed two annas each into my hand, which was nice in the end.

Mrs Aylmer was rather talkative that evening as I helped her to dress. She was direct as usual, asking me if I knew Lionel Cooper, saying she thought he wanted to speak to me.

'He asked me to marry him, Mrs Aylmer, about a year ago when I was seventeen, and I said no. I think he still hopes I'll agree.' I then wished I hadn't said anything.

'He seems a nice young man, Rose.'

What was I to say to that, Dear Diary? What would she know about Lionel Cooper and his type? So, I said nothing. I had to bite my tongue hard to keep from telling her that Michael and I are as good as engaged after that day in Madras. Mrs Aylmer didn't press me any further – but that's the way she is. No doubt she will question me again about that lout Lionel sometime soon.

There was a gay atmosphere around the camp this evening. Gajjapati had surpassed himself with his arrangements. A large rug had been rolled out in the centre of the camp and folding armchairs had been arranged on it. Small teapoys were placed between the chairs, and the surrounding trees were hung with small lamps, which looked so pretty once they had been lit. Six small braziers with hot coals dotted the camp, and dried eucalyptus had been left to smoulder on them; it's the best way to keep the mosquitoes away.

I sat with the children at a separate dining table, and we saw the head man of Masinagudi village arrive; the wizened old man squatted on the ground at the edge of the dhurrie and went through all the arrangements that had been made in great detail.

Alice and James went to say good night, and once I'd managed to get them off to sleep, I lay in our tent on my stomach near the netted flap and watched the hunt party cutting into their roast haunch of venison that Gajjapati had served with a rhubarb sauce, roast potatoes and little cabbage parcels stuffed with rice. Everyone looked so happy, and I could see the glint of the crystal glasses as one toast after another was raised, to the King, the Viceroy and the Regiment, and with each toast I joined in silently.

Dusk fell and the jungle was full of chattering, hooting, screeching, grunting and shrieking. Gajjapati had cleared dessert and Mrs Milne had been coaxed to sing. She has a beautiful voice, really, she does.

But suddenly, she stopped singing and her hand flew up to her mouth. We all heard it at the same time – and it silenced the whole camp. There it was again! What a fearsome sound a prowling tiger can make, even when it's a couple of miles away. Mrs Milne shuddered and sat down, and now the darkness was full of the hysterical warnings of the troops of langurs crashing through the trees around the camp. Colonel Aylmer raised another toast, this time to the tiger.

Dear, Dear Diary, I know – I just know that tomorrow will be an exciting day!

CHAPTER SEVEN

Masinagudi Camp, July 1920

Not for the first time since he'd left Ireland Michael wished his mother could see him. She would have been speechless, he was sure, just like he was a few minutes ago when Meena Kumari had wound her leathery trunk around his waist and effortlessly lifted him off the ground, gently placing him into the small wooden howdah on her back. *I will remember this always,* he thought, as he knelt and reached out between the rails to pat Meena Kumari on her head. In that instant when he had been level with her, Michael could have sworn the elephant's bright brown eyes were twinkling with amusement as she hoisted him into the air.

Last night had been miserably hot and noisy. Paddy Cummins and Ger O'Callaghan had cursed all night long, swearing that if they'd known the Forestry quarters had no running water or punkah-wallahs they'd never have asked to accompany their officers.

The three soldiers were billeted in a small room beside Lionel Cooper's and from their vantage point on the verandah they could see the spacious tents of the shikar party pitched on the opposite bank in the most picturesque bend of the Moyar River. They watched as the lamps were lit just before dusk and could hear conversation and laughter and the occasional clink of glasses as the sounds from the Colonel's camp wafted across the water.

'How does the brass always manage to get things looking like a scene from The Arabian *Sodding* Nights?' Paddy Cummins was talking with his mouth full and two thin mongrel pups, their tails wagging, quickly scoffed up bits of bread and meat blowing out from the side of his mouth as he spoke.

As the light faded, the elephant camp came alive with jungle sounds, till it seemed that the very air was thrumming like the skins on the regimental drums on parade. After a momentary lull, the whole crazy orchestra would start all over again till Michael felt the racket would quite literally bore a hole right through to his brain.

Earlier, Lionel Cooper had swaggered on to the verandah and without so much as a by-your-leave had sat down beside them, swinging his legs over the arms of his rattan chair, lighting a cigarette as he did so. He then asked if they wanted to buy some toddy. 'The tribals brew it here locally. Helps dull the sting of the insects.'

The Anglo-Indian had some nerve, thought Michael. 'Toddy's for you native fellows,' he said brusquely. 'We'll stick to our own drink, if you don't mind, and you can bugger off now – we're in the middle of a private conversation.'

Lionel Cooper pulled on his cigarette again before pointing to his room. 'I live here. You are sitting on my chairs, so *you* can bugger off and have your conversation elsewhere. Why don't you cross over the bridge and tell the Colonel his arrangements weren't private enough for you? They're drinking port – he might let you have some.'

Paddy Cummins had the man by the scruff of his neck in an instant. 'Fucking half-caste, you think you're funny? Your smirk will be gone before you can say t-o-d-d-y.'

'Put him down, Paddy, we don't want any trouble.' Ger O'Callaghan had jumped up, too.

'Go on, soldier,' Lionel sneered. 'Tell him it's not like the old days. You can't just beat up civilians anymore.'

Paddy Cummins dropped the young Forester into his chair. The man straightened his shirt and collar, and smoothing his hair bent down to pick up his cigarette. 'The toddy's good,' he said as he regained his composure, 'The first bottle is on me, okay, fellows?'

That was last night and this morning, as they waited for the Colonel to arrive, Lionel Cooper came up behind them.

'Ever been on an elephant?' he asked Michael, then reached up and rubbed the animal at the base of her tusk. 'Meena Kumari was bred in captivity and we bought her, especially picked her actually, from the stables of the Raja of Travancore. We couldn't train the wild elephants that we catch without her and those two chaps there.' He pointed out two other elephants who were playfully winding their trunks around each other. 'Those two came from Travancore, too. Only elephants can train elephants. Men can't do the job on their own.'

Michael was still coaxing Paddy Cummins and Ger O'Callaghan to step closer to Meena Kumari when the Colonel's Rolls-Royce swept into the camp. The entire camp immediately came to attention, along with the three soldiers who saluted the officers smartly.

'I can see you're raring to go, Private Flaherty, but it'll be a while yet. The bait was taken all right, but the trackers have yet to return. Once we know where the tiger's lying up, we can plan for the beat.'

The trackers returned with the news that the tiger was much further away than had been expected. There was a frenzy of activity as the elephants set off for Masinagudi Forest with the mahouts. Lionel Cooper drove into Masinagudi village with Michael, Paddy Cummins and Ger O'Callaghan and eight Forestry Guards who had piled into the back of the jeep, while three more stood on the footboard and clung on to the metal frame of the vehicle as the Forester drove like a man possessed. Within minutes of them arriving in Masinagudi, nearly two hundred people had gathered around the enormous banyan tree at the centre of the village – men, women and children all waiting for the sahibs to arrive and the spectacle to begin. The shikar party followed shortly afterwards in the three cars. Michael craned his neck to see if he could spot Rose but the memsahibs and children chose to stay in the shade of the cars and Rose with them.

The Colonel gave detailed instructions to the beaters who were to skirt the cover that was to be driven, giving the tiger a wide berth until they got behind the ravine to where it had been tracked. They headed off with all the village dogs, drums, cymbals, horns and bells ready to beat the tiger out of the ravine towards the sahibs on their howdah elephants.

Collector Myers and his wife took charge of the all-important 'stops', the men who would from their positions high up on trees stop the tiger from quietly slinking away into the forest to the left – and right-hand side of the cover. The stops had been handpicked and were veterans of many a tiger hunt with the Collector and his Memsahib.

Once the beaters had departed and the stops had been placed into their positions, the Colonel's party hurriedly left to meet up with the elephants at the edge of Masinagudi Forest. Following directly behind in Lionel's jeep, Michael could feel the adrenalin in the air, and he turned to look at Paddy Cummins and Ger O'Callaghan. 'Say lads, do you think this is one better than taking pot-shots at rabbits in the fields back home?'

They were still laughing when they arrived at the large clearing where the elephants were waiting patiently, down on all four knees. Ladders had been placed against their sides and the ladies were being helped up into the howdahs. James, Alice and Rose were already on their elephant and Michael looked up and waved at the children, who had called out to him as soon as they had spotted him jumping out of the jeep.

'I walked up the elephant's trunk, Michael! Walked right up the trunk and into the howdah!' James Aylmer called out.

'He crawled up the trunk and fell into the howdah, actually,' Alice said bossily. Michael grinned at them both and gave Rose a quick smile too. She looked happy and twirled her lace umbrella lightly. Lionel had been assigned to stay with the ladies, and Mrs Aylmer, Mrs McArdle and Mrs Milne held on to the howdahs and steadied themselves as their elephant rose to his feet.

Within a few minutes the entire party was mounted and on its way, the elephants walking in a rough line towards the cover where the tiger was expected to break.

When they arrived at a large expanse of four-foot-high grass the mahouts directed the elephants carrying the trackers and the howdah elephants to form an impressive wall across the cover, just two hundred yards wide. All the beaters and stops had to do was to keep their nerve and send the tiger down an ever-narrowing funnel for the sahibs.

Now began the long wait. The elephants stood quiet and still, just the tips of their trunks nuzzling the vegetation around their feet for any tender titbits that were to be had. The Collector and Mrs Myers were scanning the forest in front of them with binoculars, while Lionel pointed out things of interest to Mrs Aylmer and the two ladies. Beside them, on the largest elephant in the shikar party, James Aylmer, his new set of binoculars around his neck, was talking to the mahout while Alice leant against the side of the howdah and sketched the scene around her.

Rose had her umbrella at an angle and all Michael could see was the white satin sash of her pale-yellow voile dress as it fluttered in the hot breeze. He loved the way she looked in that dress; it was the same one she had worn to church, that first time he had laid eyes on her. Since his return from Madras, Michael had been thinking about ways to approach the Bacon-wallah with regard to Rose. Perhaps the man would be happy that his daughter was being courted by an Irish soldier from his old Regiment, because suitors of Michael's calibre were hardly going to turn up at the door every day.

The real problem was not Sean Twomey but Father Jerome; Michael knew he had to have the priest on his side before he could make any plans for himself and Rose. He already knew what the priest felt about half-castes, regardless of how they looked or how well they spoke. Father Jerome and Sergeant Tom Nolan were of the same opinion – with their repertoire of first-hand horror stories of unexpected darkie children, and Tom even insisting he knew a case of a set of twins, one white and the other black as a kaffir . . .

All of a sudden, one of the mahouts on a pad elephant stood up on the animal's neck and raised a flag, waving it frantically, and the entire line froze. And there it was: the muffled sound of drums, indistinct barking and then whoops and the faint clamour of bells.

'It won't be long now,' the Colonel hissed. 'Keep your eyes open, Flaherty, and hold the silence till the beast breaks cover.'

All down the line, similar instructions were being relayed to the whole party. Birds began taking to the air – a pair of woodpeckers, followed by kingfishers, bee-eaters, pigeons and crows. Then an enormous swathe of green flashed by above their heads: hundreds of parrots flying out of the jungle all at once. As several frightened peahens hurried out from the tall grass, behind them, a peacock, the tips of his magnificent train shimmering as it caught the sun, screeched his strident warning.

Lionel Cooper raised a flag and then pointed in the direction of a large flowering Jacaranda in the distance. The binoculars revealed a lone chital buck, his magnificent lyre-shaped antlers at least two and a half feet high, standing rigid for a moment, before he raced across into a dense grove of teak and eucalyptus and disappeared.

The Colonel and the Collector both looked anxiously up and down the line, each hoping that all the others would hold fire till the tiger appeared. It would take just one trigger-happy hunter to spoil the chance of bagging a tiger and would also put the beaters in danger.

The beaters could be heard clearly now, shouting and yelling at the top of their voices. The frenzied beat of their drums and the barking of their dogs grew louder by the minute: they were less than half a mile away. All eyes were on the stops on their trees. If they raised their flags, this meant that the tiger had passed under their tree. Michael spotted the first flag at the same time as the Colonel did, and hands were raised in the other howdahs, too. The stops raised their flags one by one: the tiger was moving closer.

'This is it, Smythe, won't be long,' breathed the Colonel, cocking his rifle and signalling to Michael to keep the second one ready should he need it. Superintendent Smythe grunted in reply. Down the line, guns were cocked and raised, everyone held their breath and Michael was struck by how the elephants and their mahouts remained still as statues.

The last stop three hundred yards away to the left flung his flag up and the Colonel muttered, 'I see it, Smythe, to your left, in the tall grass, ten yards from the last stop.'

Michael saw a streak of orange move in the grass and slink into the brake of clumping bamboo. Beyond the brake rose a steep bare rock. If the tiger left the shelter of the bamboo and tried to leap up the rock, it would be bagged with no great difficulty. If, on the other hand, it made a move unseen into the tall grass to the right, there was a small chance that it might manage to reach the far end of the cover and sneak away.

On Collector Myers's signal, the mahouts on the pad elephants at either end slowly fanned out, turning the straight line into a semicircle. From their vantage-point in the howdah, it was clear to Michael that the tiger had little chance now of slipping away: it would be forced to break cover as had been planned.

The tall grass in the middle of the cover swayed slightly and suddenly a shot rang out. The Collector's wife Mrs Myers had fired and was very calmly getting ready to fire again.

'Damn that woman! I'm sure the beast hasn't left the bamboo!' Colonel Aylmer still had his gun trained on the green brake.

On hearing the first shot ring out, the beaters swiftly converged into one heaving, quivering tight group, yelling and screaming, this time with fear. If the beast had been merely wounded, it was many times more dangerous, and they were safer in a group if the tiger turned around and charged.

Michael held on to the side of the howdah and, with his heart thumping, heard an unearthly roar rent the air as the tiger charged out of the bamboo brake, and in five or six bounds leapt onto Meena Kumari's trunk. The elephant was quick to react. Lowering her head and lifting the beast with her tusks, she shook it off with a violent toss of her head. The mahout held on for dear life as the wounded elephant readied herself for the tiger's next charge; the Colonel and Michael were thrown across to the other end of the howdah. Michael was holding on to the rails, when he saw the tall grass on the other side part for an instant – and shocked at what he saw, he shouted as loudly as he could: 'Sir! There are cubs, sir! Cubs in the grass, sir!'

The Colonel, who had his rifle to his shoulder, yelled out, 'Hold your fire, Smythe! Myers! *Hold fire!*'

His shout was drowned out by Meena Kumari's warning trumpet and the loud retort of Mrs Myers's gun. The cornered tiger fell back in mid-charge with a final bloodcurdling roar, its head hitting the ground first with a loud thud.

Meena Kumari rushed towards the tiger, trumpeting in fury. The mahout tried desperately to calm her down, but the enraged elephant stamped on the carcass of the tiger, the howdah pitching like a dinghy in a stormy sea, threatening to capsize.

'Sir! There's a pair of them, sir!' Michael was bawling at the top of his voice.

Colonel Aylmer bellowed in turn to Lionel, who was on the elephant a hundred yards to the left. 'Cooper, the nets, man – and quick.' And then he stood up as best as he could on the heaving howdah and screamed in the other direction towards the Collector: 'Myers! Cubs, a pair of them. We must keep the damn dogs at bay, shoot them if need be.'

Michael watched in horror as Meena Kumari flung the tiger's body around like a rag doll.

'The Collector Mem won't be too happy, Smythe, will she? The beast won't be worth skinning.' The Colonel looked grim, his face bruised where he had crashed into the rifle rack.

Police Superintendent Smythe, who was wiping blood off a gash in his elbow, nodded. 'Poor Myers. He'll be in for a rough time trying to console the Memsahib. She's a fine shot though. The mahout thought he was done for.'

All eyes were now on Lionel and the trackers, who had descended and were cautiously circling the spot in the tall grass at which Mrs Myers had aimed her shot. Moving inwards in an ever-decreasing circle they finally found the cubs, who snarled loudly when they were discovered, their paws slashing and swiping the air in front of them even as they cowered, their backs against each other in a heap. The nets were flung over the creatures without much ado, and a burst of applause rang out from the hunt party. Lionel kept the dogs well away from the cubs while a makeshift cage was expertly put together by the trackers, using rope and thick bamboo poles cut down from the brake.

The poor mahout was still trying to calm Meena Kumari. The big elephant had trampled the tiger to a pulpy mess and was reluctant to leave. *Thank God that Rose and the Aylmer children can't see this awful madness*, Michael thought. Just like Mrs Aylmer and the ladies, they were shielded from the gory sight at Meena Kumari's feet by the elephant's own bulk. The air reverberated with accompanying loud trumpets from the rest of the elephants.

Finally, when Meena Kumari had been coaxed by her mahout to walk away, Mrs Myers, who had been waiting rather impatiently, cut off the tiger's tail, the only bit of the animal that remained intact, and stemming the blood with a handful of the tall grass, she wound it around her neck.

'One must have something to show for it,' she called out.

Later on that evening, back at the Ranger Headquarters at Theppakadu, the Colonel was busy supervising the arrangements to transport the two tiger cubs down to the plains. Alice and James stood beside their father, not taking their eyes off the two cubs for even a second. The cubs paced the wooden crate they had been transferred into and they continued to snarl at anything that moved despite being obviously exhausted after the day's events.

The Colonel turned around to his children. 'You'll see them again,' he promised Alice and James. 'I know they'll be well cared for, pampered even. Uttam Singh will deliver them to His Highness the Raja of Pudunagari this evening. The crate will go into the back of the Rolls-Royce and the Rolls-Royce goes back to the Raja. My small thank-you gift to him for the loan of the car, what do you think of that?'

James Aylmer kicked a stone. 'You said no shikari would ever kill a tigress with cubs.'

Alice wiped away a tear and her father knelt down beside her. 'Come now, Alice,' he said kindly. 'If we'd known she had cubs we would have called off the beat, but she was cornered and then it was too late. It was a chain of events – and sometimes they're difficult to stop.'

CHAPTER EIGHT

Nandagiri, August 1920

Sergeant Tom Nolan had his eyes closed and Michael wondered how in hell's name he could have fallen asleep at a time like this. Michael looked around the small cell at the five other men sitting around him, all subdued and thoughtful, quite different from the blustering group that last night had marched into the Guard Room and volunteered to be locked up, trying to register a formal protest in the oldest way known to a regimental soldier. The hot, crowded cell had sobered them up fast and Michael wondered if, like him, the past weeks of simmering discontent, fired by information filtering in from letters arriving from Ireland had now been replaced by worries about the very real consequences of this, their impulsive reaction.

Much of the news from home had been about the terrible things being done by the Black and Tans, and the mail that had arrived a few days ago had sent even the steadiest of men completely crazed with anger. In the wet canteen last night, Sergeant Tom Nolan had urged those of the Galway lads who were literate to read their letters out aloud, one by one.

Frankie Gaffney, a strapping hulk of a soldier who could pull a gun carriage unassisted more than one hundred yards, trembled as he read how his three sisters had had their heads forcibly shaved while they were made to watch their father and younger brother stripped naked and beaten senseless. The Tans had shot all the animals and set the family farm on fire before they left. The men of B Company gathered around as Frankie broke down and wept. He made way for the next soldier whose letter told of his father being shot dead like a rabbit in a field. Others pushed forward then, climbing atop the rough trestle table to read of a sister shot at for no reason as she hung out the washing, of shops looted and ransacked, livelihoods destroyed and, in parts of the country, whole villages terrorised.

But it was one thing to be sitting in the regimental canteen on a Saturday night, their collective anger increased by Tom Nolan's accounts of Black and Tan atrocities gleaned from detailed reports in American newspapers, and quite another to have goaded each other into this obviously futile gesture.

Tadhgh Foley, who had been sitting next to Michael on the hard bench in the Guard-Room cell, began whittling away at a small piece of wood that he pulled from his pocket.

'I'm carving a tigress for my son,' he said, his eyes squinting in concentration as he exerted precise pressure with a small penknife. 'It's a mother for this little one,' he went on, taking out a tiger cub from his pocket and handing it to Michael.

Michael looked down at the wooden cub in his hand and ran his fingers down the animal's back. 'They're beauties, Tadhgh, every one of the animals that you've carved. Your little son is a lucky lad.'

Tadhgh grunted an acknowledgement and stopped his work just for a moment to take the cub back and slip it into his pocket.

A sudden thought drew Michael to his feet in shock. The church! He cursed, resisting the urge to cross himself. Father Jerome would be at the vestry within the hour, expecting his vestments to be ironed, the brass polished and the altar all set for Sunday Mass.

Michael had planned to make use of those quiet few minutes before Mass to petition the priest about Rose. He had seen her just once since the tiger hunt at Masinagudi, a hurried half-hour snatched in the shade of the back verandah of the Colonel's bungalow while Mrs Aylmer lay in a darkened room, a cold compress on her forehead, waiting for her headache to pass. Rose had been tearful at first, calling their situation hopeless and wringing her hands in despair.

Michael had tried to comfort her. 'Listen to me, Rose. I'll speak to Father Jerome. He's a priest and he'll know what to do.'

'Will he agree to marry us, do you think?'

'Even if he doesn't, Rose, it won't matter. You have my word and I will be true.'

'But the Regiment could be sent to the plains – you could be gone in weeks! There are rumours that the Indians are getting out of hand in Madras, with more threat of rioting, and Mrs Aylmer told me this morning that if Gandhi and the Congress Party were planning anything big there, the Rangers would be on the troop trains immediately.' Her face was full of anguish. 'I'll never see you again.'

'Hush, Rose. I think I know what to do – I won't just talk to Father Jerome, I'll speak to your father, too, this weekend, on

Sunday after Mass. I'll tell him of my intentions towards you.'
He put his arm around her waist and pulled her close.

'Will you speak to Father, really? Oh Michael, how I dream
of finally going home to Ireland! I can never understand what he
sees in this country full of Indians or why he has stayed so long.'

'There's no living to be made in West Cork or in the whole
of Ireland for that matter. Rose, your father makes an easy buck
here in Nandagiri.'

Michael was just thinking of the way she had leant forward
and kissed him when he was jolted back to the present by the
loud click of boots as the sentry at the Guard-Room door
presented arms and Sergeant Willis walked in briskly. His
mouth flew open when he saw the cell full of soldiers.

'What the fuckin' hell's going on here?'

Tom Nolan stood at the grille and said quite calmly, 'You
can tell the Colonel that none of us soldiers will bear arms any
more. We're sick of the news from Ireland. He knows what
we're talking about.'

'Nolan, are you out of your fuckin' mind? How much drink
was had last night? The Colonel knows nothing of this nonsense
as yet, so go back to your barracks, man, before the whole
Company's sent on route march. Nolan, d'you hear? Take your
men and get out! For God's sake, it's Sunday and too bleedin'
hot already for any of this foolish carry-on.'

'You heard me right the first time, Willis. We aren't going
anywhere. Ireland is being fucked in the name of the King and
we Irish will serve that King no more.'

Sergeant Willis unlocked the door and flung it open. 'Nolan,
that's mutinous talk. D'you know what they do to ringleaders?
Flaherty, Foley, Cummins – and the two of you at the back,
Williams and O'Callaghan – you've one second to step out

smart and head straight back for the barracks. The men will be falling out for parade in half an hour. You're bleedin' lucky it was me who stopped by the Guard Room first.'

Tom Nolan walked back to the wooden bench and sat down.

'You'll find the rest of the lads are all of the same mind. There just wasn't room enough for the whole lot of us in the Guard Room.' He turned around to the men behind him. 'Get back now and sit down you lot, we aren't going anywhere. Sergeant Willis here's going to take a message from all of us Irishmen to the Colonel.'

Sergeant Willis took a step into the cell. 'The door is open, Tom. Let the lads go, you don't need them to fight your fight.'

Tadhgh Foley moved back to the bench and sat down. 'I'm staying. This is my fight, too.'

Paddy Cummins and Ger O'Callaghan, who had been standing next to Tom, stepped back, as well. O'Callaghan clutched Michael's arm firmly and turned to Sergeant Willis, whose ruddy face was now covered in beads of sweat. 'We're Irishmen, all of us, and you can count in every lad in the barracks, as well. This is as much our fight as Tom's. We'll bear arms no more.'

Sergeant Willis shook his head. '"We'll bear arms no more" – you're going to need a bleedin' better explanation than that when you're lined up in front of the Colonel. You'll be doing a fuckin' route march in full Christmas kit to Timbuctoo, I reckon. And all in the bloody heat, too, you damn bloody fools.'

They watched in silence as he ordered the sentry to lock up the cell and mount a double guard before hurrying off in the direction of the Officer's Mess.

Michael was overcome with apprehension, and along with the others he, too, looked to Tom Nolan, expecting him to say something, but the Sergeant had pulled out a piece of paper and a pencil from his pocket and was writing furiously.

It was Tadhgh Foley who spoke eventually. 'Are you drawing up plans, Tom? What d'you think they'll do when the rest of the company refuses to parade this morning?'

'It's not a plan, Tadhgh. This here's just a letter to my mother.' He stopped writing and looked up at the five men around him. 'Whatever the outcome, I'm sure of one thing – our actions will not be in vain. Now's the time to weigh the odds for yourselves. If any of you still want out, say so when Sergeant Willis returns.'

Michael felt his legs go weak and he sat down on the bench. He wished he hadn't gone into the wet canteen after sundown, his pockets jingling with his week's wages, or sat at the table with Tom and the rest of them only to be carried away by their dangerous mood. His sense of outrage was as real as anyone else's on the table, and when the Sergeant declared that talk was cheap and they ought to do something about it, Michael had shouted in agreement as loudly as the man next to him. *But this was not the action I would have chosen*, he thought. *I was just in the wrong place at the wrong time.*

Michael dropped his face into his hands. Those were the very words which that earnest Indian doctor had said to him and Rose in Madras, four weeks ago. 'Sir, you and your good wife are most unfortunate to be in the wrong place at the wrong time.'

That evening in Madras had also begun harmlessly enough, with plans to set out in the gharry for Marina Beach with a picnic of cheese sandwiches, some pickled beef and flasks of tea that Rose's Aunty Mags had insisted they take.

The couple had strolled along the Marina, past the high rotunda of the Ice House and the elegant buildings of Queen Mary's College, stopping short of the fishing villages that surrounded the Light House and turning back, headed for the park around the bandstand, where they had left the gharry-wallah waiting.

Rose had an insatiable curiosity about all things Irish. 'In the hot season, my father closes his eyes and recalls how green the fields were around Crossterra. When I was a child, he was able to describe for me the lake in the hollow of the high mountains, the peat fields and the bog cotton. He talked of soft rain that moved sideways across the valley and fine mists that swirled in from the top of the Caha Ridge all the way down to the river. He remembers people all right, all my relations. Of course, I know most of their names and even what they look like. Did you know I'm the spitting image of my father's eldest sister Mary? She married a man from Bantry. Father says market day in Bantry town is a sight to behold: every Friday the whole of West Cork is there. I just can't understand – why on earth did Father have to sweat away thirty years amongst monkeys, snakes and bats? He could so easily have taken us home long ago, Mother and I.' She shuddered. 'I hate snakes.'

'There's no snakes in Ireland, Rose,' Michael said, as he poured out the tea from the Thermos.

She took his hand and squeezed it. 'I still can't believe it could be possible, a country with no snakes. Why did you join the Army, Michael? How could you bear to leave Ireland?'

He spluttered into his tea. 'There's no jobs to be had, Rose, nothing at all. Enlisting's the best chance of making a regular earning for us Irish lads. When I finished with school, I helped my father out sometimes if there was a fishing party up in the

Big House. There was a hot dinner in that at the end of the day and a chance to eye all the local talent below stairs.'

He laughed as she made a face at him. 'The Aylmers often had guests from Dublin, mostly high and mighty sorts from London, and sometimes even Americans, and they had all heard of the great fishing in the Liffey. There's nobody that knows that river and the fish as well as my father. Old Donnie, they call him; he helped the Colonel bag his first salmon and that was when the Colonel was only eleven years old and the fish weighed nearly as much as he did. My father was given a half-bottle of whiskey for his trouble and he was found the next morning by the priest, passed out in the graveyard up at Oughterard Hill.'

Rose leant her head against his shoulders. 'My father gave up the drink when Mother died,' she said. 'He told Aunty Mags that he needed his wits about him at all times.' She flicked her hand impatiently at the flies that had appeared from nowhere. 'Shall we go? There won't be any flies at the Connemara.' She linked arms with him. 'I just love dancing, don't you? Did you know that the Connemara has the best bands in the whole of the Madras Presidency? My Cousin Ronnie used to play the piano in the afternoons in the tearooms. But that was before he left for Australia, lucky boy.'

The gharry-wallah needed a kick on his shin before he woke, and his skinny nag took some calming down when her bag of feed was yanked off from around her neck. They set off rather slowly at first, for they had to negotiate a veritable crush of vehicles at the entrance to the Promenade.

When they broke free from the melee, the gharry-wallah cracked his whip and at the sound Rose pushed aside the flimsy curtain that separated the passengers from the gharry-wallah's seat and berated him in Tamil.

She turned her head back a minute later, her eyes still flashing with anger. 'That poor horse! I've just told that fool of a gharry-wallah not to go all the way down Marina Beach Road but to go via Triplicane. That way, you'll get to see the ancient Hindu temple – you know, the one that's on all the postcards they sell in Wheeler's and Higginbotham's.'

Michael nodded and put his arm around her waist. As they wound their way into the heart of Triplicane, they passed a few gharry-wallahs who were returning as fast as they could from the opposite direction; these men shouted out warnings to everyone, pointing back and gesticulating. Pedestrians immediately quickened their step, and some shopkeepers looked alarmed and pulled their shutters down. Several native women, babies hanging on their hips, screamed at older children to follow and came scurrying down the nearby alleyways making for their homes, locking doors and bolting windows shut.

Michael turned to Rose. 'There's something going on. Quick, ask the fellow what's happening.'

The gharry-wallah had already begun to pull up the nag when Rose shouted out to him, but over her voice Michael heard the distant volley of gunfire.

'Tell him to turn around,' he snapped. 'We need to get out of here double quick.'

'He says the other gharry-wallahs are warning of a mob of hundreds coming this way, burning English flags and effigies of the Viceroy. There's already been some rioting, he says, and even looting near the temple.'

Michael jumped out of the gharry and strode up to the nag. Taking hold of her head-collar, he attempted to coax her to turn around. 'Rose, tell the gharry-wallah to use the whip,' he said. 'We must try and head back towards the beach – we'll be safe there. The Military Police are sure to go first to where the Europeans are.'

But the stubborn nag refused to budge, and as more people came fleeing down the road, Michael could very clearly hear the shouting and chanting of slogans now only a few streets away. Panicking, the gharry-wallah stood up on his seat and lashed out hard with his whip; the nag reared, lifting the gharry's shaft up in the air and unceremoniously tipping Rose out on to the street.

Michael rushed to help Rose to her feet. Looking up, he realised that the gharry-wallah had run off down a small side street to the right.

'Come back, you coward!' He shook a fist at the disappearing shadow. 'Come on, Rose, quickly now. We had better just start walking back the way we came.'

She was shaking, and Michael was horribly aware that they were the only Europeans he could see in the fast-emptying street. 'We must hurry,' he said. 'Can you manage to walk faster still?'

An urgent whisper coming from a window above stopped them both in their tracks.

'Sir, madam, wait there a moment, please. I'm coming down – wait there, please.'

A few seconds later, a door opened and a bespectacled figure beckoned them in. 'Sir, you must come in quickly. Come, come in, madam. That mob is full of rowdy troublemakers from Black Town. I offer you the shelter of my home and you can wait it out here as long as required.'

The Indian stepped out of the doorway for a brief moment, looked to left and right, and urged them into his house again.

'You can deliberate inside the house,' he said. 'These hooligans, they're only one street away from the Police Chowki and that, sir, has been set on fire. You can see the smoke from my roof terrace.' He bolted the door firmly after Michael and Rose had stepped inside. 'Follow me, please. You'll be safe upstairs in my father's room, for it doesn't overlook the street.'

Rose held on to Michael's arm as they followed their rescuer upstairs. 'This man is right,' he told her. 'It's better we wait it out till the mob has moved on. If the police station has been set on fire, reinforcements won't be long. They'll teach the bastards a lesson they won't forget.'

The Indian turned to Michael with a smile. 'We Indians have learnt many things that we won't forget,' he said and then, pushing open a door, he ushered them into a small dark bedroom. Michael headed straight towards the window.

'No, you won't see anything there,' their host informed them. 'That window overlooks the inner courtyard. It's my room that has a view of the road. Admittedly it's extremely noisy on an everyday basis, but as you can see, very useful when it comes to keeping an eye on a riot.' The man put out his hand and said pleasantly, 'I'm Dr Swamy, Assistant Civil Surgeon, at your service, presently in the employ of Kilpauk Medical College and late for duty even as I speak.'

Michael shook his hand, thanking him. 'We're both very grateful for your help. However, we'll need another gharry in order to return home to Egmore.'

'The situation in the city could be volatile so I'd advise you to remain here till daylight. I'll return by seven in the morning, earlier if I can manage. And I'll bring a gharry for you.'

Rose was shocked. 'We couldn't possibly stay out for so long. My uncle and aunt in Egmore will be worried sick.'

'My dear lady, they'd worry more if they knew you were on the streets on a night like this. It would be most unwise to leave now. I'll send a peon to Egmore with a message. Perhaps you wish to write a note to your family, to reassure them?' Dr Swamy turned to Michael. 'You won't be disturbed here at all, as my father has gone to Benares on his annual pilgrimage.' He took out some notepaper and a pen from the desk in the corner of the room and handed them to Michael. 'Give me the address and I'll make sure the letter will be sent tonight – as soon as possible.'

Rose sat at the desk and taking the pen, wrote to her Aunty Mags. Michael asked: 'What is your address, Dr Swamy? They'll want to know. I am sure Mr Roberts, Rose's uncle, will bring a gharry himself, first thing tomorrow morning, to collect us.'

Dr Swamy gave Rose the address and then, looking at her handwriting on the envelope, he said unexpectedly, 'What a feminine hand your wife has, sir, so wonderful to look at.'

Michael was about to correct him when the doctor put his finger to his lips. There was a moment's silence followed by loud shouts, some gunfire and the sound of running on the street below them.

'As expected, I think they're heading for the beach. There have been rumours flying around all day that Mahatma Gandhi will be arrested as he steps off the train when he arrives in Madras. The Mahatma gave the Viceroy notice of Non-Cooperation just a few days ago, but this is exactly what he didn't want to happen. But that's a discourse for another day. For now, sir, I'll say goodbye, but rest assured I'll be back early tomorrow morning. There is a small kitchen downstairs, though not much in the way of food, just some biscuits and tea. There is fruit, of course, plenty of it.' He slammed a worn solar topee onto his head. 'Since I'm alone I eat in the hospital canteen nowadays. Sir, you will bolt the door behind me?'

Rose stood up. 'How will you go to Kilpauk? There could be rioting there, as well.'

'Yes, but I'm not the one in danger. This, madam, is my own country.'

When Michael came back upstairs, having bolted the door, he found Rose sitting on the bed fanning herself.

'I hope the note will reach them in Egmore before too long. Oh dear, what if it doesn't and Uncle Dennis comes looking for us? Something could happen to him. This doctor may have helped, yes, but did you see how he couldn't help making a dig at us? His attitude was rather superior, don't you think?'

Michael smoothed down her hair and tried to reassure her. 'Well, they won't be expecting us back till ten anyway and I'm sure the doctor will have the note sent by then. He has a bicycle and before he went out, he told me that he would send a peon on it to Egmore.'

Rose got up and wandered around the room. 'Can you hear anything at all now? Shall we see if we can spot anything from the room that overlooks the street?'

Michael sat down. 'Let's wait awhile. The man was adamant that we should stay out of sight and I'm responsible for you. I mean, what am I to say to your aunt and uncle in the first place? It's a good thing I'm on two days' leave or I'd have some explaining to do to the Sergeant, as well.'

'Oh, how could Uncle Dennis possibly hold you responsible? Who could have known that the Indians would choose this evening to riot? Aunty Mags said Mr Gandhi wasn't expected here till next week.' She sighed loudly. 'We're going to miss all the dancing.'

Rose began to inspect the photographs on the wall. 'Oh look – this studio photo was taken at G. K. Vales on Mount Road

– that must be Dr Swamy's father. He looks like his father all right, especially in this little frame here. But no . . . here it says *Trafalgar Square, June 1919* so it has to be the doctor himself. Imagine, the man's been to England! No wonder he was so smug.'

Michael was looking out of the small window into the enclosed courtyard. Not much could be seen in the fading dusk except clothes drying on very slack clothes lines. He strained for any tell-tale sounds from outside but, except for the occasional barking of dogs, all seemed quiet. Maybe Rose was right. There would be no harm in having a quick look through the window slats from the room overlooking the street. He turned to tell Rose what he planned to do and found her opening the doors of the large wardrobe that occupied a whole wall opposite the bed.

'Rose, you can't do that!'

'I'm only looking, Michael. I won't touch anything and the doctor will never know anyway. Oh goodness, look – the Indian has a gramophone. A brand new one, by the looks of it, and some records, too. What a very strange place to keep it – in a wardrobe with his clothes. I'd have it out on a table in the sitting room if I was him.'

'Rose, close the door.'

'No, Michael, let's wind it up and dance. I know how to get it going. Cousin Ronnie had a gramophone, not as new but they must all work in the same manner. Oh, come on!'

'Rose, close the door and forget it. The man must have bought it in England and it must be valuable. That's why it's in the wardrobe, so nothing happens to it.'

She put her arms around his neck and wheedled, 'Oh, be a sport, just for a few minutes. We can put it on the table and we'll be ever so careful. I'll even let you kiss me.'

He hugged her close and kissed her, lingering over her lips until she pushed him away gently. 'Rose, you're a minx: you get me to do the strangest of things.' He picked up the gramophone and carried it carefully over to the table. She chose a record, and soon the room filled with music. The couple danced around the room, twirling around in the small space, until they were both in a sweat.

When the record ended, Rose flopped down onto the bed and began to fan herself. 'Come here, Michael, and I'll share my little punkah with you.'

'Well, I never thought I'd make a punkah-wallah out of you,' Michael joked as he sprawled across the bed with his head on her lap.

'You could make anything out of me,' she whispered, and bent down to kiss him.

She offered no resistance when a few minutes later he slid his hands under her shift or when he began unbuttoning her dress, but instead seemed to urge him on wordlessly with little intakes of breath and acquiescent movements of her hips.

Afterwards she clung to him, her slim body covered in a film of sweat that mingled with his own. He reached down to the floor where her fan lay and unfolding it, he fanned them both and with each waft of delicious air she smiled and slowly drifted into sleep. Propping himself up on his elbows, he looked down at her lovely face framed by locks of damp hair and wondered dejectedly what he was going to do – about her, about them.

He awoke with a start about an hour later and had to lift her arms from across his chest before he was able to ease himself out of the bed without disturbing her. Taking a seat on the windowsill, he contemplated the possible consequences of what they had just done. *I love her*, he told himself. *I love her and that alone should make everything all right. My intentions are good and honourable, I'll marry her as soon as I can, and that means our situation isn't as hopeless as it looks.*

His thoughts should have cheered him up, but instead Michael found himself putting his head in his hands in despair. The grim reality was that there wasn't a hope in hell of being able to marry her in the near future.

Yes, Dr Swamy had been absolutely right, thought Michael, when he had said his goodbyes at the door. 'Sir, you and your good wife are most unfortunate to be in the wrong place at the wrong time.'

Michael still had his head in his hands, recalling that July night in Madras, when Tom Nolan called out impatiently, 'Flaherty, answer me, man! I need to know before Sergeant Willis returns – are you in for the Cause?'

CHAPTER NINE

10 October 1920

Dear Diary,
How wish I had Mother beside me. She loved me, she told
me that every day, even on the day she died. It didn't matter
what I did, she still loved me. She would have loved me
now, disgraced as I am. But Father, he won't speak to me,
won't even look at me. When he guessed what was wrong,
I fell at his feet like I've seen the Indian servants do, but he
just called for his horse and rode off. I screamed after him
that I might be dead when he returned but I don't think he
cares.

It's four days since he took me to Black Town. We went in
a covered gharry that came to the servants' verandah at the
back of the house. More than once Father took out his cane and
struck out at the crowd of urchins who were trailing us. I began
to think he might use it on me, because when I put my hand on
his to beg him to turn back, he lifted the cane, but then turned
away as if he couldn't bear to look at me.

I thought of Michael then. I have prayed to Mother and so I know she will make it happen: his sentence will be commuted and when that happens, mine will be, too.

We turned off the bazaar into a side street and stopped in a narrow alley. Father ordered me to alight as he jumped out himself and knocked on a large wooden door. He asked for Mumtaz Bibi and a minute later the door creaked open.

I was terrified. I begged Father to take me home but he was mute, never said a word to me, just swung his cane round and round about him till an old woman appeared at the door with her hands on her hips. Father spoke and she listened, then taking the money that he gave her, she signalled me to follow her.

'Don't be afraid, daughter,' she said. That's when I began to cry for Mother. As I crossed the threshold to look back, I saw Father slash the air with his cane and then get back into the gharry to wait.

'I don't want anything done,' I said to the old woman, 'I just want to go back home.' She nodded wordlessly each time I repeated my plea. I held her hand tightly, saying feverishly, 'Michael's too young to be shot. Even Father Jerome said they would never want to make an example of such a young man.'

But it made no difference. The old woman pushed me along, down another corridor into a smaller courtyard with a mighty peepal tree. I saw four native girls sitting on a charpoy, oiling and combing each other's hair, and I was so relieved to see them I smiled. The old woman said something and they milled around me, gently wiping away my tears. To think I let them touch me, those dirty native girls with their callused skin, their hands stained with henna, the rank smell of oil in their hair.

My knees were trembling so much that I had to sit down on the charpoy. The girls caressed my hair, and then they stroked my face and my lips. They'd never seen anyone so fair, so pretty, they said. 'And look at your hair – so beautiful. No wonder you are in trouble,' said one, and they all laughed.

The old woman returned with a cloth bag and it all happened so quickly I didn't stand a chance. They had me pushed down on the bed, the girls, each holding down an arm and a leg. The pain of what she did was so intense it shot through me right into my chest. When I came to, I could feel something hot and wet drip out of me, and my insides were twisted and on fire. The girls were bent over me; two of them rubbed my feet and they all smiled at me again, stroked my hair and wiped my tears, and I no longer cared about their shabby clothes or grubby hands as they cleaned me and carried me out to my father in the gharry.

He wouldn't look at me at all, and when I told him I couldn't bear the pain, that Mother would never have let him do what he had just had done to me, he said she'd have been as ashamed of me as he was.

I lay in bed for four days and waited for news of Michael. For the first two days I couldn't walk, but when I was able to take a bath I scrubbed every bit of me till I was red. I wish it was as easy to drive away bad memories. How will I ever tell Michael what my father has had done to our baby?

I haven't had the energy to write these last few weeks, Dear Diary. I feel better today though. Father didn't get his way, after all. I felt my baby move for the first time yesterday – we both have survived. I take it as a sign that Michael will survive, too: we'll know in a week that the Viceroy has commuted all four death sentences, though why Tom Nolan's should be commuted I don't know. Lord forgive me, but wasn't he the ringleader who led Michael astray?

The reason I write today, Dear Diary, is to tell you that Father has decided to send me off to Madras to Aunty Mags and Uncle Dennis. They'll keep me while I have the baby and I'm happy to leave this town, away from the gossiping neighbours and from Father, who hardly says a word more than necessary. I hate the way people look at me. Yesterday in church was so difficult, and that Dolores Cooper kept staring at my belly when she called at the house on the pretext of buying honey. Mrs Aylmer has been absolutely horrid, sending the dog boy with a note for Father, telling him I was dismissed and was not to call at the house. Well, I don't have to beg her or live with Father's silent anger because tomorrow I board a train to Madras where Aunty Mags will be kind and Uncle Dennis will talk to me as we walk at Marina Beach, and if Mother hears my prayers, someday soon Father will love me again.

CHAPTER TEN

Nandagiri, December 1920

Father Jerome would never forget that wretched day in August 1920. He had been summoned urgently by Colonel Aylmer, and on hearing of the unrest, had run nearly all the way across the parade grounds and into the wet canteen that served as the impromptu headquarters of the mutiny, only to be confronted by that hothead Sergeant Tom Nolan.

Still panting with the exertion, Father Jerome had begun with a straightforward appeal to good sense. 'Tom, if you and the men feel so strongly about the goings on back home with the Black and Tans, there are plenty of other ways of making your feelings known. What you've done is nothing short of mutiny – you know the punishment for that.'

The priest sat down on the chair that had been pushed forward for him and caught his breath before starting again.

'Look here, I know Colonel Aylmer's willing to be reasonable. If you men will all return to barracks straight away, this matter of the laying down of arms and all of last night's carry-on in the Guard Room will be handled with greater leniency than is warranted. I have the Colonel's word on that. And as I speak,

Adjutant Milne is relaying the same message to the men in B and C Company in the barracks. The Colonel's promised that he'll put your grievances and outrage at the situation at home in writing and submit it to the authorities at the very highest level. Surely that is better than mutiny: you all know the punishment for that.'

Tom Nolan stood up slowly. 'Father, the Colonel will promise anything to get us back into the barracks. We are well aware that the officers are worried about this action of ours spreading to the other Irish regiments in the plains below, maybe even beyond the Madras Presidency – to all of India even – and that, Father Jerome, is exactly what we plan to do. This is our chance to rid Ireland of the English! What say you, men? Are you true to the Cause of Erin?'

The response was deafening and Tom Nolan looked at the priest briefly before punching the air and bawling, 'Godspeed Michael and Tadhgh! They must be on the train by now, halfway down to the regiments in the plains.'

The priest's groan was drowned out in a roar of approval from the hundred or so men gathered there, while some broke into song.

Father Jerome stood up and lifted both his arms in order to get the men's attention. A hush returned eventually and they waited to hear what he had to say.

'Godspeed? This isn't God's work they're doing. You've sent young Michael Flaherty and the already unfortunate Tadhgh Foley to their deaths. Spreading mutiny isn't God's work. You men seem to forget you've taken a solemn oath before the very same God to be true to the Crown.'

Sergeant Tom Nolan was quick to counter. 'Country comes first and oaths to a foreign king next.'

'You face ruin, Tom, and you'll bring the same ruin and misfortune upon these men and their families.' The priest entreated those present. 'Go back to your barracks, lads. Think of your fathers, mothers and sisters, your wives and children who wait for you to send home money. Times are tough in Ireland – you know yourselves they depend on you.'

'Erin depends on us!' shouted Nolan.

A loud cheer followed this declaration.

'That's futile talk, Tom, and the men know it. And you, for God's sake, *you* should know it better.'

'There's nobody here being forced, Father. These men, these brave men, are patriots of their own volition. Ask them! Lads, listen up. Are you present here in this wet canteen of your own free will?'

Father Jerome shouted over the roar of assent, 'You'll be shot, don't you know? This is the Army and mutineers will be shot. *That* is the penalty for mutiny.'

A deathly silence fell in the room. Father Jerome was shaking uncontrollably. He looked at the men one by one, trying to make eye contact with as many as he could. 'Sergeant Nolan here, Tom, he's a good man but this is no way to fight for Ireland. Think of your families, lads, think of the honour and glorious name of this Regiment you serve. Think above all of the solemn pledge of allegiance, the sacred oath you made before God Himself.'

Tom Nolan jumped up onto the table before him. 'Father Jerome has asked for you to think hard, so do that, lads. Leave if you wish, and you have my word that no ill will will be directed towards you.'

A few men shuffled to the door and the crowd parted to give them way.

Tom Nolan called out to them as they left. 'It's all right, lads, every man must do what he thinks best. You were with us all along and we know you'll be with us in spirit.'

The priest began to walk amongst the men. He knew each of their personal circumstances and he reminded them of their obligations, clasping them by the shoulders and holding their hands in his. Some were unwavering but fell on their knees and asked to be blessed, some turned away guiltily as he approached them, and a few men took heed and quietly left the room. Finally, he confronted Tom Nolan once again. 'Why in God's name did you have to get Michael Flaherty involved in this madness?'

'He was with us from the start, Father, and fair is fair, he drew the shortest straw, and Tadhgh the next, to take the train to Salem to inform the Fusiliers down in the plains of our plans. The Fusiliers will come on board for sure, as will the rest. No Irishman could refuse.'

'Michael had much to live for, Tom, and you've put all that in jeopardy.'

'Michael will live on for Ireland.'

'You're talking nonsense, man – you'll have the blood of many innocents on your hands. This talk of freedom for Ireland has no place in India. For God's sake, Tom, it's not too late. I beg you again to give up this foolishness! Revolting in India isn't going to get Ireland anything – it's just going to get good Irishmen killed and all for nothing.'

But even as he said it, Father Jerome knew he could plead no more. He hurried back to Colonel Aylmer's office, aware that he would have to inform the Colonel of the two men – the emissaries, Michael and Tadhgh – who had slipped out of camp and taken the train down to Salem where the Fusiliers were now in imminent danger of being encouraged to revolt. But of greater urgency was the need to make a case to the Colonel and his officers for a calm and considered reaction.

Father Jerome was aware that at the top of the list of Colonel Aylmer's immediate concerns was the potential danger to all Europeans if the Indians in the cantonment got wind of a mutiny. The massacre at Amritsar in the Punjab was still a raw wound, and if events turned ugly at the barracks in Nandagiri Cantonment, the news would be eagerly seized upon by the leaders of the Indian insurgents; there were plenty of that ilk who didn't care for the half-naked Gandhi's insistence on peaceful protest. God forbid the Indians should find out that the Colonel was not in complete control of his men: the consequences were unthinkable.

As Father Jerome hurried up the steps to the Colonel's office, he touched the rosary beads in his pocket. He needed a miracle if he was to be successful in pleading restraint with Colonel Aylmer.

Father Jerome was still waiting for that miracle four months later, as he walked into a bitterly cold cell before a misty winter dawn, to hear Michael Flaherty's last confession.

'There isn't word of a pardon then, Father?'

The priest shook his head. 'I'm truly sorry, Michael my boy.'

'The word is that Tom didn't allow himself to be blindfolded, is that right, Father?' Michael was looking out of the tiny barred window towards the central courtyard of the prison, where arrangements had been made overnight for his execution at dawn.

Father Jerome nodded. What did it matter whether the man had been blindfolded or not as he faced the firing squad? Death was what was ordered and death was what was delivered.

'I don't think I'll be that brave. Oh Lord, it was never meant to be like this.'

'Be strong, Michael. Remember, Jesus will receive you in heaven.'

'I don't know, Father, whether there'll be a place there for me. God will never forgive me for what I've done to Rose.' The young man removed his shirt and struggled with something around his neck before handing it to the priest. 'It's my sister Bridget's scapular. Would you give it to Rose?'

'Michael, she's left Nandagiri.'

'If she doesn't return you will find her in Madras, with her Aunty Mags. They live in Egmore – number 32, Railway Lines, Egmore. Aunty Mags will know where she is. Promise me you'll give it to her. Take it as my last wish – I beg you do this for me. And Father Jerome, this letter is for my dear mother.'

The priest slipped the scapular and letter into his pocket. 'I will, Michael, I promise I will. And God *will* forgive you, my boy. He is compassionate. Come, let us pray.'

Dawn was just breaking over the cantonment, and for a moment the patch of sky that was visible through the window was blocked from view by an enormous flock of crows that settled in the trees.

Michael was sobbing quietly. 'What'll become of her, Father – my poor Rose? She wanted Ireland, but I've left her to hell on earth. I never meant for it to turn out this way.'

The priest knelt in front of Michael and held the young man's hands in his. 'Come, Michael. Let us pray in the time we have left.'

They prayed and as they did so a fearful stench arose around them.

'Forgive me, Father, I can't help myself, I'm so afraid. Hold me, stay with me till the end.'

The priest remained where he was, unflinching, and when the rifle party came for Michael, he insisted the condemned man be given a clean set of clothes before he was marched off to be shot.

In the final moments after the white paper target was pinned on to his chest over his heart, Michael was more composed. He shook hands with the priest. 'Thank you, Father, for all you've done for me.' He spoke briefly to Sergeant Willis, telling him that he held no ill-will towards the men in the firing squad. He smoothed down the paper target on his chest and then said he was ready.

As the stone courtyard reverberated with the noise of the rifles being discharged, the trees outside erupted with hundreds of startled crows that took to the air, cawing as if they were possessed. It was all over in an instant and as Father Jerome undid the blood-splattered blindfold and anointed the limp, bullet-ridden body, he wept for the complete and utter waste of a promising young life.

CHAPTER ELEVEN

Madras, August 1922

Father Jerome asked the gharry-wallah to slow down as they approached the Railway Lines in Egmore. Michael Flaherty had given him the name and address of the Bacon-wallah's relatives, where the priest would definitely find Rose. But that was two years ago, and the priest wished now that he had written the address down. It soon became clear to him that he was going to have to get down from the gharry and make some door-to-door inquiries.

He briefly looked heavenwards, asking for a speedy conclusion to his quest. The August humidity was unendurable, compared with the milder climes of Bangalore where he was now living.

His prayers were answered, for the very first door that he knocked on yielded an answer.

'The Roberts? They live in the house next door – that one, yes, number 32. I know them well, the best of neighbours they are, but I'm certain Mags is not expecting you, Father. I was in there with her this very morning and she never said anything about anyone coming.'

The priest thanked the neighbour and turned to walk back to the gate, but she was faster than him despite her size, arriving at her gate first and effectively blocking him from moving any further.

'Rose isn't here, Father. You're here about Rose, aren't you? We all feel so badly for the poor child. I've always told Mags that she should have written to you at the very start. I'm Mrs McKay, by the way.'

Father Jerome had grown to pity Anglo-Indian women even though sometimes, and this was one of those times, he felt they deserved the disdain with which they were treated. Here, for instance, was one who just didn't know her place.

'Thank you, Mrs McKay. Now that I know where the Roberts live, I can carry on with my business.'

She shuffled aside very reluctantly and even as Father Jerome headed into number 32, he was very sure that Mrs McKay would not wait long before she came across to investigate.

The large woman sitting on the verandah of number 32 had fallen to sleep in a worn rattan chair, the bright pink lace doily that she had been crocheting lying limp in her lap. Her mouth had fallen open, and as she snored, her ample bosom heaved in rhythm. Father Jerome stood at the steps to the verandah and called out to her.

She woke with a start and when she saw the priest she clasped the chair, grunting softly several times as she lifted herself to her feet, the crocheted lace, needle and ball of thread all clutched to her chest.

'Mrs Roberts, I'm Father Jerome.'

'Father Jerome of the Kildare Rangers? Oh Lord, I never thought I'd see the day!' She collapsed straight back into the chair and began to cry silently.

'Is your husband here?'

'Dennis has taken the ayah and the child to the beach. Rose's little boy – we called him Maurice. He is the image of Michael – oh, the very image of him.' She wiped her tears as she spoke but there was no staunching them.

The priest plucked at his collar, trying to let in some air around his neck. The sight of the weeping Anglo-Indian woman was distressing, and the mention of Michael Flaherty's name made his hair stand on end. He fanned himself with his canvas hat. There was another chair on the verandah, but it was right up beside the Roberts woman and he was afraid to sit so close, since women in her state were prone to reach for his hands and he could not, in this clammy heat, bear the touch of anyone's skin on his.

But he didn't have to stand for long because Mags Roberts suddenly got up, making a big attempt to compose herself and then, with much fussing and ado, she ushered him into the slightly cooler interior of the sitting room, plumping up the cushions on the sofa before asking him to sit. She stepped towards the inner door and called out to her cook, and then walked back to the verandah and let out a yell for the punkah-wallah to get going, before sitting down heavily on the armchair opposite the priest.

She wiped away the tears that had welled up in her eyes again, saying, 'I thank God every day that I married a good man, or what would I have done? Dennis, God bless him, has been very good to Rose when you think she isn't even related by blood.'

Father Jerome was taken aback. 'I was so sure Michael said you were Rose's maternal aunt.'

'Oh, Father Jerome, where do I even start? You see, Rose's mother Evie and I, we were as good as sisters, closer than most sisters I ever knew anyway. It isn't surprising we were so attached to each other. We both arrived in the Military Asylum for Orphan Girls in Madras on the very same day, December of 1880 it was. Both of us took ill that very first evening and were kept isolated in the infirmary block for two whole weeks with just each other for company. We were only six years old, or so they told us, and we cried most of the time. They thought we had the cholera but thank the Lord it wasn't – we were just sick with dread, and that's what made us ill.'

The punkah creaked overhead, slowly coming to life, and the priest dabbed his face with a handkerchief. He hadn't the time to listen to the woes of an Anglo-Indian woman. They were all the same, these chee-chees. When they let down their carefully tended guard, the truth of their tainted origins and half-caste blood came tumbling out.

He interrupted her just as she was about to launch into the rest of her story. 'Is Miss Twomey here? I wish to speak to her.'

Mrs Roberts clasped her hands together. 'Rose! Oh, Father Jerome, Rose isn't here – she hasn't been here with us for the last two months.'

The priest stood up. 'Then I'm afraid I've wasted your time, Mrs Roberts. I was hoping she'd be staying with you. I could have written to her father in Nandagiri and checked with him, but as this matter is to do with Michael, I thought it best to leave Sean Twomey out of it. Perhaps you'll be good enough to tell me where she is? I made a promise to Michael that I have to keep.'

Mrs Roberts remained seated, her head lowered, lamenting, 'Where did it all go wrong, Father?'

The priest looked down at the portly woman. 'Their liaison was ill-advised, Mrs Roberts,' he said sternly. 'I had indicated that to Michael very early on, and as for Rose – Mrs Aylmer was vehemently disapproving of followers from the start.'

'That heartless lady! She can't have an ounce of pity in her. She turned my Rose out, treated her like a common Indian servant. All those letters Rose sent, begging the Colonel and his Memsahib to consider her desperate situation, fell on deaf ears. They returned them unopened and Dennis wrote two on his own account as well. They were returned, too. Was that Christian of them, Father? How could Rose be held to blame for the deaths in the barracks? She had no part in that foolish mutiny!'

'Ah now, Mrs Roberts, when you've been betrayed, as Colonel Aylmer was . . . The Aylmer family have been good to the Flahertys – it goes back a few generations. There was a history of loyalty – mutual loyalty, I might add – that went beyond just the Kildare Rangers and regimental honour. A difficult notion for you civilians to understand in any case. Now Mrs Roberts, you must tell me how I can get in touch with Miss Twomey. I've but a few days in Madras and many other matters to take care of, as well, before I return to Bangalore.'

The woman wiped away her tears and looked up at him defiantly. 'Rose's mother and me, we could teach those Aylmers a thing or two about loyalty. The day Sean Twomey came to the Female Asylum to pick a bride and chose Evie, she and I were terrified we would never see each other again. You might find it hard to believe, but they were married the next day.'

Mags Roberts sniffed into the lace-edged handkerchief that was balled up tightly in her fist. 'There was never an orphan in the Female Asylum who had refused a chance to leave, even if it meant marrying a total stranger. And do you know why he chose Evie – over me or any of the others? Sean Twomey had declared to the Warden that, above all, he didn't want to marry trouble; he wanted someone biddable and the Warden assured him she was the meekest of the ones available to marry. When Evie said goodbye, she promised she wouldn't forget me and I tell you, Father, she may have been the meekest, but she was the most persistent. She begged Sean constantly for a year to find someone who would have me for a wife. *That's* loyalty: she didn't forget me.'

She folded the handkerchief on her knee with great precision, smoothing it out with firm strokes of her hand. 'Dennis had gone to Nandagiri to work on the survey for the mountain railway and he heard about the Bacon-wallah, the old soldier who cured the finest bacon in South India. He bought bacon from Sean all right, but when he returned home to Madras, he came to the Female Asylum the very next day and asked for me by name. "Evie Twomey insisted you'd make a fine wife" is what Dennis said when I was brought out to be shown to him.'

The priest was about to speak when Mags Roberts pre-empted him. 'Don't leave without something cold to drink, Father. I've asked the cook to bring in some lemonade and a bit of the almond and rum cake I baked this morning. Please, Dennis would be upset if he knew that you'd left without a little something.'

Father Jerome made a show of looking at his watch. Anglo-Indian women were, if nothing else, famed for being superb cooks, and he was always partial to cake at any time of the day. 'If you insist, Mrs Roberts, but I haven't long to stay and as I said earlier, you must let me know how I can get in touch with Rose.'

Mags began to speak but, overcome with emotion, she started to cry again.

The priest sighed in exasperation and wished he hadn't agreed to stay to eat something. 'How long did you say Mr Roberts was going to be?'

Mags hadn't heard him. She sobbed, 'She tried to kill herself a few months back, God help her. It was a terrible business, Father.'

Another tragedy, another wasted life! 'Is she dead?' Father Jerome asked. 'Where is she now?'

'She waited it out for two years, waiting when there was no hope at all. Just her own letters to Ireland returned, unopened. She has been hospitalised, Father, for the last few months – and now there isn't any hope at all for her.'

'Mrs Roberts, you're talking in riddles. I really must insist that you tell me what exactly has happened and where the girl is.'

Ignoring him, the big woman rambled on: 'I had to write to Sean to tell him that Rose tried to take her life – in our house when we were meant to be looking after her! It happened with no warning. She jumped into the well at the back of the house. She thought it was very deep, but the rains have failed two years in a row now, and the water-level is the lowest it's been for years – barely three feet or so. Oh Lord have mercy on her, she didn't know that and her suffering was terrible. She broke both legs, her ankles and many ribs and some bones in her face.' Mags shuddered as she spoke.

'She's in hospital in Madras?'

'Yes, Kilpauk. She is being kept in Kilpauk.'

'The mental asylum? Why on earth?'

'She was moved there from the General Hospital a month ago after the bones in her leg had set. The doctors told us Kilpauk was only going to be temporary, that she needed to be treated for her acute melancholia, but in the mental asylum she contracted TB. She's wasting away. She hardly speaks and hides her face if we take little Maurice to see her. That is why we don't take the child there anymore.'

'What about her father, Sean Twomey? Why has Rose not returned to her own father?'

'Return to Nandagiri? Sean might have brought her up single-handed after Evie died but which father, living in such a small cantonment town, could cope with the shame of what happened to her? Rose came to us to have the child, and we all hoped and prayed the Aylmers would take pity on her and do something, give her something to hope for – if not for her sake, then for the child's. If they'd given her a situation in their household in Ireland perhaps, since she was as good as betrothed to Michael, her father would have willingly supplied the money for her passage there. Maurice could have been brought up by Michael's people, as is right and proper. Now Sean sends us money for Rose and the child, but he can do no more. How could he look after Maurice? The boy is barely a year and a half.'

'But Mrs Roberts, this unfortunate situation can't be solved by the Aylmers,' the priest objected. 'What I mean is, they're not responsible for Rose by any stretch of the imagination. As for the Flahertys in Ireland, they are a respectable family. Why, it would be nigh impossible for them to explain the arrival of a child out of the blue.'

'No matter now, Father Jerome, it's too late for help at this stage. You see, Dennis and I have accepted the reality that she won't live long. She doesn't *want* to live, you see.' Mags began weeping piteously and the priest felt sorry for her.

The khitmatgar appeared at that very moment with a tray of lemonade and cake and looked alarmed at the state of his mistress. Mags pulled herself together as best she could. She smiled wanly at the man and asked him to put the tray down on the table beside her.

'He,' she said, looking at the khitmatgar, 'he was the one who found Rose in the well. He heard her moaning. We were out that evening – we had taken Maurice to the beach. I think more than anyone, the khitmatgar understands what we've been going through.'

'Lord have mercy, who would ever have thought it would come to this.' Father Jerome shook his head in disbelief. 'I'll visit her tomorrow morning, Mrs Roberts. I'll pray for her and please God she will recover. And if that's not what He wills, I pray her suffering will be short.'

He slumped back into the sofa as she poured out the lemonade. He had known for the last few weeks while planning this visit to Madras that meeting Rose Twomey would be very difficult, but as it had turned out, the situation was far worse than he could have ever imagined. He gritted his teeth in frustration. This was what his sermons were about all the time – the consequences of one's actions and inactions – but whoever listened?

'A little more lemonade, Father?' Mags Roberts was holding the jug up.

'No, Mrs Roberts, thank you but I must go now. Rose has been much on my mind – indeed, it has been my intention for the last two years to meet with her, and if not for my own illnesses I would have done so earlier. I'm glad I've located her before it was too late.'

'You've been ill yourself, Father? Are you well recovered now?'

'I contracted malaria in Nandagiri in the aftermath of that dreadful mutiny, and I was in the hospital in Bangalore for

130

nearly a year and a half, unable to shake it off. Still, the last five months have been much better and the doctors seem to be happy enough with my recovery. I'm alive today, and in the end, the malaria was nothing compared to the hardship of others.'

'I wish you could have met my husband Dennis. If you stay awhile, he'll be back. Michael's little boy, Maurice, will be with him.'

Father Jerome felt guilty for his initial impatience with the woman. 'Mrs Roberts,' he said gently, 'you and your husband will be blessed. Not many would have taken on such a burden as you have with the care of Rose and the child, too. I've two other appointments this evening and one of them is in the Garrison Headquarters at Fort St George that I can't miss under any circumstance. I'll definitely call again when I come to Madras next. I'd very much like to meet your husband and to see Michael's son for myself.'

'He is Evie's grandson, and for me that's as good as family. If only, and I ask this of Our Lord every day, if only we can live to see Maurice grown and settled, I'll have done my duty by Evie. As for Rose – oh Father . . .'

The priest consoled the distraught woman as best he could. 'I'll keep you in my prayers,' he promised her.

As the gharry pulled away from number 32, he watched Mags Roberts stand at her gate with Mrs McKay by her side. It was obvious to Father Jerome that he had misjudged Mags Roberts. She had been left to pick up the pieces, the consequences of a futile act in the name of a country she did not know and would never see. He took out his rosary beads, and as the gharry picked up speed, he prayed for her and little Maurice.

CHAPTER TWELVE

Madras, February 1934

When Father Jerome arrived in Madras Central Station that February morning nearly twelve years later, he took a gharry straight to the house in Egmore, where Mags and Dennis were waiting for him on the verandah along with the boy and a few neighbours.

Mags stood up to greet him, urging the young lad, 'Remember your manners, Maurice. Father Jerome's come all the way from Bangalore to wish you a Happy Birthday.'

The boy shook hands politely. He was a quiet child, rather shy, and over the years each time Father Jerome saw him, the likeness to Michael was painful to observe. It was no different today, on his thirteenth birthday. When Maurice smiled at the rupee that the priest pressed into his hand, he could have been his father Michael Flaherty in the flesh, expressing a similar delight when he was given some small treat for his work as altar boy.

The priest had let Mags fuss over him as he tucked into some excellent pressed tongue sandwiches followed by small, crumb-fried fish cutlets with a tartare sauce, and then a piece of her fabulous lemon cake, all washed down with tea served in the best china in the house. It was clear from his previous visits that Mags Roberts found feeding other people therapeutic and Father Jerome wasn't one to deny her that pleasure.

When he finally put his plate down, Dennis asked if he would like to step into the sitting room for a chat. This had become something of a routine in the one or two visits that the priest managed to make to Madras each year. Mags wasn't capable of giving him any news about Rose without breaking down inconsolably, and Dennis had taken it upon himself to brief the priest on her condition, even though he himself had been rather emotional the last time.

Inside the room and away from the rest of the neighbours, Father Jerome spoke without hesitation. 'Has it made any difference to Rose, Dennis, this new treatment? I'd like to be able to visit her this time. Even if you say she won't know me anymore, I'd still like to see her again.'

Dennis Roberts sat down heavily in the armchair beside the china cabinet. 'The doctors say they'll need to give her several sessions of the electric shock treatment before they can begin to see any improvement. But Father, it seems so cruel. She bit her tongue the last time and it needed to be stitched. The nurses said they hadn't realised she would struggle so violently, enough to dislodge the wooden bit in her mouth.'

Father Jerome wiped his brow. 'I've had the chance to speak to a few of the doctors in the asylum in Bangalore and they have only high praise for this new method. We must pray that they're right and that Rose might begin to take more interest in life.'

Dennis Roberts glanced towards the door leading to the verandah. 'I haven't told Mags about this as yet – I thought I'd wait till the young fellow's birthday had passed. The

Superintendent says that the problem now is she's developed a fear of being touched. I blame the shock treatment, Father, you can sense the terror, see the animal fear in her eyes.' The man began to cry silently, tears rolling down his cheeks. 'To think I welcomed him into our house, that snake in the grass Flaherty, to have taken advantage of Rose like that. In my day we would have shot him, Sean Twomey and me. We should have shot him.'

Father Jerome sat back in the sofa, regretting that he had eaten so much. It was his belief that Rose was as much to blame and yet, although he was not one to question God's methods, it did appear to the priest that her suffering seemed out of proportion to Michael's.

'He paid the price, Dennis,' he said aloud. 'He gave his life. Come now, let's not talk ill of the dead.'

Dennis Roberts rose out of his chair in anger. 'Forgive me, Father, but he paid the price for being a mutineer! He dishonoured his Regiment. His death was *not* about Rose. What he died for was not a punishment for having left Rose in disgrace with a child, nor for having placed this burden on us. Don't mistake me, Father, I love the girl as if she was my own, and her child as if he was my very own grandson, but not knowing what'll become of Maurice if Mags or I should die or fall ill . . . it gives me sleepless nights.'

Father Jerome closed his eyes. There was nothing he could say that would comfort Dennis Roberts. Over the years, the priest had looked at every possible solution to the desperately sad situation. He had thought of writing to the Bacon-wallah in Nandagiri to say that it wasn't enough to just send money each month to the Roberts, it was time for the man to resume charge of his daughter and take responsibility for his grandson. However, Rose was not well enough to come out of Kilpauk Mental

Hospital. Her recovery from TB gave way to severe melancholia and she had remained in the asylum in a silent world of her own. And so, Maurice stayed on with Mr and Mrs Roberts in Madras.

Sean Twomey died suddenly when Maurice was ten, without ever having seen his grandson. Despite that, the Bacon-wallah left all he had to Maurice: the dilapidated bungalow in Nandagiri that housed the piggery at one end, and the grand sum of seven thousand rupees. Mags Roberts cried for days when it was revealed that he had saved for forty years to buy a passage to Ireland for himself and Rose when he was, as he stated in his will, 'fed up of the Orient'.

Father Jerome belched uncomfortably. 'Dennis, I'll accompany you when you go to see Rose tomorrow. Is she still in the European wing?'

'She is, Father, though we've to pay a little extra to the warders to make sure she remains in the room with the biggest window. Superintendent Dr William Corbett retired last month and he's to be replaced by an Indian. Mags fears the new man might get rid of the European wing, and club those patients in with the rest. We'll fight it tooth and nail, of course, but one has to be careful not to antagonise these Indian doctors. They can get quite uppity.'

Father Jerome sighed. 'The times are certainly changing, Dennis, and we'll just have to move with them. The Assistant Civil Surgeon in the hospital in Bangalore, a young Indian, proved to be quite competent when I was recovering from malaria. In fact, he was very eager to show his superiors that he knew what he was doing.'

'Yes, but we always find that Indians, especially if they are well educated in any way, suffer from an unwarranted superiority complex. They are particularly off-hand with Anglo-Indians.

Still, money talks and it's a good thing that I was able to lease out the Bacon-wallah's house and piggery on an annual basis to the new Jesuit seminary in Nandagiri.'

'And you're receiving the rent regularly?'

'It pays for most of Rose's care, and the rest we manage. The boy has to be looked after, as well, and Mags is bent on making sure he's educated. It's his only hope if he's to be able to stand on his own two feet after we've gone.'

'Does he ask for his mother at all? I mean, where does Maurice think she is?'

Dennis Roberts stood and walked over to the wicker table beside the sofa. He picked up a photograph in a frame and handed it to the priest. 'That's how he remembers her, and that's how it will remain. It was taken on her eighteenth birthday.' Rose, confident and smiling, was seated on a mahogany Grecian-style stool against a backdrop of marble columns and grape-vines.

'What he's been told for a good many years now, is that she's gravely ill away in a hospital in England, too ill to write to anyone. When you first came to our house, Father, you might remember Mags telling you that Rose would refuse to look at the little fellow when we took him to the hospital. It was quite upsetting, so we stopped taking him there for his own sake. That was more than ten years ago. Now, he hardly ever talks about her.'

'I agree it was for the best, Dennis. And does *she* ever ask about Maurice?'

'No. It's the same as I said to you the last time – she remains mute. Not even Mags can coax a smile or a word of recognition. She won't allow herself to be washed and tries to refuse food. It's a wretched thing for her to live through. Death would be kinder. I pray the Lord takes her sooner rather than later.' Dennis blew his nose to hide his emotion.

'And I pray He will help her recover,' the priest said quietly.

When the gharry pulled up outside Kilpauk Mental Hospital, Father Jerome paid the driver while still seated in the vehicle because the sight of an open purse, to the waiting rows of lepers outside the gates of the hospital, would have led to a torrent of cries for alms.

He had decided to have a private word with one of the medical staff about the efficacy of the electro-convulsive treatment and whether it was truly worth their while putting Rose through the agony of it. He had arrived earlier than he needed to, well before Dennis Roberts, so that he could have a frank talk with her doctors. Even though he was not kin, the fact that he was a priest in his cassock meant there would be little difficulty getting them to give him the true picture.

The European wards and secure rooms were housed in a separate set of barrack-like structures that formed a quadrangle. There was just one entrance into the complex and it was secured by metal grilles and a locked door. He signed the visitor's book and asked if any of the doctors were around. The orderly pointed down the corridor towards the female wing of the asylum.

'The doctors have all gathered for a meeting, have they? Where's the matron?' asked Father Jerome.

The man was about to reply when his eyes widened and he nearly came to attention. Father Jerome was relieved to see a half a dozen white-coated doctors walking down the corridor towards him, followed by the matron and some nurses. The man leading the posse was Indian and he looked very much in charge.

'Good morning, Father,' the man said. 'It's not a Sunday, but we welcome the religious at all times. The word of God almost always has a calming effect on our patients. Are you from the Madras Mission?'

'No, indeed no, Doctor. I've come on a private visit to see Rose Twomey. However, I'd appreciate a few minutes of your time to discuss her treatment before I see her. I need some clarifications on a certain issue.'

'Of course. I'm Dr Swamy, the new Superintendent here. I just took over last week and am in the process of familiarising myself with the patients. As it happens, this Rose Twomey you talk of has caught my particular attention. The fact is, I wish to ascertain some details about her for myself, just to satisfy my own curiosity.'

Dr Swamy instructed the orderly to take the priest to the Superintendent's office.

'I'll be no more than ten minutes, Father,' the man promised. 'The orderly will bring you tea if you wish.'

Father Jerome looked around the small office, where several shelves were lined with medical texts and journals. A large baize-covered desk sat in the middle of the room and strangely enough, on a smaller table in the corner of the room overlooking the garden was a beautiful gramophone, its mahogany case buffed so well that the polished shiny brass speaker was reflected in it, dazzling the priest's admiring eye.

He was bent over the small collection of 78 records that were stacked in two wooden boxes, intrigued by the collection of jazz and Dixie, when the doctor walked in.

'Are you fond of music, Father? There's nothing like it to take your mind off the madness of life around us, don't you think?'

Father Jerome was not sure whether to agree, so he decided to establish his credentials instead, and shaking hands with the Indian, he introduced himself.

'That's interesting, an ex-military chaplain – but you stayed behind in India after your Regiment left. Surely that wasn't out of choice?'

Father Jerome explained: 'I was very sick for two years in '21 and '22 with malaria, and in that time the Regiment I was attached to, the Kildare Rangers, had finished their tour of duty and returned home to Ireland, only to be disbanded in the wake of Irish Independence. My religious order wanted me to stay on in India to help with ministering to the growing cantonment parish in Bangalore, and that's where I've lived and worked since.'

'You're related to the patient, Rose Twomey?'

'I'm a family friend – of her father, her uncle and aunt. She remains in my prayers every day. Please tell me, Doctor Swamy, what's the outcome to be for her? I hear that the convulsive therapy is very debilitating and has made her uncooperative.'

'We'll come to that in a moment, Father. You see, I do believe that I've met this lady before. Did she live in Madras? Did she have relations in Egmore?'

Father Jerome nodded. 'Yes, her uncle and aunt live in Egmore. They're her only kin.'

'In that case I'm quite certain it is her. I recognised her even though she has none of that youthful spark of life left in her. You see, she and her husband – he was an Army man, I do believe – they took shelter in my house many years ago, at the time of the Triplicane riots. They stayed the night and I remember sending a peon on a cycle with a note to her relations in Egmore, to let

139

them know that Mr and Mrs Twomey were safe. I was heading into the hospital for duty that night, and though I had promised to be back in the morning, we had so many injured brought in overnight that when I did get home late the next day, the couple were gone. I think a gharry came to pick them up, or so my neighbours said. Her uncle wrote me a very kind note subsequently.'

Father Jerome reached for his rosary beads in his pocket and closed his eyes for a brief second. *Oh Lord, You truly work in mysterious ways, bringing things to a full circle.* This man was the reason Rose was here, and this man might be the reason she would get better.

The priest nodded to the waiting doctor. 'Yes, I know that story. That *was* her, that *was* them.' He sat forward in his chair. 'You saved her life once, Dr Swamy, and I can only think the Lord has put you in a position to help her again.'

'Yes, in this line of work we sometimes have to pray for miracles. Mrs Twomey is one of the first patients in Madras to have been selected for the convulsive therapy by my predecessor. I've had a very good chance to study and observe the application of this technique in England at the famous Maudsley Hospital and I intend to continue this for her.'

Picking out a record from one of the boxes, the doctor wound up the gramophone and then clicked his fingers to the beat of the soulful jazz, looking at the priest as he spoke. 'They've a great success rate at the Maudsley, and we hope to follow their example. But Mrs Twomey has more than her fair share of problems and now can you tell me, Father, why her good husband, Mr Twomey – why isn't he listed as kin?' Dr Swamy had Rose's file open at the desk and was flicking through the papers.

Forgive me, Lord, I do this for Rose. 'Mrs Twomey's husband died just a few months before his Regiment returned to Ireland,' Father Jerome lied. 'Not having a single relative in Ireland, she elected to stay behind in India with her uncle and aunt. Her father has since dies, as well.'

'Ah! We know that sort of situation only too well in this country. With widowhood always comes big misfortune.'

CHAPTER THIRTEEN

Malaria Hospital, Bangalore, 15 August 1947

Father Jerome tried to lift his head and look around. He was so sure that someone was in the room with him.

A hand on his shoulder exerted a gentle pressure and pushed him back against his pillow. 'It's only me, Father, it's Sister Charity.'

'Oh, I thought it was Mags. She used to come from Madras to visit me every year.'

Sister Charity tut-tutted. 'Now Father, there you go, harking back to old times again. The Robertses died, don't you remember – two years ago now, Mags and Dennis, both of them within months of each other. You forget – you yourself told me the story. So very tragic. But you mustn't dwell on it too much. After all, Father, you told me that they would most definitely have gone straight to Our Lord in heaven.'

'They would have gone straight to heaven, yes. They were good, saintly people.' He could smell her now; Sister Charity always smelled of Cuticura talc.

'Now Father Jerome, how do you like this news for today – the Matron has ordered a special lunch for all.' She stood beside him and took his hand in hers. 'You know why, don't you?' she said. 'Today is Independence Day. The Indians have got what they wanted – Independence.'

Father Jerome closed his eyes. 'As good a day as any to die then.'

Sister Charity slapped his hand lightly. 'Today is definitely *not* a good day to die. Everyone's gone to Cubbon Park for the celebrations and it's just me and the Matron holding the fort here at the sanatorium. We're expecting two more admissions in the next hour despite it being a holiday, so I just wanted to make sure you were comfortable before I got busy with the new patients.'

Father Jerome nodded slowly. What was the use of her even asking how he was or if he needed help, when she couldn't really do anything? Only death could stop the wanderings of his fevered mind, as it slip-slided back and forth down the years, from the barracks in Nandagiri to the trenches in France and then back in this room hoping that the ayahs would come and take away the commode so he could breathe easy again.

But on a good day he could be back in the Emerald Tearoom in Nandagiri, ordering a slice of fruitcake or the jam sponge or both, and if he found himself drifting into Mags Roberts's house in Egmore in Madras, he willingly allowed himself to go there. She made a fine lemon cake, Mags did. He couldn't wait to see her again . . .

Sister Charity and the matron were in the corridor talking about him. Father Jerome couldn't hear them very well, but if he held his breath for a few seconds he could catch a few words.

'I do feel badly for the Father, Matron. He told me once a few months ago that he sometimes hated the places his mind takes him to.'

'It's a lesson then, Sister Charity, isn't it? If one stays on a righteous path, that's all the mind will ever know.'

She could be cruel sometimes, that matron, the sick man thought.

I stayed on the righteous path, Lord, You know that I did, he prayed. *I just wasn't able to help others in my care to do the same. Lord, will You forgive Rose. Take pity, Jesus, and end her suffering. Heavenly Father, look at her! She sits in the very corner of her room with no one and nothing to call her own. Give her back her conscious mind so she can repent.*

He called out softly to Rose. He was sure it was her he could see in the dim light of her small room, slowly turning away from him, her back hunched over her drawn-up knees. He called again and again, because he had promised Mags and Dennis that he'd never give up. One day she would break her silence.

It was Sister Charity calling him now, and when he opened his eyes, she was bent right over him, a look of alarm on her face.

'Thank the Lord, Father. I was just about to send for the orderly. You were sobbing in your sleep and you just wouldn't wake. Didn't you feel me shaking you?'

'I was calling to Rose,' he said hoarsely. 'She has no one now. Will you visit her for me, Sister Charity? Will you go to Madras? I'll ask the matron if you can.'

The nun sighed. 'Now, Father Jerome, there you go rambling again and you know it does your blood pressure no good. Rose isn't in the asylum any more, remember? She's safe with Our Father in heaven. Let me tell you something that'll cheer you up – we're going to have a tri-colour cake with custard for dessert, given what day it is today. You remember what day it is, don't you, Father? It's the fifteenth of August, Independence Day.'

'Yes, I know what day it is,' the sick man answered. 'It's my day to die.'

'Oh shush, Father, I won't have such talk of dying from you.' Sister Charity lifted his hands and placed them on his chest. 'Now stay like that for a minute while I draw the curtains a bit.'

Father Jerome closed his eyes and a slow smile spread across his face. He knew what day it was – and he knew he was right.

PART TWO

1982

The Sitar-Guitar Girl

CHAPTER FOURTEEN

Nandagiri, March 1982

Mohan Kumar sat back in his rattan armchair and reached for the old brass bell, pressing it down several times. A short while later, little Appu appeared at the door.

'Soda, Saar?' he asked.

'Where's your father?'

'Bazaar, Saar. He's gone to buy white flour. He told my mother he needed it for the special high-class bread he was going to make for the vellakaran, Saar. Are you wanting some soda, Saar?' The boy posed the question in English this time. He enunciated each word very carefully, then waited for a reaction.

Mohan smiled as he corrected the seven-year-old: 'Do you want some soda, sir?' The child mimicked his every inflection and Mohan continued in English, 'Yes, cold, so make sure you bring it from the fridge.'

The boy was delighted at this but then reverted to his native Tamil as he replied, 'I'm not allowed to touch the fridge, Saar.'

'Yes, I know that. Ask your mother to give it you.'

Mohan watched the boy leave, pondering on the news that an ordinary sliced loaf from the Nilgiri Bakery wasn't good enough for the visitor from overseas, the 'vellakaran'. He wondered what else his housekeeper Ishwar had planned for tomorrow.

Mohan was well aware that his servants were in a high state of excitement. As Collector of Nandagiri, and despite being just thirty-two years old, Mohan Kumar was the most senior civil servant in the small town, his remit covering three divisions and their outlying villages, which stretched over the thickly forested hills and valleys of the Nandi mountain range. The government offices over which he presided had a notoriously efficient grapevine – and the news of this particular visitor's impending arrival had spread with more than the usual speed, arriving back, embellished with atrocious inaccuracies, at the Collector's own bungalow residence in a matter of days.

Mohan pulled a little rattan stool close to the armchair and put his feet up. He was tired and could have done with an early night. Instead, two boxes of official papers lay in his office room waiting to be dealt with before the weekend was over. And to top it all, starting from tomorrow, Saturday, he had to play host indefinitely to an unknown Irishman for whom old Ishwar was going to personally bake bread.

The soda had not yet arrived. His servants were slow, painfully slow, and he had nobody but himself to blame. His mother had pointed that out when she had visited him at his first posting in Assam. "Run your home like your office, she had said. The word is that you have an iron fist at work, so why this poor management at home? 'A home is to relax in,' he had insisted. That's the whole point, son, she had countered. If you keep the servants on their toes, you can really relax." She had been thoroughly disapproving, and his beleaguered Assamese servants were not the only ones who were relieved when she left.

'Your soda, Saar.' Appu's mother Kala placed the glass on the table, her face modestly averted, then left as quietly as she had come into the room. Mohan was about to call her back and enquire about the boy's progress in school but there was no point in preaching to the converted. Kala was ambitious for her son, dead set on ensuring he did well, for Appu was a bright little fellow.

Mohan got up from his chair, crossed to the old sideboard, unlocked it and peered inside. He was low on rum, he noted, and had just half a bottle of gin left and no tonic water at all. He needed to stock up. This Irishman might enjoy a drink, and it wouldn't do to run out. After all, the District Collector had made it known to Mohan that the Chief Secretary himself had personally requested that Richard Aylmer be well looked after. The Irishman was obviously well connected, for the District Collector had immediately dismissed Mohan's plan to put him up at the government guesthouse on the Ooty Road.

'That would be too impersonal, Kumar, and we both know the food there is terrible. Somewhere more homely would be more suitable.'

'What about the Nandagiri Club, sir?'

'He's here for four months, Kumar! We can't confine him to one room. I've received written instructions that he's to be made very welcome. The Chief Secretary was most emphatic. You see, this Aylmer fellow's grandfather was Colonel Aylmer. You've heard of him? Yes, he was something of a legend in these parts. A first-class artist and I believe he had a great affection for the people of this district. All of which is a little surprising because he was essentially a military man. He commanded the Regiment of the Kildare Rangers when they were stationed here in the 1920s.'

151

'Richard Aylmer will have full use of the Club, sir – the library and the bar, as well as the billiards room.'

'Actually, Kumar, I was hoping *you'd* offer to put him up at "Knocknagow". Surely that big Collector's bungalow of yours has more rooms than you need? The Chief Secretary would be very satisfied.'

Mohan had sighed inwardly. He should have known what was expected of him. 'That shouldn't be a problem at all, sir. I'll make the arrangements straight away.'

The District Collector was relieved. 'Good, good. I'll leave it in your capable hands. By the way, how's your mother? Still doing her sterling work on the Tribal Crafts Board? She's marvellous for a woman in her circumstances; widowhood never held her back, did it? Do give her my regards when you next speak to her. Bring her down to Coimbatore when she visits you next time. I'm always looking for a partner at the bridge table.'

Mohan thought now about the way that conversation had ended. The Indian Administrative Service was all about knowing your place – and if you proved that you did, you could then make enough of an impression to move a rung higher on the career ladder.

He settled back in the armchair with his whiskey and slowly poured in the soda. The unknown Irish visitor might even prove a pleasant distraction, he thought, cheering up. It would be nice to have someone to talk to and have a drink with in the evenings without having to make the effort of going to the Club. He hoped the newcomer was a sociable sort or he would be condemned to four months of polite misery.

Mohan skimmed the surface of the whiskey with his fingertip and picked out a very tiny insect that was floating lifeless in the alcohol. What would Richard Aylmer make of all these creatures? Flying cockroaches, lizards that dropped down unexpectedly from the ceiling, flies that appeared the minute food did, marching ants, biting ants – and just last week a small snake curled up in the cool, dark shadows of the enormous brass water drum in the bathroom.

Mohan wasn't quite sure why the man was coming to Nandagiri in the first place. Nevertheless, he had instructed Ishwar to thoroughly clean out the two rooms at one end of the house in preparation. The Collector's bungalow was, like many of the older houses in Nandagiri, just a glorified soldiers' barrack, a relic of the Raj days. Ten identical rooms led one into the other in one long row, and every room had a front door that opened on to the very wide verandah that ran the length of the front of the house. Additionally, each room also had a door at the back, leading on to a much narrower rear verandah. The latter functioned as a service corridor, which was used in the main by the servants as they went about their daily chores. Here, every afternoon, Kala sat peeling potatoes, shelling peas or topping and tailing spinach or green beans as instructed by her much older husband Ishwar in preparation for the evening meal; their son Appu would sit cross-legged on the cement floor beside her doing his schoolwork.

Mohan had occasionally come across them just as he was about to return to work after his lunch and afternoon nap. Although Kala herself couldn't read or even write her own name, the boy's neatly completed homework was looked over and corrected by Murali the watchman each evening at five, when Kala took the man a glass of tea and a plate of savouries from the kitchen. The watchman had her permission to twist Appu's ears really hard if he made careless mistakes or if his handwriting was less than perfect. All this Mohan knew because the watchman, so proud of his input into the child's education, gave him occasional updates when Mohan sat outside on a Sunday morning, having his breakfast while reading the weekend papers.

The front verandah overlooked a large, immaculate lawn that was watered twice a day and hand-cut with an old-fashioned scythe by a fanatical mali. The latter had looked after the garden in the Collector's bungalow for thirty years and was an exceptional gardener. The wide rose beds that bordered the lawn on three sides were simply breathtaking: they were, without doubt, the most famous roses in the whole valley and surrounding hills. The mali was fiercely protective of them and would get agitated if any of Mohan's admiring visitors asked for cuttings. He would very grudgingly part with a few if he was certain the visitors were from far afield, like Coimbatore or Madras – or preferably from the other side of the country like Bombay or even Delhi. But if the request came from any amma or saar who was local or lived anywhere in the Nandagiri range, he would cook up the most ingenious horticultural excuses for not taking cuttings there and then.

'The Collector's bungalow has always won the prizes – we don't want to end up in a few years competing against our own blooms,' was his explanation.

Mohan was never sure why he indulged the mali and let him get away with this. Perhaps it was because the man's behaviour reminded him of his own mother, who would firmly insist that family recipes stayed in the family. If pressed by a particularly stubborn enquirer, she would cunningly reveal most but not all of the ingredients; some, but not the entire method. Her evasive tactics were a great source of entertainment for Mohan and his younger sister Asha. So, when it came to his mali, Mohan would laugh and tell any complaining guests that, in anything to do with the garden, the mali was the boss and that even he, the Collector, would not dare to interfere in the matter of the roses.

In the evenings towards sundown, particularly if he had had a stressful day at work, Mohan liked to relax on the verandah on one of the old-fashioned planter's armchairs, his drink resting on one long rosewood armrest and his weary feet slung over the other. Spectacular sunsets were followed by blue and purple dusks that seemed to cool down the valley before his very eyes. Later, as darkness blanketed the hills, he would listen to the nightly chorus of crickets and frogs until Ishwar came and stood behind the chair to give him the daily update on what had transpired in the Collector's bungalow since the morning. Ishwar insisted on following this with a menu check for the next day and even though Mohan was confident that his experienced cook would turn out a delicious meal whether he was consulted or not, he had quickly realised it was easier to comply with the ritual than leave the old man fretting about the next day's culinary arrangements.

Over a period of forty years or so, the old regimental barracks had been moulded to suit each Collector's idiosyncrasies. Mohan, for instance, had turned the first room in the bungalow into an office, which he used early each morning during the working week and often late at night as well, to catch up on the endless paperwork – reading and signing reports, requisitions, petitions, orders and authorisations.

The office opened into his bedroom, which had two exquisite Assamese Sitalpati mats on either side of the bed and, against the window overlooking the front verandah, a small rosewood desk with brass inkwells that Mohan's great-grandfather had brought back from Burma. Two bookshelves framed the window from floor to ceiling. The room, which had no other furniture, was dominated by a five-foot-square charcoal sketch of a group of local Yurava tribesmen squatting in a forest clearing beside a catch of fish and eels in a woven basket. The artist was a retired Nandagiri railway engineer.

Mohan had bought the piece within a few weeks of taking up his position in Nandagiri, struck by its incredible realism. The Yuravas' faces were weathered and leathery; two of them smoked thin beedis as they prodded the squirming eels, while three others strung more of the basket traps together. A lone tribesman sat a little apart from the others, staring back defiantly at the artist, daring him to capture the moment if he could. Mohan never tired of looking for details that he hadn't spotted before – the way a blade of grass had been flattened by a cracked and dirty heel or how the whiskers on one catfish seemed to be entangled between the thin fishing lines.

Mohan's bedroom opened into a dressing room, which was rather cramped because of the sheer size of the two cavernous free-standing wardrobes that Ishwar kept meticulously tidy, with not a handkerchief or sock out of place: Mohan's shirts and trousers lightly starched and hanging neatly, his belts rolled up and stacked in a cane basket and his shoes polished and precisely arranged on a very large and ancient shoe-rack that still had the worn remnants of military-style red baize on its sloping shelves. The furniture in the dressing room was typical Public Works Department issue of pre-Independence vintage, fashioned locally from cheap country wood, marked with rusting metal plaques bearing the name *Wilson's Furniture Yard*, no doubt a prosperous establishment from a bygone era when Nandagiri was still a thriving garrison town.

Mohan's home in Nandagiri was simple and uncluttered, although he had picked up a few things over the years: small durries from his time in Chettinad, some old rosewood furniture from the auction of a tea-planter's household effects in Assam, and a large iron mural, very intricate in its depiction of a Tree of Life, that he had had made to order by Bastar craftsmen using a design sketched for him by his sister Asha.

Over the last eight years as an officer in the Indian Administrative Service, Mohan had become well used to making the best of whatever accommodation came with a new posting. His immediate concern was always for his books. Left too long in packing cases they inevitably suffered; the unrelenting humidity left pages stuck together with grey-green mildew and prone to attack by silverfish, which were nearly impossible to eradicate.

Within a week of arriving in Nandagiri he had ordered bookshelves to be built in three of the rooms. In Mohan's bedroom, paperback fiction, heavy academic tomes and leather-bound official government publications that reflected his fascination with the social history of the Indian subcontinent sat side by side with the poetry of Tagore, the writings of Khushwant Singh and the 1980 Census of India.

Mohan's first few years in the IAS had been difficult. The tenures in remote up-country outposts were lonely, the social life non-existent unless you wanted to count the odd drink shared with unknown government officials passing through for a night or two, and even that didn't make for entertainment, as the revelation that Mohan was in the IAS normally made the others keep a respectful distance. Lonely, he had depended on his love of reading to keep him going, buying dozens of books whenever he was in a town that had a bookshop, often getting his mother or Asha to parcel up a good selection to whatever rural backwater he was stationed at. Even now, the memory of those dingy rooms in dilapidated government dak houses had not faded fully and, like other young IAS officers scarred by the experience of their early years, his very first instinct when informed of a transfer of post was to pick up the phone and pull as many strings as possible to make sure he had the first call on the best possible house available for his seniority.

Mohan had loved 'Knocknagow' from the very first time he laid eyes on the house. It had been vacated by the previous Collector barely a week before his own arrival, and when Mohan's car pulled up outside, having made the four-kilometre journey from Nandagiri railway station with the three-car official welcoming party still in tow, the entire household staff, led by a beaming Ishwar, had lined up to meet him on the steps of the verandah.

It had been surprisingly warm for a January afternoon, and taking in the vista for the very first time, Mohan had been enchanted by what he saw. The Collector's bungalow was situated on a small plateau on the gentle Nandi mountain range of the lower Nilgiris. The rose beds, which were always at their best in the winter months, served to frame the view of the small green valley that stretched out below.

Unlike the pristine and orderly tea-estate terraces that dominated much of the Nandagiri mountain range, this valley had remained part-scrub and part-jungle – an Eden of sorts, where plants that had disappeared from other parts of the range had managed to survive the relentless onslaught of agribusiness. Mohan had walked all the way down to the bottom of the garden, which ended at the edge of a steep slope that fell away to the valley below. Rhododendrons, poinsettias, rambling dog roses and thorny blackberry brambles smothered the slope, while lower down in the valley, thickets of small trees and pockets of grass and fern vied for space with scores of very large trees, some of which were venerable specimens with orchids growing in the mossy nooks between their branches. A thin stream meandered through the valley, forming tiny pools wherever rocks and small, smooth boulders dammed its flow. The water glinted in the afternoon sun, and even at this distance Mohan could see a lone kingfisher waiting patiently on an overhanging branch.

The official entourage had followed Mohan on to the lawn and were jostling each other, eager to point out to him the various geographical landmarks in the far distance, rattling off the names and heights of several peaks, filling him in with details about the old military cemetery that could be seen below and telling him about the disused road that ran along the northern flank of the valley towards the abandoned Army shooting-range.

It was at this point that Ishwar had come forward, having discreetly edged his way towards Mohan. 'If Saar would like to rest, the bedroom is ready,' he murmured. 'The hot water is also ready, if Saar wishes to have a shower.' Minutes later, when Mohan had shaken the round of hands and accepted the heartfelt welcomes to the district once again, he had watched the three cars leave with huge relief, knowing that his arrival had gone down well and that this old fellow Ishwar, his new housekeeper and cook, was a clever man.

Mohan's first impressions of Ishwar's efficiency proved to be accurate, which was why instructions to the housekeeper regarding the Irishman's impending arrival had been very simple: 'The vellakaran Saar will use two rooms – make up one as his bedroom and in the other put a table and some chairs,' Mohan had requested. 'Use the cane sofa out of the storeroom as well. Make sure Kala cleans the windows and checks for insects.'

Mohan was confident that Ishwar would make adequate arrangements. As a housekeeper and cook to every single Collector in Nandagiri over the last forty years, Ishwar knew the routine off by heart. It wasn't surprising really, for his father, and grandfather before him, had both worked in the same capacity, though the huge colonial households they had managed were remarkably different from Mohan's small retinue. Ishwar had, on Mohan's arrival in Nandagiri two years ago, produced a file of testimonial letters written by previous Collectors who, being bachelors in the main, were quick to acknowledge his culinary skills and his ability to manage the rest of the household staff.

When Mohan had finished leafing through the file, Ishwar had produced an ageing manila envelope from which he had pulled out several sheets of foolscap paper on which were listed, in Tamil, the names of every single dish in his culinary repertoire, divided into Indian, European and Chinese sections.

'I can cook anything Saar wishes,' Ishwar had declared proudly.

Within weeks, Mohan knew that his posting in Nandagiri would be tolerable because of Ishwar's gastronomic abilities. The man's housekeeping was also faultless though he tended to bully the other servants into submission, threatening them with quick eviction from the staff quarters if they did not toe his line.

Mohan preferred to keep out of the domestic politics of his household. It was unnecessary to get involved in the day-to-day running of 'Knocknagow'. In fact, he was aware that any interference would upset the natural balance of things. The pace may have been slow and unhurried in the Collector's bungalow, but things got done, and done well. Lunch was invariably ready for him when he came home each working day, and the household maintained a quiet when he took his twenty-minute afternoon nap before heading back again to his office, which was just two kilometres away. In the evenings he looked forward to sitting down to eat, with Kala hovering outside the dining room and bringing in the hot chapattis and soft parathas as Ishwar made them in the distant kitchen.

It was a warm evening for March, Mohan thought as he got up and walked outside. It was nearly dusk and the air was still. The mali was on his haunches, weeding the rose beds, and when he saw Mohan, he raised his hand to his forehead in a quick salaam. Mohan nodded in acknowledgement and walked down the front verandah towards the two rooms that had been prepared for the visitor.

The bedroom smelled slightly musty, so Mohan switched on the ceiling fan. It whirred into life, sending ripples through the fine mosquito net that hung to one side of the bed. He opened the large wooden wardrobe and saw with satisfaction that Ishwar had lined the shelves with fresh sheets of newspaper, with a few neem leaves tucked in between. Leaving the fan on in the bedroom he walked into the adjoining room where Ishwar had fashioned a small sitting area that faced the front verandah. A desk and chair had been placed in one corner of the room. Both rooms looked rather bare and spartan, however, prompting Mohan to walk back out and call to the mali, who wasted no time in presenting himself, wiping his hands vigorously on the thin loincloth that was all he wore.

'Pick four nice flowerpots and place them on either side of these doors,' said Mohan, pointing to the two rooms. 'Be sure to clean off any dirt on the pots and check for ants as well.'

The mali nodded enthusiastically. 'Right away, Saar. There are two bougainvillaeas, one pink and one orange, and I'll bring in the nasturtiums from the side of the house.' He wiped his hands again, this time on his bare chest, and then hesitated before saying, 'If Saar has the time, can I remind him about my brother-in-law? He's still without a job, Saar, and my sister . . . her child will be born any day now.'

Mohan was used to being petitioned; it was a daily occurrence when you were an officer in the Indian Administrative Service. He had early on in his career realised that the more people he obliged, the greater the number who were indebted to him. This meant that he had, in his own hands, the power to build up a great reservoir of goodwill to be tapped whenever he needed it. Everyone had something to offer in return – whether it was the station-master who made sure Mohan got a train ticket when he wanted one, or the Chief Secretary who would remember him favourably when the time came, or this lowly mali who would ensure that the Collector's bungalow had the best flower beds in Nandagiri.

'Did he put in his application as I'd told you?'

'Yes, Saar, for a ward orderly's post in the hospital.'

'All right. Tell him to come to the office on Monday and I'll give him a letter for the hospital superintendent.'

The mali salaamed smartly and went back to his weeding. Mohan stood for a while on the verandah, looking at the garden and beyond. In another ten minutes it would be dark and the view would be shrouded by nightfall.

Nandagiri was one of the smaller garrison stations that had grown around the larger town of Ooty during the days of the British Raj. Ooty had achieved legendary status during that period as the summer capital of South India. Its elevation at 2,240 metres ensured that summers were cool and sometimes even dust-free, its woods and gardens reminiscent of England. The quaint stone churches, the polo grounds, little tea rooms and lush cricket greens transported the homesick rulers of British India, if only for a season, back to a romanticised notion of home.

Ooty still retained some of its past glory but the same could not be said of Nandagiri. Eighty kilometres south of Ooty and at a slightly lower altitude of 1,850 metres, it was no longer the bustling garrison town that it used to be in its heyday immediately after the First World War. The town had, for about eighty years leading up to 1922, been the regimental home of the Kildare Rangers, but today its main street, Kildare Avenue, was much quieter – a bit shabby and listless. The once-colourful bazaars were drab and deserted, for the summer visitors had all but stopped coming. The famous public school was well cocooned in its own extensive grounds on many hundreds of acres, all of Nandagiri completely out of bounds to its boarders, while the small Army cantonment remained fully self-sufficient with its own shops, school and club.

The Collector's bungalow and its garden faced west, and Mohan had grown to love the view of the small shady valley with the old British cemetery that lay on the lower slopes. In the afternoons, schoolboy goat-herders would arrive whooping and whistling, rushing up to a large wingless marble angel only to gleefully rub her breasts, laughing at their audacity as they took turns. Then they would sit cross-legged on the neglected tombs, coughing over a shared illicit cigarette or playing a game of marbles in the dusty mud around the numerous graves. This evening however, the valley was quiet, and despite the dusk, Mohan could still see the fractured marble angel with the gleaming chest, the rest of her body covered in grey green lichen.

Mohan called out to the mali: 'Is there still a track to that graveyard from the Ooty Road?'

'Yes, Saar. It used to be a tar road, Saar, but now you wouldn't know that,' said the mali, looking down the valley in the direction of the graveyard. Mohan dismissed him with a nod and walked to the guest rooms, where he switched off the fan and closed the doors before heading back to the drawing room for his second whiskey. *I'll take Richard Aylmer down there one of these days,* he decided. Vellakarans were known for their penchant for graveyards.

CHAPTER FIFTEEN

Nandagiri, March 1982

How much longer was Richard Aylmer going to sleep? He had arrived on the last train on Saturday night, politely but firmly declined dinner, showered and gone to bed. It was now nearing lunch the next day and Mohan, who had managed to work through both boxes of files that had accompanied him home on Friday evening while he waited for the visitor to surface, was getting a bit impatient. If lunch was late and dragged on past three in the afternoon, he would almost certainly have to cancel his Sunday-afternoon game of tennis with Captain Satish Pillai.

Captain Pillai was a difficult man to lose to at tennis. He fancied himself as a bit of a coach and if Mohan lost, what usually followed was a tedious game-by-game analysis of the entire match. There was no point in playing tennis if it was too soon after lunch, for the slightest bit of post-lunch sluggishness would ensure that Mohan would lose to the quick-footed Army man.

A shadow fell across the doorway just as Mohan dropped the last file into the box by his feet.

It was Ishwar, his face animated with excitement.

'Appu's bringing him this way, Saar. Richard Saar has woken and is all dressed and ready!'

Mohan pursed his lips. The normally unflappable Ishwar seemed to have lost his sense of decorum completely.

Richard Aylmer stooped as he passed the doorway and walked into the room, his arm stretched out for a handshake. 'Thank you very much for letting me sleep,' he said pleasantly. 'It was a frantic few days in Ireland before I left for India. You're very kind to have me stay with you.'

Mohan shook hands and pointed to the two despatch boxes crammed with files. 'I'm glad you slept well. I'm with the Indian Administrative Service – as Collector of Nandagiri I find the paperwork never ends, but I've actually managed to clear my desk completely, which is great. The rest of Sunday now awaits us. Would you like some tea or coffee, Richard? Or if you want to have lunch straight away – perhaps you'd like a beer or a gin and tonic to start?'

'Tea, please, and yes, lunch would be fine. What an amazing view you have from the verandah, Mohan. I am pronouncing it right – Mo-han, isn't it?'

Mohan laughed. 'My name isn't the usual South Indian tongue-twister – you're spot on with the pronunciation. I hope your room is comfortable enough?'

'Very comfortable. I haven't slept so well in a long time.'

Mohan ushered Richard out of the study. 'We'll sit here on the verandah, shall we? Yes, it's a lovely view, I never tire of it.' He called out to Ishwar, who had backed out of the room and was standing on the rear verandah: 'Tea, please, and you can serve lunch soon after.'

The two men sat outside and talked, just courtesies at first: about the journey, the weather and vaccinations. *He looks the same age as me,* thought Mohan, *though at thirty-two my hair isn't quite receding as yet.* The Irishman was very tall, six foot at least, with rather unruly short, dark hair that was thinning at the temples. He looked fit, maybe he played tennis; he might even show Captain Pillai a thing or two. Nice friendly smile, rather fair – no, *very* fair-skinned actually – and no vellakaran airs and graces as yet. *And if I apply one of my mother's many obscure tests: the one that decrees 'a gentleman knows how to relax into a sofa',* Mohan thought to himself with a smile, *this fellow passes with high honours.*

Ishwar brought the tea and then lingered near the dining-room door, staring at the back of Richard Aylmer's head before Mohan dismissed him with a request to get lunch going.

Richard put down his cup.

'I've to confess, Mohan, that when Mr Baneerjee told me he'd made arrangements for my accommodation, I assumed it was in a guest house or hotel of some sort. I'm embarrassed – I really can't impose on your hospitality for more than a day or two. There must be a hotel that I could stay in?'

Mohan got up and strolled to the edge of the verandah. 'Ah yes, Mr Baneerjee, the Chief Secretary. You won't be imposing at all – to be honest I'm glad of the company. Moreover, I'm gone the whole day and my servants have nothing to do, running a household for one. Let's see if they can stand up to the pressure of two for a while.' Mohan laughed and continued, 'In fact, they've been in a state of high excitement since the word went around about your arrival. You see, Nandagiri is a small town and the bush telegraph is terribly efficient. My cook, Ishwar, he's the man who just brought in the tea, I believe his father Gajjapati was khitmatgar to your grandfather, Colonel Aylmer – a sort of housekeeper, cook and butler rolled into one. Ishwar's barely been able to contain himself these last few days before you arrived.'

Richard looked genuinely surprised. 'Really? That's amazing! It never even occurred to me that there might still be people around who'd recall my grandfather. The Regiment, I knew, would be remembered – after all, they were stationed here so many times – but an actual connection with my grandfather and the family? If I believed in signs, I'd consider it a good omen.'

The Irishman ran his fingers through his hair. 'You're probably wondering why I've come to Nandagiri. You see, Grandfather was a soldier, but he was also a talented artist, as was his daughter, my Aunt Alice. The project I've in mind concerns the large collection of his work that we have in Ireland.'

Mohan nodded. 'Yes, I know he was a fine artist. Only a week ago, when I mentioned your visit to Captain Pillai, a good friend of mine, he pointed out the two watercolours that hang in the billiards room at the Nandagiri Club and told me they were painted by your grandfather. Colonel Aylmer had gifted them to the Club. It was exclusively a services club then, of course. There were no civilian members, and certainly no Indians ever darkened its doors.'

He realised his gaffe immediately. 'I'm sorry, that didn't quite come out the way I meant it. What I was trying to say was that the Club has changed considerably since your grandfather's time. It was a different era altogether, the 1920s. Nandagiri was different, too. It was more of a military town then. These days, it's quite commercial, with tea estates, spice plantations, logging, that sort of thing. But I'm rambling now. You were about to tell me about your grandfather's work and how it's brought you here.'

Richard sat forward and put his cup of tea down.

'What I want to do might turn out to be a bit of a wild-goose chase. You see, our family have a portfolio of a hundred or more watercolours that my grandfather painted while he was here, commanding the Kildare Rangers. I'd like to photograph the very same views that he painted. The idea is to have an exhibition in tandem, my grandfather's paintings side by side with my photographs – and I've had some expression of interest from the National Gallery of Ireland. But of course, this may or may not be possible, because Grandfather was a prolific painter and didn't always give a name or place to his paintings. I'd need a local guide of some sort, someone who'd know the geography of the area intimately. I realise that this is a tall order, but Mr Baneerjee said he would talk to a couple of people.'

Me, most likely, thought Mohan.

'Mr Baneerjee can certainly move things along and quickly, too,' he said. 'Have you known him long, Richard?'

'He's my father's friend actually. He studied law at Trinity College in Dublin, and my father James and he were in digs together for four years before the war and stayed good friends over the years. In fact, Mr Baneerjee was one of the few people who could get my grandfather to talk about India. He even tried to persuade him to come back to Madras for a holiday.'

'And did he?'

Richard shook his head slowly. 'After what happened with the Regiment here in Nandagiri? No, Grandfather would never have come back. He loved India, but – hell, it's a long story. You see, he blamed himself for that dreadful mutiny that took place.' Richard turned to look over the garden towards the Nandagiri hills. 'You know, he used to speak of the Blue Hills, but I never thought they'd really be blue.'

169

I'll have to get more details about this mutiny from Captain Pillai, thought Mohan. 'It's the way the light falls,' he said aloud. 'I mean, there's a scientific reason for the blue haze.'

'It was the light that my grandfather loved. "An artist's dream", he used to say. It creates great opportunity for photography, too.'

'So, is that what you do? Are you a professional photographer?'

'Yes, I do it for a living, landscapes mainly, but I do some bread and butter stuff as well – industrial catalogues, factories, manufacturing processes and machinery. Mohan, is that a cemetery down in that valley there?' Richard had his hands up to his eyes, shading them from the intense glare.

Mohan walked back to his chair. 'Yes, an old British one. Some of the graves are quite ancient; they even predate the graves in St Andrew's Church in the middle of the town, which was built in the late 1890s. This one contains mostly soldiers' graves, I believe. I could arrange for you to see it, if you wish. There's a rough track that runs to it off the main Ooty Road.'

'I'll definitely take you up on that offer, thank you, Mohan. Who maintains it?'

'No one, really.' Mohan felt compelled to give a reason for the neglect. 'It's the fate of most old cemeteries, I'm afraid. We're a poor country, with no money to spend on the dead.'

'It's a pity.'

'You'll see worse. Is this your first time in India?'

'You can tell?'

Mohan laughed. 'Ah, I can see Ishwar heading this way, so lunch must be ready. Shall we go into the dining room?'

The lunch took Mohan totally by surprise. Ishwar waited till they were seated and then returned, proudly bearing a platter containing a large roast leg of lamb with a herb crust. Kala stood just outside the dining room, holding a large tray from which the cook retrieved one at a time and with much ceremony, roast baby potatoes and mashed potatoes. This was followed by glazed carrots, buttered peas and a large tureen of gravy. A plate of bread rolls was placed beside the gravy and then Ishwar moved to stand behind Richard, admiring his own handiwork for a few seconds, after which he looked at Mohan before he spoke.

'This was Colonel Aylmer Sahib's favourite meal. My father had noted it down in his ledger, along with all of the Burra Memsahib's particular recipes. The Colonel Sahib liked to have roast lamb every Sunday lunch, followed by fruit and sherry trifle because it reminded him of home. The children loved mashed potatoes the best. For dinner then, the whole family would just have soup.'

Though taken aback at his cook's initiative, Mohan translated the small speech for Richard.

Richard pushed his chair back, stood up and held his hand out to Ishwar. The cook took it hesitatingly and the two men shook hands briefly.

'Thank you, I'm very touched. Would you say that to him, Mohan? Tell him how much I appreciate it and I'm sure I'll enjoy this lunch as much as my grandfather must have, every Sunday, all those years ago.'

Ishwar looked like he was going to burst with pride and was all smiles as he carved the joint with an expertise that Mohan had not expected.

'Your grandfather must have been quite a man to evoke such sentiment in this old fellow,' Mohan told Richard. 'He thinks he's about sixty-eight years old, which means he was just a child when your grandfather was in Nandagiri. Ishwar's father, of course, would never have forgotten his years of service and would have kept all those memories alive, for he belonged to that old school of loyal native retainers. Indians made a great servant class – they were biddable and faithful.'

'You're being a little harsh maybe, Mohan?' Richard responded. 'They did what colonised people do, didn't they? Self-preservation, it's called. They did make a choice in the end though. You guys weren't quite so biddable in 1947, if I remember right.'

'Hmm. Thirty-five years on and we still haven't been able to shake off that colonial mentality – the unquestioning acceptance of any higher authority, the deference, the fatalistic acceptance that someone else knows what's better for you.'

'I guess you come up against it all the time, being in civil administration.'

Mohan drummed his fingers lightly on the table. 'Oh, this is where I have to bite my tongue and admit my role in perpetuating that belief. As a civil servant I'm part of the machinery that keeps that defeatist way of thinking alive and well. Is it any different in Ireland?'

'We were colonised by the English and immediately after that by the Catholic Church. From the frying pan into the fire is what I think.'

'I take it then you aren't a practising Catholic?'

Richard chuckled. 'No, I'm afraid I'm truly damned. I'm Protestant.'

'Part of the ruling class, am I right? That's what we learnt in history.'

'Ruling class? No, not for a long time now. But like you Indians, we haven't been able to shake off the name-calling. We are still only Anglo-Irish even after all these years. We have a complicated social history, and apparently, we've yet to redeem ourselves. Really you'd have to be Irish to understand – it wouldn't make sense to an outsider.'

'Don't feel too badly. Most of India doesn't make sense to outsiders either.'

Later, having done the meal justice, they moved back on to the verandah again, where Mohan adjusted the two planter's chairs, pulling out the extra-long arms and then sitting down in one of them and swinging a leg over an arm of the chair to show Richard how it was done.

'Just picture it: it was this chair, the thought of a welcome chota peg, someone to ease the boots off your tired feet . . . this is what kept the English sahib going in these parts. There wasn't much else in these densely forested hills except the opportunity to make a fortune in tea. Nandagiri was just a planter's town all year round and a busy cantonment whenever a regiment was in station. Ooty was where the high life was and is, even now.'

Mohan decided to change the subject. 'Do you play tennis, Richard?' he enquired. 'I have a regular game organised on Sunday afternoons – perhaps you'd join us later and I could even show you around the Club. I know Mr Baneerjee has arranged a temporary membership for you, but the Club offices are closed on Sunday, so you'll have to sign in during the week maybe.'

'Tennis sounds good. I haven't played in a long time though. About my project, Mohan – I'll need to unpack first so I can show you the portfolio and explain what I want to do. I've some brief notes that you might read if you've the time.'

'What about tomorrow mid-morning? I'll send the car out for you and you could come up to the office. I'll be able to pick up the phone and put you on to the right people straight away.'

Richard agreed and Mohan stood up. 'I hope you don't mind, Richard, but I'm going to go inside for a short nap, about half an hour or so, before we head to the Club.'

'You carry on with your routine, and please don't let me get in the way. In fact, I might start unpacking and sort some things out to show you tomorrow.'

Mohan stopped at the door. 'I should have asked you earlier – I hope your room is okay?'

'Absolutely, and the fact that your house is called "Knocknagow" makes me feel very much at home.'

'Knocknagow is an Irish word? I've always wondered who named the house and what Knocknagow means.'

'It's the name of a famous nineteenth-century Irish novel actually, about life in rural Ireland: and the story is set in a village called Knocknagow. My guess would be that some Irishman, very nostalgic for home, named this house after the bestseller of its time.'

'I must ask my sister to order a copy for me if it's still in print. She sends me parcels of books every two months or so from Delhi. The one thing – no, let me rephrase that – one of the *many* things that we don't have here in Nandagiri is a decent bookshop.' Mohan pointed out the doors to the sitting room. 'However, I've plenty of books in there if you want something to read. The dining room here has maps and local interest stuff – history and a good few books on the Nilgiris itself.'

'Thanks, Mohan, I'll have a browse. Why don't you carry on and catch that nap?'

Mohan stifled a yawn. 'I've asked Ishwar to organise the adjacent room as a sort of study-cum-sitting room for you. If you need anything else – more pillows, stationery, anything of that sort – just ask. Right, Richard, I'll see you at four then. I think you'll enjoy the Club and we'll start by having a look at the two watercolours I mentioned.'

Mohan switched on the fan in his room and lay down on his bed, crossing his arms behind his head. Ishwar, who knew his routine on Sundays, had been in the room ahead of him and had drawn the curtains closed and left a glass of water by his bedside table. Without the glare of the afternoon sun the room was dark and cool, and Mohan knew it would be only a matter of minutes before he fell asleep. It was going to be interesting having Richard Aylmer around, a change from the small social circle to which he was confined, restricted as he was by his position as Collector.

As he drifted off to sleep, he thought about the two close friendships he had cultivated in the fourteen months since he had come to Nandagiri. He had met Sonal and Bala Mishra at an official function within a week of his arrival. They were both doctors, college sweethearts who had married in their intern year and who had, to the utter dismay of their families, decided to sacrifice potentially lucrative careers to concentrate on rural medicine.

Mohan had got to know the Mishras quickly from having to frequently liaise with them on an official basis, for the couple ran a large NGO-funded health centre in the belly of the old town, in the crumbling maze that was Raja Bazaar. There, in a large sprawling house that was rumoured to have been a thriving brothel long ago, the couple worked with a total disregard for officialdom, running the busy clinic with ruthless efficiency and a cleanliness that was nearly other-worldly, given the decaying and fetid surroundings of the once-bustling bazaar. Sonal and Bala were frequent visitors to 'Knocknagow', often dropping in unannounced after dinner for coffee. Then there was Captain Satish Pillai, the Adjutant of the Corp of Engineers Regiment stationed in the cantonment, who had started off as a tennis partner at the Club but was now a good friend.

There was no doubt that they would all enjoy meeting Richard Aylmer, thought Mohan as he fell asleep. The Irishman was an interesting and personable addition to their circle.

CHAPTER SIXTEEN

Nandagiri, March 1982

It was just a week since he had arrived in Nandagiri and Richard was impressed by the speed with which Mohan had organised introductions for him to help lay down the initial groundwork for his photographic project. Over breakfast earlier that morning, Mohan Kumar had warned him about the brusque manner of the District Forestry Officer whom Richard was to meet.

'Gerry Twomey's an oddball,' he said. 'Don't take any notice, because he'll do as he's asked. The problem is, he has a big chip on his shoulder – even a whole tree, perhaps – but then these Anglos are like that. Can you imagine what it's like to have both a superiority *and* an inferiority complex on the go at the same time?'

'Anglos? Who are they?' Richard was curious.

'Anglo-Indians – they were called Eurasians in your grandfather's time. Gerry's an Anglo – you can tell them just by their names. They descend from mixed-race liaisons dating back to the days of the Raj. At that time the authorities believed that abstinence was dangerous, especially for soldiers, and there are plenty of Anglo-Indian offspring around who are the result of that belief.'

'I thought I hadn't heard right when you mentioned the name Twomey. That's as Irish a name as you'd get.'

'If you scratch, you'll probably find some Irish blood. Anyway Richard, Gerry Twomey will be extremely useful to you so don't take a bit of notice of his gruff manners. Technically, he comes under my remit so he has no choice but to be helpful. The fellow was born here in Nandagiri and there's no one who knows these mountains better than him. He'll find your locations – in fact, I bet you he'll know those views the minute you show him the copies of your grandfather's portfolio.'

Forewarned about Gerry Twomey's idiosyncrasies, Richard had left 'Knocknagow' at mid-morning in Mohan's official car and was driven to the Divisional Forestry Office fifteen kilometres outside Nandagiri, where the arrival of the Collector's vehicle caused a commotion. A peon came running to the car, unfurling an umbrella over Richard's head as he stepped out. It had taken barely a few days for the Irishman to realise that it was easier to go along with the fuss, even if it meant that the peon was practically on his tiptoes to keep the umbrella over Richard's tall frame.

Gerry Twomey had kept him waiting for ten minutes on the redbrick verandah where a chair was brought out and dusted before four peons urged him to please be seated. Two of them stood at the grilled windows of what was obviously Gerry Twomey's office, occasionally peeping through the gaps in the curtains to see if their boss was done. Suddenly, there was a scraping of chairs from inside the room and the peons stood smart and alert as two men emerged, clutching files and papers, followed by an unsmiling man in a khaki uniform holding a polished wooden baton. The men with the files thanked and salaamed Gerry Twomey repeatedly, and one bent down to touch his feet. He shooed the fellow away perfunctorily and, slapping his baton lightly on his palm, turned to face Richard.

'That feet-touching nonsense,' he said brusquely. 'It's the Indian equivalent of kissing my arse.'

Richard stood up and put his hand out. 'Gerry Twomey? I'm Richard Aylmer. I have to tell you how grateful I am for your time. I see you're busy.'

The handshake was returned. 'Ah, the Collector's friend. No need to be grateful, we scratch each other's backs all the time. It's the way things work here.'

Gerry Twomey was a tall man, well built, with unruly brownish hair that may have even been red years ago, and a handsome though weather-beaten face. He was smartly dressed in the khaki uniform of the Indian Forestry Service and wore an old-fashioned solar topee.

'I've a meeting with the Highways fellows in a few minutes,' he went on. 'You can come with me or wait here. I'll be finished with them by lunchtime and I normally go home for a bite to eat, so you can tell me what you want me to do for you over lunch.'

'I'll come along if that's okay. It'll save you having to come back to pick me up.' Richard had hardly said it when he found himself having second thoughts. 'Actually, I don't really want to barge in on your lunch, so perhaps I should wait here till you return.'

'We were expecting you at home because I told Mohan Kumar it would be easiest to discuss your plans over lunch and really, our house is the only clean eating place around here. I've a busy day today and the rest of the week, too.'

He gave Richard no chance to reply. 'So that's settled then, yes? Right, let's get a move on – the jeep's here.'

With that he climbed into the canvas-topped rear of the jeep and Richard followed, stooping low to avoid the metal roof bars as he sat down opposite Gerry. A peon hopped into the front passenger seat with the driver and with two loud thumps of his fist on the door, gave the signal for the vehicle to move off. Richard looked out behind them and as the jeep sped away, he saw the peons at the Forestry Office slide into the squatting position favoured by the lowly. It had taken the Irishman barely a week to figure out that the administration of India was not so much about running the country but about providing employment to millions.

'I believe you've an unsurpassed knowledge of the local area,' Richard said, looking at Gerry.

'I was born here in Nandagiri – our family has been here since my great-grandfather's time. My father was the District Forestry Officer and I've lived here all my life. But what I or anybody else in the Forestry Service knows doesn't matter much because my opinions aren't very popular and as a result, they are considered irrelevant and never taken into account.'

The man was turning out to be just as surly as Mohan had said he'd be.

'What do you do?' Gerry demanded then. 'Are you a journalist?'

'I'm a photographer.'

'For a newspaper?'

'I work for myself. I sell my landscapes, like an artist would a painting.'

'And what can I do for you? Mohan Kumar mentioned that you had some old paintings and that you wanted to find the locales – is that all?'

'There are over a hundred paintings, and I've copies of each. If you could identify the views – if they still exist, that is – I'd be most grateful.'

'So much trouble just to know where they were painted? You've travelled from Ireland, isn't it?'

Richard nodded and briefly outlined the project as he had envisaged it.

Gerry Twomey listened with interest. 'So, when you're done in Ireland, will you bring this exhibition to India? Your grandfather's watercolours, side by side with your photographs taken sixty years later, would really open up some eyes in this country. I've been shouting for years about the urgent need for conservation. They are quite unique, the flora and fauna of these hills – has Mohan Kumar told you about the Nilgiri sholahs? They're one of a kind, nothing like them anywhere in the world. There's been indiscriminate felling and terrible deterioration in forest cover here in Nandagiri. People need to see the ruin that we've brought upon ourselves. At the current rate of destruction, I'll be without a job in twenty years. There'll be no more forests left here, just tea plantations.' His voice was bitter, impassioned.

'Well, I've never thought about showing my work here in India. So far, I've simply concentrated on the feasibility of the project itself – you know, just being able to find the views and photograph them. Bringing the project to India would certainly take the idea the full circle . . . Yes, now that you ask, I *would* bring it here. Definitely, yes,' replied Richard. The idea that his fledgling project could have a real legitimacy in India excited him.

The jeep pulled into a compound and Gerry alighted swiftly. 'I'll be about twenty minutes. You can wait on the verandah, I'll tell my man Friday to make you comfortable. Friday! Switch on the fan and keep the chokras away from the Sahib.'

The peon who had been sitting in the front of the jeep nodded agreeably. 'Yes, Saar. No problem, Saar.'

Minutes later, Richard went through the same procedure as at the Divisional Forestry Office. A chair was dragged out from one of the office rooms, hastily dusted and placed in the middle of the long verandah. The ceiling fan came to life with a frightening shudder and then clacked around slowly and noisily, letting out an excruciating whine every now and then.

Friday, who had taken a proprietorial interest in Richard, stood at the edge of the verandah and glared at the small ragtag crowd of urchins and some toothless crones who had gathered at a short distance to point and stare. This Highway Engineer's office had not been graced by a vellakaran for many decades and the crowd grew by word of mouth.

They called out to Richard repeatedly, 'Hello, Mister! Hello!' One little boy came forward and began a fanciful song and dance routine, wiggling his hips suggestively in the manner of the latest Bollywood hit song. The rest of the urchins began to clap to the rhythm, when one of the old crones suddenly stepped up and gave the nimble dancer a sharp clip across his ears. The rest of the urchins fell about laughing and the old woman screeched a few obscenities and then calmly resumed her place in the crowd.

Richard sat unmoved. He knew that to show any emotion – appreciation or anger – would draw them closer, till they would be touching, pawing at him, begging for loose change, the pen in his pocket, a comb even. He'd been divested of his things in this fashion twice before and was now impervious to these little collective street dramas.

There was sudden silence when a bottle of Coke arrived on a tray; Richard politely declined it. As Friday took it back, a cacophony of voices rose from the crowd, each child volunteering to finish it. Friday stopped and put the tray down on the verandah floor and, with the umbrella in his hand, made a rush at the crowd who scattered immediately, leaving just the three crones who ignored the peon and proceeded to dig around the folds of their dirty saris for little cloth pouches from which they took small plugs of tobacco, placing them carefully in the corner of their mouths.

It wasn't long before some of the urchins began to creep back, holding scraps of paper in their hands. Soon there was another round of 'Hello, Mister!' and the scraps of paper were waved in the air. Friday yelled at them and they shouted back and he laughed. Richard was curious and he signalled to Friday to explain.

'They are thinking Saar is famous cricketer.'

'And who told them that?'

'All of India watching cricket in television. Only one TV in village but all of village boys knowing cricket teams, India, English, Australia. That boy, he say you famous English. They looking for your sign on paper.' Friday turned to point to the Bollywood dancer and at that, the crowd stood hushed and still in anticipation of some new development.

Richard sighed. 'Tell them I'm not who they think I am.'

'They be sad, Saar.'

'Yes, I know.'

Friday's shoulders dropped and he turned to the urchins to inform them. They hung around for a while more just staring and pointing, then fed up with Richard's unresponsiveness, wandered off, discarding their scraps of paper wherever they had stood.

Gerry came out shortly after. 'Hope you weren't too bored just sitting here. We can head home for some lunch now. Then we can start our business of looking at your paintings.'

Richard stood up, stretched himself and laughed, saying, 'India could never be boring.'

Gerry Twomey's house was a surprise. Richard had expected a smaller, more modest version of the Collector's bungalow but in fact it was much larger. They drove in, past freshly painted light-blue wooden gates, and down a long avenue of very old and very upright yews, right up to a set of three old barrack houses that were linked to each other and set in a U-shape around a very large, sunken rectangular courtyard, the latter planted in the style of a walled cottage garden.

Richard was struck by the colours in the garden. Every shade of pink and purple and white was there, along with some lavenders and mauves, but not a single red or yellow; no marigolds or nasturtiums, no asters or cannas, none of the varieties that he had admired in Mohan Kumar's garden. The whitewashed walls of the house were covered at regular intervals with wooden lattices that supported lush green creepers heavy with plump white buds of jasmine. The avenue of yews carried on past the house to several very large modern farm sheds, beyond which acres of fruit orchards rose into the low hills that ringed the property.

'Do you farm cattle here?' Richard asked as he got down from the jeep.

Gerry was about to reply when a labourer came running from the direction of the sheds. There was a rapid exchange between the two men and then, dismissing him, Gerry turned to Richard. 'No, not cattle, we have a piggery here. I can show you around later if you're interested. The fellow just came to tell me that we haven't any electricity and are running on the generator. It happens at least three times a week because the electricity board linesmen are trying to screw around with me.

I've been forced to buy generators to beat them at their own game. It's the usual story, they want a regular pay-off to keep me connected. But it's too hot to stand around here talking about power cuts – let's go inside.'

They crossed the verandah, with its polished red cement floor, and entered directly into a small but comfortably furnished sitting room. Making a motion with his hands towards the sofa, Gerry disappeared past a curtained door without a word.

Richard could hear him calling out, his voice getting fainter as if he had moved to the part of the house on the other side of the courtyard. Richard switched on the fan and sat down. He looked around the spotless room with its old-fashioned crocheted sofa backs and the volumes of *Reader's Digest* lining the glass cases on either side of a plain cast-iron fireplace that very obviously hadn't seen a fire for years. Instead, a bunch of plastic roses covered with clear acrylic raindrops sat in a brass bowl inside the grate, and above the mantelpiece was a magnificent old mirror, its ornate gilt edges barely scuffed.

Richard heard voices approaching again and Gerry came back into the room followed by a tall, strikingly elegant woman in a lavender sari.

Richard put his hand out. 'Mrs Twomey, I'm sorry to be barging in like this at lunchtime.'

She shook his hand and turned to look at Gerry in amusement. 'Oh no, I'm Miss Twomey – May. I'm Gerry's sister. He'll be hard-pressed to find a wife.'

'You put them off, May, you scare them away,' said Gerry.

Richard laughed, delighted that May Twomey was not the grouch that her brother was. 'Oh, my apologies, I'm Richard Aylmer. Your brother has been very kind . . .'

185

Gerry pushed the curtain aside and showed Richard through. 'Come on, let's eat lunch before May's piano students start coming in for their lessons. We won't be able to hear ourselves think.'

'Gerry!'

'*Für Elise* drives me mad.'

May rolled her eyes. 'Please don't mind my brother, Richard. He gets very childish when he's hungry, but just wait till he's eaten. He can be quite sweet if Cook has made dessert as well.'

They ate a simple lunch of chicken curry and rice followed by little bowls of cold caramel custard, and Richard told May about his photography project. Later, after lunch, when the table was cleared, Richard began laying out a selection of photographed paintings in rows, and to his surprise both Gerry and May became instantly animated.

'Lansdowne Ridge – these two were definitely done from Lansdowne Ridge. Look, he even took in the Bishop's Nose.' Gerry held up two pictures in his hand.

'This one as well, Gerry. There, that's the view from the lower ridge – you know, the old footpath to Lovers Leap. Richard, your grandfather had an eye for detail and that's going to prove very useful in pinning down the locations.' May was circling the table slowly, pointing to various pictures.

'The way to do this,' she said, 'is to pick out the ones we can identify positively and then arrange them according to locations. We can work through the rest gradually; there'll be other people as well who can help. You'll find it easier that way.' As she spoke, May began rifling through the bulk of the pictures still in the plastic portfolio. 'You'll need some extra files and labels. Gerry, Richard will need an Ordnance Survey map of the district, as well. Make sure you get a laminated one.'

'You see that, Richard? Now it's my turn to apologise. May's a teacher at Nandagiri Public School and therefore thinks she can treat everyone like a twelve-year-old.'

Richard smiled at May. 'But she's being so helpful, Gerry. You both seem to have identified some locations already; I'll put those aside.'

Gerry looked at his watch. 'Funnily enough, I have to head in the direction of Lansdowne Ridge later this afternoon. Richard, it'll suit if you come with me today. It's only another five kilometres to the Ridge from where I have to go and it'll save me from having to make another trip just to show you the place.'

May tutted in disapproval and Gerry put his hands in the air. 'What now? What did I say? It actually *is* only another five kilometres, and if Richard comes with me this time it'll be a journey saved.'

May turned to their visitor. 'You can see that he wasn't educated by the nuns, can't you? But that's my brother for you: no finesse but he means what he says and says what he means.' She grinned. 'Come on, let's have a proper look at these pictures.'

Richard had watched their faces as they exchanged their exasperated observations about each other. The affection between the brother and sister was obvious, and he knew straight away that their collective confidence in being able to help him wasn't just talk.

They quickly identified eight views that they were certain were all painted from the Ridge. Friday was summoned from the kitchen, where he had been gossiping with the cook, and sent to the office room to fetch a few spare files.

After twenty minutes or so Gerry yawned. 'I usually nap for half an hour after lunch. Would you like to grab some shut-eye in the guest room, Richard?'

187

'No, half an hour would leave me groggy, not rested. I probably wouldn't wake for a good few hours if I slept now, but please don't let me stop either of you. I can linger over a cup of coffee, May, if that would be possible.'

Gerry was gone even as his sister ushered Richard back into the sitting room. 'My brother works hard,' she explained to him. 'He starts at six in the morning when the temperature is just bearable, and there really is no point in going back out in this heat. This way, you'll be on the road after three and by then the worst of the afternoon sun will be over. This is only March – in June, Gerry won't stir from his afternoon nap till four.'

'Don't let me keep you from your routine. I'll be fine here on my own. You know, I haven't read a *Reader's Digest* in years.'

'Oh, those. We stopped subscribing after our mother Betty died, but she used to treasure them and I haven't the heart to give them away even though the servants are constantly moaning about having to dust the whole lot every week. Don't worry, I don't nap in the afternoons. You see, school starts early at seven in the morning so that we are finished by one o'clock before the heat of the day. Most of the pupils have sport in the early evening, starting at four. I've a handful of day pupils coming to me for some extra tuition, and the first one will be here in twenty minutes. I teach music at the school, the piano mainly.'

Richard watched her as she stood looking out of the window on to the verandah and beyond. She was the most attractive woman he had seen since his arrival in India, though he would never have described her as a traditional Indian beauty. Her eyes were not almond-shaped or kohl-lined, nor were her lips full or her figure very shapely in the Indian cinematic fashion. She had instead a slim boyish figure, with an honest face that was lit up by the friendliest and lightest brown eyes that he had ever seen. Her straight hair had been styled into a simple bun at the nape of her neck, and every now and then she tucked away the loose strands that had worked their way out. She carried her sari with casual grace, and when she had stretched across over the dining table to examine the copies of the paintings, he had seen flashes of her neat, nut-brown belly, and his eyes were drawn to it again as she leant over the windowsill and shouted across to Friday who had dozed off in the jeep parked in the courtyard.

'The workers' children aren't allowed in the swimming pool. They pluck the flowers indiscriminately and that fellow Friday should know better than to turn a blind eye,' she explained without turning around.

May watched for a minute more and then with an exasperated sigh opened the door and went out. Richard caught the glint of a silver ring on her toes as she stepped over the threshold, and when he followed her out into the verandah, he was just in time to see three children scamper across the courtyard in the direction of the farm sheds.

'Where's the swimming pool?'

'You're looking at it,' said May, pointing to the courtyard. 'That sunken area used to be a swimming pool, built for the Kildare Rangers. We live in what used to be the barracks that housed the changing rooms, the showers and recreation areas. Our dining room, where we ate lunch today, was once a canteen, that's why it is so big. The sitting room and the room next door were originally one room, the gymnasium, with weights and boxing bags. My mother had it divided into two because it was too huge to heat with just the one fireplace. As for the pool, that was filled in about fifty or sixty years ago by my great-grandfather Sean Twomey, who bought the property when the Rangers left. The pool had been disused and empty for a year before he bought the house and, soon after, a servant's child fell into it and broke an arm. So, my great-grandfather had it filled up immediately. We still call it the swimming pool though.'

'That's quite amazing. Living in this house must be like living in a piece of history. My grandfather was with the Rangers.'

'I know. My grandmother, Rose, was your grandmother's maid.'

Richard looked at May, totally at a loss for words. 'I don't know what to say. Gerry never mentioned a word.'

'Gerry's like that.'

'Is she still alive, your grandmother?'

'Oh no, she died quite young, of tuberculosis and a broken heart. I never knew her.'

'I'm sorry to hear that,' Richard said awkwardly.

The cook appeared at that moment with a tray of coffee and they watched him in silence as he poured and sugared the cups and then waited, tray in hand, to be dismissed.

'I wouldn't know much about my grandparents' time here in India,' Richard said quietly. 'They didn't speak of it . . . and my father, James, who was only ten when they left Nandagiri, he doesn't remember much. We discovered the paintings four years ago, in a wooden trunk, in the attic of my grandparents' home when it was being re-roofed — and this was nearly twenty years after both of them had died. It was a miracle the watercolours had survived in such good condition. They'd been packed with such care, triple layers of tissue between each one, and tucked into all the corners were little muslin bags filled with some sort of dried herb.'

190

'Oh, that wasn't a herb,' May said immediately. 'That would have been neem leaves. They keep away insects of all sorts.'

'Yes, you are probably right. We know the paintings had been packed away in India because the newspapers that lined the trunk were all Indian.'

She twirled the rings on her finger. 'Gerry will be very useful to you, Richard. He knows these parts like the back of his hand. You see our father, Maurice Twomey, was a District Forestry Officer, as well, and he was a conservationist at a time when such people were considered the loonies who got in the way of jobs and progress. It was a different time – then we had elephants, panthers, plenty of wild boar even, and he fought to keep it that way. He was powerless, of course, just a forestry officer with no clout. The forests around here were relatively untouched in those days before the tea companies started clearing whole swathes of hillside for the latest money-making export crop: pepper, vanilla and cardamom. Gerry tagged behind Dad wherever he went, even as a child; it used to drive my poor mother mad with worry.'

'Mohan Kumar said the same thing, that Gerry would be the key. I'm staying with Mohan. Do you know him?'

'Yes, I know who he is.' May sipped on her coffee and looked down at her feet. She bent down and fiddled with her toe ring, pulling it off and putting it back on again.

'Do those rings mean anything? You know, like the dot on the forehead?'

'Toe rings? They used to symbolise your married status, for Hindu women, that is, but now everyone wears them; it's a fashion thing. I put them on if I am wearing a sari. It completes the look, I think. I have to wear a sari to work, the school insists. None of those immoral slacks or skirts.' Smiling, she tidied the pleats of her sari.

191

'Where is the school? Is it in Nandagiri?'

'Yes, it's in Nandagiri, but you can't really see it from any of the approach roads. It is set within a four-hundred-acre campus, and is totally out of bounds to the public. It has a bit of water frontage on Lake Victoria as well.'

'Is that the lake in Nandagiri town? I thought it was called something else. Mohan mentioned an Indian name.'

'It now bears the name of a dead politician, but it will always be Lake Victoria to me. My mother loved walking there, along by the bandstand and in the gardens by the shore. In this part of the world politicians think history can be altered by changing names or removing statues from the places they've stood at for several decades, even centuries — from crossroads and the town hall, from the clock-tower, the front of the libraries and civic buildings, and even hospitals — as if it would change history or make a difference to who we are.'

May was about to go on when they heard a car pulling up outside. 'That's my pet rant out of the way,' she said, 'because here comes my first pupil for her piano lesson. Richard, excuse me, will you, as I must go now. Will you be okay here till Gerry wakes up?'

Richard stood up. 'I'll be fine. Would you and Gerry join me for a drink at the Nandagiri Club? Mohan sorted me with a temporary membership there. How about this weekend? We could have dinner.' He was surprised to see her colour slightly.

'That would be very nice, but I think you should check that out with Gerry. I must get on now — here she is. Good afternoon, Rekha. I hope you haven't forgotten your sheets today?'

'Good afternoon, miss. No, miss, I have them with me.' The child looked at Richard wide-eyed before following May out of the room.

A few minutes later, Richard could hear Rekha practising her piece – *Für Elise* – over and over again. He relaxed into the sofa and as he waited for Gerry, he closed his eyes and tried to conjure up the unlikely image of his grandmother in Nandagiri.

Richard Aylmer was certain that at any moment now, he would deposit the entire contents of his stomach somewhere on the dashboard of the jeep that was hurtling down the narrow forest track. Then suddenly, a shout from behind caused Gerry Twomey to brake without warning. Richard lurched forward and then back again, his dark glasses dislodging from the bridge of his nose. He bent down to pick them up but a hand on his arm signalled him to be still.

'Don't get out of the jeep. Not till I tell you, okay?'

Richard nodded, not sure if he was even allowed to turn his head to look around. The canvas window between the cab and the rear of the jeep flapped open and a rapid exchange of words took place, then one of the uniformed men in the rear stood up and eased himself though a gap in the metal-framed roof of the jeep, cupped his hand and called out into the thick forest. They waited in the jeep for what seemed like an eternity, and then stepping out from behind the thick foliage to the right of the track, as if they had been standing there all along, a pair of bedraggled men appeared and then another and then more till about forty of them waited at the side of the track, some squatting, some standing.

Richard turned to Gerry Twomey, who was at the wheel and who, anticipating questions from Richard, had put his palm up.

'Just wait for my say-so. No cameras as yet, all right?' With that, Gerry hopped out of the jeep and walked towards the group of men.

The canvas window opened up behind Richard and Friday poked his head through.

'No need frightened, sir, these being just tribals, just Yuravas.' The flap closed and Richard tried hard not to laugh. *I'm in a Monty Python sketch,* he thought, *and if all goes according to script, they'll soon be negotiating a price for my scalp.*

Gerry spoke to the two men who had first stepped out of the forest and they began pointing and gesticulating in the direction that the jeep had been headed. This was followed by a lot of animated conversation, during which the rest of the group came closer, squatting around in a semicircle. Nearly half an hour passed and Richard, drenched in sweat, watched as twigs were used to scratch out what looked like crude maps in the dusty mud. Several times there were disagreements and the dust was smoothed over with a few sweeps of Gerry's boot and the maps were redrawn again.

'Richard, you can come now. Leave the camera for later.' Gerry had turned around and was signalling him to come out.

The tribals remained squatting as he approached, and conscious that they were watching his every move, he put his palms together and bowed slightly in the traditional form of greeting. They burst into applause, pointing at him and laughing.

He wiped the sweat off his brow and faced them along with Gerry.

'These men are Yuravas, one of the local forest tribes,' the Forestry Officer explained. 'They keep me informed about animal movements and occasionally they can tell me about poachers operating in the area, as well. Sorry for the drama and to keep you waiting in the jeep, but the minute they see a white face they begin to look for more bottles of rum than I can give them. But they won't argue once a bargain's been struck.'

Richard could think of a million things that the Yuravas would be better off with than bottles of rum. They looked terribly unhealthy, and the black stumps of their rotting teeth gave them a fearsome appearance. They wore the remains of old clothes so torn and threadbare, tied up and kept together with bits of rough coir, that the rags were barely recognisable as once having been items of clothing. Some of them had filthy cloth bags slung across their chests and a few others sat with old fertiliser sacks at their feet, sacks that Richard could see were shifting and moving of their own accord.

'Have they told you anything interesting? Was it maps they were drawing in the mud for you?'

'Oh, just a herd of black buck, which they spotted moving west of the ridge in the direction we're heading. I'll get these fellows to show you their traps; they often catch interesting things, all of which they eat.'

Gerry turned to speak to the Yuravas, making clicking noises and mimicking the actions of a camera. There was some talk back and forth and some of the Yuravas got up and vanished back into the forest.

'They're willing to be photographed,' he said. 'I've told them they can have one more bottle.'

'What about some money? I'd be happy to give them whatever you suggest.'

'No, money isn't a good idea. They'll go straight to the illicit liquor stalls on the Madras Road and those bastards mix the country arrack with anything at all that they feel will give the brew a good kick. About six months ago, they added paint stripper – eight men died and twice as many were hospitalised.

No, money isn't a good idea. Better it be drink that I can vouch for.'

'Whatever you think is best but look, are some of them leaving?' asked Richard, as he walked over to the jeep to fetch his camera. He pointed to the men who had disappeared into the forest.

'No, they'll be back with the traps. They love to show off.'

Gerry was right, because the Yuravas came back with several wicker baskets draped with nets, and as Richard worked with his camera, photographing the men with the small animals and birds that they had caught – several live porcupines and some rabbits with their feet all tied together, limp wood pigeons with their necks severed and a couple of eels in an earthen pot – he felt guilty for having let Gerry organise the Yuravas to show him their pathetic catch. *This is voyeurism gone mad,* he thought, as he signalled to Gerry that he was done.

Ten minutes later, the Yuravas had taken their rum and had melted as quickly and silently into the forest from which they had earlier emerged.

Gerry was driving like a maniac again and Richard debated for a while about asking him to slow down. Reluctantly, he decided that such a request might be taken as a criticism of the Forestry Officer's driving abilities. Instead he would try to distract the man with questions, hoping that talk would make Gerry drive more slowly.

'Do these tribals, the Yuravas, live in villages?'

'They're nomadic but stay within the forest, rotating from camp to camp. Of course, the forest is shrinking, which is a real problem – it restricts their way of life. I don't really know what the future holds for the poor buggers. The younger ones make forays into towns and like what they see, but they are ill-equipped for town life. No education, no skills that are considered useful outside the forest, and you've seen their rags. Why, they wouldn't be able to put together an old vest and a clean dhoti between the whole lot of them. Did you notice those woven basket traps?'

'Yes, in fact I was going to ask you about them. The weaving was very intricate and the traps are really quite ingenious. Works of art, really.'

'The women do all the weaving, but it's a skill that's of no use outside their own environment. The rest of India has converted to plastic and aluminium – nobody uses reed baskets any more. They are skilled in many other ways but their skills are useless. The only thing they can barter is their knowledge, and I'm the sole buyer.'

'With bottles of rum?'

'Why not? Drink is the only thing that lets them survive a night in a forest full of biting insects. You didn't take many photographs. I thought that's what you wanted.'

Richard was taken aback by the accusing tone. 'To be honest, I felt dreadful, their catch seemed so meagre. I felt sorry for them.'

Richard waited for a reply, but none was forthcoming. When they did finally arrive at Lansdowne Ridge, about half an hour later, he was thinking only of his stomach. He tried to take in gulps of air to stop the nausea, but it was too late. With Gerry and Friday watching on, he threw up the contents of the chicken curry and rice over the very spot where his grandfather had sat painting his impressions of the stunning views of the hills of Nandagiri.

'The curry was too spicy for you, I guess.' Gerry was looking at him in near-disgust.

Friday nudged his elbow gently and handed him a bottle of water. 'Washing mouth and drinking water, Saar will be feeling better soon.'

Richard smiled feebly at Friday and then turned to Gerry. 'I'm sorry, I just haven't the stomach for such speed. I'm a slow-lane kind of guy.'

CHAPTER SEVENTEEN

Nandagiri, April 1982

Mohan rapped his fingers impatiently on the steering wheel as he looked out for Richard Aylmer in the rear-view mirror. This was an annoying start to what he already knew was going to be a very awkward evening. Richard had prompted a minor crisis with his dinner invitation, and now this impulsive stopping off at the bazaar for flowers . . . it was bad enough that the Irishman had asked that Forestry fellow Gerry Twomey and his sister to a meal at the Club, but buying flowers for her seemed over the top, and Mohan was certain it would embarrass the woman.

Richard didn't seem to think so and had looked surprised at Mohan's suggestion that a box of laddus might be better received.

'Come on, Mohan, there isn't a woman in the world who doesn't love getting flowers and I'm sure May is no different. I won't be a minute.' With that he had hopped out of the car, leaving Mohan with an uneasy feeling about how the evening was going to turn out.

If anyone was to blame for the potential disaster, it would have to be Gerry Twomey. Yes, Richard had done the well-intentioned inviting, but it was Gerry who had accepted, Gerry who bloody well knew that this was the same club that had blackballed his application for membership just a year ago. The rumour was, he had over the years had run-ins with three of the more influential committee members over logging permits and had consistently been obstructive when the Honorary Secretary had tried to acquire a fifty-acre parcel of Forestry land on behalf of a tea estate. It was quite obvious that Gerry Twomey had accepted the invitation in order to cock a snook at the Membership Committee.

Mohan spotted Richard hurrying back to the car and sighed. Small-town politics, that was all it was, and he should know better than to let himself get sucked into it or worse still, drag this unsuspecting vellakaran into it. Let him buy flowers, laddus or both – everyone would know to say just the right thing regardless.

Richard got into the car and placed a small packet wrapped in damp banana leaves over the air-conditioning vent. 'Mohan, if this is mild weather, what does it get like here in summer? That flower chap hadn't any decent bunches of anything but recommended this string of jasmine. I think I got fleeced, though he insisted he was giving me two lengths for the price of one.'

Mohan groaned inwardly at the sight of the jasmine. He pressed down on the horn and beeped his way out of the crowded market. *Will I tell him or will I leave it?* he fretted. In the end he turned to Richard and apologised. 'I should have come with you and then this wouldn't have happened.'

'Oh, I'm not complaining, Mohan. It was only a few rupees anyway.'

The heady scent of jasmine filled the car. Richard breathed in the fragrance deeply. 'This is what India smells of in the best of times,' he said dreamily. 'Eastern promise.'

Mohan looked at the voluptuous creamy white buds poking out from their moist envelope of banana leaves and decided to explain. 'It's loaded with plenty of promises, all right. Richard, that jasmine is the Indian equivalent of giving a woman a single rose. That's what I meant when I said I should have come with you to the bazaar, or I should at least have told you what *not* to buy.' Mohan added kindly, 'But we Indians are very forgiving of cultural faux pas. It gives us a good reason to laugh at the white man's expense, so don't panic.'

Richard put the jasmine back on the dashboard and sat back. 'No panic, Mohan, none at all.'

They drove in silence for a few minutes, Mohan fiddling distractedly with the music system, putting in cassettes at random and ejecting them with a disapproving index finger at the first tentative sound.

'Why don't you tell me what you want to listen to?' Richard suggested. 'It wouldn't do for the Collector to crash his car.' He began rooting through the dozen or so cassettes crammed into the glove compartment.

Mohan bit his lip. What he really wanted to hear was why the Irishman was suddenly looking so smug. Could it be that the fellow was infatuated with the Twomey woman? Why else would he want to spend an evening with her uncouth boor of a brother? He realised then that Richard was still waiting, half a dozen cassettes in hand, and he sighed. 'Oh, forget it, Richard, we'll be there in a few minutes anyway. I need a new car, not this desperate government-issue behemoth that does its own version of rock and roll.'

'I thought you were spoiled rotten in the IAS, always got what you wanted.'

'Is that what the Forestry Officer has been telling you?'

Richard chuckled. 'Actually, Mohan, you confessed as much last week. No, Gerry Twomey is a man of few words. Very helpful as you know, delivers what he promises, though he does drive too fast.'

'What about the sister?'

'May?'

'Is that her name? Sounds typically Anglo. Does she have a chip on her shoulder like her brother?'

'You've never met her then? I got the impression she knew you.'

'Everyone knows the Collector.' Mohan looked at Richard and shrugged. 'I'm not being conceited. Everyone does know the Collector, who I am, where I live, what I ate for breakfast and what landscapes my Irish guest likes to photograph. I govern a very big district, but it is a very small town.'

'Well, thank God for small towns. If nobody knew the Collector I wouldn't have got as far as I have with this difficult project of mine. I'm truly grateful, Mohan.'

'So, what's she like, the sister?'

'Oh – the kind you'd want to buy flowers for.'

Mohan thumped the steering wheel and laughed. 'I knew it, I guessed as much!'

They were driving in through the Club's once-ornate gates and Richard pointed to an empty spot in the crowded car park, saying, 'You'll like her, too, she's quite charming.'

'I was warned off Anglo-Indian girls all my growing years. When I was in school, I had a few in my class, and do you know what I remember? They could really jive, those Anglo girls, all cap sleeves and sweetheart necks. My mother would have none of it.'

'I've no idea what you are talking about, Mohan.'

'It's complicated. Let's save the lesson in social history for another evening; remind me the next time old Ishwar keeps us waiting for dinner.'

They had walked into the Club, both men acknowledging the obsequious salaams and 'Good evening, Saars' that issued forth from the Assistant Steward, who scurried across the wooden floor of the lounge, expertly skirting the maze of sagging, tired sofas in order to get to them before the head barman; the latter, having spotted them through the glass double doors that led into the Planter's Bar, was making his own speedy way in their direction. This had happened before – in fact, it happened every time he had come to the Club with Richard, and though Mohan had found it amusing the first time, it irritated him no end, this sucking up to the vellakaran just because the man could only think in his own currency when it came to tipping.

'I've asked for a table in the Blue Mountain Annexe, but perhaps I should make sure my guests aren't already here, waiting in the bar or at a table outside on the lawn.' Richard headed towards the Planter's Bar to check.

Mohan smiled to himself. Gerry might well be skulking on the dimly lit lawn to avoid bumping into any of the committee members, or more specifically the three who had blackballed him. Maybe it was his sister who had twisted his arm to make him agree to come. Anglo-Indian women had the reputation of knowing how to have a good time. 'Good girls aren't in the business of giving anyone a good time,' was the oft-repeated warning from his mother in his growing-up years. 'As broad-minded as we are, Mohan, never a Muslim, no Anglos – and remember, your father won't countenance anyone with a nose ring, no, no, not even if it's just a small diamond stud.'

He could picture his mother shuddering ever so slightly as she said 'Muslim', and then continuing to lecture him while she decorated her lemon soufflés with bits of green angelica and quartered glacé cherries.

Mohan cast his eye around the Club lounge with its groupings of shabby sofas, worn armchairs and rickety teapoys. The 120-year-old institution had remained largely unchanged in the years since Independence, and the photographic evidence that hung in various parts of the Club was testimony to the reverence the members had for just letting things be.

A few people went through the motions of rising respectfully from their seats on seeing him, and Mohan acknowledged them with brief nods. Petitioners were a hazard of the job and yet they were the catalyst for benevolence, which when dispensed gave him that heady feeling of power and affirmation that he was an enabler of many things to many people.

'Mr Richard Saar's table is ready, Saar, in the annexe. AC is turned up, Saar.' The steward was hovering to Mohan's right.

'Very good, Raman, very good. Has Captain Pillai arrived?'

The steward pointed towards the Buttery Bar. 'Mr Richard Saar is talking to Captain Pillai, Saar. I've asked Bearer Muthu to attend to the table, Saar. His English is being good for Mr Richard.'

Richard and Captain Pillai emerged out of the bar laughing. The Irishman had settled in at 'Knocknagow' better than Mohan had expected and had quickly turned out to be one of the most interesting and amiable house-guests to have ever been foisted on him. And Mohan had had plenty of those – his parents' friends and acquaintances, his sister Asha's weird and wonderful collection of artistic buddies and plenty of known and unknown relatives who turned out to be both demanding and disapproving. No, Richard Aylmer was none of those. He ate everything that Ishwar made, ready to try anything once, hadn't caused a fuss with any household arrangements except to express his shock when he found that his socks had been ironed by the dhobi, and had the good manners to insist on signing the tab every single time they went to the Club.

Sonal and Bala, who had met him twice, had warmed to him very quickly, even inviting him to visit their clinic in Raja Bazaar, where he had taken many pictures of them at work. He had told Mohan that he hoped his photo-essay recording a day in the life of the rural health clinic might get accepted for publication in the *Illustrated Weekly of India*, raising the profile of the NGO that funded it. As for Captain Satish Pillai, the Adjutant wasted no time in loaning Richard one of his good spare rackets and was playing tennis with him nearly every evening, relishing the challenge provided by the tall and physically more powerful Irishman.

A week ago, Satish had given Richard the tour of the cantonment, showing him some of the older, more historic buildings, which in true Army fashion, unlike the buildings in the civil lines, had never been allowed to fall into disrepair. Satish had taken it upon himself to do a little investigation, locating the bungalow in which Richard's grandparents, Colonel and Mrs Aylmer, had lived. The place had long been downgraded and divided into four unmarried officers' quarters, though the servants' lines at the back had remained just that, the stables having been converted into garages for the officers' vehicles.

Satish had spotted Mohan. 'Collector Sahib, good evening, good evening. I was just telling Richard about our last attempt to organise a dawn safari.'

Mohan shook the outstretched hand. '*Your* last attempt, Satish, not mine. If I'd been in charge of the arrangements, I would have left it all to my trusty fellow Ishwar. He would have sounded the wake-up call and brought in coffee for everyone at three in the morning. All very civilised, with a drop of rum in our cups, and we would have been on our way and in position before dawn.'

Satish put his hands up. 'Okay, point taken, how could I ever compete with Ishwar? But there's something I can do and that's thrash you at tennis tomorrow. I've a court booked.'

Mohan punched him lightly in the shoulder. 'You're on, my friend, though I can't see any reason for your overconfidence.'

Richard was looking at his watch. 'You don't suppose Gerry and May could have got the day wrong, do you?'

Satish Pillai suggested, 'Let's head for the annexe. The steward informed me that the air conditioning has been turned up and I know it'll make waiting for your guests more bearable. Great service! Just how much are you tipping these fellows, Richard?'

They headed into the Blue Mountain Annexe, a small dining room that had been air-conditioned about three years ago by Mohan's predecessor, Collector Tiwari, whose agonising psoriasis was aggravated by the tiniest bit of sweat and who consequently dedicated all official resources at his disposal to air condition every place that he frequented on a regular basis. As a result, the billiards room, the reading lounge and the dining annexe of the Club were all now havens of comfort.

The steward had outdone himself with his napkin-folding skills, and when the three men sat down, they found themselves face to face with plump pink paper swans with ruffled concertina feathers squatting on their plates.

Bearer Muthu wasted no time in aiming to please, appearing at Mohan's elbow. 'Drinks, Saar?'

Mohan was about to answer when Richard suddenly scraped his chair back. 'Ah, they're here at last and the Mishras are with them as well. Everyone's accounted for now.'

Gerry Twomey and Bala Mishra were deep in conversation as they walked down the corridor towards the annexe, with Sonal and May following close behind, laughing about something that was obviously very funny for May was clutching Sonal's elbow with one hand to steady herself while dabbing the corner of her eyes with the other.

'What's the joke, May? I didn't realise that you and Gerry would know Sonal and Bala.' Richard was kissing her one cheek at a time, his tall frame obscuring her from view.

It was Sonal who replied, still laughing as she sat down beside Captain Pillai. 'Oh, we're very old friends. May and I were in school together here in Nandagiri, though I was a boarder. So, all you have to do, Richard, is to quickly introduce May to our Collector and Captain Pillai, after which we can get you to order drinks. I could kill an ice-cold fresh lime soda – who'd believe it's just the first week in April?' She looked at Mohan. 'Can't you do something about the heat, Mohan? You IAS guys are famed for your ability to sort out any type of crisis.'

'The country expects too much of us and anyway, Sonal, that particular file seems to have gone missing.' Mohan kept a straight face as he shook hands across the table with her husband Bala Mishra. He then turned to meet May Twomey, who was just then wrapping the length of jasmine around one of her wrists, raising it up to her face to breathe in the delightful fragrance. Her obvious pleasure was so beguiling that when Richard made the introductions, Mohan found himself tongue-tied for just an instant, bestowing instead an unnecessarily hearty hello on her brother Gerry. He turned back to make amends, but she was already sitting, talking to Captain Pillai.

Mohan tried very hard not to stare, wishing suddenly he could exchange places with Bearer Muthu, who was now standing attentively to one side of the table from where he could gawk at all of them with complete freedom, examine if he wanted every aspect of May Twomey, her looks, her sari with its unusually short pullav, her long straight hair that was swept to one side with a knot in it, a knot that sat in the crook of her neck. *I mean, whoever in this day and age ties a knot in their hair, for God's sake?* He began to search for words to describe her to himself; as his father would say: *Tell me in two words, two words will say it all. Remember, son, brevity is the measure of a man.*

Naturally beautiful. Mohan shot her a quick glance. No – she was no beauty with that crooked eye-tooth. She could get it set right, but then she would lose her charm. *Charming with a crooked tooth* – no, that was five words. Two words. *Interesting and intelligent.* She could be, but he didn't know that as yet. *Poised and confident.* No, that was more like Miss India's job description. *Intriguing and unusual?* Yes, that might just do, till he got to know her better. She was looking at Richard, smiling, now turning to Satish, listening seriously, and then it seemed they were all looking at him now, all of them, the whole table.

Bala tapped his fork on the table officiously. 'Mohan, are you going to give us the inside story on the Special Areas of Conservation list? Is Nandagiri going to make it on to the list?'

His wife joined in. 'I heard that a crew from *National Geographic* are coming to photograph the Yuravas, which I hope you all know is a real coup for Gerry here. With a ten-page photo feature in a few months' time, surely the government's hand will be forced.' Sonal had her hands clasped together. 'Come on, Mohan, you can tell us. After all, you are the Sarkar.'

'I'm not the Sarkar, Sonal. I'm the Collector, a mere servant of the Sarkar. Yes, I've had some correspondence with the magazine, as has Gerry, regarding permits and related paperwork. The Central Government is under pressure from so many ecological interest groups that it's difficult to say who will make it on to the Special Areas of Conservation list.'

'The only voice the government will bow to is the baying of commercial interest groups. Ecological lobbies are banging on doors that lead nowhere.' May Twomey was looking at Mohan directly. 'People like my brother, and my father in his time, have been accused of crying wolf for so long, I just don't believe anything will make a difference. I'm afraid this is just a ruse. Okay, Nandagiri gets on to a list, what then? A couple of backs get patted, the list goes into a file, the file goes missing, the government sits down for tea with the planters and before anybody realises, they have both crept into bed together again.'

Mohan knew they were all waiting for a reply, but he was drowning in a sea of words, clutching at possibilities as they floated past him. Was she *feisty and ferocious* or *plain and honest*? Not plain in looks, he thought, but honest-looking perhaps?

Sitting opposite Mohan, Satish was shifting uncomfortably in his seat. 'Come on, Mohan, hope you haven't taken it personally.'

'Oh no, I never meant that any of it was Mohan's fault.' May looked at Satish Pillai in surprise. 'Why, the Collector is only just getting to know us here. Nandagiri was ruined well before his time. It started during the Raj.'

Richard, sitting to her left, protested: 'But May, there were conservationists amongst the colonisers, as well, you know.'

'You could never accuse me of generalising, Richard. But since you mentioned it, don't forget that in the years when the Kildare Rangers were stationed here, three taxidermists made a very good living in Nandagiri. Between them, they stuffed many hundreds of tigers.'

Mohan knew he would have to say something soon and leave the elusive two words for another time. 'Look, I can tell you that Nandagiri will be on the list, most definitely,' he intervened. 'I was tipped off by Mr Baneerjee himself.'

Bala raised an eyebrow. 'The Chief Secretary?'

Gerry Twomey, who had been silent all along, had a cynical smile on his face. 'Yes, Mr Baneerjee would know all right. The Chief Secretary has just bought twenty-eight acres along the forest bordering Lansdowne Ridge, and you can add that to the nine he already has all the way up to the Ladies' Point. Now that he owns a piece of paradise, he has a reason to make sure it stays that way.'

Richard interrupted at this point: 'Shall we leave this important topic alone for the moment? I'd like to start the rest of the evening by saying how very much I want to thank Gerry and May for all their help. I wouldn't be nearly halfway through my project if it wasn't for their generosity with time and their willingness to share their intimate knowledge of these hills.'

'Oh Richard, you don't have to be so formal,' May chided with a tap on his arm.

'No, May, I've to say it like it is. When I arrived in Nandagiri I was not entirely sure of what I wanted to achieve. But thanks to Mohan's hospitality and the help I've received from both of you, this fancy of mine has turned into something concrete, something with purpose. And,' he paused dramatically for a moment, 'I've some news to share as well. My brother rang this morning to confirm that the National Art Gallery of Ireland have expressed a firm interest in this project – the juxtaposition of the old paintings side by side with my photographs. It means a curated show in a year and a half's time, with a good chance of funding to bring the exhibition to India, travelling to the major cities. May, Gerry and Mohan, I owe you.'

'Wonderful news, Richard,' Sonal congratulated him.

Mohan looked at May just in time to catch her glancing in her brother's direction. *I wonder how they get on, the brother and sister?* He stole a look at her hands. Her nails were neat, unvarnished, and her skin looked soft, well cared-for. She had lifted her jasmine-wrapped wrist up to her nose and was taking in the fragrance again when she caught him looking at her.

'Nice flowers,' he blurted out, trying to cover up his embarrassment.

'Yes. Richard's so sweet, isn't he?'

'I was the one who took him to the bazaar to buy them.' Mohan had no idea why he hadn't just nodded his head.

Richard laughed aloud. 'Yes, he took me to the bazaar all right, but guess what he thought I should have bought you? A big box of those sickly-sweet laddus.'

'Oh, but I love laddus, Richard! There isn't an Indian who doesn't.'

'I'll have to remember that for the next time.'

Sonal groaned lustfully, 'Laddus! Mohan, next time drive Richard straight to Madras Bhavan and get him to ask for their boondi laddus. And then, Richard, you're allowed to drop off a big box to me, as well. My husband won't mind, would you, Bala?'

But Bala was in a serious conversation with Gerry, who looked as if he was drawing a map on his napkin. Bala looked up only when his wife called out his name for the second time. He seemed excited.

'Have any of you ever seen a wild dog?' he asked. 'Gerry says, just today, the Yuravas let on to him that a pack of wild dogs has been spotted three days in a row in the sandalwood forests. The pack's been drinking at the rock pools around the Trishul Falls area. It's a large pack, the biggest they've seen – twenty or more apparently.'

'They're so elusive and shy, I've never seen one myself,' said May. 'And I've been on so many of my brother's mad tracking trips. Gerry's fortunate to have the Yuravas as his eyes and ears in the forest.'

Bala was grinning from ear to ear. 'Well, I might just have managed to persuade the Forestry Officer to share his particular privilege. Who's up for a pre-dawn trek tonight to the Trishul Falls?'

May looked eagerly at her brother and then at Richard. 'Do you remember, I told you that the series of four paintings, those small ones, were probably painted close to the areas around the Trishul Falls? The rock pools there are quite distinctive – the colour of the water is different from others in the Nandagiri area. You'll see for yourself.'

'I don't know if this'll be everyone's cup of tea, May,' Gerry said, looking concerned. 'You've been before and you know it's a good two-and-half kilometre trek on foot before we get to the machans, and we'll have to be there and settled in before four in the morning. Working backwards, we'll have to be at the Forestry supply hut by three, which means we'll have to head off in the jeep by two o'clock in the morning at the very latest, which is later tonight, after dinner. No, tonight's out – it wouldn't be feasible. I'd need to make arrangements for extra walkie-talkies, Petromax lamps, a couple of coolies – and I'll have to get word to one or two of my Yurava trackers to meet up with us at the Forestry hut.'

'How about tomorrow night then?' Mohan suggested. 'Surely you'll be able to sort those details out by then. We'll still have the whole of Sunday to recover from the early start. Is everyone up for that?'

The consensus was immediate, and Mohan slapped the table. 'There you go, Gerry, we're all set and ready. I can provide any assistance you need from my office. I'll speak to my chaps tomorrow if you think we need another jeep.'

Gerry looked at his sister and then at Mohan. 'It should be possible,' he said. 'Yes, I should be able to organise that. Another jeep won't be necessary, though.'

Mohan knew that he'd forced the District Forestry Officer's hand, but looking around the table it was apparent that no one else had noticed the subtle pressure exerted on the man in the guise of geniality – no one except Gerry himself, that is.

The latter was being bombarded by rapid-fire questions from all around the table and Mohan went through the motions of looking interested, at some point even inviting everyone to return to the Collector's bungalow for a post-safari breakfast on Sunday morning. But all the while he had eyes only for May. He watched her as covertly as he could, for she fascinated him – the way she used her hands to explain herself, to cover her mouth when she laughed, to flick her napkin at Richard or to tear a rumali roti neatly in two and give one half to Satish. He observed her as she listened intently to Sonal's description of a recent wedding, and the way the corners of her mouth twitched as she wiped away tears of laughter when Sonal elaborated on the bridegroom's temper tantrum during the nuptials.

He glanced briefly around the table, only to catch Gerry's eye. *The man is watching me watch his sister,* thought Mohan, *and he doesn't seem too happy.* 'Gerry,' he said aloud, digging deep into his memory bank, 'I hear you're planning to expand your piggery operation. The District Engineer mentioned you've had a long-standing problem with electricity. Let me know the details and I'll do the needful. Is it a small-scale commercial set-up that you have?'

'It's a long-standing problem only because I've refused to cough up,' Gerry grunted. 'Bloody linesmen are so blatantly greedy we've had to resort to using generators. I've been planning to install some modern pressurised cleaning equipment for the last six months, but of course we can't move ahead without the necessary upgrade to the electricity supply.'

So, does he want me to intervene or is he too proud to ask? wondered Mohan. And as if reading his thoughts Gerry leant forward and said, 'I'd be grateful for your intervention. They wouldn't dare refuse you.'

As the evening progressed, Mohan drifted in and out of conversations, increasingly distracted by the presence of May sitting opposite him and astonished at his own behaviour. He had pushed for the trek into the forest at an unearthly hour of Sunday morning, then invited the whole crowd back for breakfast at 'Knocknagow' just to impress May Twomey and have a chance to be in her company again. Mohan wondered if Richard had sussed out the effect May had had on him; it was obvious that Gerry had some idea. It had been a while since any woman had got him into such a heady sweat. Of course, Nandagiri wasn't quite the place to meet women; they were either married, dragged kicking and screaming to this provincial backwater by husbands unfortunate enough to have jobs that required them to be in Nandagiri, or if they were single, they were not to Mohan's taste, being too bookish, too demure, too loud or too eager.

Two hours later, not wanting to make a complete fool of himself, he hovered behind Richard in the Club's pillared portico as everyone went through the prolonged ceremony of goodbyes, thank yous and good nights, amidst jangling car keys and complaining sighs about the heat.

It was Satish who finally supplied Mohan with the two elusive words, summing it all up as they watched Richard walk the Twomeys up to their car. 'Some dame, isn't she?'

CHAPTER EIGHTEEN

Nandagiri, April 1982

Ishwar was still waiting up for them on the verandah when they returned, and as he hastily stubbed out his beedi, Mohan filled him in on the plans for Sunday's pre-dawn start and the breakfast afterwards back at 'Knocknagow'. The old man's eyes lit up; Ishwar loved to show off his culinary ability and Mohan had to tell him, very firmly, to hold off from discussing the menu, the exact time for the wake-up calls, the packed snacks, hot drinks and cold water for the trek and the individual breakfast preferences of the guests till the next morning.

'He's wasted on you, here all on your own, Mohan,' Richard teased. 'A man like Ishwar was born to run the Viceroy's household, not a one-man establishment.' He yawned, stretching his arms above his head. 'I'm looking forward to this safari. And so are they, you know – Gerry and May. Gerry told me so at the Club as they were leaving. You made quite an impression I believe.'

'I did? Why, what did she say?'

'I meant Gerry – you made an impression on Gerry. He said you were "different".'

'What's that supposed to mean?'

'I don't know, but it sounded like a compliment. I hope you enjoyed the evening. I certainly did, and I know I'm going to be asleep as soon as I hit the pillow. Good night.'

Mohan had no such luck. He lay in bed thinking about May. He had never had a problem attracting women; his mother insisted he was handsome and his sister Asha's friends all turned quite coquettish whenever he was around, which was flattering. He was tall like his father, with straight hair, which when he left school and the painfully strict Jesuits, he swore he would never cut – a resolution that he kept through the first two years of college till he tired of being a rebel. He got his dark brown eyes from his father, too, but – as his mother often said – he thankfully did not inherit his father's big nose.

He was confident as a child, and that stayed unchanged when he went to St Stephen's College in Delhi. A privileged upbringing had made him self-assured early in life, while frequent run-ins with his mother had given him the ability to talk himself out of the most awkward of situations with aplomb.

No, he had never had a problem attracting women but for the first two years in college he was happy to remain unattached; instead immersing himself in study, playing for the college cricket team and eventually getting himself elected to the Student Union.

In his third year, he was interviewed for the college newspaper by the newly appointed editor, an English major also in her third year. She was a dusky Malayali, in a tie-and-dye churidar kameez that was tailored to fit her slim figure, the dupatta wound twice around her neck. She had very short black hair that framed a face with the darkest, blackest eyes he had ever seen. She smoked languorously right through the interview, blowing rings into the air as she recorded him on a troublesome tape recorder, asking him questions for a profile that she was going to run on new office-bearers in the Student Union.

At the end of the interview he asked Roshni Nair out, for coffee or lunch or even a movie if she fancied it, but she declined, saying she hadn't the time, not this week or the next.

'I'll get back to you if I've any queries about this,' she had said. 'But that's unlikely. These profiles are quite routine, you know,' she added with a shrug. The rejection stung him and he moped for a week unable to shut out the image of her catlike grace, those lovely eyes and her long-limbed elegance.

He used all his resources, networking with every girl that he knew on the college campus before he managed to get her phone number. She agreed to meet him at Kwalitys for lunch, and over dessert he asked her why she had fobbed him off the first time.

'Don't take it personally, Mohan,' she said. 'That bit of playing hard to get – it separates the wheat from the chaff. I knew you'd ring sometime.'

'And I knew you'd be different, not like any of the other girls on campus.'

Roshni Nair blew a slow ring of smoke towards the ceiling. 'I'm a poet.'

'A poet who writes mundane profiles?'

'Unfortunately, poets have to live in the real world; it's good practice.'

'You should thank God for the real world, or what on earth would poets have to write about?'

They had sparred in that vein several more times, meeting often, and he lingered as long as he could in her company. Three weeks later, he had managed to persuade her to consider giving up smoking and to let him read her work, short poems, beautiful and elegant like her, about love and life, many of which he took upon himself to memorise. Her parents were both doctors who lived in Bombay and she had spent the last three years in Delhi as a paying guest with a retired Punjabi telephone engineer and his wife. She invited Mohan home to her place one afternoon after college, two months after they had first met. The Punjabi couple were not at home, nor would they be every Tuesday and Friday she informed him, taking him by the hand as they walked up to the flat on the terrace, for the telephone engineer had been diagnosed with renal failure and needed dialysis twice a week. Their electrical-engineer son in America was paying for the treatment; it almost made the dialysis a pleasure, the couple had told her, wiping away tears of pride and joy.

Roshni unlocked the door into a large room that looked much smaller because it was crammed with books and plants. They sat next to each other on the single bed, holding their faces out towards the table fan which oscillated wildly, and when the sweat had dried off, she placed a dictionary and a thesaurus, one on top of the other on the bedside table and lifting the fan onto this raised platform, she tilted it so that the breeze blew down towards the bed. They made love on the hard mattress, Mohan for the first time. She was uncomplicated and played no mind games, was unashamed of her body and what she wanted done to it, spoke her mind without hesitation, and many Tuesdays and Fridays passed in similar fashion, with them lying satiated, as far away from each other as possible on the narrow bed, the afternoon heat making the touch of skin unbearable. They grazed fingertips instead.

One day, before the Christmas break, he asked her home to meet his parents.

'Why?' she asked, putting down the little notebook in which she was furiously scribbling.

'Why not? They know about you – I told them you write poetry. Don't worry, they won't eat you. They're just curious.'

Mohan didn't tell her that his mother had been more than curious about the girl who was taking up so much of her son's time.

'A poet? Is that how she describes herself?' His mother was in the middle of her monthly tidying-up of potted plants when Mohan decided to expand on the subject of his new girlfriend.

'Yes, a poet.' He waited for his mother to speak, prepared for the comments that he knew would follow.

'Well, it's a good thing she's not a man.'

'Yes, it is a good thing, I suppose. I'm not interested in men.'

'Chee chee, what nonsense you talk, Mohan! Anyway, what sort of a man would want to describe himself as a poet?' She cut away sharply at straps of dead canna leaves with a pair of gleaming secateurs that the mali had spent a whole evening sharpening.

Mohan flopped into the cane chair beside her. 'She is not a man.'

His mother wagged the secateurs at Mohan. 'Yes, so it's okay for her to call herself a poet. She won't have to support a family and pay the bills. You'll pay the bills, and she, lucky girl, can call herself a poet.'

'I'm not marrying anyone as yet and she can call herself anything she wants – it doesn't matter to me.'

'So why are you bringing her home then? Is this one of those latest things, what are they called . . . flings? It's the right word for it. Flinging your life away, that's what it is.'

Mohan leant forward and grabbed her hand, stopping her mid-snip. 'I like Roshni very much. She's a poet and she's not a man. I want you and Dad to meet her, so can she come home this weekend?'

'Did I say no? Bring the poet home! It's most unorthodox, this girlfriend-boyfriend business, but your father has sworn he will never arrange a match for you or Asha, or let anyone else do it, so what choice do I have?' His mother resumed her snipping. 'Is she vegetarian? Don't give me that look! What use are my chicken sandwiches if *your poet* only eats cucumber?'

Mohan looked at Roshni Nair as she slowly flipped the pages of her notebook, tapping the pencil against her lips. 'Come on, Rosh, you're going to have to meet them at some point.'

'Why?'

Mohan got up from her bed where he had been lying and pulled on his jeans. 'I'd have thought that was pretty obvious.'

'I'm not that type of girl – I thought *that* was pretty obvious.'

'I love everything about you – your eyes, your lips, your poems, your body and your soul. You're exactly my type of girl.'

'I'm not the marrying type. I've told you that before.'

Mohan wrapped his arms around her. 'Yes, but who's talking marriage? Not me, not for the moment anyway.'

She agreed eventually, and though that first meeting had gone off rather well, Roshni was reluctant to come to his house again and they argued a lot about it.

221

'There's no need to disappoint more people than necessary, Mohan. You know what it's going to lead to – a few more times and your mother will want to get in touch with my parents, then I'll be ambushed into meeting relatives passing through Delhi, and then there'll be talk about rings and engagements. I'm not going down that road, tying myself to a man and then by default to his family.'

He tried to reason with her. 'I haven't figured out what I'm going to be doing next myself – a Master's maybe, or I might spend a year preparing for the IAS exams – so who's talking about tying anybody down, you to me or me to you? I'm too young anyway. I'm happy to just be with you.'

He placated her as best he could, but it soon became obvious that he had triggered something that he couldn't reel back. She became paranoid about spending as much time with him as she had in the past. 'I'm weaning you off me,' she said to him.

He was amused at first and went along with it, agreeing not to see her for a week. It was difficult. He missed their trysts, the longed-for touch of her skin, so smooth and brown, and he missed reading her poetry back to her, gossiping about friends, arguing with her about the latest movie they had seen or just listening to music that they had bought together.

In retrospect, it was too good to have lasted. Mohan was a brilliant student, inquisitive, argumentative and a good essayist – and in Roshni Nair he had found his intellectual equal. She had just as much confidence and swagger as he had, with the same touch of arrogance that came from never having had to doubt herself.

Even before the current impasse, they had had many arguments about the institution of marriage, but he had misread the depth of her conviction.

She was adamant. 'I'd be totally stifled knowing that I had to kowtow to someone else's expectations. I want to be able to live my life, to write with none of the old-fashioned restraints weighing me down.'

'It's a selfish attitude. What about how I feel about you?'

'I've never led you to believe anything else. Maybe I'm the first person you've met who actually meant what they said. I'm honest, I've always been – remember, Mohan? You used to like that once.'

A few weeks later, hurt by her continuing obstinacy, he had countered with false bravado, suggesting they take a long break from each other. But she called his bluff and they ended up avoiding each other studiously. Very unhappy with the way things had worked out, Mohan once again buried himself in his books and the cricket season and graduated with a distinction in his final exams.

Roshni Nair's rejection, even months later, had left him glum and he dwelled a lot on what he wanted out of life and the kind of woman he would want to share it with. He thought about his parents' marriage, which had been carefully arranged to suit both of them and their families, too. It was a typical marriage of that generation, in which the wife deferred in most matters to the husband but was, most of the time, able to influence his decisions from behind the scenes. It was the one aspect of his mother's behaviour that Mohan thoroughly disliked, and yet he was never quite sure if his father was aware that he was being manipulated or whether he went along with it because that was a happy pattern that they had fallen into, leaving him with the pleasure of the last word and her secretly satisfied.

A marriage of equals was Mohan's ideal, and he knew that Roshni Nair would have been that equal. But though losing her had hurt him, he trusted her honesty. She would have done the same to any other man who had come into her life at that time.

Mohan shied away from any serious relationships for two years while doing his Master's, dating a few girls but not finding anyone interesting enough to pursue wholeheartedly. His parents were delighted that he had decided to sit for the IAS examinations and he took a year out to prepare for it, reading extensively during the day and spending many evenings being grilled by his father in readiness for the tough interview panels.

When he was selected, his parents had been very proud. His father had formally shaken his hand and told him: 'The Civil Service needs people of integrity, son, people like you. I know you'll go far.'

Mohan was twenty-four years old when he left the famous National Administration Academy in Mussoorie for his first posting as an IAS officer. He had been sent to Assam as Sub-Divisional Magistrate in Dibrugarh and arrived quite nervous and excited, ready to plunge into whatever was required of him in his role as head of the subdistrict. Here, he was wholly responsible for everything that happened within his jurisdiction, and to a large extent was expected to make independent decisions.

Mohan's training days in Mussoorie seemed a million miles away as he grappled with the complex reality on the ground. There was ongoing socio-economic and environmental legislation to be implemented, and as well as numerous laws dealing with revenue, food and land – and all of it required adept juggling of the expectations of vested local interests. Hierarchy, precedence and protocol had to be taken into consideration, and religious and caste sentiments had to be factored in at every instance.

He got his first heady taste of power from day one: people jumped to attention when he appeared, tobacco was extinguished and paan spat out hurriedly, petitioners began shuffling their papers and documents the minute they saw him, caps were doffed, salaams proffered; there were attempts at grovelling and bribery both in equal measure.

Within a short few weeks he was totally immersed in his work, invigorated by the knowledge that he was solely responsible for the administration of this part of India.

Three months later, towards the end of the monsoon, the mighty Brahmaputra River had wreaked havoc in the district, and he was caught up in the organisation of extensive flood-relief works, co-ordinating between various NGOs, civil contractors and the Army Corps of Engineers. The Assistant Collector had rung him in Tinsukia, asking him to call into the Himalayan Tea Estate on the outskirts of Dibrugarh town to check out reports of a possible outbreak of typhoid in the labour lines. The District Medical Officer was already on his way and would meet Mohan at the Estate Manager's residence.

After six days on tour, Mohan had nothing on his mind except a hot bath and a stiff whiskey on his arrival home in Dibrugarh, but first he had to get through the inspection with the DMO. The Himalayan Tea Estate manager's house was a sprawling low bungalow with a red-tiled roof and a verandah that encompassed it on all sides. Mohan was feeling tired and hungry, having eaten just a small packet of biscuits for lunch.

Monisha Dutta came down the steps of the verandah to greet him.

'Mr Kumar, we've been expecting you – please come in. I'm Monisha, Mr Dutta's daughter. My parents have been stuck in

Calcutta for the last three days trying to get back, but you know the situation with the flights and now these landslides. Please sit down. What can I get you? Some tea or coffee maybe? The DMO rang to say he's held up but expects to be here before dark.'

Mohan went through the motions of greeting her and agreeing to have tea, but all he could think of was how dishevelled he looked, how dirty and sweaty his clothes were. How unprepared for the appearance of such a beautiful creature in this remote rural backwater. Who was she, and what was she doing on a tea estate?

He realised he was staring at her when she said politely, 'Just look at the way it's pouring! I doubt the airport will reopen soon, though the Assistant Collector told me the landslide should be cleared by tomorrow.'

Mohan looked in the direction of his jeep, which his driver was manoeuvring into position under some corrugated-tin awnings by the side of the house. 'Yes, the Corps of Engineers have brought in some heavy earthmoving equipment. And you're here on your own?'

'Oh, it's safe enough. The Assistant Manager and his wife live about a quarter of a kilometre from here on the other side of the estate, and we've very good servants here in the house. They've known me since I was a baby.'

An elderly servant came out to the verandah and she spoke to him in Bengali, giving the old man precise instructions for tea. Monisha Dutta was slim and petite, dressed in a black and white block-printed salwar kameez with a white pashmina shawl wrapped around her shoulders very casually. She was definitely the most exquisite-looking woman he had ever met, her round face typical of a Bengali beauty. Her small nose was slightly upturned and when she smiled, a pretty dimple in her left cheek added to her charm. She had the kohl-lined eyes of a dancer and long black hair, which was swept to one side and plaited; she fiddled with the ends of the plait as she spoke.

'So, you are involved in the running of this estate, Miss Dutta?'

'Oh no, I left Dibrugarh three years ago, but I suppose I'll remain a tea planter's daughter for the rest of my life. The daily life on the estate, the seasonal routines, are all ingrained in me and I used to be of great help to my father when I lived here at home. But I'm just visiting my parents for a few weeks. They had to go to Calcutta at short notice – my mother's sister wasn't well, you see, but they were only meant to be away for two days.'

'It must have been very quiet, growing up here.'

'Well, it was quite lonely, but there were other isolated estate children like me – "the tea and jute kids" we called ourselves. We all went to school in Dibrugarh on the same bus. But when we finished school, we scattered all over India for college. Have you been in Dibrugarh for long, Mr Kumar?'

'No, just a little over three months. It's my first posting. Do you come to stay with your parents often, Miss Dutta?' Mohan, who was wondering how he was going to get to see more of her, was hoping she would say yes, that she came regularly.

'Please call me Monisha. Back to Dibrugarh? No, not as often as my mother would like me to. My father's more understanding though. He knows I can't just keep asking for a week off work. I live and work in Bombay. It's a bit of a rigmarole getting here.'

A Bombay girl – it shows, thought Mohan. 'My younger sister has just joined an advertising agency in Bombay,' he said. 'Asha – she's a trainee graphic designer.'

'What an amazing coincidence! I work in advertising, too. I'm a senior copywriter with Hindustan Thompson. Where does she work, Mr Kumar? I mean, which agency is she with?'

'Please, it's Mohan. Asha is with Lintas, on probation with them for a year.'

'Our rivals. We're competing for accounts all the time. Does she like it? Does she like Bombay?'

'She did her degree at JJ College of Art and these days swears she could never live anywhere else. She's a Bombay girl, through and through.'

The tea arrived on a very large tray and Mohan wolfed down two of the hot samosas and waited as Monisha poured out the tea. 'I'm glad the DMO is running late or I might have missed these samosas,' he said.

'No IAS officer has ever left our house without something to eat,' Monisha told him. 'You'll realise that soon enough – it's the way of the estates. You see, it's the only opportunity the women get to meet anyone and hear about life outside the tea gardens. If my mother was here now, she would have finished her first round of questions and you'd be steeling yourself for the next. She'd consider an IAS officer an absolute fount of information.'

Mohan was amused. 'But I see that you don't buy into that myth.'

Monisha put her cup down on the table. 'I've a theory about big fish in small ponds, but we'll have to talk about that some other time because here comes the DMO.'

Mohan stood up and joined her on the steps of the verandah. 'Yes, we must talk about it. I have to redeem the reputation of the IAS. I'm sensing you don't believe we are descended from gods.'

She laughed aloud. 'Definitely a debate for another day. But now to the labour lines. It might be best for us to go in the DMO's vehicle. His driver is familiar with the estate's roads, or what's left of them. I'll change my shoes and join you in a minute.'

A week later Mohan engineered to meet the DMO at the Himalayan Tea Estate for a follow-up visit, arriving earlier than planned, hoping he would meet Monisha again. When Mrs Dutta told him that her daughter had left for Bombay the previous evening, he was furious with himself for not having rung or come earlier.

Mrs Dutta was a portly Bengali matron whose nose for opportunity had not been dulled by the many lonely years spent on the tea estate managed by her husband. In fact, the isolation had honed her skills to perfection, and it was obvious that she had picked up on Mohan's disappointment. She questioned him, not indiscreetly, about himself, his parents and the number of unmarried sisters he had and then, apparently satisfied with his answers, she proceeded to ply him with delicious spicy snacks. And finally, summoning the elderly servant, she ordered him to make a fresh pot of tea using the last season's reserve first-flush tips.

Mrs Dutta then turned to the subject of her daughter, filling him in on Monisha's childhood and schooling, listing her many accomplishments. Mohan nibbled on the tasty snacks, smiling at the woman genially while he pondered his next course of action. He was just wondering what Mrs Dutta would say if he asked for Monisha's address, when Mr Dutta emerged from the house.

'Ah, Mr Kumar Sahib, I'm very grateful for your concern,' the man greeted him. 'The DMO said you'd requested this follow-up visit. You're very kind. I've informed the Assistant Collector of your thoroughness in these matters.'

'The government wouldn't want a full-scale outbreak of typhoid, Mr Dutta. You'll remember what happened in 1965, I'm sure. I was only following proper procedures.' Mohan wasn't surprised that the Assistant Collector had been informed – it was the way things worked in officialdom.

Mrs Dutta clapped her hands cheerfully. 'Forget the Assistant Collector, did you know Mr Kumar's father is Chief Secretary in the Finance Ministry in Delhi? Mr Kumar, he says we should call him Mohan, has been enquiring about our Monisha.'

She turned to Mohan, her eyes shining at the thought of all the possibilities. 'If you're visiting your sister in Bombay, will you be so kind as to take a parcel for our child?'

Mohan nodded enthusiastically. 'Actually, I might be going to Bombay next month. My sister's turning twenty-one and I've promised to be there. I can pass on anything to Monisha if you want.'

Mrs Dutta looked like she was going to burst with delight, and she turned to her husband excitedly, but Mr Dutta pre-empted another monologue with a wave towards the driveway. The DMO had arrived and Mr Dutta and Mohan immediately headed for the labour lines, but not before Mohan had thanked Mrs Dutta, who looked very disappointed at the sudden end to the conversation.

'Those kachoris are quite irresistible, Mrs Dutta,' he said in farewell, 'and thank you for the tea. I'm all set up for the rest of the day now.'

As the two men walked down the stairs to the waiting jeep, she called out to him, 'Monisha makes better ones! Just taste her cooking and you'll see what I mean.'

A month later he arrived in Bombay, the brief conversation he had had with Monisha Dutta still fresh in his mind. There was no doubt that she had mocked him – very politely, of course. It had never mattered before, what anyone thought of him as an IAS officer – so why should it matter what she thought of him? He tried to analyse his feelings and the reason for his totally impulsive trip to Bombay. He wanted to impress her, this woman that he had known and spoken to for barely half an hour.

Monisha was expecting his call and when they met, she came to the point very bluntly. 'You realise that my mother set you up? You can be honest – she tries stuff like this all the time.'

Mohan laughed. 'Well, I suppose she did, but I was complicit in the plan. I did want to meet you again. Remember you said you'd a theory about big fish in a small pond?' He wondered what she would say if he told her that he hadn't stopped thinking about her since they had met on her father's tea estate.

They were sitting by a window in the Sea Lounge of the Taj Mahal Hotel at the Gateway of India. An unseasonal storm was brewing in the Arabian Sea and in the far distance, container ships and oil tankers, waiting at anchor, were silhouetted against a murky and darkening sky.

Thus began 'The Great Pursuit' as his sister Asha called it. He came to Bombay as often as possible, sometimes just for a weekend. It was an expensive business, costing him nearly all of what he had to spare from his salary each month. He wasted no time in telling her how he felt, but although she was obviously flattered, she made it very clear that she wasn't interested in a relationship.

'I'm sorry, Mohan. I can't see myself as an IAS officer's wife. Your sort of life just isn't for me, years of moving from one remote district to another, followed by postings in provincial towns. I just couldn't bear it, not after having managed to finally get away from Dibrugarh.'

He tried to make a case for small-town life, adding that it would have to be borne just for the first few years of his career, but she was very sure of herself.

'I actually have a life in Bombay,' she explained. 'I love this dirty, crowded urban jungle and everything that comes with it, the anonymity of being one amongst millions. I can do what I want and I don't have to answer to anyone. I'd never be able to give up that sort of freedom.'

He understood her reasoning but wasn't ready to admit defeat that easily. He continued to woo her unashamedly, writing her long letters and still making trips to Bombay, hoping that as long as she was unattached there was a chance she might change her mind. She was happy to meet up with him when he came to Bombay, taking great pleasure in introducing him to a new restaurant that she had discovered, or insisting that he sample the charcoal-fired delicacies of some roadside stall at Colaba, where she rented a tiny one-roomed apartment above the Leopold Cafe.

Sometimes Asha and her friends joined them when they went dancing at the Oberoi Hotel, and they would head for late-night snacks from the stalls at Chowpatty Beach. They watched movies at the Regal Cinema and spent whole Sunday mornings browsing second-hand book stalls. But she broke his heart each time when she insisted that they could only be friends.

His sister Asha sympathised with him but was quite blunt from the start. 'You're wasting your time, Mohan. What's the point in pursuing her, when she's told you that herself? You know, I'd be the same – nothing would drag me to any of those desperate Dibrugarhs of India. Not even for a guy twice as nice as my lovely brother.'

It was difficult to explain the madness of it all to anyone. Monisha had captivated him with her looks, her way with words and her candidness, cruel as it was – and looking back at it he was able to say there had been a certain amount of thrill in the chase itself. He wanted her like he had wanted no other. Eighteen months after he had first met her, she wrote to tell him she was engaged to a documentary film-maker and they planned to travel around the world for a year or two before they settled in Bombay.

He moped for a week, questioning his choice of career, unable to get himself to write back to her or ring her, and was about to make arrangements to fly to Bombay yet again, not knowing exactly what he was going to say to her when, very unexpectedly, his father died. It was a terribly sad time and he spent the two weeks of compassionate leave with his mother and Asha, crushed by the finality of his father's passing and the knowledge that he had lost Monisha Dutta, too. He mourned them both as he stayed by his mother's side, watching her as she controlled her grief and went through the motions of acknowledging the steady stream of visitors – the Prime Minister, nearly all of the Cabinet, politicians of every party, government officials, relatives and friends.

The ashes were immersed in the Ganges at Varanasi and ten days later, Mohan insisted that both his mother and sister come to Dibrugarh and stay with him for a few days. In the peace and quiet of his Assamese bungalow, they sat on the verandah drinking tea and reminiscing about his father, marvelling at the number of people who had come to the funeral just to acknowledge what he had done for them. They read and reread aloud the newspaper obituaries that called him one of the finest, most upright and capable senior civil servants in post-Independence India.

The death of his father had blunted the loss of Monisha Dutta, and when Mohan returned to work, he flung himself wholeheartedly into fulfilling his administrative remit. Two months later, he was posted south, to Cuddapah for a year, where he had to wrestle with the calculations of local annual land revenue settlements, and then to Nellore, where he worked for eighteen months, arriving the day after the town had been hit by a tropical cyclone that had ripped the roof off of the government house allocated to him. He was then sent to Madras for six months in the Secretariat before getting his first Collectorate, in Nandagiri, a year and a half ago.

He hadn't paid much attention to women since Monisha, not until now, not until this evening at the Nandagiri Club when Richard Aylmer had introduced him to May Twomey.

CHAPTER NINETEEN

Nandagiri, April 1982

The trek to the machans at Trishul Falls got off to a very early start. Sonal and Bala Mishra had arrived at 'Knocknagow' at one-thirty in the morning and Ishwar had fussed over them with tea and biscuits. Gerry and May Twomey arrived shortly afterwards and the six of them set off a quarter of an hour later. May and Sonal sat in front with Gerry, who was driving, while at the back an armed Forester pressed himself into the corner against the half-door of the jeep, clearly overawed by the august company of the Collector, the doctor and the vellakaran.

'Why the rifle?' asked Richard as soon as he saw it.

'Lone bull elephants,' May answered, turning around. 'They can occasionally be a problem.'

'Actually, May, *we* are the problem,' interrupted her brother. 'The elephant corridors existed long before these hills were populated.'

'Okay, I suppose I'd better spare everyone the long lecture that I suspect my brother's itching to give you.' May held her left hand up and counted off on her fingers: 'Illegal encroachments, logging, tea, coffee and new roads – they all add up to this.' She held her right hand up in a fist. 'Very upset elephants.'

'I'll never tire of saying it, May, or lecturing as you call it. You know yourself that the wildlife corridors are on the verge of becoming bottlenecks. The only way to control the situation is to turn off water and electricity to all encroachments that are squeezing the elephant corridors shut. No exceptions.'

'The stay orders and injunctions will only end up squeezing the corridors in the High Court,' Bala said. 'I can see a lot of lawyers getting rich.'

'Getting rich and then building summer homes in squeezed-out elephant corridors,' added Sonal.

Mohan stayed quiet. Administering India was quite often a depressing business and he had heard that view confirmed even by his father, the man who had often been called the best of the best. His father's advice had proved invaluable so far. 'Small victories at the start, Mohan, are what you are looking for. They are attainable and they make the fewest enemies at the time when you are most vulnerable.' On another occasion, when he'd visited his parents, just before heading off to Assam to take up his first post, his father had been unhesitating in his pragmatism. 'You don't want to get a reputation too soon. Remember, son, only survivors can actually make a difference.'

Mohan realised that Richard was looking at him curiously. 'You seem a million miles away, Mohan.'

'Not really, I was just thinking of practicalities. Gerry, would a gun really scare off an elephant, stop it from charging?'

The jeep had turned off the main road and they were driving on a rough track, having entered the outskirts of the forest a few kilometres earlier. Gerry slowed to a near halt as he negotiated his way around three very large potholes before replying, 'In theory it should. But it's hit and miss really. Some of them are well used to gunshot noise at this stage, and one never knows if they move on because they're afraid or if they just couldn't be bothered to actually charge.'

'That's so reassuring, Gerry. Please tell me there's a back-up plan to the gun,' Sonal put in.

'Yes. It's called "slamming the jeep into reverse".'

'Pay no attention to him, Sonal. You should know what he's like by now. Of course, there's a back-up,' said May as she elbowed her brother and then, opening the glove compartment of the jeep, she pointed to a half a dozen plump red plastic sticks. 'That supply of flares normally does the trick.'

Gerry was smiling but Sonal was far from mollified. 'What happens when we leave the jeep and start trekking? I thought we were going to see wild dogs, not have encounters with lone tuskers.'

'Well, Richard asked what the gun was for. I was just answering his question.'

'Okay, blame it all on the White Man, why don't you?' said Richard, throwing his hands up in the air.

Mohan riposted, 'Actually, it was an Englishman, John O'Sullivan, who discovered the hills around Ooty – in about 1820, I think. He built a house for himself and recommended building a sanatorium for convalescing soldiers of the East India Company in the neighbouring hills. Historically speaking, the elephant corridor problem can be traced right back to him. So yes, let's blame the Englishman.'

Richard stretched his legs out, crossed his arms and leant back against his seat. 'I'm Irish, so I blame the Englishman, too.'

Sonal turned around to face him. 'In that case, why were you guys in India, serving the Crown?'

237

Richard groaned. 'Sonal, believe me, there are entire academic departments, ideological wings of political parties, whole communities, branches of families, TV shows, radio programmes and very many pubs the length and breadth of Ireland torn apart by that very question on an ongoing and daily basis – and no one has ever come up with a satisfactory answer.'

'Well, what about your own family – your grandfather? What made him join an English regiment?' she persisted.

Richard sat up straight. 'There was nothing remotely English about the Kildare Rangers.'

'Except they were in India to keep the Raj ticking over and that's reason enough for us Indians to lump them in with the English. I'm just curious you know, no offence meant.'

Richard took his time answering. 'Sorry, I've to think this through carefully; it's so complicated. You see, in Ireland you can be many things other than being Irish. You could call yourself Anglo-Irish – you don't mind calling yourself one, but you certainly don't want to be labelled one. You could be a Nationalist, which almost always means you are Catholic – and yet every Nationalist rebellion was shaped by Protestants. You could be a member of the Protestant Ascendency or a Castle Catholic, and either way you'd be despised and envied both in good measure. So, coming back to your question, Sonal, my grandfather was an Anglo-Irish Protestant, and that's what men like him did if they wanted to be soldiers. They joined Irish regiments.'

Mohan patted Richard on his knee. 'And Richard, I thought *our* caste system was complicated.'

But Sonal wasn't satisfied. 'So, what about the Catholics – why did the Catholics join? I thought they hated the English.'

'It was a job when there were no jobs to be had. I guess that would be the most obvious reason. Many still chose to enlist in the British rather than the Irish Army, but almost always into Irish regiments.'

Sonal was nodding. 'When the Kildare Rangers mutinied here in Nandagiri, surely your grandfather . . . what I mean is, where did his loyalties lie?'

Richard sighed. 'My grandfather was a career soldier – that's how he would have described himself. So, there was no crisis of identity really. For him it was all about the Regiment – the Kildare Rangers' honour – and loyalty to it was paramount.'

'I'm just fascinated by the way the English managed to play people against each other so they could hold on to their Empire,' said Sonal, just as the jeep arrived at a Forestry hut.

Two more armed Foresters, who were fast asleep in a jeep parked right up at the hut, were hurriedly woken by the two coolies who had been waiting, their Petromax lamps beside them. Leaving one Forester behind, and without much ado, Gerry led the group on foot, with Bala beside him, down a deeply rutted track that was quite steep in places. Sonal and May walked together, with Mohan and Richard following behind. The night forest was very dark, with just a sliver of a new moon obscured by the abundant rhododendron and wattle that formed a canopy over their path. Without the Petromax lamps the party would not have been able to see their noses in front of them.

'Walking in twos like this, I feel as if we're back in school again. Sonal, do you remember Mrs Dalhousie and her insistence on singing as we walked?' May asked as she scrambled over a rocky uphill section of the path criss-crossed with huge roots that had pushed out from the forest floor. She turned around to lend a hand to Sonal and when her friend had managed to clamber up, the two young women gave each other the Girl Guides salute and burst out laughing.

'I haven't sung "Ging gang Goolie Goolie" in fifteen years,' said May.

'That's because it sounds positively rude fifteen years later. Come on, May, let's do "Kumbaya" the way Dalhousie used to,' Sonal giggled.

'I can't, Sonal, not with these guys watching.'

'Oh, I don't mind. Do you, Richard?' said Mohan, who was right behind them. 'The Dalhousie method sounds fascinating. Please don't let us hold you back.'

'I didn't mean you guys, I meant them,' said May, nodding in the direction of the Foresters and the coolies.

'Okay, but this means we'll hold you to a command performance later,' said Mohan.

Gerry turned to see why they had stopped. 'Come on, May,' he said briskly. 'There'll be time for chat when we get to the machans, plus I have trackers waiting ahead.'

They moved on quickly, but Richard's curiosity had been aroused. 'Who was Mrs Dalhousie?'

'She was our troop leader. We were Girl Guides.'

'Indian Girl Guides sang "Kumbaya" and "Hava Nagila"?' Richard chuckled.

May was quick to respond. 'And why not? I'll have you know, Richard, that Baden Powell was in India when he came up with the idea for the Scouts.'

Richard put up a conciliatory hand. 'Okay, I don't want to cause an international incident here.'

May smiled. 'So, were you in the Scouts?'

'No, I wasn't. My father had a notion that it was all play-acting at adventure, that it was too childish. He remembered real adventures in India, and nothing ever compared to them, I suppose.'

'What about you, Mohan?'

'Unfortunately, May, I didn't have Mrs Dalhousie. Our Scout Master was dismissed for having supplied us with our first bottles of beer, and after that nothing was adventure enough. No, my mother decided my sister and I were better off going to chess class.'

'See if you can beat May. She was the Inter-school Champion two years in a row.'

'Oh, that was so long ago, Sonal. I haven't played in ages.'

Mohan didn't hesitate for a moment. 'We'll just have to rectify that, May. Satish and I get the chessboard out during the rains – you know, when the tennis is a washout. He's very competitive. If he can't win on the court, he has to win at something else.'

'It's a pity he couldn't make it today. I didn't think he would miss this trek,' said Richard.

Sonal knew the details. 'The lamb's being led to slaughter. His mother's been after him to go and visit relations in Ooty. You see, they've friends up from Coimbatore staying with them who've brought along an eligible daughter.'

Richard was quite surprised. 'You don't mean an arranged marriage?'

'What Satish said to me on the phone was that he couldn't possibly tell his mother he wasn't going to go and meet this girl because he preferred sitting up a machan waiting to spot wild dogs!' Mohan added.

They were still laughing when they arrived at a small clearing where, as expected, two Yuravas were waiting, squatting on their haunches, chewing what looked like pieces of root. They spat loudly before getting up to speak to Gerry, gesticulating as he questioned them and pointing several times in various different directions. *This is going to be a bloody wild-goose chase all over this forest,* Mohan thought irritably, but Gerry looked pleased with what they had told him.

'This is good news,' he announced to the group. 'The Yuravas say that the dogs were at the rock pools again yesterday so there's every reason to hope they'll come this morning, too. Another forty-five minutes and we should be there. Mohan, are you okay bringing up the rear? We just have to follow this tracker here, while the other one will keep behind you and the Petromax coolie. We'll keep going till we pair off at the machans.'

Mohan nodded but he would have preferred to have been walking behind May as he had been earlier. Striding along barely a few feet behind her, he had become an unashamed voyeur, taking in every detail of her slim figure and the assured way she carried herself, tucking wisps of hair behind her ears with one hand as she pushed away thin whippy branches of eucalyptus that nearly blocked the track with the other. Her light blue jeans, casually rolled up to her ankles, skimmed her sturdy, well-worn boots and her cotton kurta was still crisp and starched.

I've found the elusive sitar-guitar girl, thought Mohan, suddenly remembering a treatise on women that he had submitted to his college magazine in his first semester. Characteristics of aloo-gobi home birds, tiresome khadi-kholapuri pseudos, bookish Brahmins, cash cows and buxom beasts had peppered his detailed analysis and had nearly got him expelled. The sitar-guitar woman, he had theorised, was any young college fellow's dream: the right combination of jeans and kurta, more hints of Hollywood than Bollywood, intelligence was assumed, a little craziness was to be hoped for.

Mohan was thinking about the fallout from that overly honest literary submission, copies of which had circulated like wildfire despite being summarily rejected by the editorial board: his parents' disappointment, the righteous horror emanating from the Head of Sociology and the temporary but painful disdain of every girl in college . . . when Gerry gave the signal for them to move on.

They headed off again, this time in single file, and the chat dwindled to nothing as everyone concentrated on not getting clothing and knapsacks snagged in branches that overhung the trail. The Petromax lamps cast maniacal shadows that danced on the trees, hung from the vines and leapt out from the dense wattle bushes that closed in on them as they walked.

An hour later they could hear the distant sound of water and, closer to the waterfall, the trail widened slightly just as they arrived at the first machan – the tree-house-cum-hide. Gerry sent Bala and Sonal scrambling up the rather rickety ladder, along with one of the Petromax-bearers. The rest of the group skirted the rock pools that lay to the right of them and walked a further ten minutes to the next machan.

'I'll take Richard with me to the last one. It has the best view, 360 degrees.' Gerry was looking at his sister as he spoke. There was an awkward pause as Mohan and Richard both looked at May, who was about to speak when her brother interrupted. 'If the pack comes a little after dawn and there's enough light, Richard might even get some photographs from that machan. Mohan, you and May can head up to this one.' Gerry directed one of the Yuravas to start climbing. 'This fellow will stay with you both. Keep the walkie-talkie switched on, May. I'll signal you as usual, as soon as we see something.'

243

Mohan had stood beside her on the machan as they watched Richard, Gerry and the Petromax coolie disappear into the darkness following the Yurava tracker.

'Gerry doesn't approve of the interest he takes in me.'

'Do *you*?' said Mohan, surprised at her confession.

She seemed taken aback. 'Do I what?'

'Approve of the interest Richard takes in you?'

'Oh, did I just speak out aloud? That wasn't meant for your ears.'

Mohan, not quite sure what to say, waited for her to add something more in explanation. The Yurava was squatting in one corner, preparing a plug of what looked like tobacco to slip into the corner of his mouth. The machan was barely ten foot square and about thirty feet off the ground, supported on three tiers of bamboo scaffolding that were lashed together with rope and anchored to nearby tree trunks; roofless except for the overhanging branches of a gigantic rain tree. Mohan slipped off his knapsack and sat down, leaning against the bamboo wall. The forest was in near-darkness, but dawn would break within an hour and then they might not have to wait too long. May sighed and sat down beside him, leaning against her small backpack, her knees drawn up under her chin.

'It's not that my brother doesn't like Richard, he's gone out of his way to help him,' she murmured. 'If Gerry disliked him, he would have done only what was expected, the bare minimum that you'd requested.'

Mohan contained his curiosity. 'Will you have some coffee?' he asked. 'I've a flask here and some biscuits as well.'

'Coffee? I have tea. Do you want tea?'

They laughed quietly and settled on the coffee which he poured out and handed to her before sitting back again, crossing his legs and wrapping his fingers around his mug. *I'll give her a minute,* he thought.

He could feel her hesitate before she finally spoke.

'Gerry's quite wary of most people – not that I'd blame him. I know what it's like when you work in Forestry. He has a reputation for being gruff and I'd be the first to admit that he is, but in his line of work, he hardly ever comes across anyone who doesn't have some sort of agenda.'

'Isn't he used to it? My father was in the Administrative Service, as well, and one of my earliest childhood memories is of petitioners arriving at the house even as my parents were having their morning tea on the verandah. In later years, my mother just wouldn't allow it, or my father would have had no peace even at home.'

'It's not that type of petitioner that Gerry's ever had a problem with.'

'You don't need to elaborate, May. I deal with the same sort of scum all the time. In fact, I've got a meeting set up next week with Superintendent Rao, to get to the bottom of those incidents of arson last month.'

'Oh yes, Gerry mentioned it to me. He's convinced that it was, as you've just said, arson and not just random unconnected accidents as the newspapers had initially reported. Nandagiri would have been destroyed, if it wasn't for people like my brother and our father before him. You need that anger, well-stoked too, to keep these hills from being turned into one big tea plantation.'

'Your father was a Forester?'

'Yes, he was, and it killed him. His name was Maurice Twomey. He was so reluctant to share the burden of responsibility because he never thought anyone else would be capable of loving the hills like he did.' May sighed. 'It was the death of him, and our poor mother Betty never forgave him. He had promised her all sorts of things, most of all his undivided attention, after he retired.'

'He died in service?'

'A heart attack, while he was inspecting the elephant camp at Theppakadu. Everybody said it's what he would have wanted – you know, to die quickly, and doing what he loved. Dad was only fifty-four so I can tell you we certainly didn't find any consolation in that. As for my mother, she tried her best to persuade Gerry to transfer out of Forestry, but by that stage, he was a few years into the Service and was just as wrapped up in it as Dad had been.'

'My father died fairly young, too,' Mohan told her. 'He was just sixty-six and it's nearly the same story. It was his first heart attack, but it was a massive one. It's just the three of us now: me, my younger sister, Asha, and our mother.'

They sat in silence for a minute or two after that.

"Gerry will go the same way, you know,' May said quietly. 'The stress will eventually kill him. In a few decades there won't *be* a forest to protect. It's scary. Every day, some part of this forest faces a point of no return. Once a sholah is cleared it's lost forever. We are suffering a new kind of coloniser – the tea companies.'

Mohan nodded. 'I don't dispute that at all.'

'Life's tough for Gerry because he's an honest, old-fashioned Forestry man – not that he ever harks back to the glory days. That was what my parents' generation did.'

'Glory days?'

'Yes, when Anglo-Indians all thought they were on the verge of going home, to where their hearts belonged – the land of their fathers and grandfathers: England, Scotland, Wales and Ireland. The glory days before we became dingoes, the bastards that no one wanted to call their own. You must know – isn't that what you call us?'

Mohan put his cup down slowly. *I must remember this isn't about me,* he thought. *This is about her brother.* In the very faint light he could see she had her fingers pressed to her forehead.

Before he could say anything, she spoke again. 'I'm sorry, Mohan, that wasn't fair. It was uncalled-for, and anyway, I began by talking about Richard and none of that has anything to do with you.'

It has everything to do with me, thought Mohan, *but I'll leave it for a while.* 'All right then, change of topic?'

'You pick, I seem to be out of form.'

Keep it neutral, Mohan warned himself. 'Very well: what do you think that fellow is chewing? Is it tobacco?'

May looked at the Yurava who had his eyes closed and head rested back against the bamboo rails. 'That stuff is made from yemuth. It's a plant that looks like the datura and must be from the same family. The Yuravas harvest parts of the plant and its root and make a gum-like paste out of them. It's a hallucinogenic, keeps them semi-permanently tranquillised.'

'Maybe I should ask him for the recipe. A permanent tranquilliser is just what we need in the Indian Administrative Service – something to dull the pain of dealing with politicians and petitioners.'

May laughed softly. 'But that is the very essence of your remit, isn't it? You surprise me, Mohan. I thought you were one of the dedicated new breed, ready to face old challenges with new vigour and that sort of stuff.'

'Yes, don't remind me. I'm embarrassed by that earnest bullshit with which we all sallied forth. I'm sure you aren't any different. After all, you have been a teacher for a good few years, so you must know what it's like to be jaded.'

She didn't reply and Mohan clenched his fists in regret. He was about to blurt out an explanation, even a tentative apology, when she pre-empted him.

'Yes, I suppose we all start out with the best of intentions and the grandest of hopes. It's not the worst way to start, is it?'

'Do you like teaching?'

'I do. Yet I often feel, I don't know, that there might be something else I could do, something I might enjoy more.'

Mohan sipped his coffee and waited. *Go on, you go first and tell me more about yourself. Give me a hook to theorise about why I am behaving like a schoolboy around you,* he pleaded silently, and found himself holding his breath as he willed her to speak.

'There's the piggery, of course,' she went on. 'Not that I'd ever look at that as an alternative to teaching music. Gerry wants me to get more involved with the day-to-day management, and I suppose that'll be inevitable when the capacity increases. My great-grandfather started the business with just a few dozen pigs in the beginning, selling bacon and pork to the regiments that were stationed in Nandagiri. He was called the Bacon-wallah. Everyone in the district knew him by that name. Not Sean Twomey, but the Bacon-wallah. Oh, I nearly forgot! Gerry told me last night that you'd offered to sort out the hassle with the linesmen. Those bastards need a kick – nothing a small cattle-prod up their butts wouldn't sort – but the Collector's word would be just as good, so I must thank you.'

Mohan chuckled quietly. 'That's the first time I've been likened to a cattle prod.'

'What do you think of Richard?' May asked suddenly. 'You must know him quite well – he's been staying with you for a while now, hasn't he?' She gave an awkward laugh. 'I'm being unmannerly and also very nosy, so you don't have to answer that.'

'Well, he seems a decent chap, wants to pay me for board and lodge, has already tipped the servants well in excess of their salaries, buys you jasmine, makes your brother feel good, occasionally lets Satish win at tennis – yes, I suppose he's an okay sort.'

May sighed loudly and put her forehead down on her knees.

Mohan bit his lip. *I should just tell her – tell her what a great guy I am, how I haven't thought of anything else for the last twenty-four hours. Nothing but thoughts of you, Miss Twomey.*

Her next question was more to the point than he expected. 'Does Richard talk about me?'

'Yes, he talks of you a lot – so much so that I felt I knew you even before we met last night.'

'Did we really meet just last night? And look how much you know about me already! I've broken every rule my mother dinned into me. Don't show your hand, never show your hand.'

'The truth can be disarming, May.' Mohan might have said more, shown his own hand even, when the walkie-talkie suddenly crackled to life.

'Everything okay?' Gerry sounded business-like. 'Dawn should break within the next ten or fifteen minutes, and then hopefully these dogs will turn up and we'll see some action.'

May handled the walkie-talkie with ease, adjusting the volume and frequency as she spoke to her brother. When she finished, she placed the walkie-talkie on the floor between them.

249

'You do this often,' Mohan asked, 'come out to the machans with Gerry? You grew up here in Nandagiri, I believe.'

'Gerry and I used to come here very often with our father. If you'd asked my mother, she would have said far too often. She was secretly terrified of the forests, the sholahs and everything they held, but would never admit it to Dad. Of course, the cover was much thicker then and the animals more numerous, particularly elephants. I was five years old when these machans were built. Dad supervised the building of the first three and Gerry commissioned the other two soon after Dad died. Gerry takes his role as custodian very seriously.'

'Yes, I'm well aware of that. It explains the more than cordial reception he gave to Richard's project once he realised that there was something in it from a conservation point of view. Your brother was not very enthusiastic when I first asked for help for Richard.'

May gave a small laugh. 'Why should you be surprised? Anyone else would have refused point blank. My brother may be honest but he's no saint, Mohan. He can't help but dwell in the past sometimes.'

Mohan looked baffled.

'Ah, I see. You don't know about the Aylmers and their history in Nandagiri. I thought Satish might have mentioned it to you.'

'I was aware that Richard's grandfather was Colonel Aylmer of the Kildare Rangers, and that while he wasn't soldiering, he loved to paint local scenes. Yes, of course, I did know that.'

'My grandmother, Rose Twomey, was a lady's maid to Colonel Aylmer's wife – Richard's grandmother, that is.'

'Is that good or bad?'

'It's a long story.'

But before she could say anything more, the Yurava who had been squatting and peering out through the cracks in the bamboo slats stood up suddenly and motioned to them to be quiet. The walkie-talkie came to life, its green light flashing urgently before May picked it up and signalled an acknowledgement. They squinted through the viewing gaps and waited, looking down at the forest and the clearing in front of the rock pools. Less than a minute later, just as Mohan was beginning to wonder if this was a false alarm, he heard distant calls that sounded like whistling, first one and then more.

The dogs came into view and May clutched his arm, excited. 'Have you any idea how lucky you are?' she breathed. 'Very few people get a chance like this.'

Mohan wondered if she could feel the shiver that electrified his body. 'Yes,' he whispered back, looking in the direction she was pointing at. 'Oh yes, I know how lucky I am.'

CHAPTER TWENTY

Madras, May 1982

May's hands clutched the book on her lap and her head rested
to one side against a small pillow that she had brought with her
for the long car journey to Madras. Mohan sat next to her, wide
awake. In the last four weeks since the dawn trek to Trishul Falls,
he had met May, and Gerry, too, several times, and each time
the effect May had on him had revealed a startling truth. His
mother was right: he *was* missing a woman in his life. He was
ready – very ready – to be domesticated.

A week ago, when he found out that May was planning a few
days away in Madras visiting her elderly Grand-uncle Ronnie,
he had quickly arranged an official trip to the Secretariat and
offered May a lift to Madras in his car.

'It's no trouble at all, honestly,' he told her. 'The car is air-
conditioned, plus I have the driver. You could sleep all the way if
you wanted, or chat or whatever you prefer, really. If we left by
five in the morning, we could stop in Salem for a late breakfast
and then we should be in Madras by six in the evening at the
latest. And you can hitch a lift back with me, as well, if you like.'
I've four days of work scheduled at the Secretariat and I'll be

ready to head back on Saturday or even Sunday if you wanted to stay on longer. My mother would be delighted to have me stay for an extra day.'

Even now, Mohan could hardly believe that he'd managed to engineer the whole situation as well as he had. But then, if he hadn't got a move on, Richard would most certainly have done so. The Irishman had become increasingly enamoured of May, and it was obvious that she was well aware of this. Mohan looked down at her slim fingers and neatly filed fingernails and wondered if she'd guessed that he, too, had fallen for her straight-talking, simple charm.

She was woken by a Mofussil bus that overtook their car in a reckless fashion, the driver blasting his musical horn as the bus lurched past them. The dangerous bend in the road ahead forced the bus driver to swing the vehicle back to the left-hand side of the road in front of Mohan's car, and its overloaded roof-racks threatened to discharge all manner of goods across the road.

Both May and Mohan instinctively grabbed hold of the door handles and prepared for impact, but miraculously the bus managed to steady itself and with a sigh of relief Mohan instructed his driver to keep a distance.

But the driver was all fired up, his ego seriously bruised. 'Saar, if I can just overtake him, I'll block him completely all the way to Salem and teach him a lesson he won't forget. The disrespectful fool will never dare overtake a government car again.'

Mohan didn't hide his exasperation. 'And there won't be anyone left living to tell the tale. He'll probably turn off the highway soon, anyway.'

The driver nodded his head silently, but it was obvious that, left to himself, he would have let the bus driver know who really was the king of the road.

'Where are we?' May asked sleepily. 'Are we nearly in Salem, Mohan? I'm ready to demolish a paper masala dosa and a hot filter coffee.'

'Make that two of each, I'm hungry as well. Another half an hour and we should be there. Is there anywhere to eat that you particularly like? I usually stop at the Saravana Bhavan near the Clock Tower. It's the cleanest one can get and the service is fast.'

'No, I've no favourites at all because I can't remember when I last travelled to Madras by car. I take the train because I always go on my own. You see, Gerry hates Madras and he has got worse over the years, refusing to come even when it's to do with family.'

'I find the car less of a hassle. There's no waiting around in Coimbatore or Mettupalayam.'

'Yes, that's true. Richard was talking recently about doing a tour of South India after he finishes his project, and I suggested he do it by car. It might take longer, but he'd be able to get off the tourist track and see the real India – and eat in Saravana Bhavans.' She grinned.

'And he'll get to race with crazy, but authentic Indian bus drivers for free. Has he asked you to join him?'

May looked at Mohan for a few seconds too long for comfort before replying. 'No, but I think he may and if he does, yes, I might be tempted. I find I appreciate this country more when I see it through his eyes.'

'That's a common enough syndrome, not appreciating what's under your nose. It's no reason to go with him.'

She was taken aback. 'Have you been talking to Gerry? You sound just like him!'

Mine is not brotherly concern, thought Mohan in a panic. *I've been sending all the wrong signals, or maybe no signals at all.* He looked at the road ahead in despair. *Shall I just say it?* he wondered. *Turn to her now on the outskirts of Salem and say it?*

'Can I ask you an honest question?' She was looking at him quite earnestly.

'Not brotherly advice, I hope?' Mohan asked and then added, 'Because that wouldn't really be appropriate.'

She ignored what he thought had been a strong clue from him. 'Oh no, not when I've Gerry to deal with already. What I want to ask you is very appropriate: what do you really think of Richard's project?'

'From what I can make out, it's going to be a game-changer for him professionally, especially since he got confirmation that the National Gallery of Ireland will showcase the work,' Mohan replied.

'That's what Richard thinks and hopes. No, I want to know what does the Collector Sahib think?'

'Me? I have to say I envy him a bit, to be able to combine his professional ability with something so close to him personally. They are his grandfather's paintings, so nothing could be closer; the satisfaction must be immense.'

'I didn't know you were the sentimental sort, Mohan.'

'You'll just have to get to know me better, May.' He cleared his throat.

May ran her fingers through her hair, flicking it to one side. 'Gerry was only saying yesterday evening when I was packing my case that he could hardly believe that we met you just three months ago. I suppose we've Richard to thank for that.'

'And what about me, for having introduced Richard to Gerry?'

She smiled. 'Yes. We've to thank you. He's a nice man, and he can't be blamed for what his grandparents did or rather

255

wouldn't do. I realise that now, and so does Gerry. He actually likes Richard. I do know that.'

'And do you?'

'Like Richard? Of course I do.'

'That morning at Trishul Falls you were going to tell me a long story, that's what you called it – about the connections between the Aylmers and your family. Something to do with your grandmother. She worked for Richard's grandmother; I believe that is what you said.'

'Oh God, it's a long story all right. We've known about the Aylmers all our lives, but would you believe it, Richard can't remember anyone even mentioning a lady's maid. Apparently, India was a taboo subject with his grandparents. His father James and his aunt – I think he said her name was Alice – had only their own childhood memories to rely on when they reminisced. Alice is still alive, and when Richard showed her Colonel Aylmer's watercolours, she recognised a few of the views but couldn't put any names to them. I believe she's a well-known artist herself in Ireland. "Highly collectible and much sought after" is how Richard described her work.'

'It's understandable, May, people shut out bad memories. It happens all the time.'

'And Anglo-Indians, by contrast, have made an art of keeping those memories alive. God, how we live in the past.' She turned away to look out of her window.

Mohan wished he hadn't brought up the subject of whatever it was that had happened sixty-odd years ago.

'Nostalgia is a dangerous thing, don't you think?' she mumbled. 'A whole community strangled by dreams of what we never did have in the first place.' She didn't wait for him to reply before asking: 'Have you ever been to McCluskiegunj, Mohan?'

'I have, actually,' he said, surprising her. 'My father was posted in Ranchi in the late 1960s and my sister Asha and I went there as children a couple of times. A local Anglo-Indian family organised fishing trips in season on the Damodar and my father loved fishing that river. Our mother was bitten by a snake the very first time we went there. God, there's a memory!'

'And what happened then?'

'To the snake? It didn't hang around long.'

'Very funny, Mohan.'

'It turned out to be harmless and the only fall-out from that incident was my sister has a serious fear of snakes. But getting back to McCluskiegunj, why did you ask?'

'It always comes to mind when I think of the Anglo-Indian penchant for the past, a past that was never the way we'd like to think it was. If ever there was an example of nostalgia gone badly wrong, McCluskiegunj is it.'

'That's a bit cruel, don't you think, May?'

'No, actually I don't. You know, my mother's parents put every bit of their savings into buying a house on a small piece of land there, in the middle of nowhere, in this so-called Chota England. I mean, what a foolish idea it was in the first place, to think it'd be possible to create a homeland for Anglo-Indians, a 9,000-acre enclave stuck in the middle of India, that would forever be loyal to the Crown. But so many hundreds of families bought into it. My mother always said it was one of the saddest places in all of India. Her brothers all left one by one, two headed off to Canada and one to Australia. She only ever saw one brother again. My Uncle Eddie came back for her – to take his little sister Betty "home" he said, but she'd met Dad by then and it was too late. She always said that – *too late*. As if Canada could ever have been home!'

'Your mother was from McCluskiegunj? How did your parents meet? It's a long way between there and Nandagiri.'

'Our mother had been sent to Nandagiri to stay with relatives the summer she turned seventeen, and it wasn't just for a holiday, either. She was to find herself a husband, which she did. She met our father, Maurice Twomey, at a dance and was married within a month.'

'What happened to the house in McCluskiegunj?'

'It was left to my mother, and after she died four years ago, we sold it to a man from Calcutta who was buying up property in the town. He had plans to start a boarding school. I'm glad we got rid of the house. I couldn't bear McCluskiegunj and everything it stood for. An Anglo-Indian little England – a shrine to isolation.'

'You could also say McCluskiegunj was an attempt to preserve a collective identity.'

May smiled sadly and shook her head, saying again, 'Anglo-Indians just won't admit it, but there was nothing good about the good old days. Oh look! I think we're approaching Salem.'

Mohan looked at his watch. 'We've made good time and I'm sure the driver's ready for a break and something to eat, too.'

After the stop for breakfast, the couple spent the rest of the journey talking about their jobs, chatting and gossiping about Nandagiri and all the people they knew who lived there.

'How long before you get posted out from Nandagiri?' May asked

'God, I haven't thought about that for a while,' said Mohan. 'It could be a year or more – I've no idea.'

'It must be tough, having to move constantly, changing houses, leaving behind friends and starting all over again with new faces and colleagues every few years. I feel sorry for you, Mohan.'

'Have you never wanted to leave Nandagiri to live somewhere else, May? You know, move to a bigger town, a city with more to offer than one bazaar and an ageing club?'

'Yes, I do feel like that once a year, during the monsoons when all my leather slippers turn green and every crawling insect wants to take refuge in my bedroom, but when the rains are over that feeling passes off easily enough.'

'What about Gerry?'

'Gerry? Oh, he's married with two wives, don't you know? The forest and the piggery. You can laugh, Mohan, but you and everyone in Nandagiri knows that's true.'

'He's never married?'

She dismissed the notion with a wave of her hand. 'No. Which Anglo-Indian girl would want to get married to someone stuck in Nandagiri?'

'He doesn't have to marry an Anglo-Indian.'

'Indians don't care to marry Anglo-Indians – you should know that.'

'That's old-fashioned nonsense.'

She shrugged. 'It maybe nonsense yes, but Anglo-Indians have never been in fashion. Not now, not before.'

Mohan nodded wordlessly. *How the hell did I let the conversation slip back to that subject again?* he wondered.

May was looking down intently at her fingers as she said in a low voice, 'We're tainted – we were never white enough then and will never be brown enough now.' Then she looked up at him and said in her normal voice, 'Will you come and meet my Grand-uncle Ronnie tomorrow, at the house in Egmore? He's a real character and I know he'll be impressed to have an IAS officer, a Collector Sahib at his house.'

'I will, if you promise to have dinner with me on Friday night. We could go to the Connemara.'

She didn't hesitate. 'I love the Hotel Connemara! It has an olde-worlde charm that reminds me of Nandagiri. It must be all that colonial teak furniture and the potted palms.'

Towards the end of the journey as they approached Madras, she fell asleep once again and Mohan wondered how he could possibly get himself off this road to nowhere that he seemed to be travelling on. *I won't wait longer than Madras to tell her how I feel,* he vowed. *I'll have to say or do something before we return to Nandagiri at the end of the week.*

Mohan sat in his car outside number 32, Railway Lines in Egmore. The house was typical of old railway colonies dating to as long as a hundred years ago that had been allowed to slide into total disrepair. The Indian Railways were playing a waiting game, waiting for their long-retired employees to move away in despair or eventually die. The latter was the preferred outcome because the value of land, in the heart of the city as Egmore was, had escalated beyond anyone's wildest dreams, and vacant possession of these old houses was essential before the value of the land banks could be realised.

The small wooden gate creaked as Mohan opened it. He walked down the short path that led to a large verandah overlooking a small enclosed garden to one side. The garden was overgrown, he saw, with tree-sized bougainvillaeas, a gnarled frangipani and large hibiscus bushes. A very old jasmine, its base twice as thick as his arm, had gone rampant all over the roof, trellis and pillars of the verandah. The smaller shrubs and plants appeared to have been given a drastic pruning recently, and piles of cut branches lay in neat heaps along the borders.

The door to the verandah opened and May, dressed in jeans and a short sleeveless top, came down the steps to meet him.

'It's such a mess, isn't it? Every time I come to Madras, I get the garden tidied up as much as I can.' She shook her arms out in front of her. 'They're aching from all the pruning I've had to do. Uncle Ronnie won't have a mali come on a regular basis. He doesn't trust the natives! I'm not joking, he'll actually tell you that himself. Come on, he's waiting to meet you.' She ushered Mohan into the sitting room, which unlike the garden was spotlessly clean.

'Uncle Ronnie, this is my friend, Collector Mohan Kumar. I came in his car from Nandagiri.'

The old man shuffled to his feet even as Mohan asked him not to get up.

'Ah, the IAS man. May's been telling me how helpful you have been to Gerry. Sorted out the electricity for the piggery, I believe. Always useful to know someone in the Civil Service, always very useful. Sit, my boy. Here, come on, this armchair's the best in the house.'

Mohan was about to protest as the old man moved towards the sofa but May made eyes at him and Mohan did as he was told. She sat beside Ronnie and he hugged her close, putting his arm around her.

'In the old days you needed a child in each service. One each in the police, the railways, telephones and electricity board. One in the Auditor General's office and one in a bank. That would set up the parents for life. No palms to grease and everyone in the family got a leg-up every which way you wanted to go. It worked well you know – we looked out for each other.'

May laughed out loud. 'Nobody has more than 2.2 children nowadays, Uncle Ronnie.'

'It's time for you to get married and have those 2.2 children then. I want to play at your wedding, it's the reason I came back from Australia. See these fingers, Mohan? They are eighty-six years old, but they can still hammer out a fine tune on the piano. All this lass needs to do is find a nice boy.'

Mohan replied with a smile, 'We'll have to get working on her then. How long were you away in Australia, Ronnie? And have you been back long?'

'I was a young man when I left here in January 1921, twenty-four years old, with five pounds in cash, a few porter cakes that my mother thought would keep well during the voyage, all my sheet music and the new suit I was wearing. I started out in Sydney and stayed a railway man all my life.'

May patted Ronnie's arm gently. 'He missed India, so he came back here last year. I keep telling him to come and live with us in Nandagiri, but he refuses.'

'I came back to Madras because I wanted to die at home,' Ronnie confessed. 'I never felt that Australia was home, especially after my wife Beryl, God bless her, died. She was Anglo-Indian, too, but my sons, the lucky fellows, married Australians and my eight grandchildren are Australian – with no surprise darkies amongst them, thank God.'

May tutted. 'Uncle Ronnie!'

'The truth can be embarrassing, May, but the colour of your skin always matters, anywhere in the world – it matters all right.' He was looking at Mohan as he spoke. 'Tell her it matters, Mohan.'

Mohan leant forward and reassured the eighty-six-year old: 'It shouldn't matter, but you're right, Ronnie, it does.'

The old man slapped his knee in delight. 'There's honesty now! May let's drink to that. Get out the bottle of Old Monk. I'm sure Mohan would like to start the evening with rum and cola.'

May backed out of the room, wagging her finger and shaking her head disapprovingly behind Ronnie's back. Mohan was trying to figure out what it meant when the old man shuffled along the sofa closer to him.

'Our families chose the ones that got the ticket to leave India – to migrate to the home country, you know. We fair-skinned ones were given a chance, but the darkies were always left behind here. Darwin's theory of natural selection, Anglo-Indian style.'

Mohan tried to change the subject. 'Do you miss Australia, Ronnie?'

'You know, all the years I was there I longed to do something really outrageous – but I never did. You see, I always felt that I had to be on my best behaviour because even after sixty years in Sydney, it still wasn't my own place.'

Mohan teased him gently. 'Are you telling me you came back to India just to break some rules?'

'No, I came back because this is my *baap ka raj* and even when I do flout the rules, I can do so with my head held high.'

Mohan nodded. When you were in your *baap ka raj* you assumed a confidence that you could never have anywhere else in the world. It gave you the freedom to swagger, to go about about without fear, the licence to defecate, urinate and spit anywhere with ease, permission to bribe, cheat and defraud, the sanction to do as you pleased, with bravado, and all because it was your *baap ka raj* and there were no pretences to be kept.

'Tell me, boy, are you courting young May?'

Mohan was as surprised at his own speedy answer as he had been at the question. 'Yes, but she doesn't know it as yet.'

The old man threw his head back and laughed loudly.

'If you are, she'll know. Trust me, women are quick on the uptake, much quicker than us men.'

Mohan could hear May approaching the doorway, holding drinks and glasses on a tray.

'Mohan, maybe you could pour out the drinks? I'll be back in a minute with the ice.'

Ronnie watched her as she went out of the room. 'May and Gerry's father Maurice Twomey was a good man. He did a lot for Nandagiri and its environs, worked very hard all his life, though he hasn't yet had any credit for it at all. He was brought up from a tiny tot by my mother Mags, and Mum was so proud when he qualified as a Forestry Officer and when he married Betty.'

'What happened to Maurice's own mother?'

'It was the 1920s and she was unmarried. That's what happened, poor thing.'

'This is May's grandmother Rose you are talking about?'

'You know of her? So, May has told you the story then. I'd only been in Australia a few months and wasn't on my feet yet. There was some talk of sending my Cousin Rose across to Sydney, but it didn't happen. Back then you needed to be tough to make a start at living and working in Australia, and a woman with a babe in arms didn't really stand a chance.'

'Are you telling Mohan Aussie stories, Uncle Ronnie? You could have waited till I joined you.' May set the ice on the table along with a platter of savoury snacks and sat down.

'May, I wish you had visited us in Sydney before Beryl died. She always hoped you would.'

'I know, but overseas travel on a teacher's salary is an impossibility. It was much nicer to have you come here every few years instead. Mohan, you should have seen the presents he brought us. Shark's-tooth necklaces and musical pencil cases, roller skates and once a small, stuffed, talking kangaroo. God, I remember my first set of felt-tip pens – they came in a two-foot-long tin box emblazoned with a picture of the Sydney Opera House. Mum kept them in the cupboard in her room and didn't let me use them except for project work.'

'I remember getting one of those, too,' Mohan put in. 'Only mine was bought from the customs-notified shops in Burma Bazaar, and to my dismay the pens dried up in a week. My mother was sure I had left the caps off and, long after they'd been binned, they were often quoted as an example of my lack of regard for hard-earned things.'

'That's nothing but a universal mother mantra,' Ronnie said comfortably. 'Does your mother live in Madras?'

'Yes, she lives here. She bought a house in Adyar a few years after my father died. He was in the IAS too, retired as Chief Secretary in Delhi.'

'A big shot, eh?'

Mohan drained his glass before he replied. 'I suppose he was, though we only thought of him as Dad, my sister Asha and I. Would you like to meet my mother, Ronnie? I tell you what, why don't you and May join us for lunch on Friday? I should be done in the Secretariat by mid-morning. I can pick you both up and we could be in Adyar by noon.'

'It's very nice of you, Mohan, but don't you want to check with your mother first? Will she be free?'

'Hush, May, the fellow knows what he's doing. There are no steps to climb at your house, I hope? I'm wary of steps, you know, and it isn't because I can't walk – I've two artificial hips and they should last two lifetimes.' He tapped his chest. 'No, it's the old ticker actually. It shouldn't be strained.'

May stood up, walked to the door and looked out through the mosquito netting on to the verandah. 'I don't know why you won't come and stay with us, Uncle Ronnie. It's a worry for Gerry and me, you know, with you all alone in this house.'

'I'd be afraid to die anywhere else, May. I want to die in my own house, the same as my father and mother.'

'Okay, let's be morbid. What's the difference between dying here and dying in our house in Nandagiri, knowing you'll have us with you all the way till the end?'

It was obvious to Mohan that the old man had been cornered like this before. He found himself cajoling Ronnie. 'May has a nice home in Nandagiri, a sprawling bungalow, with no steps at all.'

'I never saw my father or mother after I left for Australia, you know that, don't you, May? They died within months of each other, in 1945, and it was only much later, a good fifteen years after the war, that I was able to afford that first trip back.' Ronnie was looking at Mohan now. 'I can't wait to see them again, and as long as I die in my own house, the same as them, I just know I will.'

Mohan watched May steady herself against the sofa, her voice choked. 'Oh, Uncle Ronnie, you will, surely you will.'

The old man put one hand up in the air. 'And while I wait, I intend to be merry. Let me play you young ones a few tunes.' He got up and made his way to the piano, handing his empty glass to Mohan. 'Fill it up, please, my boy. Plenty of ice and a good dash of that Old Monk.'

May and Mohan stood around the piano as he picked out a few keys, limbering up with flair. 'Did May tell you that I used to play the piano at the Connemara? There was dancing in the ballroom every evening, and in between sets the band dispersed. We would try our best to canoodle with any willing girls behind the velvet drapes and potted palms. I was a regular Romeo!'

May laughed. 'I bet you left plenty of broken hearts when you sailed off into the Aussie sunset.'

Ronnie sang the names out aloud: 'Clarice Hopper, Dulcie Dudman and Grace – goodbye my darlings. Goodbye Maude, Evelyn, Blythe and sweet Mable – goodbye!' Then, grinning widely, he continued, 'Those are just the ones I remember!'

He stepped up the tempo and began playing some rock and roll. It was foot-tapping stuff, and after a minute or so he said to May even as he continued to play, 'Get the boy out on the floor – show him how well you jive.'

'Not really, Uncle Ronnie . . .'

'I can see him keeping time with his feet so stop being a granny and get on with it!'

May was apologetic as they pushed the coffee table to one side. 'Sorry, Mohan, my grand-uncle can be rather stubborn sometimes. We don't have to really, maybe just one dance.'

'It's fine, May. I haven't jived since my college days and better to do it here, where no one's watching.'

'No one except Uncle Ronnie.'

She was a good dancer, as Ronnie had promised, and lost her inhibitions quickly. By the end of the first dance, she was instructing Mohan as he fumbled with the steps. Ronnie kept playing, and as Mohan twirled and swung May around, he was struck by the Anglo-Indianness of the whole tableau. This is what he had been warned Anglo-Indians did – they drank, played music and danced.

Waiting in the lobby of the Connemara Hotel for May, Mohan watched the piano-player in the far corner of the lobby bar. Another Uncle Ronnie in the making, give or take fifty years. He must be a Dominic or an Edwin or perhaps even a Basil, and he probably knew how to jive. Anglo-Indians stood out a mile – it was a fact that his mother had pointed out to him when he told her that he had invited May and her Grand-uncle Ronnie over for lunch. 'Who are they?' she had asked, her eyebrows arching as she poured out her cup of fragrant Ceylon orange pekoe.

When he had explained, she sighed in resignation. 'After your sister insisted on marrying Rahim, I decided there was no point in putting my foot down when you did choose a girl. But Mohan, an Anglo-Indian – they stand out a mile further than Muslims!'

'Well then, we'll just have to tell Rahim that he has competition, won't we?'

'Your father encouraged this sort of liberal behaviour, and happily for him, he died before me – leaving *me* to put up with the consequences.'

'There haven't been any consequences!'

But his mother ignored his protest and carried on, 'Still, you are your own man now, and if I couldn't stop Asha from doing as she pleased, I can hardly say anything to you.' She stirred her cup with frustrated vigour. 'If it is Anglo-Indian you fancy, then it's Anglo-Indian I have to live with.'

They had drunk their cups of tea in silence which Mohan took as a sign of victory for him.

'What should I serve for lunch?' she said finally. 'Cutlets, Coronation chicken and buttered peas – the sort of things you get at the Club?'

Mohan looked at his mother and laughed. 'You did this with Rahim the first time he came home, remember? We had to eat lamb trotters and drink rooh-hafzah.'

'You can joke – I was only trying to be hospitable. Muslims do eat those sorts of things.'

He got up to leave for work at the Secretariat and she was suitably mollified when he hugged her and said, 'Okay, hospitable will do fine tomorrow.'

There was a small smattering of applause from the far side of the lobby and the piano-player acknowledged it with a modest smile. From the corner of his eye, Mohan saw the two businessmen sitting near him stop their animated conversation to look the other way, at the heavy double doors to the hotel, and Mohan knew instinctively that it was May who had caught their attention.

'Uncle Ronnie wouldn't let me go,' she greeted him. 'I think secretly he wanted to come, as well.'

Mohan must have looked uncertain because she said in alarm, 'Oh no, I didn't mean to say you should have invited him. No, what I meant was – I think he's taken a real shine to you.'

'Yes, but I don't think my mother quite knew what to make of all his flirting at lunch today. As far as she's concerned, by the time you hit eighty-six, good decorum suggests that there are only two things that you should think of. One is how long you've left to live and the other is how soon before you die.'

May laughed. 'It's difficult to kick an octogenarian under the table, but there were times this afternoon when I nearly did.'

'Come on, the legendary food of the North-West Frontier awaits us. I booked the table for nine, so we're going to be just in time.'

Sitting opposite her in the restaurant Mohan couldn't help but stare at her as she fiddled with her handbag, first trying to hang it on the back of the chair, then putting it under the table and then finally on the chair-back again. He would never have described her as a classic beauty, but she had irresistible charm, those big eyes and a simple but adorable face fringed by hair through which he longed to run his fingers.

'So,' she said with her forearms on the table, twisting the ring on her finger, 'did you manage to finish all your work here in Madras?'

'In the main, yes, though I might have to come back here next month for a day or two to attend a seminar on water management. By the way, May, my mother has sent samples of the basket weaves that she was discussing with you at lunch. They are in a box and I'll leave them in the boot of the car till we get back to Nandagiri tomorrow.'

'She was very helpful, Mohan. If I can pull this off with her help it'll mean a great deal to the Yurava women who come to the Tribal Women's Welfare Unit. Their weaving is exquisite, every basket a work of art. Gerry must have told you already that in the old days, before they ever came out of the forest, the tribe depended on the baskets to fish and trap and to hold and carry their prey. The catches and hinges are pure genius and they are woven, too.'

'I hadn't realised till yesterday, when you and my mother got talking about it, that you volunteer at the Welfare Unit.'

'Gerry roped me in – no, that's not strictly true. Our father was very committed to ensuring that the Yuravas could continue to live in their traditional ways. My involvement was inevitable, I suppose.'

'My mother was suitably impressed I can tell you. You see, the Tribal Crafts Board is her pet project and she uses a good deal of Machiavellian cunning to steer the Committee in the direction she wants it to go. The fact that she was the Chief Secretary's wife helped her consolidate her position there in the initial years, but she doesn't really care when people call her autocratic. She says the ends justify the means – she has the clout to get products into high-end craft boutiques. By now she's become quite an expert on the tribal weaving traditions of South India.'

'She sounds like Gerry – he is quite abrasive when it comes to his remit as a Forestry Officer. And you know, it's so difficult for him when he is up against the senior administrative cadres who drift in and out of the district with no desire to really get to the bottom of its problems.'

Mohan sat back in his chair. 'I think you are talking about me!'

'To be fair to you, Gerry does say that you are the straightest Collector he has ever worked with.'

Mohan put down the menu in his hand. 'That's all? The straightest?'

'Well, we don't blame you, Mohan. Nandagiri is just the staging post in the scheme of things for the IAS, and nobody expects a whole lot of commitment to the place.'

'Actually, May, that's where you are wrong. My commitment is to my job. I do my job and I do it well wherever I am sent.'

'Oh, I didn't mean to offend you, Mohan, but you have to agree that small towns like Nandagiri aren't served well by the office of the Collector when that Collector changes every two years. I know that by the time you've actually come to grips with the peculiarities of the district, you are moved off to another one.'

271

As the rest of the evening progressed, it became clear to Mohan that May was indeed the very epitome of the ideal girl he had eulogised in that ill-fated college essay. He looked for an opportunity to hint at the way he felt or even make an outright confession, but she was clearly having such a good time, that not knowing if she felt the same way, he was reluctant to spoil the mood and embarrass her. They talked about everything and her honesty encouraged him to own up to idiosyncrasies that had her laughing helplessly.

'You prefer your parathas triangular unless they are aloo parathas, in which case you insist they are round? Oh Mohan, that's totally nutty!'

'That's how my mother made them,' he said unashamedly.

'That's even worse – no man would admit that!' When May had finished laughing, she was more solemn. 'Our parents were quite hard up when we were children and the one thing I learnt from my mother was thrift. Ours was more of a bread and homemade tomato jam kind of household, with butter only on Sundays. It's Gerry who really made a go of the piggery on a commercial basis, though my parents didn't live to enjoy its success.'

'What about you, did you always want to teach music?'

'I had a really mean piano teacher as a child and I was her charity student. They did that in those days – take on one or two "deserving cases" as we were called. She chain-smoked and would pinch us if we made mistakes. If we cried, she'd pinch even harder. But far from being put off, I was determined to learn to play and study to be a teacher myself, a good one at that. I had lofty ideas as a ten-year old. I wanted to save as many children as I could from horrid, smelly piano teachers.'

'A right little musical Mother Teresa, then.'

'My God, that's exactly what they used to call me. Did Gerry tell you that? Come on, how do you know?!'

Mohan laughed. 'A lucky guess, May. Now, how about dessert?'

'I fancy a really decadent chocolate pick-me-up. Will you share it with me, Mohan?'

'Why not, May. You choose.'

He watched her as she scanned the dessert menu and changed her mind several times before settling for an almond kulfi with sliced fresh mangos. He knew he was taking heart in something that meant nothing. She was doing what all women did in offering to share dessert – they were just assuaging their own guilt. Yet the anxiety he had experienced at the start of the evening, at the prospect of telling her how he felt without sounding like a corny teenager had somewhat abated. They'd had a great evening together and maybe if he said nothing for the moment, she would mull on it herself.

'By the way, Mohan, I forgot to tell you that Richard phoned just before I left Uncle Ronnie's. He asked me to let you know that he was holding the fort at "Knocknagow", and that Ishwar was continuing to spoil him. He wanted to know if I was going to be back on Sunday in time for the movie night at the Club. It's an Irish film, *Ryan's Daughter*, have you seen it? Apparently, it's very good.'

'Yes, I have, a few years ago in Delhi. He could go with Sonal and Bala or Satish even, if he wanted. Sonal loves the movie nights, they never miss it.'

'Oh, but Richard's great company and it would have been fun to see an Irish movie in the company of an Irishman. He was disappointed we wouldn't be back in time. I told him I'd probably be too tired after a day's drive anyway.'

'I think Richard's taken a fancy to you,' said Mohan, regretting his words even as he finished speaking.

She looked up at him and smiled. 'Yes, I know.'

He waited for May to say something more, but she seemed to be more interested in chasing the last chunk of mango round the rim of her bowl.

He reached forward and tipped the bowl to a slight angle. 'Try cornering it now.'

She ate the mango, her mouth covered with her napkin, then pushing the bowl away from her, she said, 'I hope he doesn't think I have encouraged him. I wouldn't, you know. After all, he might just be looking for some holiday diversion, unconsciously even.'

'I don't think any man in his right mind would consider you a mere diversion.'

She toyed with her coffee spoon, stirring imaginary sugar lumps that were refusing to dissolve. 'That's very sweet of you, Mohan, but I don't want to be made a fool of. I think that's what Gerry's afraid of as well, though it's none of his business.'

'That's a very clinical approach to being attracted to someone, May. You have to go with your gut feeling, you know.'

She sighed loudly. 'I wouldn't call it clinical, Mohan. In fact, I'd call it being realistic. My gut instinct is dulled by caution – it's a family affliction.'

'Still, being smitten involves throwing caution to the wind.'

As he poured out the coffee, she said archly, 'You know all about it then, do you – being smitten? I can't see *you* ever throwing caution to the wind! I know you civil-servant types – you're all governed by protocol, procedure and process.'

'I'm curious, why did you call it a family affliction?'

'Reliability counted for everything in my father's opinion. He only listened to the BBC, he shaved with Gillette blades, kept

Labradors all his life, wouldn't drive anything but a Land Rover and really believed in the power of Bournvita. It didn't matter if you were a person or a plug, you had to be trustworthy. If you let people down – you weren't worth a second glance. He was quite unwavering in his expectations. People and things had to do what they promised.'

'And do you take after him?'

'I suppose I do, but I'm sure most people have their own ideas based on issues of trust.'

Mohan nodded. 'Yes, you're right, but don't you think many of our opinions – what we think of as our own personal opinions – are really preconceived notions? It's the rare person who truly has an open mind about everything.'

'Well, this is India we're talking about. What everybody else and the next-door neighbour's aunt thinks is the most important thing, isn't it?'

'The next-door neighbour's aunt's opinion certainly loomed large when Asha and I were growing up,' Mohan agreed. 'My mother thought it quite important while my father asked us to ignore it completely.'

'We've something in common then, Mohan. My mother was just the same and my father used to drive her mad with his don't give a damn attitude.'

Mohan was quick off the mark. 'I'd say we've much more than just that in common. We must, May, because otherwise I wouldn't have enjoyed dinner as much as I have this evening.'

'Oh, I've had a really lovely time, too, but this trip has just flown by so quickly, hasn't it? What time are you planning to leave on Sunday morning, Mohan? I'll be ready for an early start, as early as you want.'

'I guess six o'clock will be fine: we should be in Nandagiri by seven at night. Shall we stop in Salem for lunch? Ceylon egg parathas and Chicken 65?'

'You mean they'll make triangular ones just for you?'

'I knew I'd regret telling you.' But even as he said it, he knew he had no regrets at all because there was a comfortable familiarity about May's gentle teasing that gave him hope and made him feel good.

'Six o'clock on Sunday morning is no problem at all. I'm not going anywhere tomorrow – I thought I'd spend the day with Uncle Ronnie at home. Every time I leave Madras after a visit like this one, I feel I may not see him again. This morning he asked me to help him sort out some of his old papers. I'm sure most of it is pure junk, but he carted them back with him all the way from Sydney so he must have some sort of sentimental attachment to them. He says he's quite sure he kept several bundles of letters written to him by his mother Mags, some of which had news about my father Maurice when he was a child. Uncle Ronnie said there might even be a photograph or two.'

Mohan held the car door open for May. 'That should be worth having a look at, letters going back sixty years. You never know what interesting bits of family history might turn up. The stamps could be worth something, too, May, so just keep that in mind.'

'My father was so reticent about his childhood, even though I know that Uncle Ronnie's mother Mags was so very kind and brought him up as her own, after his own mother Rose died. You're right, Mohan – there might be a photo or two that will make it worth a root through. I might even find something to show Richard.' She was smiling contentedly, with her hands crossed on her lap, as they drove out of the hotel car park.

CHAPTER TWENTY-ONE

Nandagiri, June 1982

Richard Aylmer was looking at himself in the mirror when Ishwar knocked gently on the door and then came in. The delight on the old man's face was plain to see. Having placed the pile of ironing down carefully on the bed he said, 'Richard, Saar, you looking so fine, Saar, finer than bridegroom.'

Richard thanked him. Today, in honour of the wedding of Captain Satish Pillai, he was wearing borrowed finery – a cream silk veshti with a thin gold-thread zari border. The previous evening, Mohan had shown him how to wrap the 3 metre-long piece of material around his legs and waist, before knotting it securely at the waist; over the veshti he wore a splendid silk kurta – a long, collarless shirt – also in cream.

Ishwar picked up the narrow piece of folded red silk with a gold brocade border from the wooden clothes horse by the mirror and draped it over Richard's left shoulder. He then stood back again in admiration. 'Saar looking superfine, Saar.'

'Saar is looking superfine indeed, but are you comfortable, Richard?' Mohan was standing in the doorway.

Richard made a wry face. 'I wouldn't quite call it that. How am I to keep this damned silk sarong from slipping down and falling off? It wouldn't do for the whole thing to unravel just as Satish is about to exchange garlands with his bride, would it?'

'Let's see, did you put a belt over it?'

Richard lifted his kurta to reveal a broad leather belt, tightly strapped over the veshti. 'Indeed, I did. I wasn't taking any chances.'

'Well, you've nothing to worry about then, so just relax. As Ishwar said, you look superfine. We should have time for a cup of tea before Sonal and Bala arrive. I'll see you on the verandah when you're done, yes?'

Richard nodded and headed into the adjacent room that had served as his office and study for the last few months. He checked through all his camera equipment, packing it into two cases. He had promised Satish that he would take photographs at the wedding, and their friend had been delighted.

'An Irish take on a South Indian wedding,' he had rejoiced. 'It'll be something different.'

'Curious' didn't even begin to describe how Richard felt. Four weeks ago, after a game of tennis, Satish had casually told him that his marriage had been fixed and the wedding would take place within the month. 'I'll know the date in a few days. You see, our astrologer and the astrologers on the girl's side haven't been able to agree on an auspicious date.'

'I didn't even know you were seeing someone.'

Satish was towelling the handle of his racket. 'I saw her in April, don't you remember? The weekend I missed the trek to Trishul Falls. The meeting took place that Sunday.'

Richard couldn't hide his shock. 'You mean that arranged marriage date? But you haven't seen her since — or have you?'

'No, I haven't. That's not how it works, you see, Richard. I liked her, but my parents weren't in a rush to say anything to the girl's side, as they didn't want to look too eager. It's called negotiating, my friend. We did the same for my sister, when we married her off three years ago. We wanted the best for her and we had to play our cards carefully. And to answer your question, I'll be meeting her this weekend. She's coming up to Nandagiri with her parents. My parents will be coming, too.'

'I just can't get my head around this whole business of an arranged marriage, but one thing I do know is you're going to have to stop calling her "the girl". So come on, what's her name?'

'"The girl" has a lovely name,' Satish said proudly. 'Kavitha. It means poetry.'

At that moment, Ishwar knocked on the door, bringing Richard back to the present. 'Saar! Tea ready, Saar.'

Richard carried his camera bags out to the verandah, sat down and waited for Ishwar to pour the tea. He was still feeling rather concerned, and it showed on his face.

Mohan put his cup down. 'Richard, don't tell me you are still worrying about Satish. You shouldn't – this is a time-tested method.'

'Oh, I know, you've given me all the happily ever after statistics and Sonal and Bala seem to concur, but it hasn't escaped my attention that none of you ever opted for an arranged marriage.'

'My father always said it was too much of a responsibility and as for my mother, God knows she has tried to set me up with suitable girls dozens of times.'

'Would you trust your mother?'

Mohan smiled. 'Don't look so shocked, Richard. Those girls were all carefully vetted and every one of them could probably have discussed the inner workings of the International Monetary Fund or the subtle nuances of a particular Indian raga – and all of it while turning out a perfect lemon soufflé. In fact, any of my mother's choices would have made a good wife. It was me who was the problem. Compatibility was my mother's mantra but it's a frightening word because it implies a degree of making do. I've never wanted to just make do about anything I wanted for myself, let alone a wife.'

Richard looked across the valley where the early-morning summer sun had already begun to leave its mark. 'I won't ever be able to understand it,' he shrugged, 'but I hope Satish will be happy. He's a nice guy, a very nice guy.'

There was a loud honk at the gate and Sonal called out to them as the car swept up the drive. 'Let's go if you both are ready. I want to be there early.'

Richard climbed cautiously down the steps of the verandah in his special costume, saying, 'I'll get the hang of it eventually, Sonal so don't laugh, please.'

'On the contrary, I'm upset. I just lost a fifty-rupee bet with May. I said you'd chicken out and she said you wouldn't – about wearing a veshti, that is.'

Reversing out of the gate, Bala looked round at Richard. 'Don't worry,' he told him, 'the last time I put on a veshti was at our wedding three years ago and I, too, was terrified that it would fall off.'

Richard lifted his kurta. 'Insider tip, Bala – wear a belt. And Sonal, I have to say that you look like a real princess today. You should dress up more often. You look so – how shall I put it – so Indian.'

There was a collective groan from the other three.

'Oh no! Richard, you sound just like my mother,' sighed Sonal.

Bala nodded. 'Or like mine – her prelude to a lecture.'

'Come on now, don't you feel like a princess?' Richard went on. 'All that jewellery, and your sari is exquisite, that amazing colour and the intricate embroidery . . . I'll have to get a nice photograph of you and Bala.'

'This was one of my wedding saris. I wore it at our reception and it's the first time I'm wearing it since. Yes, it is a lovely colour, isn't it? But . . .' Sonal was still talking about how she had battled against custom and tradition to limit the colossal waste of money that her trousseau had entailed, when they arrived in Ooty half an hour later

'I must look for May and Gerry, they are probably here already,' she said as she got down from the car.

That's exactly what I want to do as well, thought Richard. He hadn't seen May since she had returned from her trip to Madras with Mohan ten days ago. She had told him over the phone that she was very busy with extra tuition classes for her piano students, preparing them for their Royal College of Music exams.

Richard followed Mohan into the large banqueting room of the hotel, aware, very quickly, that all eyes were on them. Even after four months he found the way Indians stared, with no inhibitions and no attempt to disguise their curiosity, very disconcerting and it was immediately obvious that at a wedding staring was what everyone did. By the time they got to the pandal – the temporary structure erected for the wedding – at the top of the banqueting hall, several small children were standing on their chairs to get a better view of them.

'You are going to steal the bride's thunder at this rate,' Mohan joked. 'A white man in a veshti and kurta is a rarity in these parts.'

But Richard wasn't paying attention. He had caught sight of May walking in through the doors to the left of the pandal, trying to pin a string of jasmine on her hair. Sonal had seen her, too, and called out to her.

May waved back. 'We have places saved for you all,' she told them. 'Come up here to the front.'

Gerry Twomey shook hands with Richard and Mohan and slapped Bala on his back. 'Satish's brother has particular instructions to look after all six of us for the rest of the day,' he said, 'and he made sure we were seated upfront so Richard can take his photographs.'

Richard was looking at May, and quick off the mark, Sonal held on to May's arm and said archly, 'Another Indian princess, don't you think, Richard? May, this Irishman's been very generous with his compliments today.'

But it was Mohan who spoke first. 'You look absolutely lovely, May.' There was an awkward moment or two and then he grinned and said, 'It's obvious we should all be listening to our mothers and should dress up more often. What do you think of our Richard here?'

'Satish will be very touched that he's made the effort, and half the mothers in this banqueting hall are wondering if they could find a son-in-law as fair-skinned as him,' May said, beaming at Richard.

Just then, the musicians on the small platform rose to their feet and the high-pitched fanfare of the nadaswarams – the long metal and wood reed pipes – rent the air. Conches were blown and the drumming grew frenzied. The bridegroom and his family had arrived, and everyone craned their necks to watch Satish's feet being washed ceremoniously by the bride's younger brother. Minutes later, the hullabaloo died down and the banqueting hall returned to its earlier state. There was a steady hum as everyone went back to chatting, staring, greeting relations, matchmaking and gossiping. Sonal and Bala headed off to the other side of the hall, having spotted old classmates from medical school.

'Keep our places, we'll be back just before the tamasha begins,' said Bala as he followed his wife.

Richard took his camera out of the bag. The priests were getting the sacred fire ready. The whole ceremony centred on the fire, he'd been told, as the vows were witnessed by Agni, the god of fire. He looked through his lens at the pandal and began to take some photographs.

'I have to hand it to Satish,' he murmured to May, who stood beside him as he worked. 'The fellow looks so calm. The symbolism of fire couldn't be more apt. I mean, it's like baptism by fire, don't you think, marrying someone you don't know at all?'

'I couldn't say, Richard. I've known too many happy arranged marriages to agree completely.' She stopped and covered her face with the back of her hand. 'Please Richard, don't point your camera at me – I'm not photogenic at all. Save your film for the bride, she'll be out soon.'

As he sat back down next to her, he asked, 'Those earrings you're wearing, with the links attached to your hair – are they an heirloom, handed down from your mother?'

May ran her finger along the many tiny pearls that hung from the delicate three-tiered gold and turquoise pieces. 'Certainly not. My mother absolutely hated jewellery like this. "Vulgar Indian ornaments", she used to call them. No, Gerry bought these for me the year after she died. He was in Delhi at a conference and purchased them on impulse at a Rajasthani shop in the hotel.'

'So, what did your mother wear then, when she wanted to dress up or go to weddings like this?'

'She'd only a few things, just a string of pearls and an opal pendant and earrings that were her pride and joy. Uncle Ronnie brought her the opals from Australia one time when he came home on holiday, and she saved for two years from her housekeeping money to have them set. You see, our father being in the Forestry Service meant they didn't have much – it all went into our education. "I invested in my children" was what he used as an argument when our mother badgered him about saving for a pension.'

Before Richard could ask her anything more, she added hastily, 'Oh, but don't get me wrong. Our mother was a slavish follower of fashion, regardless. She used to get the *Woman's Weekly* sent over from the UK. I think she was never quite sure whether she liked Queen Elizabeth best, so gracious and good, or whether she preferred the jet-setting, naughty Princess Margaret who was so glamorous. Mother was a great dressmaker and she'd recreate their outfits down to the last bow and button. The Queen's jewellery was often just a string of pearls, and if that was good enough for the Queen, it was absolutely perfect for my mother. She never went to Mass on Sunday without her white kid gloves, either. Those were a gift from Uncle Ronnie, as well. He really was as generous as he could be.'

'Mohan said the old man was quite a character. I think he found your uncle very interesting.'

May smiled. 'Oh, they were definitely members of a mutual admiration society that weekend. Uncle Ronnie took a real shine to Mohan.'

'Your mother sounds as if she was a real character, as well. White kid gloves, in this weather.'

'It was all about keeping up appearances, you could nearly say that that was the Anglo-Indian motto. You must swear you'll never say anything to the others, but my mother used to dress Gerry up exactly like Prince Charles. He wore blue romper suits, shirts with ruffles and huge Peter Pan collars embroidered with ducks and bunnies till he was seven at least, poor old Gerry.'

Richard burst out laughing and nearly dropped his camera at the picture May had painted. 'And what about you? Which of the royals were you masquerading as?'

'Princess Anne, of course. Pinafores, box pleats, headbands to match, white lacy ankle socks and white shoes. I even had a tartan skirt like hers. I used to hate it. We always stuck out, you know.' She sighed. 'That generation, they felt they didn't belong in India, but they also knew they'd missed the chance to head "home", to England, and so this was Mum's way of showing her loyalty to the Crown, the long-lost Empire.'

'But May, I thought you said you had Irish roots.'

'Yes, but it didn't matter to the people of the Colonies. Irish, Welsh or Scots, once they were in India, they were English; they were here serving the Crown and that's where Anglo-Indian allegiance had always lain, with England. We're a mixed-up bunch not just by parentage but even in our own heads.'

'You know, don't you, that your Irish ancestors will be turning in their graves with all that deference to the Crown.'

She coloured slightly. 'I haven't told you this, but my paternal grandfather was in the Kildare Rangers; and he was one of the mutineers. Yes, I suppose he would be turning in his grave.'

Richard, who had his lens focused on a close-up of Satish listening intently to the priest, lowered his camera. 'May, you've mentioned your grandmother Rose, but you've never before said anything about your grandfather being involved in the mutiny.'

May looked down at her hands. 'It's not the kind of thing you'd want to advertise. It was a shameful business: he was court-martialled, dishonourably discharged and shot at dawn by firing squad, leaving our father Maurice, who was born six months later, a bastard. And then when Dad was two years old, he became motherless to boot. We don't know much more than that anyway.'

'What was your grandfather's name?'

'Private Michael Flaherty. Our father was never told much by Uncle Ronnie's parents, Dennis and Mags; they brought him up, you see, after his mother Rose died. And of course, Dad had no interest in digging up the dirt about court-martials and mutinies. My mother wouldn't have let him anyway. There weren't that many left in Nandagiri who knew the family story and she wanted it to remain that way.'

Richard let out a big sigh. 'I know what you mean. My grandfather just couldn't bear the thought that history books had, even in his lifetime, recorded the fact that the only slur on the Regiment's glorious history happened on his watch as Commandant. He would never talk about India. In fact, my father James and his sister Alice didn't even know anything had happened till many years later. They learnt about the mutiny when they were in their teens, from gossiping aunts. The Kildare Rangers were disbanded just before Irish Independence, did you know that? My grandfather presented the Colours to the King at Windsor Castle in June 1923, if I remember right.'

'Yes, I heard that from my father a few months before he died. It was an odd thing. We had just visited the grave of my great-grandfather, the Bacon-wallah, in St Andrew's Church – you know, the one at the top of Kildare Avenue. His name was actually Sean Twomey but even his tombstone bears the inscription *The Bacon-wallah*. Anyway, it was Christmas morning and Dad was a bit emotional; he always got like that at Christmas-time and Mum put it down to him missing his Uncle Dennis and Aunty Mags. In the churchyard, completely out of the blue, he told us of his father's disinterment. Mum wasn't there to hold him back, and perhaps that's why he spoke of it that day. Did you know that the bodies – my grandfather's and that of another NCO – were taken back to Ireland?'

Richard shook his head. 'No, May, I didn't.'

'Neither did my father at first. He was working in Theppakadu at the time, at the elephant camp there, around 1956 or '57, and he told us that he only read about it a day or two later in the newspapers. Apparently, a delegation came from Ireland, there was a small ceremony and the two bodies, those of Michael Flaherty and Sergeant Tom Nolan, were disinterred and taken back to Ireland. The *Nilgiri Times* quoted the Irish Ambassador, who was present at the graveside, as saying that the Irish government had declared them heroes for the Irish Cause and that's all my father ever knew.'

'Did Maurice make himself known?'

'To whom?'

'To the Irish authorities.'

'And claim he was Michael Flaherty's bastard son? No, to what use? Dad just let it go. And so did we.'

Gerry and Mohan headed back towards them and sat down beside May. 'You both looked like you were discussing doomsday,' Mohan remarked. 'Why so serious?'

May tucked a wayward strand of hair back into place. 'Just bits of history.'

Richard was still digesting what May had told him. Bits of history, true – but who would ever have thought that they shared those bits of history?

May leant forward. 'Look – the musicians are gearing up again and here come Sonal and Bala, so it must be nearly time.'

And just as she had predicted, the fanfare of the nadaswarams filled the air again, and moments later the bride emerged through a door on the left. Richard had his camera ready, and as he took his photographs, May and Sonal filled him in on what was going on.

'Satish never told us she was so pretty,' said Sonal.

'The bride's name, Kavitha, means poetry. So, what did you expect?'

Both Sonal and May laughed at this. 'You're well-informed, Richard. Who told you that?'

'The man himself – our friend on the pandal, looking pleased as Punch.'

'Well, at least that confirms that Satish is a romantic at heart. Do you know what I got from Bala for my last birthday? A table fan!'

Bala was not going to let that pass unchallenged. 'All the better to keep you cool, my dear.'

May tapped Bala on his arm. 'You don't need to play the big bad wolf, Bala. I know how you spoil your wife.' She nudged Richard. 'Look, Satish is pointing us all out to the bride.'

Satish waved before saying something to his bride, who gave them a shy smile. Richard had his camera at the ready for just such an opportunity.

'I think they make a lovely couple,' said May.

Through his lens, Richard looked on fascinated by the detail he was able to capture.

The musicians had stepped up their tempo and the bride's mother, dressed in a splendid peacock-blue sari with a silver brocade border, hurried on to the pandal, having spent the last half an hour along with her husband meeting and greeting people as they arrived. The bride's gangly young brothers, self-conscious and awkward, positioned themselves beside Satish and his parents, while the priest, who had been sitting cross-legged in front of the fire for over three-quarters of an hour, stood up and loosened his joints as discreetly as he could.

'That must be the bride's maternal uncle. He'll be giving her away,' said May, pointing to a tall lanky figure walking up the steps of the pandal accompanied ceremoniously by the bride's father.

'Her uncle gives her away?' Richard said, baffled. 'What about her father?'

Mohan said quietly, 'I think it's because there could always be doubt about your paternity but never a doubt about who your maternal uncle is. So traditionally the marriage contract was between the bridegroom and the bride's maternal uncle.'

'I thought Indian women didn't play around.'

Sonal dug him in the ribs. 'We don't, Richard, but men created these rituals.'

Richard stood up then squatted on his haunches facing the rest of them. 'Okay, Bala, it's time to make up for the table fan,' he announced. 'An arm around your wife now – as if you mean it.'

Husband and wife held each other and posed, smiling as Richard kept up the banter until he realised that the ceremony was finally about to come to a climax.

The bride's maternal uncle placed the young woman's folded palms in Satish's, and then with great pride and satisfaction pressed both pairs of hands together. The priest, muttering loud incantations, gave the musicians a final signal and Satish placed the thali around the bride's neck.

'That's the equivalent of putting the ring on her finger. They are married now,' Sonal explained as the couple were blessed with flurries of rice thrown on them by all on the pandal. Eager relatives joined in the blessing from all directions, leaving those in the front rows also dusted with rice.

Then to Richard's astonishment, the room began to empty rapidly as the guests streamed out of the two double doors at the back.

'Do they know something we don't?' he asked. 'Everybody's leaving.'

Sonal burst out laughing. 'The wedding-breakfast buffet is being served in the banquet room next door and now that the show is over, everyone's getting down to business. Most of them will eat and run – it's a weekday, remember?'

Mohan stood up. 'I'm starving, too. Shall we head for the buffet?'

When Richard had first arrived in Nandagiri, the thought of having a spicy cooked breakfast with sambar and chutney seemed unpalatable, but he had very quickly, and to Ishwar's complete delight, become a willing convert. He was partial to rava dosas, the semolina pancakes dotted with tiny bits of onion and green chilli, and the accompanying coconut chutney to his mind created a marriage made in heaven.

'Have you missed sausages, bacon and eggs?' enquired Bala, as Richard tore off a piece of the rava dosa and dipped it in the coconut chutney.

'Not really. I can't imagine not being able to eat Indian food of the standard that I've got used to these last few months.'

'Does your father remember his years in Nandagiri?' asked Sonal. 'James was just a little boy, wasn't he, when your grandfather was commanding the Kildare Rangers? He must have been the same age as Ishwar was then. So strange to think they might even have played together – it wasn't unusual in those days. So many of the little Baba sahibs were lonely and often the servants' children were all they had for company.'

'Father has hazy memories of watching polo matches, tiger hunts and cobras being killed by servants. He was in India for just nine months before he was sent back to school in Dublin. He had a friend with him on the voyage, a boy due to start at the same school. He was the Prince of Pudunagari, the only son of the Raja. The poor chap died in Italy in 1944 – the Battle of Monte Cassino. He was a Lieutenant in the Rajputana Rifles. I know that his father, the Raja, could never come to terms with it – you know, his son dying at the hands of the Germans, fighting for the very same King Emperor who had summarily annexed Pudunagari for the Crown in the 1930s. The Raja died of a broken heart in Switzerland, where the family had moved after Indian Independence. I know the Rani and her two daughters continued to live there, moving to Paris in the 1960s. My Aunt Alice wrote to the Princesses for many years. I think she had been secretly in love with the Prince.'

'The one that was killed in Italy?' said Sonal.

'Yes. He used to spend the school holidays with my father at my grandparents' home. Later, he went off to military college and then to Sandhurst. They saw him only once after that, when he came to Ireland apparently to visit my Aunt Alice before heading back to India to join the Rajputana Rifles. The story is that my grandparents stamped out the fledgling romance and she was terribly sad when he died; they had been writing to each other despite her parents' disapproval. My father doesn't remember much but Alice, who remained with my grandparents in India till the Regiment left, has an incredible eye for detail and recalls a good deal about her childhood in India. When I go back, I must ask her about Ishwar and see what she says.'

'She should write a book, a memoir perhaps,' suggested Bala.

'Look, there's Mohan – and May with him. I was just beginning to wonder where they were. They haven't even started eating, and Mohan was the one who said he was starving.' Sonal waved to them.

Richard watched as Mohan shepherded May towards the buffet tables. They had their heads close to each other as they talked, laughing at something the maître d' had said to them at the dosa counter. Richard would have made nothing of it if he hadn't seen Sonal look at Bala with a nearly imperceptible lifting of one eyebrow. He took a sideways glance at Gerry, who was wiping his mouth with the corner of his napkin and gazing intently at his sister as she and Mohan approached and sat down next to each other at the shared table.

'We're a bit late as Mohan bumped into Stanley Cooper, the General Manager, and he arranged for us to see an amazing private garden behind his residence,' said May.

Gerry looked surprised. 'Here at the hotel?'

'Yes. You know Stanley, don't you, Gerry – Lionel Cooper's grandson? I meant to tell you that, Mohan. Lionel Cooper was our father's mentor when he joined the Forestry Service but had retired by the time Gerry started. Anyway, I'm surprised we never knew of this little gem. It's the kind of paradise my mother tried to create all her life – a walled cottage garden straight from a Jane Austen novel. Hollyhocks and huge old-fashioned cabbage roses, beds of lavender, violas, alliums, peonies, sweet peas climbing the wrought-iron pergola and a gazebo overhung with wisteria. I could have lingered there all day.'

Sonal put her napkin down on her plate. 'You missed Richard telling us this really sad and romantic story about his Aunt Alice and the heir to the Pudunagari seat.'

Bala rolled his eyes. 'Sonal, you make it sound like a Merchant Ivory production.'

'Yes,' she said, 'I can just see it through sepia-coloured lenses.'

Mohan was curious. 'Pudunagari? Those lands are revenue lands now, they belong to the government. I think the title was never passed on; it died with the last Raja. Richard, did you say your aunt and the Pudunagari heir . . . how on earth did they even meet?'

Richard told Mohan and May what he had told the others earlier. 'But the reality was that Aunt Alice couldn't have done any better than the Prince of Pudunagari. I mean, it was the 1930s and there weren't any decent young men left.'

'In all of Ireland?' said Bala.

'No, amongst us – I mean the Anglo-Irish. The well-off ones had upped and left for England in the aftermath of the Civil War. Some got out before they lost everything, while others were burnt out of their homes, many shot and killed by the Republicans, the IRA. The ones that remained in Ireland did so because, almost without exception, they couldn't afford to leave. Of course, there were a few like my grandparents, who whether they could afford it or not, couldn't imagine leaving a country they called their own, a house that had been home for generations, regardless of what the Catholic majority thought.'

'So, it was all about religion then?' asked May.

'Religion was a big part of it, though retribution was the driving force. I must say, that having been to India, I'm only now able to appreciate what it must have been like for them when they returned to an independent Ireland. To go from being the Colonel Sahib and Burra Mem, with the whole of Nandagiri and the rest of the district salaaming them at every turn, to arrive back in Kildare openly despised by all the locals, envied by all who worked on the estate for them, and living in fear that their home would be burnt down . . . anyway, that was what it was like, and poor Aunt Alice would have been hard-pressed to find a suitable husband.'

'There must have been other men in Ireland,' said Sonal.

'Catholics? They won't touch us with a bargepole.'

'You speak in the present tense, Richard.'

'We're still Anglo-Irish. Not Irish enough yet.'

'That's an awful way to feel. Doesn't it bother you?'

'Not on an everyday basis, but occasionally, when you get somebody's back up and you know it was only because they heard your accent – yes, it bothers me then.'

'You have a different accent?'

'That's right. I've only to open my mouth for people to make up their minds about what a posh prat I am.'

Sonal tapped her glass with a spoon. 'Richard, finish the story. Your Aunt Alice, did she marry in the end?'

'She did, after the war, quite late and just when everyone in the family had given up hope that she would find someone. She married an art historian, a quiet man who adores her. They live in West Cork. She paints and he writes, they lead a simple life. I see them a few times a year and she seems happy. Loves to talk about India, and as I said earlier, I must ask her if she remembers Ishwar. In fact, I must ask *him* if he remembers *her*.'

'He'll more than likely tell you what he thinks you want to hear, Richard,' Mohan warned him. 'His aim in life is to please his masters. It's part of Ishwar's survival mechanism. How do you think he's managed to stay on in the servant lines at "Knocknagow" and see about eighteen of us Collectors come and go? No, I've nothing but admiration for the man. He's good at his job and a diplomat to boot.'

Before anyone could speak, the bride's parents escorted the newlyweds into the banqueting hall. The bride and groom looked exhausted but Kavitha managed a weary smile as she struggled to keep her head above the garland.

Everyone shook hands with Satish and congratulated both of them.

The groom turned to his bride and introduced them one by one. 'And this is the Irish friend I was telling you about,' he ended. 'This is Richard.'

Richard put his palms together and bowed his head slightly. 'Congratulations,' he said politely. 'It was a beautiful ceremony. I've some lovely photographs and maybe I'll get a few more after you both have eaten. Mohan might even be able to get us into this private garden at the hotel that's apparently quite idyllic. I hope to take some nice shots of you both there.'

The bride thanked him before she said, 'You're the first Irishman I've ever met. Do you live anywhere near Sligo?'

'Sligo? No, that's in the north-west of Ireland, and I live just outside Dublin. But it's a small country, and Sligo's just a three-hour drive away. Why, do you know someone there?'

She beamed at him, saying, 'Well, I know *of* someone buried near there. W.B. Yeats – I've been studying him for the last two years. My M.Phil. thesis is on the relationship between Yeats and our own Rabindranath Tagore. They were great friends, you know.'

'In that case, Kavitha, when Satish brings you to Ireland – and I'm going to make sure he doesn't leave it too long – I'll take you there myself. Yeats is buried in the churchyard at Drumcliff in the shadow of a mountain called Ben Bulben. It's a beautiful spot, I know it well.'

'Oh, I hope we'll be able to, sometime,' said Kavitha. 'I have to submit my paper in the next four months and my supervisor at the University wasn't too pleased about the wedding interrupting my work.'

Richard followed the wedding party camera in hand, as they mingled with their guests. He had been dumbfounded in the car, on the way to Ooty, when Sonal casually mentioned that there were going to be twelve hundred guests at the wedding and now, looking at the newlyweds as they patiently smiled and shook hands, over and over again, he was filled with admiration for them both. What would make two seemingly modern, tennis-playing, Yeats-reading people trust their parents so much that they'd agree to marry total strangers and be quite happy doing so? Kavitha seemed so unafraid, and Richard knew Satish was pleased with his lot. He watched the newlyweds look at each other now and then, at ease with themselves, despite the fact it was only the third time they'd ever met.

As he moved around the large banqueting hall taking pictures, he faced a barrage of questions from the older ladies there. Why had he come to India, how old was he, was he married, why hadn't his parents found a girl for him as yet, maybe he had sisters to be married off first, did he have sisters, did they have dowries, each of them? And when he told them he would have to fall in love with a girl before he could marry her, the same ladies laughed before issuing another round of questions. Tell us about your family, everything starts with a good family. Is the family house mortgage-free, does your father have life insurance, vegetarian or non-vegetarian, are your parents God-fearing? He left them excitedly mulling over what he had told them. *It's an unfathomable country,* he thought to himself. *People say India is a country of contrasts, but they don't know the half of it.*

A little later, he was back at the table with Sonal and Bala. 'Where are the others?' he asked.

'May dragged Gerry off to meet the General Manager and Mohan went looking for you some time back.'

'Ah – there's May, and Mohan's with her,' Sonal interrupted. She watched them walk across the room towards the dessert counter then said thoughtfully, 'They make a lovely couple, don't you think, Bala?'

'Sonal, you are not ready to be a matchmaker as yet.'

'But they do, don't you think?'

'I can't think because I'm off to get some dessert myself. Coming, Richard?'

Richard needed a moment before he could reply. 'You both go ahead,' he said. 'I shall just sit here for a while and take it all in.'

CHAPTER TWENTY-TWO

Nandagiri, July 1982

Mohan was woken by a persistent but gentle tapping on his door. It was Ishwar.

'Your tea, Saar, it's ready on the verandah,' the old man said. 'Richard Saar is awake and reading the paper. Shall I come in and draw your curtains open?'

Mohan groaned and reached out for his watch on the bedside table. It was six-thirty on a Sunday morning. He would have preferred to stay in bed for an hour or so longer, but as he clearly recalled, the previous night before going to bed he had instructed Ishwar to wake him the next morning as soon as Richard was up and having his morning cup of tea.

'I'll be there in a few minutes,' Mohan said and yawned. 'You can do the curtains later.' He got dressed then switched off the air conditioner and hurried on to the verandah, where Richard sat hidden behind a newspaper.

Richard lowered the weekend supplement. 'You're up early, Collector Sahib. Last night at the Club, Satish said you'd cancelled your Sunday-morning game of tennis so I reckoned you were going to sleep in late.'

'I was, but that blasted air conditioner makes such a racket in the mornings. All that shuddering and juddering – must get it serviced.' Mohan sat down but not before walking to the end of the verandah and hollering for Ishwar. 'I thought we might have an early breakfast out here – what do you think? Looks like it might be a cooler day than yesterday. If we're lucky we might even get a few thundery showers. You'll have to see some tropical rain before you leave next week: there's nothing quite as dramatic as the first rains.'

'Breakfast on the verandah sounds good. I'm quite hungry – famished actually.'

'How was your dinner with May and Gerry last night?'

Richard stretched his arms out behind his head and sighed. 'It's a long story. Gerry couldn't stay for dinner – said he had arrangements to make for some VIPs.'

'Yes, I'm tied up with the same thing, too, later on this evening. The visitors arrive tonight and leave tomorrow night. Gerry has to get his trackers ready for an early-morning safari, like the one we did last month, plus they are going to visit a Yurava camp.'

'Oh, right. I thought he seemed preoccupied and May was in a strange mood.'

'What was the matter, did she say?'

'Well, Satish and Kavitha joined us for a while and May talked to Satish at length about the workings of military court-martials. This is all to do with her paternal grandfather – Private Michael Flaherty – who was shot for his role in the mutiny of the Kildare Rangers.'

'Yes, I think it stems from all that old correspondence she's been reading. Did she tell you about it? It's a box of old letters and photographs that her Grand-uncle Ronnie gave her in

299

Madras a few weeks ago. It must have thrown up a whole lot of family stuff for her to deal with.'

'She wasn't very forthcoming about it with me though,' Richard said quietly. 'Brushed me off when I asked her.'

'Didn't your grandmother have something to do with hers?'

'Yes, but I already knew that. May told me about it the very first time we met. My grandmother had taken her grandmother on as a lady's maid.'

'She'll probably tell you more in her own time. Another cup of tea, Richard?'

'Yes, please.' They sat drinking their tea in silence for a few moments.

'I have to thank you for all you've done for me,' Richard said impulsively. 'Your hospitality, your friendship – I do appreciate it, you know.'

'Come on, that sounds like a very final farewell. You're back here in Nandagiri in the autumn, after the rains, aren't you?'

Richard stood up and walked to the edge of the verandah. 'Yes, I'm still on for a return trip. I need to tie up a few loose ends with the India part of the project before I can make a submission to the Arts Council.'

The clouds suddenly parted and the rose beds were illuminated by a single shimmering shaft of orange morning sunshine. The two men watched as the beam of light lingered for a minute or so and then seemed to retreat just as quickly as it had arrived, as if it were being pulled back on some urgent heavenly command.

'I could have sworn there was someone up there orchestrating that special effect,' Richard murmured.

Mohan was amused. He commented, 'I think I heard May describe that as a "Ten Commandments" sky.'

'May — she's a bit of an enigma, wouldn't you say? She seemed close to tears a lot of the time last night. I didn't know what to make of it. I felt she wanted to tell me something, but nope — she held back the whole evening.'

'She's certainly not normally the weepy sort, is she,' Mohan said thoughtfully.

Richard looked at him and hesitated for an instant before he spoke. 'I sense you've changed your opinion of her quite a bit. If I remember right, that evening when we were driving to the Club to meet the Twomeys for dinner the very first time, you said she was the kind of girl you had been brought up to avoid at all costs.'

'I admit I was very judgemental then. People change their minds.'

'And you have?'

Ishwar's arrival at that moment gave Mohan some breathing space. As he gave instructions for breakfast, his mind was not so much on the dishes that he was asking the old servant to make as it was on the answer that Richard was expecting to his question.

'Would you like eggs and toast as well, Richard? I've asked Ishwar to make puri and aloo.'

'Puri and aloo will be just fine, though maybe I should specify how many I want to eat — just four perhaps, instead of being tempted to indulge in as many as I want when they arrive.'

Mohan grinned. 'Ishwar will be devastated if I tell him you want just four — his aim in life at the moment is to fatten you up before you leave for Ireland. He was shocked to hear that you do your own cooking.'

'I'll have to tell him myself,' said Richard, and using sign language and broken Tamil, made his intent to eat in moderation known to Ishwar.

Mohan watched as his cook's face fell. Ishwar cleared away the tea cups, muttering grumpily as he left.

Mohan waited until he was gone before he said, 'Here's a man who never gives up. He just said he's going to make the puris twice the normal size, so regardless of the numbers, you're going to be eating more than you plan to anyway.'

Richard sighed. 'A man who never gives up. I should be one of those but I've a horror of being labelled as the one who didn't know when to stop.'

He stood up and leant against one of the wooden pillars, gazing down the valley towards the old cemetery below. A few young goatherds squatted there, on the cool marble tombstones, sharing a cache of cigarette stubs that they must have scrounged from the pavements around the bazaars.

'You know, Mohan, my grandfather painted prolifically when he was in India – yet he hardly ever spoke of his time here. India was a taboo subject, never to be mentioned in case he had one of his "turns". It became one of those mysterious ailments of which my sisters and I were mortally afraid. It wasn't till I was much older that I realised "having a turn" meant he could slip into a prolonged bout of depression.'

'Did he live with your family?'

'Yes, though the truth is that we lived with him. The Big House in Straffan was too much for him after our grandmother Beatrice died, and at the time it seemed the most logical thing for my father to do, to move his family in with him. I was a baby and my mother, who was expecting one of my sisters, was most unhappy about moving from her comfortable suburban home in Dublin to a draughty, damp old house in Kildare. Even today, and despite the fact that the house is held up as one of the finest examples of sympathetic restoration in the country, she never loses an opportunity to remind Dad of the life they could have had if they didn't have a big Georgian country mansion leaching horrendous amounts of money on a daily basis.'

'I'm curious, Richard. Why did your grandparents neglect their own house?'

'I think things were tough for them when they got back from India. Things were tough for all Anglo-Irish families in those days; they had to keep their heads down while the fledgling Republic thrashed out how it really felt about us.' Richard gave a wry smile. 'We were the Ascendency, you see. We kept Ireland in good working order for the Crown – rulers by proxy, you could call us – and most importantly, we were Protestant. Now as any Catholic will tell you, there is no absolution for being Protestant.'

'So, you were like the Anglo-Indians in the sense that you didn't quite fit in. However, with Anglo-Indians it's nothing to do with religion. They just denied ever being Indian and then it came back to haunt them after Independence. They're in limbo and that's an awful place to be in. May spoke about it when we went to Madras together.'

Richard sat down at the table. 'It's a pity we can't just wipe the slate and start afresh. I hate being labelled, having to battle assumptions all the time.'

Mohan, who had spotted Ishwar pushing the ornate wooden trolley on to the verandah, laden with puffed-up puris, aloo and an assortment of chutney, drew his chair closer to the table. 'Okay, my friend, here is breakfast and as you'll see, there are more than a dozen of those extra-large puris. Let's tuck in.'

Ishwar handed Mohan an envelope before transferring the food onto the table, saying, 'One of Twomey Saar's servants cycled up with this an hour ago but our watchman, the fool that he is, waited till now to give it to me. Saar should have a word with him – I think the fellow's drinking again. His eyes were bloodshot like the devil's.'

Mohan looked at the handwriting on the cover as he spoke. 'Send him here after we've eaten and I'll have a chat with him.'

'Saar must cut his salary if he's been drinking. You are too soft on him, Saar. Just threatening him won't do.'

Mohan nodded in Ishwar's direction. The note was from May. The phone lines were down at their place since the previous night, and she wondered if he might be able to call by to the house. *Come for lunch, if you have the time*, she wrote. Mohan reread the note and wondered what to say to Richard, who must have gathered from Ishwar's mention of Twomey Saar where the note had come from.

He stuffed the letter back into the envelope and put it on the table. 'It's from her. Their phone lines are down. She wants me to call by sometime today.'

Richard looked thoughtful. 'You are talking about May?'

'Yes. I'll head on there later this morning. What about you, have you anything planned for today?' Mohan busied himself tearing his puri precisely and hoped he sounded casual.

The Irishman was matter-of-fact when he replied: 'You look like the cat that got the cream.'

'I won't count my chickens, not yet. I don't know how she feels about me,' said Mohan, looking straight at Richard.

Richard slapped the table with his napkin. 'Mohan, you could have said something sooner! Or perhaps I should have guessed sooner.'

'I couldn't really tell anyone since I haven't told May herself how I feel. But I know I want to marry her.'

Richard put down his fork. 'Marriage – you are offering her marriage. Mohan, you've a distinct advantage.'

'It's not an enticement, Richard. I want to marry her. I've never felt as strongly about any woman before. I've loved, but not like this. I've dallied, pursued and lusted after a few, and apart from those, God knows my mother has tried to set me up with suitable girls dozens of times.'

The Irishman didn't reply straight away and Mohan felt a bit self-conscious. 'What about you?' he enquired.

'The strange thing is that we aren't too different,' replied Richard. 'I wouldn't have known what I wanted either – until I found it. And yet, I wouldn't rush into marriage as fast as I might into a relationship. I too find May very attractive. She is guileless, very straight and direct, nothing coquettish about her. I know that she was only flattered by my interest, nothing more.' He pushed his plate away and stood up, smiling. 'It doesn't look like it'll be pistols at dawn for the two of us.'

Later that morning before he headed off to the Twomeys', Mohan made a phone call to his sister Asha. They chatted for a while and he listened patiently as she ran through the list of friends she and Rahim were expecting for Sunday lunch.

'Suchi has promised to come. She and her husband are in Delhi for a week. You should have grabbed her for yourself when she was available.'

'Asha,' Mohan interrupted. 'Remember the sitar-guitar girl?'

'She doesn't exist, brother of mine, except in an essay you wrote in college. That was a million years ago and you are now a zillion years older and ageing even as I speak.'

'Sisters are cruel things by definition, so I'll let that pass. But she does exist, and her name is May Twomey. I'm going to ask her to marry me.'

'She's a foreigner? What is she – English or American?'

'She's from Nandagiri.'

'What's she doing there?'

'She teaches music at Nandagiri Hills Public School.'

'No, Mohan, I mean what's a foreigner doing in the sticks?'

'She's Anglo-Indian, she was born in Nandagiri.'

'A hill-station Anglo-Indian?'

'Yes, Asha. Is that a problem?'

'I would have thought it would have been a problem for *you*.'

'Well, it obviously isn't.'

'Look, it's the truth, Mohan, so don't be so touchy. Have you told Mum?'

'They met last week in Madras.'

'What! She never said a word to me and I spoke to her last night.'

'You know Mum. She wasn't any different with Rahim in the beginning, remember? She probably hopes May will just disappear. They got along quite well though. May's involved with the Tribal Women's Welfare Unit and the pair of them got talking weaves and baskets.'

Asha laughed out aloud. 'No wonder you are the IAS's rising star. You're pure devious to have set her up to do that.'

'It wasn't anything to do with me. In fact, I had no idea that May was involved with the Yuravas at all. Her brother Gerry is the District Forestry Officer here.'

His sister sighed loudly. 'I hope you know what you're doing, Mohan. When will we get to meet her?'

'It could be a while. You see, I have to tell her first. I'm waiting for the right moment.'

'You don't tell a woman to marry you, you ask her.'

'I need to tell her how I feel before I ask her to marry me!'

'Let me get this right, Mohan. You haven't told her how you feel and you took her to see Mum?'

'Yes, I know. Nothing makes sense, I'm just making it up as I go. I'm heading there now, to May's house.'

'Listen, Mohan, there's no such thing as the right moment. Just spit it out. If she's a woman worth her salt, she'll have known how you felt anyway.'

'Hmmm. Listen, can you get away for a few days, come to Madras even? I want you to meet her.'

'In a week or so, maybe. Actually, now that I think about it, I'm due for a few meetings in Pondicherry so I should be able to wangle an official trip fairly soon.' His sister gave a little laugh. 'This brings back memories! I remember when you met Rahim the first time, all big brother and gung-ho to start with, but you were putty in his hands when the evening was over.'

'That's *your* version of it. How is Rahim?'

'He's trying to convince me that it's time for us to have a baby.'

'And?'

'I'm thinking about it. In fact, I think he's right.'

Mohan was overcome with sentiment when he put the phone down five minutes later. It looked like life was going to change for his sister, and as he picked up the car keys to drive over to the Twomeys', he was filled with hope.

May came out to the door when he pulled up and parked outside the house.

'I got your note,' he called. 'Are the phone lines still down?'

She was wearing a pair of jeans with a blue checked blouse, and she stood on the edge of the verandah with her hands held up to shield her eyes from the sun. 'Yes, they're still down and the neighbours have lost connection, too.'

'That's a nuisance but I'll get the fellows on to it first thing tomorrow morning. Is Gerry around? I hope I'm not too early.'

She led him into the small sitting room and switched on the fan. He had been watching her face, looking for a sign that would give him an idea of how the morning was going to progress, and was completely taken by surprise to see her eyes well up.

Mohan immediately reached out and put both hands on her shoulders. 'May, is everything okay? Where's Gerry?'

She moved towards the armchair near the old fireplace and covered her face with her hands. 'I'm sorry, Mohan. I wish now that I hadn't bothered you.'

Mohan remained standing. 'I'm here now, and it must be something important to have upset you so much.'

She walked to the window, her back to him, and clutched the wrought-iron grilles tightly. 'I've slowly been going through the letters and papers in the boxes that Grand-uncle Ronnie gave me last month; it's taken quite a while. On Friday, I found my Grandmother Rose's diary and a bundle of letters that Aunty Mags wrote to Ronnie.' She took a deep breath before going on. 'How can I describe what it was like reading them? Just heart-breaking. My poor Grandmother Rose. Mohan, she suffered so terribly! We knew she'd died of TB, but all these years none of us ever knew what she went through – in hospital, in the mental asylum. We never even knew she was in the asylum in Madras! She paid such a heavy price for that mutiny by the Kildare Rangers. She bore the brunt of it all, physically, mentally.'

May turned away from the window towards him, her face wet with tears. 'I just wanted to tell someone. I just wanted to tell *you*, Mohan.'

CHAPTER TWENTY-THREE

Nandagiri, August 1982

Standing on the veranda in the late afternoon, Mohan looked out at the cloudless blue sky and was glad that he had decided to have Richard's farewell do on the lawns of 'Knocknagow', even though Ishwar himself had been most reluctant. For the last three days the old man had been looking up at the rain-laden sky at every given chance, wringing his hands in despair. Mohan, however, knew the storm was unseasonal and would dissipate in a couple of days, and there could be no better time to have a dinner in the open air than in the cool but brief aftermath of a summer downpour.

The dinner was an important event for both men, master and servant, and though neither would admit it to themselves, they were equally nervous about how the evening was going to turn out. For the old cook, it was the most elaborate party he had been in charge of since his master had arrived as Collector in Nandagiri. For Mohan, it was a night filled with anticipation, for tonight was the ideal opportunity to tell May how he felt about her.

Standing looking out at the distant graveyard, he could see the three coolies down at the tombs, squatting patiently beside their Petromax lamps. They had been asked to report there before dusk but weren't taking any chances and had arrived well before time. Mohan nodded to himself in satisfaction.

A few days before, when discussing his farewell party with Mohan, Richard had requested an early night; he would have to leave Nandagiri by four o'clock. the morning after for the long car journey to Madras, where he was going to catch his flight to Dublin via London at midnight.

Mohan had agreed immediately. 'I'll get Ishwar to serve dinner at seven and everyone will be informed that the gates will be closed to late-comers.'

Richard laughed loudly. 'I'm afraid your Collector's strong arm doesn't extend to the invitees, Mohan. I've never seen people take such pride in keeping Indian Standard Time. I'd change it to eight o'clock, if I were you.'

Mohan clicked his tongue. 'Are you mocking us even before you've left? And here I was, thinking how happily you'd slipped into the same terrible habits as us.'

'The same and more. Imagine, in forty-eight hours, I'll have to iron my own clothes and even water my own house-plants. Park my own car, carry my camera bags myself and pour my own drink. I can understand now why expats find it hard to settle when they return from the East.'

They had sipped their whiskeys on the verandah, watching the rain pouring down in sheets. When they spoke, it was together and Mohan stopped short. 'Go ahead, Richard – you first.'

'Have you spoken to May this week?'

'No. She said she was going to be busy again, preparing the last four of her senior students for their piano exams and I've been snowed under with all the preparations for the official functions next month. There will be press and politicians – local and central government – plus a good few environmentalist types, all jostling for a place on the podium for the formal announcement of the Special Area of Conservation initiative. A very dangerous mix for any administrator. You see, each wants precedence over the other: who sits where, who gets to speak and for how long, who garlands whom – it goes on and on. It's a game of one-upmanship and I'm the thankless referee.'

'I met Gerry yesterday and I've never seen a man so relieved. Now that Nandagiri has secured a place on the Special Area of Conservation List, he must have high hopes for the future of the Range.'

'I think he's too smart a fellow to be relieved just as yet. It's a temporary respite, this SAC business. Once the initial media hype dies, the logging and the poaching will slowly but surely creep back to old levels, and then there's the eternal paradoxical problem of the place becoming too popular with day-trippers from the cities down below in the foothills. Gerry knows that the policing of the SAC status of the forest will forever be an ongoing and uphill task.'

'Don't remind him, will you,' Richard said gently. 'It's nice to see him loosen up a bit.'

'Yes, he has, hasn't he? I thought so myself when he called into the office to collect the press releases. He told me he's placing great store on your completed project returning to India, and if you can manage the tie-up with this *National Geographic* chap, Raoul Garcia, it would give Nandagiri an even better chance. In

311

this country, the minute stuff appears in a foreign publication, it's suddenly accepted as the gospel truth. Still, we have to play the game. I've invited Garcia for the dinner on Friday night.'

'That's great, Mohan.'

'Have you any idea when you'll be back exactly? Do you have a definite date in mind?'

Richard looked thoughtful for a while. 'A few weeks ago, I would have been hurrying back as quickly as possible, but that was when I thought May was . . . you know, when I thought there might have been a spark of interest. So yes, I guess it'll be the end of September as planned.' He paused awkwardly, watching the rivulets of water course down the slopes of the valley opposite before asking, 'What about you – have you said anything yet? I mean, does she know how you feel?'

Mohan shook his head. He just hadn't had as much time with her as he would have liked since that Sunday at her house when she had wept in helpless anger, showing him Rose's diary, and the letters to her Grand-uncle Ronnie from his mother Mags, which she had arranged on the dining table in sequential order, chronicling her grandmother's tragic life.

'The truth is, I'm waiting for the right moment.'

As he spoke, Ishwar arrived on the verandah with more ice and a bowl of fried masala cashews. The two men drank in silence, staring listlessly at the rain as it bucketed down, fat drops clattering loud and incessant on the terracotta roof-tiles of the verandah, and examining in great detail each cashew before eating it.

'The tombs are going to get a good old wash,' Richard remarked finally, pointing in the direction of the cemetery which was barely visible in the dusk.

'I must arrange for you to see it,' Mohan said. 'It was something I'd planned to do when you first arrived in Nandagiri.'

'I kept putting it off myself, but I know I can manage to walk down there on my own, Mohan. There's a track leading off from the main road, isn't there? Let's see, perhaps if the rain lets up before I leave, I might go down and take a look around.'

Mohan rubbed his hands together. 'I'll organise something for your last evening, just before the dinner. This rain won't go on forever.'

That was a few days ago and, as Mohan had predicted, the rain vanished, leaving the gardens and valley below cleansed and dust-free. The jasmine that smothered the rusty iron pergola at the edge of the garden, where the hillside fell away to the valley, had burst into bud, and Mohan asked Ishwar to arrange the chairs as close as possible to the heady tangle of fragrance. May would definitely have something to say about it, he thought. She had such a fondness for jasmine.

Mohan was expecting the Twomeys and Satish and Kavitha to arrive within the next half an hour, and he was sure Sonal and Bala would not be far behind, having agreed to first collect Raoul Garcia from the Nandagiri Club, where he was staying. Mohan had planned for the group to spend half an hour to forty-five minutes at the cemetery, and he wanted to be back by six-thirty, just before dark and well in time for drinks and then dinner at eight.

Ishwar was in his element, the star director of the evening's domestic drama.

It was a quarter past five when May and Gerry arrived. Mohan and Richard were both on the verandah watching a

313

small tandoori oven being lifted onto a large metal tripod at one end of the lawn.

'It belongs to my uncle, Saar, who has a small stall in the bazaar,' Ishwar explained. 'I've borrowed it at no expense.' The cook looked at Richard before adding, 'Richard Saar loves tandoori naan, so I'm making three types.'

While Richard thanked the man in Tamil, Mohan nodded distractedly, for from the corner of his eye he had seen the watchman stand up and salaam Gerry Twomey as he drove in through the gates. Richard pushed his chair back immediately and was headed down the steps of the verandah before stopping and looking back at Mohan sheepishly.

Mohan laughed. 'Okay, you go on first. After all, with you leaving tomorrow, you're the one in the Last Chance Saloon.'

He tried hard to lip-read May's response as Richard kissed her one cheek at a time. It was just a hello, and now she was looking straight up towards Mohan with a big smile. 'Where are you taking us?' she called. 'It seems a bit morbid, visiting the old cemetery before dinner.'

'It's Richard's last night here, for a while anyway, and I thought I'd show him what happens to careless foreigners in these parts.' Mohan touched her elbow lightly as he ushered her on to the verandah.

'That sounds very much like a threat,' said Gerry, shaking Richard's hand and then Mohan's. 'I'd watch this Collector if I were you, mate.'

Richard joked, 'He's invited me back in the autumn and he sounded sincere, so I think I'm safe for the moment.'

Gerry joined in the laughter. 'On a more serious note, Mohan, it might be an idea to get in touch with the Commonwealth

Military Graves Association. They could be persuaded to make a record of all the graves and inscriptions, and maybe even take on board the maintenance. They maintain other British military graves all over the country, and they do have the funds.'

Mohan was about to reply when Satish and Kavitha drove in, Sonal and Bala following directly behind them with their passenger, Raoul Garcia.

'So sorry we're late! Shall we head down to the Ooty Road straight away, Mohan?' Sonal had rolled down her window. 'If we get out of the car now, we'll be wasting precious daylight time. Night will fall quickly.'

Mohan agreed immediately. 'I've some fellows down there already with a few Petromax lamps just in case it gets too dark while we are at the cemetery, but I think that might be a good idea, Sonal. Why don't you guys reverse out and we'll follow you.'

Whatever he might have thought of the Collector's strange request, the man from the PWD had done a good job this morning, as soon as the rain had stopped, of getting the first few rows of graves and tombstones cleared of the unruly vegetation that still overwhelmed the rest of the cemetery. The old gates with their ornate latches had been lifted off the ground where they had lain for decades and had been propped up carefully against the crumbling stone walls to which they had once been attached.

The party wandered around the graves, making for the large elaborate tombs with watchful angels that still stood guard despite having lost limbs, faces, heads and in many cases their entire torsos. Bala was the one who spotted the dull brass plaque with its precision-cut inscription in modern typeface that had been screwed on to a much older headstone. 'Look at what this says, Mohan: the bodies of two soldiers in the Kildare

315

Rangers, a Sergeant Tom Nolan and a Private Michael Flaherty, were disinterred and taken back to Ireland. This plaque is dated 1956 and says they were "Irish freedom-fighters, heroes for the Cause".'

Mohan was glad that May was out of earshot at the opposite end of the cemetery from where he and Bala stood, looking at something along with Kavitha and Gerry. Raoul Garcia had his camera out, while Gerry and Satish lingered at the graves closer to the entrance.

Mohan ran his hand over the dull tarnished brass. 'I was told a grand official ceremony was held here in Nandagiri when that happened. Ministers and diplomats came from Ireland and Delhi, and the bodies were taken back home in style.'

Bala was digesting the information in silence when Richard, who was a few rows away, called out, a look of surprise on his face: 'Would you believe this? I'm so glad you brought us down here, Mohan. I'd never have dreamt there'd be so many Irish graves and I want you to see this particular one. This man was from Ardclough, that's just a mile or so from where I live in Ireland now.'

Richard read out the inscription that eulogised a Pat Walsh for the faithful friend and fine soldier that he was. It was obvious he had been a popular man, for the large marble monument and hovering angel had been erected by his fellow soldiers to honour his memory.

May and Sonal were walking slowly past the smaller tombs, stopping at each one, sometimes having to crouch down close in order to decipher the inscriptions on the headstones, which had been pockmarked by time. Mohan left Raoul Garcia taking pictures of Patrick Walsh's grave and went over to the two women.

316

Sonal stood up and looked at him as he approached. 'It's not so creepy as I thought it would be, Mohan. I'd call this place quiet and serene actually, though it's shocking how young many of these soldiers were – mere boys, some of them.'

Mohan remained beside May. 'Yes, it's tragic really. I've looked down on this cemetery every day for two years now and would never have guessed how many stories have remained untold and unsung. I will initiate contact with the Military Graves Commission immediately, as Gerry suggested.'

When Sonal went off to investigate the older graves on the other side of the gravel path, Mohan sat down on a marble slab next to May. They stayed quietly watching Gerry and Satish, who were exploring the far end of the cemetery, where the Petromax coolies were fiddling with their lamps, getting ready to fire them up in the next fifteen minutes or so before dusk descended into the valley.

Scratching out random patterns in the dust with a thin stick, Mohan said, 'I'm so sorry, May. I just realised that this outing might be a bit upsetting for you. I had no idea that this old cemetery was where Michael Flaherty, your grandfather, was once buried.'

'He means nothing to me,' she said, her voice bitter. 'I was thinking about my poor Grandmother Rose and wondering where *she* was buried. All the while we thought she had died in England, though my father never knew where she had been sent or even the year she had died. But to find out now from Grand-uncle Ronnie's letters that my dad had been sheltered from the truth as a child, that Rose had never actually been sent away to England and that she had died miserably in the mental asylum in Madras . . . it seems so cruel and heartless. All these years, and we didn't even know.'

'Where is your father buried?'

'Our parents are both buried next to our great-grandfather, the Bacon-wallah, in the graveyard at St Andrew's Church at the top of Kildare Avenue.'

'Do you go there often?'

'I do. Gerry isn't willing, though. I have to drag him there once in a while. It's a lovely spot, very peaceful, nothing like this at all. It's spotlessly kept and has a beautiful rose garden at its entrance. The parish priest is quick to let us know if he thinks there's any neglect.'

Mohan touched her on her shoulder. 'May, if you want, I can use my official contacts in the Secretariat and make some inquiries about your grandmother. Kilpauk Mental Hospital must have some record of when she died and where she was buried. A death certificate must have been issued and signed by someone. There will be a record in the offices of the Registrar of Births and Deaths.'

May shuddered. 'The asylum – just the thought of it makes my flesh crawl. Gerry wants me to put it behind us and move on, but I don't think I could ever do that. He buries his head in the sand about who we are and what we came from. Anglo-Indians with a family history of madness? He thinks it can't get any worse so why not just burn the letters and go back to believing that she died in England of TB.'

Mohan broke the stick in his hand in two. 'Let me do this for you, May. Gerry doesn't have to know anything about it and if we do ever find anything, a death certificate or a burial record, he may feel differently.'

She put her hand out and held his arm. 'I'd be very happy if you would. For my own peace of mind, I know I have to try to put this to rest. And there's another reason. I'm absolutely

318

certain that our father Maurice would have spared no effort if he'd known this when he was alive. He grew up an orphan, and I believe that void affected him to the core of his being. He spoke of his mother, but there was no connectedness. Maybe . . . no, I'll deal with that when it comes.'

'Maybe what?'

'It's expecting far too much, I know, but imagine – just imagine – if we could bring her back to Nandagiri and lay her body next to her father and her son in St Andrew's Church, where she belongs. But I know that's unrealistic.'

Mohan didn't hesitate to put his arm around her shoulder as she wiped away her tears, and though it lasted but a brief moment, consoling her made him absolutely determined. He was going to locate Rose Twomey if he had to unearth every single grave in every single graveyard in the city of Madras. He'd start by making a few phone calls, first thing tomorrow morning.

Mohan was in Madras to see his mother and to visit Ronnie out in Egmore. He wondered why it was that he always managed to forget how totally suffocating the August heat of Madras could get. Today was one of those dog days, with the sun relentless from the minute it rose, taking the early-dawn temperatures soaring to unendurable levels within half an hour of climbing in the sky.

His mother had come into the sitting room, having been out for her morning walk.

She spoke first. 'You can have my car and the driver today, if you want. It'll give your fellow a break before the long drive back to Nandagiri tomorrow. They say this is the start of a heatwave, but then they say that every year in August. Sometimes I wish I'd stayed on in Delhi and not moved to Madras at all.'

'You said yourself that Delhi had become unsafe, and anyway that winter smog there is terrible for your asthma. Why don't you come up to me in Nandagiri?'

'No one there plays a decent hand of bridge and I don't approve of the way you let that old man, that Ishwar, have a free rein running that Collector's house of yours. Just because he's a good cook doesn't mean he can rule the roost.'

Mohan picked up his paper. 'Asha feels it'll be good for you, a few weeks in the cool weather – and the roses look lovely at this time of the year.'

'Let my bridge tournament finish and I'll think about it. We're going to win the trophy again this year so I'm not going anywhere for the moment. Did you have a nice time with your friend May's Uncle Ronnie last night? What did he serve you for dinner?'

'His next-door neighbour, a Mrs McKay, had organised the food for us in a large tiffin carrier. Prawn biryani and egg masala and a salad. She dropped it off herself and told me there wasn't any dessert because the old fellow wasn't meant to eat any. We ate early, almost as soon as I arrived, and then we talked for a while.' Mohan knew his mother would not be satisfied until she had details, and so it was better to be forthcoming at the start, rather than be questioned incessantly.

'What about?'

'May, mainly.'

'What did he tell you that you don't already know about her? I don't see how you can woo her by visiting her grand-uncle. If you have anything to say, why don't you just say it *to her*?' Mohan's mother sighed loudly. 'But I know you'll do what you want in the end, so there is no point in lecturing you. So, what did the old man have to say?'

'He rambled a lot. His memory is good for some things, but I think he likes to steer clear of difficult times. He showed me a photograph of Rose when she was eighteen – and she looked very fresh and pretty. Apparently, even as a little girl she had always been very particular about how she dressed, always very style-conscious and never, ever allowed the sun to ruin her skin. Her fair complexion was the pride of the family.'

Mrs Kumar sniffed. 'I suppose it was a natural prerequisite if you claimed your heritage was not tainted by Indian blood.'

Mohan didn't rise to the bait. Ronnie had been quite forthright about the difficulties he and other Anglo-Indians had faced when they arrived in Australia in the 1920s and 1930s. Very few of them could manage the subterfuge of passing off as anything but being of mixed race, but if one of them was lucky enough to marry an Australian, at least then they could say that leaving India had been worthwhile, because the next generation, the children, had a good chance of growing up white.

The old man had become quite emotional, too, when Mohan told him about May's distress at the information she had gleaned from the box of letters he had given her.

'Those letters brought great misery to me, too – and you might be surprised, Mohan, to hear that it wasn't because they contained upsetting news news of Rose. It was my mother Mags's naïve expectations and my father Dennis's pride in my apparent success that did it. You see, my boy, I'd been given a grand send-off from India, the best they could afford, and I left here with high hopes, clinging to what I found out were false promises. There *was* no job in the railways waiting for me as my parents had thought. In fact, I was lucky to be able to eke out a living as a porter at the station, and I was homeless for three weeks before I got that job. Could you imagine if I'd let on to them that their son was a mere coolie? I used to write back telling them what they wanted to hear – I had a job, I'd got promoted, was doing well – and they replied, their letters each one so full of happy relief. Oh, it made me ill to read them. So, I stopped reading them. I'd open them just to see my mother's familiar hand; she was so proud of her exquisite handwriting. I kept them all, including the envelopes that my father always addressed: I was nothing less than Ronald McKay, Esq. on those envelopes. God bless them, at least they believed in me.'

Mohan looked tactfully into his whiskey, letting the old man dab at his tears.

'I couldn't have done anything for Rose then. I ate at the Salvation Army soup kitchen most of the time.'

'I'm sure that May, and Gerry, too, wouldn't hold it against you, Ronnie.'

The old man looked at Mohan with a tremulous smile replacing the tears on his face. 'But it was a good thing I was desperate for a bite to eat all the time, my lad, because that's where I met my wife Beryl: she worked in the soup kitchen. Beryl was a bloody good dancer! Her parents came from Calcutta. They were of fine Anglo-Indian stock. Did I tell you that all my sons married Australian girls? I've beautiful grandchildren – they are real Australians and would you believe it, Mohan, they all want to come to India to find what they call their "exotic roots"! And this, after all those years Beryl and I tried to hide them! Life is nothing but a twisted joke, my boy, but you only see that at the very end.'

'It must please you, though, that they're so keen to know where their grandparents came from.'

322

Ronnie chuckled. 'Let's see what they make of India first.' He lifted his glass and asked for more ice. Mohan fetched it from the ice-bucket on the sideboard and topped up his own drink as he did so.

'So, May is arriving tomorrow,' the old man resumed. 'She's a good girl, you know – rings me every other day. She told me that you'd hit a brick wall with all your inquiries over the last four weeks and now suddenly you say that they might have found some records pertaining to Rose at the mental hospital. Being in the IAS is an advantage – you fellows open doors for each other, but slam them shut in everyone else's face. But don't take it personally, my boy. I like you, you know that, very much.'

Mohan grinned. 'You can't say things like that, Ronnie, and then qualify it by saying it's not personal.'

'See? That's what I like about you. I'm going to tell May that when she arrives – you are no push-over.'

'I spoke to her yesterday morning and told her what had been relayed to me by the fellow in the Registrar of Deaths and Births office. After all these weeks of no news, she was thrilled that we had some records to have a look through. She must be on the train now from Coimbatore. I'll collect her tomorrow morning when she arrives in Madras and we'll head straight to the hospital before we come back here. My mother has asked if you both will join us for tea in the evening.'

Uncle Ronnie fumbled with his dentures as they clicked out of place. 'Well-kept woman for her age, your mother,' he commented. 'Please let her know that I accept, on behalf of May and myself. But tomorrow, when you meet May at the Central Station, you must warn her not to get her hopes up too much. Sometimes these clerical fellows in government service will send you on a wild-goose chase only because they don't want to confess that they haven't found what you're looking for.'

'I'm very familiar with that problem, Ronnie. I deal with it on a daily basis. Yes, I've told her we may not find anything much more than admission records, but it's a start.'

'What about you? Have you got off the starting block as yet?'

Mohan knew exactly what he meant. 'You mean with May?'

'You Indian boys were always a bit slow. Better make a move soon, or she'll think you have nothing much more to offer than that Irish fellow.'

'I haven't been able to find the right time,' Mohan explained truthfully. 'She's been quite upset with all this business about Rose.'

Ronnie held his glass up in a mock toast. 'So, cheer her up then, boy. *Cheer her up!*'

CHAPTER
TWENTY-FOUR

Madras, August 1982

Mohan waited impatiently on the platform at Madras Central Station. The train's imminent arrival had already been announced, but he guessed it must be stuck at Basin Bridge, with everyone on board fretting at being so near and yet so far. The overwhelming stench from the nearby Buckingham Canal made it almost impossible to think of anything else.

He was about to head towards the station-master's office, when he saw the train approaching in the distance. A few pairs of wildly gesticulating coolies ploughed through the crowds indiscriminately, trundling heavy trolleys piled high with canvas sacks of mail that would be loaded on to the carriages at the very end of the train.

Mohan remained where he was, at the head of the platform, where the first-class A/C coach would stop. As the train pulled up, he stepped on top of a disused luggage trolley and waited to spot her. She was one of the first out, climbing down from the carriage with just an overnight case in her hand.

He waved. 'May! This way!'

She looked around, saw him and beamed. 'We stopped at Basin Bridge,' she said, 'and I thought we'd never get here.'

'Here, give me your bag, the driver is parked up in front.'

'Are we heading straight to Kilpauk?'

'Yes.' He put a hand lightly on her waist and guided her through the throng. 'I thought it would be best to get there before they do the usual civil-service trick of disappearing into fictional filing rooms.'

Getting into the air-conditioned cocoon of the car was a relief. Sitting unmoving, caught in the severe logjam of cars, auto-rickshaws, scooters, cycles and pedestrians all trying to exit the station simultaneously, the pair chatted for a few minutes, catching up on each other's news. It was the driver's very obvious reaction of surprise, when Mohan broke off his conversation with May to tell him to head for the Kilpauk Mental Hospital, which made her go silent for a while.

'Mohan, was it a coroner's report they found or her burial record? If there's a coroner's report, I'm sure there'll be a burial record. Even Gerry seemed pleased after I told him about your call, but he says disinterring a body is a rigmarole of a process.'

'I promised Ronnie I'd start this morning by telling you not to get your hopes up, May, but if we do get that far, Gerry needn't worry. There's nothing a few more phone calls can't sort out.'

She put out her hand and held his arm briefly. 'I really appreciate what you have done these last few weeks, Mohan.'

He had said it before he knew it. 'May, I'll do anything for you, you must know that.'

She was smiling as she looked out of her window. 'You can tell me again over dinner tonight,' she murmured. 'Is it the Connemara we are going to?'

Mohan was sure he could hear his heart thumping, but it was a young boy, his left fist hard at the window of the car as he held up his other hand. 'Saar, Mister Saar, plastic combs, toothbrush, hairbrush – all fine foreign quality, Saar!'

'Yes, the Connemara,' he said as they pulled out of the Central Station.

Kilpauk Mental Hospital was only a twenty-minute drive away, and when they drove in through the gates of the hospital, May was visibly nervous.

The hospital gates and entrance were covered in bunting and large welcome banners, and Mohan began to worry. If there was some sort of function or celebration coming up that evening or even the next day, there was no chance that anyone, even a clerk, would be free to go over patient records. He knew what these government institutions were like. From peons who would be busy whitewashing and shifting flowerpots to cover up eyesores, right up to the Superintendent who would be up to his neck coordinating arrangements to make sure no dignitary's ego was bruised by any mis-step, it would be all hands on deck and to hell with the day's normal routine.

May was thinking the same thing. 'There's no way we'll be allowed to rummage through old records if something is happening here today. They're going to fob us off, Mohan.'

As they got out of the car and walked up the steps to the offices, he tried to reassure her. 'Let's be positive. We are to ask for this fellow called Mr Gopalan by name at the inquiries desk: he is going to tell us how to proceed.'

When Mohan mentioned who he was and asked to speak to Mr Gopalan, the couple were immediately ushered into the VIP waiting room and left sitting under a noisy fan. While they waited, he thought of how he was going to tell May that

327

he loved her and how he had been smitten from the moment he had seen her at the Club with Richard's strings of jasmine around her wrist.

She fiddled nervously with her hair before clipping it into place, with just small strands falling around the nape of her neck. And then, looking about the room she said, 'I expected it to be really old and dilapidated. It's nothing like the mental asylum I had in my mind's eye.'

Mohan was about to reply when a middle-aged man in glasses walked in, many files in his hands.

'Ah sir! Mr Mohan Kumar, Collector sir, and your good wife. Good afternoon, madam. Sorry to keep you waiting but we're having super-big function this evening – the Dr Swamy Memorial Lecture. Plenty of foreign doctors, all from worldwide, and All India delegates, as well. The Superintendent, his temper is boiling over today, so I have not much time to devote, Mr Kumar, sir.'

Mohan's heart sank. 'Mr Gopalan, if you can just show us the files, we will be able to go through the records ourselves. It'll save you the time.'

'Records? I have no files or records ready for you, sir. There is some mistake for sure here. Sir, I was told you are enquiring about our Rosey Twomey. I thought you've come to see the patient. She has not had one single visitor for forty years, or is it forty-five? I was only a baby then. I came here to work in 1950, starting in the outpatients; now I am the Head Clerk in Records, sir. I will be retiring in three years, sir, after the marriage of my last daughter is arranged. God willing, sir.'

Mohan had to steady May and hold her close. 'The patient? Mr Gopalan, are you telling us that Rose – are you saying that Rose Twomey is still here?'

The Head Clerk looked shocked at the question. 'Why, sir, where else could Rosey go? She was most personal favourite patient of the late, great Dr Swamy, but now she has no one.' He looked at his watch. 'Sir, you will please be coming with me.'

May had begun to cry quietly, and as they followed a few steps behind the puzzled Head Clerk, Mohan put an arm around her shoulders. 'Come on, May,' he whispered. 'Everything about this day is turning out better than expected.' He could feel her trembling and he prayed that what they were about to see would make May happy.

They walked a lengthy route through several blocks before being led out into the open, to what Mohan was sure must be the furthermost corner of the hospital. The area was dominated by gigantic banyan trees, in the shadows of which were grouped several low, barrack-like structures.

Mohan was curious. 'Are we still in the grounds of the hospital, Mr Gopalan?'

'Why yes, sir. This being the original buildings, sir. That dispensary was built in 1890 – oldest building in the grounds, sir. When new hospital was built in 1963 under our late, great Dr Swamy's inspiration, they left these buildings like this, sir – for sorting later. But it stayed like this always – not very nice, sir, but we are keeping only the long-term institutionalised patients here. All are harmless and cooperative; some had TB, some leprosy, but now all are fully cured. I am longest-serving clerk, sir. I am knowing all these patients by name.'

They entered a gated courtyard and followed Mr Gopalan into the first set of low buildings, which he told them six rooms each, with doors on to the narrow verandah. He stopped at the doorway to one of the rooms and gestured to Mohan and May.

'She is here, sir, like I told you. Nearly died of TB, but still here, Dr Swamy's favourite. She won't come out because of the sun. Our Rosey likes to keep her skin white always.'

He opened the door and the couple stared around, holding their breath. The room was dark and cool after the scorching courtyard. A single bed was pushed up against the grille of the large window and a small table served as a bedside locker. The dressing table at the other end of the room was bare except for some well-thumbed magazines and a jug of water covered with a beaded doily. An empty birdcage hung from the ceiling.

Sitting on the bed was a small elderly woman, fair and with fine grey hair, dressed in an old maroon school pinafore. She was putting her hairbrush into a battered tin with a picture of caramel sweets on it when they walked in; alarmed, she looked at Mr Gopalan for reassurance.

May was about to enter the room when Mohan held her back. 'Wait, May, she's not going to know who we are. We must be careful not to frighten her.'

Mr Gopalan shouted, 'Rosey, it's me, Gopalan – see? You have visitors. These people, they've come to visit you.' He turned to Mohan. 'Sir, madam, you have to shout, Rosey being a little deaf now she is eighty years old.' He hesitated before asking May politely, 'How are you knowing her, madam?'

'I am – I am Rose Twomey's granddaughter, Mr Gopalan. My father Maurice Twomey was her son.'

The man's hand flew to his mouth.

May's voice broke as she continued, 'My father was only a child when he was told she had died.'

'Dr Swamy's spirit is guiding this miracle today, sir.' Mr Gopalan pressed his palms together and raised them in the air. 'He was the greatest doctor and now a real-life greatest miracle-worker.'

The Head Clerk then walked inside and sat on the edge of the bed. He smiled and pointed towards May, saying, 'Rosey, see this madam lady? She's the daughter of your son Maurice. This lady's come to see you because she's your granddaughter, she's your Maurice's daughter.'

Mohan held May's hand as they stepped into the room. The old lady turned to look at them, nervously fingering an old leather scapular that hung around her neck.

Mohan spoke first. 'Maurice lived with Mags and Dennis — you did too, Rose. Do you remember? It was in their house in the Railway Lines in Egmore many years ago, before you fell ill. Your Cousin Ronnie has returned from Australia and he lives there now.'

May walked around the bed slowly and knelt down beside her grandmother. 'Ronnie will be thrilled that we've found you.'

The old lady reached for the tin of caramels and held it close. 'Ronnie plays the piano,' she said in a near-whisper.

May looked up at Mohan and smiled through her tears before touching her grandmother's arm. 'Oh, and how happy he'll be to play for you again, dear Rose.'

The old lady pointed at the birdcage. 'The parrot was happy to sing for me.'

Mr Gopalan sighed loudly. 'That parrot died some ten years ago, Rosey.' He turned to address Mohan. 'Dr Swamy let our Rosey keep the bird out of kindness as animals are not allowed usually, but this parrot,' he lowered his voice, 'was most rude, sir. Making ladies blush, sir.' He raised his voice again. 'But you were Dr Swamy's favourite patient, Rosey. Special food and special care always, by order from the top.'

Rose prised open the tin carefully, took out the small brush and ran it through her greying hair again. 'Michael was going to take me dancing at the Connemara,' she said.

She flinched as May gently took both her thin hands in her own warm ones. 'Michael sent us for you, Rose,' she said.

Rose pulled away her fingers and, holding on to the scapular around her neck, she stared back at May intently, as if seeking Michael in every one of her features.

May spoke out again, more insistently this time. 'Michael sent us for you, Rose,' she repeated. 'To take you dancing at the Connemara.'

The old lady smoothed down her skirt before she replied: 'And then are you taking me to Ireland?'

May held Mohan's arm as she promised, 'Home, Rose. We are taking you home.'

The End

ACKNOWLEDGEMENTS

My immense gratitude to Joan Deitch, my editor, for her wisdom, humour and guidance. Thank you also to Rosemarie Hudson for all her sound advice and keeping the faith. I would like to thank Mary Stanley and Shirley Stewart for spurring me on. My mother Bollu Guruswamy, Colonel Vaskar Das, the late Colonel Hector Grant, Kishore Dutta, Rosaleen McCabe and Aisling Kearns for critical appraisals of the initial draft.

A special thanks to my soulmates Marie Carberry and Paula Fahy for living my ups and downs with me. Breda McHale, Emer Hatherell, Ida Milne, Fiona Stapleton, Annette Flynn, Indu Balachandran and Shuba Priya – your friendship is everything. I had a lot of help researching this book: thank you Kevin Myers, Eoghan Corry and my father-in-law Gopal Madhavan. Thanks to the Wednesday Wonders Book Club for your unwavering support.

I would like to thank Sue Booth Forbes for her decades of friendship and support, for always being there, my sounding board at the end of the phone.

As for you, Prakash my dearest, and Sagari, Rohan, Maya – where would I be without you?

Cauvery Madhavan was born and educated in India. She worked for a newspaper and a hotel group before getting her first taste for writing when she drifted into advertising in her early twenties, working as a copywriter in her hometown of Chennai (formerly Madras). Cauvery moved to Ireland thirty-three years ago, arriving on St Valentine's Day and, despite the Irish weather, has been in love with the country ever since. She lives with her husband and three children in beautiful County Kildare.

www.cauverymadhavan.com
@CauveryMadhavan